In the Grip of Time

In the Grip of Time

Book One of the Actum Tempus Saga

Adam Jacob Burgess

Nunmill Press

www.adamjacobburgess.com

ISBN: 978-1-8380886-6-8 (paperback)
ISBN: 978-1-8380886-7-5 (ebook)

for Karen

Contents

Prologue

'Bums.'

This was not the best introduction to one of the world's pre-eminent wizards, but this was not the best of times for Mirrah. In fact, it was right down there with the worst of times, alongside turning her vice chancellor into a cactus plant and accidentally cc'ing her boss into a letter thread about 'sexy sorcerers.'

Mirrah had walked into a booby trap. Not the pillowy one that straight teenage boys dream of, but the type that slowly erodes your memory, peeling away layer after layer of personality until you become nothing more than an empty, decaying husk of your former self. So, the bad type.

'Bums. Bugger. Balls.'

Well, what else was there to say?

Perhaps she could have raised her fists to the sky and shouted, 'Gods, why have you forsaken me! I led a good life. I did right by you all. I fought evil wherever I found it. I treated those less fortunate than me with kindness. What more could I have done?'

Or:

'I am one of The Twelve! We're the most powerful beings in the world, how could I have fallen for such a simple trap?'

Or:

'Not only have I fallen for a trap that has cursed me, but I have woken the Ancient Device: a machine capable of manipulating time and ruining the world in the process. It was built for folly. It was hidden for sense. But now it stirs, sending knowledge of itself out into the world, seeking out those that would seek to use it. And all because of me. Because I was foolhardy, reckless, and rash. I have unleashed a great problem upon the world and know not how to stop it.'

But she said none of those things.

Instead, she simply said,

'Bums.'

Chapter 1:
The Blue Forest

Many months after Mirrah was booby trapped, and many miles away, a community of gnomes went about their business as usual in a small forgotten corner of Esh'areth. Business in the Blue Forest mainly revolved around pranking one another: electric shocks, knock-a-door run, jellyfish in your pyjamas. All the classics. Most gnomes loved pranks, just as most gnomes loved how peaceful and familiar their lives were. Woven between the treetops, a blanket of old magic kept the gnomes' dwelling a secret. Travelling outside of the Blue Forest was restricted, and for most gnomes, that suited them just fine. But Sawwse Bohge was not most gnomes. For one thing, she bloody hated pranks. There's only so many times you can have your shoelaces tied together before you start to see red.[1] For another thing, she was desperate to leave the Blue Forest and travel the world! Unfortunately, the only exploration on the horizon was the depths of her own boredom at the town hall.

---

[1] And start wearing slip-on boots.

'Bums.'

'Language, Sawwse. If you're going to curse, at least do it properly. For example: big, hairy, smelly bums.' Dannse Gan looked down at Sawwse with a kindly face. Dannse was an elderly gnome whom Sawwse had befriended. The wrinkles around her eyes and her mouth revealed a long life full of mirth, lines shared by almost all the oldest gnomes. 'Anyway, I only said that you have to attend the town hall meeting.'

'But you said I could play my music for you then.'

Sawwse sat in her usual spot, cross-legged in front of Dannse Gan's rocking chair, twiddling the strings of her lute. She had never known her own parents, so Dannse had become something of a grandgnome to her over the years.

'Well, you can visit me after the meeting.'

'But the meetings are so boring.' Sawwse blew out an excessively long sigh. 'Okay, fine,' she relented, pulling a face. 'But before I go home, tell me again about your visit to the tiny kingdom of Meus.'

'I think that's quite enough story-spinning for today, child.'

At one hundred and thirty-eight Sawwse was hardly a child, but compared to the four hundred and fifty year old she was as fresh as a gnomeling.

'Just a quick story then. How about the one with the molluscs?'

Dannse had to chuckle as she remembered her time spent with the Snegell, an achingly unhurried tribe. The most dynamic thing that ever happened in the Snegell's camp was the time a gang of sloths challenged them all to an anti-race. Dannse didn't watch the whole thing, because dying of boredom was a genuine possibility, but she found it fascinating, especially the insults that the sloths threw out e.g. 'you're moving at a snail's pace' and 'you're so sluggish,' which tended to do more to spur the Snegell on.

'I'm sorry little one, I'm very tired. I'll share more stories with you tomorrow.'

'It's not fair. You got to explore the world, while I'm shut away.' Sawwse did her best grumpy pout.

'As I've told you before, it isn't all fun out there. For every Meus and Snegell, there's a Grobulax or Scarborough.[2] And that was a long time ago, mind, before the restrictions. Things could be even worse out there now.'

Sawwse looked around Dannse's small wooden room. The souvenirs from the older gnome's past adventures beckoned to her from their shelves, painting Sawwse's imagination with vivid colours.

'Look, Sawwse, do you need me to remind you again about the Magnarrian plot to steal grapefruits from the–' Dannse stopped, abruptly. Aware now that this had been Sawwse's plan to keep her talking all along. 'Promise me you'll go to the meeting tomorrow.'

'Okay, but you owe me double stories afterwards.'

'Of course.'

Sawwse broke into a wide grin, and Dannse followed suit. With her infectious smile and twinkling green eyes, it was impossible not to be charmed by Sawwse Bohge. She bowed to Dannse in the customary way, her right arm at her breast with one leg outstretched below the other, and then, left the old gnome's treehouse. She grabbed onto the nearest silk vine and swung her way over to the library.

---

[2] Not that one.

Both Sawwse and her grandgnome lived on the outskirts of the Blue Forest, leaving Sawwse a fair bit of tree-branch terrain to cover to get back to the castle-like estate at the centre of town. Not that it looked very much like a town in a human sense.[3] Three centuries ago, a travelling elf decided to build a grandiose home for himself, right in the middle of the forest. When he'd nearly finished construction, the gnomes had teased and pranked him so much about his receding hairline that he abandoned his project and fled, hair being very important to elves after all. The central point of the Blue Forest shifted as more and more gnomes moved into the unfinished castle's hundreds of rooms.

Sawwse wasn't keen on the estate. It was beautiful, and full of interesting flora set into lush sloping grounds, but it was also full of arrogant, odd and anarchic gnomes. The Blue Forest Council had relocated to the castle's upper chambers, and it had changed them and the town. For one thing, they'd relocated the library into a damp and dank cellar.

The diminutive gnome gently lowered herself to the ground by the estate and paused outside the modest library. A plaque loosely fastened to the stone wall read: 'For hearts, heads and lungs full of knowledge.'

Sawwse scoffed.

'Tell me about it,' said a voice next to her.

Sawwse turned to find a squirrel alongside her. The red and white streaks on its charcoal-coloured fur made it distinctively indistinct to the gnome. She scratched the

---

[3] It didn't have the lack of aspiration and purpose, the high street full of closed shops, or the incredibly specific local history museum.

crest of its little head, turned back to the plaque and sighed.

There was a pause before the squirrel said, 'No, I mean tell me about it. I can't read Gnomish.'

Sawwse apologised and explained that the plaque used to say: 'For hearts, heads and lungs *to fill* with knowledge.' She explained that there used to be a statue of Alia Yuhne, the first of the Gnehsehgs: the knowledge-seekers. They had been an elite branch of the Blue Forest Council and had special dispensation to venture outside the forest to explore the world, but that had stopped two hundred years ago. 'The Council couldn't give a crimp about knowledge now, they're a bunch of navel-gazing crimplords who'd be better off falling into a hole somewhere and… am I boring you?'

'No.' The squirrel looked at Sawwse with a blank expression while scratching itself. 'Please continue to explain the intricacies of Blue Forest Council foreign policy. It's scintillating.'

Sawwse shook her head at the squirrel's sarcasm and walked into the library.

Three rows of books extended on either side of the room, leading to a large, battered book kept inside a bamboo cage. Parchment of different sizes and shades were haphazardly arranged within the book, bound by vines and glued with maple sap.

'What's that then?' asked the squirrel.

'It's the Gnomeopedia. Our compendium of knowledge.'

The Gnomeopedia had been at the heart of the Blue Forest for centuries, added to over time by the Gnehsehgs. It had been placed under lock and key around the same time that the knowledge-seekers had been forbidden to leave the forest.

'Any good?'

Sawwse rolled her eyes. 'Well, obviously I've never read it. Though, I'd love to. Dannse has really bigged it up.'

'Why don't you?'

Sawwse pointed to the lock.

'I could pick that for you, easy.' The squirrel hopped onto the lock and reached its claw inside the mechanism.

'Woah, stop!' Sawwse quickly checked to make sure no one was watching. 'What are you doing?'

'I thought you wanted to read it?'

'Yes, but I'm not a thief!'

The squirrel shrugged and jumped down from the lock. 'Suit yourself.'

Sawwse moved away from the Gnomeopedia and took up her usual perch by the music section. She took a deep, calming breath and picked up Walken Musike by Emmeline Flowerdew. She flicked to the pretty maple leaf bookmark placed thirty pages from the end. Sawwse had spent a great deal of time poring over Flowerdew's other works, and had learnt loads from them, but now she was reading a memoir of sorts about the talented musician's bardic travels around the world. Of course, this kind of world tour was only ever possible without a misguided travel ban. She began picturing herself in the lands that Flowerdew had written about: the upside-down hills of Reversilius, the broken Isles of Hubris, the sunny climes of Shi'areth.

Sawwse finished the book and let out a blissful sigh. All gnomes of the Blue Forest were musical, in a manner of speaking,[4] but none loved music more than Sawwse Bohge. It gave her such a wonderful, spirit-lifting feeling when she played her beloved lute. Sawwse held the maple leaf bookmark she always carried with her and stared at it longingly. The tales of Flowerdew had drawn to a close with an expert summary of her travels, and with a plea that all hopeful musicians should travel across the Four Continents sampling as much of the world's music as possible.

Easy for her to say, thought Sawwse, forgetting about the chapter on Flowerdew's lisp. She looked upon the mighty music section of the library, and sombrely returned the book to its empty space. Sawwse had been steadily working her way through the books from left to right, bottom to top, inside out to outside in, and Flowerdew's memoir was the last one. She'd read her way through the entire library. Every book, bar one. The Gnomeopedia sat tantalisingly within its cage.

From outside came the hum of the evening reverie.

'What's that noise then?' asked the squirrel, tilting its head.

Each day in the Blue Forest ended in a kind of haze. The gnomes hummed, sang and fiddled until they entered a trance-like, night-time state. In this way, the division between one day ending and the next day beginning was blurred.

'It's the reverie,' grumbled Sawwse.

The ritual of the reveries rankled with Sawwse. Even though she'd spent year after year learning music, she had never been asked to lead. Leading the reverie was a

---

[4] That manner being lying. Just ask Hammerhands Nelsuun to play the violin and you'll wish your ears were internal.

great honour, and involved a solo of indeterminate length (the longest lasted the equivalent of nineteen human days). She suspected there were any number of reasons for the snub, but the main one was that the music she most liked to play was considered 'un-gnome-like' as it came from outside the forest.

'They'll all be laughing out the other side of their faces one day. I'm going to perform on the biggest stage in the whole wide world with thousands of people chanting my name, and then they'll see.'

'Fairy snuff.' The squirrel raised its tiny eyebrows. 'Where's that then?'

'Where's what?'

'The biggest stage in the world.'

'It was a figure of speech.'

'What's that then?'

'It's when… never mind.' The squirrel was beginning to get on Sawwse's nerves. Not just that, but as the thrum of reverie loudened, Sawwse's thoughts became more and more frustrated. 'I just don't understand why we can't play other kinds of music. I mean, Gnomish fiddling is great, but surely some variety would be nice.'

A drop of cellar water trickled down the back of her neck.

'Ugh! This place. The older gnomes have it sewn up. They had it so good, but we'll be living with their decisions while they're gallivanting round Groma-tundhi.'[5]

---

[5] Groma-tundhi was the afterlife that most Blue Forest gnomes believed in. Like all the best afterlives it was full of promises about everlasting peace, endless happiness, and bottomless ice cream.

'Knockity-knock.' An elderly gnome with sparkly grey eyes appeared at the library door at exactly the wrong moment. 'Good day to you, Sawwse. What an un-surprise to see you here.' He smiled warmly and held out his hand.

'Good day, Beghs.' Sawwse shook his hand and let out a yelp as a tiny shock ran through her body. She spoke through gritted teeth. 'Oh great, yet more pranks! Ceaseless crimping pranks.'

Beghs laughed and slapped his side, revealing the electric buzzer strapped to his palm. 'I'm sorry, couldn't resist a final joke before reverie.'

In all fairness to Beghs, there was no way for him to know how vexed Sawwse felt, or that his good-natured prank would set in motion life-altering events for the young gnome.

Sawwse patted down some of her wispy hairs, which had stood on end. 'You know what Beghs, you do such a good job attending to this library.' The sarcasm was so thinly veiled it was practically indecent. She waved her hand vaguely about, taking in the mildew-infested 'Politics' section and the piles of squirrel droppings lining the 'Art History' shelves. 'How about I lock up tonight? You should go and enjoy the reverie.'

As Sawwse prepared to double down in her subterfuge, Beghs just chuckled, passed the keys to her, and waved good night as he left.

'Well, that was surprisingly easy,' said Sawwse.

The squirrel jumped up onto Sawwse's shoulder looking at the keys in her hand. 'Would've been easier if you'd let me pick the lock.'

'As I said, I'm not a thief.' Sawwse met the squirrel's sceptical look head on. 'I'm not! I'm merely going to borrow it.'

'Whatever you say.'

Sawwse approached the bamboo cage holding the Gnomeopedia. Her heart thumped in her chest. What on Esh was she doing? She'd be in *so* much trouble if anyone found out. And yet, she found herself rifling through the collection of keys almost on autopilot.

'There.'

It was an ornate, dark wooden key and it felt right in her hand. Engraved on the key's grip were tiny open books. Sawwse placed the key snugly into the cage's lock and held her breath as she turned it. There was a satisfying click and the door to the cage swung open. Her heart was beating harder than ever. She reached in and ran her fingers across the bold lettering on the Gnomeopedia's spine.

'Am I really doing this?'

The squirrel made to reply, but Sawwse covered its mouth with her hand.

'It was a rhetorical question.'

Sawwse slipped the Gnomeopedia into her bag and stepped outside. She grabbed a silk vine and swung her way home.

Chapter 2:
Sorrow-Wraith

'"**When a living** being suffers an unspeakable emotional hurt, they may occasionally transform into a hateful creature known in the local tongue as a sorrow-wraith."'

Stretching herself out after an accidentally uncomfortable reverie trance – she'd sat on her own foot for six hours without realising – Sawwse hung upside down from the tree branch that had persuaded its way into her room. The Gnomeopedia lay on the floor, open on a page featuring an illustration of a monstrous, hulking figure.

'That sounds grim,' said the squirrel, who'd followed Sawwse all the way home.

'It gets worse. Listen to this: "These beings return from the dead to roam the land where they were hurt, searching for revenge. If one comes across a sorrow-wraith, the best course of action is to run fast and far, lest you are sucked up inside its vortex of pain and hate."'

'Vortex of pain and hate. Laying it on a bit thick, aren't they?'

'I know.' Sawwse dropped to her feet. 'I think I'd still pick them over the shadow crabs though.'[6]

Since returning home, Sawwse had spent all day glued to the Gnomeopedia. She carefully scooped up the tome and held it open in her hands, flicking to a bookmarked page. An illustration of a large, curved building was drawn over two pages. Written underneath in bold text: 'The Conservatoire of Rhyddinas.'

'Imagine studying in a place like that,' she said, dreamily.

'Looks fancy,' said the squirrel.

'They say it's the height of musical education in Esh'areth.'

'Not full of shadow crabs and sorrow-wraiths, is it?'

'No! The Gnomeopedia says the place is wonderful!' Sawwse kicked a pair of socks she'd left lying on the floor. 'I don't know why I should be any less able to study there than anyone else.'

'So, why don't you?' The squirrel tilted its head.

Sawwse scoffed. 'Did you forget about the travel ban?'

'Oh, right. They've put a big fence around the forest?'

'Well, no.'

'A magical perimeter, then? One that sends you back on yourself when you try to leave?'

'No.'

'Ah, big scary sentinels guarding the exits?'

---

[6] "Shadow crabs are horrible crustaceans that appear on sunny days, hide in your shadow, and snip at your ankles. They're not particularly dangerous, but make sure to double up on socks if visiting the beaches of Achillesthrøb." (Gnomeopedia, p. 62)

'Not that either.' Sawwse interrupted the squirrel as it was about to make another suggestion. 'It's more about the feeling of leaving than anything physical. It's a... shame-based restriction.'[7]

The squirrel nodded patiently, and then said, 'The great thing about feelings is that they can change and tend to do so over time anyway.'

Sawwse noticed that the squirrel suddenly looked incredibly wise. She looked again at the illustration of the conservatoire for a few moments before carefully closing the Gnomeopedia and heaving it back into her bag.

The quiet sounds of rustling and creaking came from outside Sawwse's little home as her neighbours took hold of tree branches and set off. It was time for the town meeting. The squirrel followed Sawwse to her window and watched as a hundred or more gnomes swung from tree to tree towards the estate.

Sawwse quickly packed a bag to bring to Dannse's. She stuffed her flute into the backpack, along with a hand drum, her hand gong, and hand viola. She packed her trumpet, a crumpet, and her violin. In the small crevice that remained she stuffed a triangle, a snare, and a circlet, and then bagged her bagpipe and piped her pipebag, and then finally, she took her lute from beside her hammock and used a long, hairy string to attach it to the front of the bag. She suddenly had a thought. 'Do you think Dannse would notice if I skipped the meeting?'

---

[7] Not literally, although the clan of gnomes in the mountainous region of Guiltoria did employ shame-based security forces to guard their perimeter. Any gnome wanting to leave was met with a flurry of tuts and sighs.

The squirrel raised its tiny eyebrows at Sawwse.

'Okay, okay.' The squirrel was right. Of course, she should go to the meeting, despite each one boring her to tears. She'd promised Dannse after all.

Sawwse placed her little backpack over her shoulders and sighed. 'Come on then, hop up.'

The squirrel ran along Sawwse's body and sat on her shoulder, ready for the journey. A couple of minutes later they were swinging their way to the grand hall of the estate.

The shape of the hall resembled the inside of a violin. Sawwse found a space near the curved back wall alongside some of the younger gnomes, while the Council opened the meeting from a stage at the long thin end of the room.

The Council rotated the chair of the meeting, and today it was due to be Fuggh Banns. He wore grey robes and despite his youthful appearance, he sported a long, wispy, white beard.

'Welcome everyone. I hope you have all had a long day of pranking, and may you continue to prank for a long time still.'

Sawwse rolled her eyes. It was customary to start every meeting with some kind of reference to pranks, as it was such an integral part of gnome culture.

'Unfortunately today's meeting brings with it worrying news. Someone has stolen The Gnomeopedia.'

'Crimp.' A knot the size of a prize-winning watermelon suddenly appeared in Sawwse's stomach. She'd assumed they wouldn't even notice it missing from the library.

A murmur made its way around the room.

'This book is dangerous. It gives false impressions about what gnomes are able to do. Yes, it is an interesting artefact that we should keep and respect, but only to illustrate the dangers that occur when certain types of gnome sit on the Council. What is a gnome supposed to do when faced with a dragon? Feed it? Zazazaza!' The Council chair laughed, and the laughter rippled around the room.

'The Fugghs of the world are so small minded,' muttered Sawwse under her breath.

The more she pondered it, the more it seemed absurd to her that she had never left the forest. When gnomes had been permitted to roam the continents freely, Emmeline Flowerdew had walked all Four Continents without harm or hindrance, bringing her music to faraway lands. *It's gnomes like Banns who keep us from sharing in the joys of the world*, she thought.

'It is important that we trust one another.' Fuggh Banns held out his open arms. 'We have no need for conflict in the Blue Forest, so please, whoever took the book, come forward now and we will forgive you.'

Silence preceded another murmur, which circulated the hall. Sawwse kept her place. She knew Fuggh's platitudes were empty, and that if she came forward, she'd have millions of pranks to deal with. Better to let them stew for a while and then quietly return it at a later point.

'I think it's time we moved on, isn't it?'

The gnomes closest to Sawwse turned to look at her. She could've sworn she hadn't said anything. Sawwse spun around to look for the voice as it continued.

'There is a place for us out there in the world, but they will forget about us if we don't stop looking at our thumbs.'

Sawwse looked to her shoulder. It was the squirrel! She tried to grab it, but the squirrel sprang onto her head and took another deep breath. 'No, shush! What are you doing?'

'Sawwse Bohge will be our envoy to the world.'

'A different Sawwse Bohge.' Sawwse continued swiping at the squirrel, but it was too nimble. 'It means a different Sawwse Bohge!'

'The future of the Blue Forest lies at the feet of our young, not in old conservative trolls like Fuggh.'

'Are we happy calling the leader of our Council a troll?' Sawwse swiped again. Another miss.

'So, it is you who stole the Gnomeopedia,' said Fuggh.

Now every face in the hall was looking directly at Sawwse. Many of the younger gnomes were smiling. For want of something more appropriate to do, Sawwse did a little bow, unbalancing the squirrel, who jumped onto a nearby gnome's head instead.

Sawwse's nervous voice failed to carry more than a few feet into the hall. 'Well, no one actually said that it was–'

'Yes, Sawwse Bohge has the tome,' the squirrel boomed, projecting into every inch of the hall. 'She will fill every page with new knowledge. She will study at the Conservatoire of Rhyddinas. She will see the world. And she will do whatever the heck she wants to!' The squirrel beamed at Sawwse, and in that moment, Sawwse could've sworn she saw the twinkle of Dannse Gan's eyes. 'Now go. Run into the world!'

Fuggh sent his attendants rushing towards Sawwse, but the younger gnomes by the entrance blocked their way. The next thing she knew she was running out of the hall, exhilarated and scared in equal measure. She clambered out of the estate, and ran to the nearest set of vines. The gnomes gave chase, swinging after her, but they were no match for Sawwse. In no time at all, she had reached the edge of the Blue Forest.

The chasing gnomes fell back at the border, but Sawwse didn't stop. Dropping to the ground, and hurtling through unfamiliar vines, bush and leaves, she ran, and ran, and ran, while her mind did the same. What on Esh was she thinking? She'd just spent the morning poring over a thousand terrifying things that could kill her in about a million different ways, and now she was running straight towards them. *Isn't that the definition of crazy?* thought Sawwse. *No, that's doing the same thing and expecting different results. What, like learning music every day and hoping you'll be picked to lead reverie, even though they never ever pick you? Ha!* Now that Sawwse thought about it, it was crazier to stay than to leave. In fact, it made quite a lot of sense to leave. She was going to experience all that the Four Continents had to offer. She was going to taste every flavour, smell every scent, see every sight, hear every note, and touch everything that it was appropriate to touch. She was going to do it all and nothing would get in her way. Not even the absolutely enormous sleeping ogre she'd just run head first into. Fear stopped her breath, her tongue, and her movement. The ogre opened one eye and raised itself onto elbows, like a sleepy bear.

Fearing that gnome-breakfast was the first thing on the ogre's mind, Sawwse's whole body shook violently as words burst from her mouth, words she had never expected to say, thoughts that she hadn't even known were possible to articulate. 'Hello, my name is Sawwse Bohge please don't eat me I'm running away on an adventure and want to be the greatest musician in the world.'

The panicked gnome inhaled deeply and watched the ogre slowly stand to his feet, towering above her. He leant his face down close to hers. 'Hello, Sawwse Bohge,' he said. 'I'm Marius, and I adore music.'

--

An excerpt from the Gnomeopedia

Everyone knows that we live within the Four Continents, and specifically the continent of Esh'areth. But how best to describe each continent? With crisps, of course! Esh'areth is very much the 'ready salted' of the bunch. It's a safe choice, often considered dull, but not without its fans. Shi'areth is naturally the 'chilli pepper' with its heat and its ability to make one sweat just thinking about it. Wed'areth is more of a 'salt and vinegar' flavour: full of sharp, tangy edges, but delicious if you like that sort of thing. Finally, No'areth is full of wizards, so it's probably 'prawn cocktail' or something. I don't know. I've lost my train of thought and I'm off to eat some crisps.

--

It turns out, there was no need for Sawwse to be scared. She'd been walking with Marius for over an hour, and she'd come to realise that he was the loveliest, most gentle, most amiable running-away partner that she could ever have imagined. Crucially, for someone who probably could've swallowed Sawwse in two gulps, he was a vegetarian. He was also a brilliant audience.

'Delightful,' said Marius. 'I haven't heard music this pleasant for a long time.'

Sawwse beamed. Until Marius qualified it by saying he hadn't heard *any* music for a long time. She swung her lute behind her back. 'Yeah, well, I'll take it. Still a better review than I ever got back home.'

'I wouldn't take reviews from Blue Forest folk at face value.'

Sawwse looked askance at the ogre. 'You know about us?'

'I do.' Marius smiled cryptically. 'Most don't.'

'What makes you so special?'

'Oh, I'm not special. I'm your neighbour.'

'Our friendly neighbourhood ogre? Gods, this is exciting! In fact–' Sawwse quickly rooted around in her backpack and retrieved a thin cone made of bark, decorated with sticky green and yellow leaves. She held it out for Marius to take. '–a party hat. To celebrate being neighbours.'

Marius chuckled. He placed the party hat on his head. A small bit of loose string was sewn into either side of the cone to keep it on. The hat looked like a tiny acorn sitting pert atop Marius' large head.

'You are pulling off that look in a BIG way.'

Marius laughed a belly-shaking laugh, vibrating the ground underneath Sawwse's feet. And then he said, 'You are a good soul, Sawwse Bohge. You've no idea how much I needed that.'

Sawwse looked up at Marius and saw a deep sadness resting behind his eyes. 'Do you want to talk about it?'

'A good soul,' repeated Marius, but he said no more. Instead, he simply sighed and continued his heavy-footed shuffle into the outskirts of the forest.

Sawwse didn't press any further. She swung the lute back around and began to play again. The trees here grew further apart and the birds and beasts of the forest gave way to the meditative thrum of cicadas against a gentle breeze. Sawwse began to reflect and refract the sounds she could hear around them. Harmonising with the cicadas' chirps, Sawwse somehow evoked their life cycle: two to seventeen long years tunnelling underground, only to emerge and perform a festival of song.

Marius smiled, a wide, warm-hearted ogre grin. 'You really should join the conservatoire in Rhyddinas.'

'That's exactly where I'm heading! Do you think they'll accept me?'

'They'd be lucky to have you.'

Sawwse blushed.

'But you do have a long trek ahead of you.'

'Oh. Like a twenty-to-thirty-minute kind of thing?' This didn't really make any sense, because Blue Forest gnomes didn't really have much concept of time.

Marius chuckled again. 'More of a three-to-four-day kind of thing.'

'Pretty similar then?'

'No.' Marius took off a large rucksack and lowered it next to Sawwse. 'I'll take you there, but we'll head back to my house first.'

'Bit forward, eh?' Sawwse flashed a cheeky grin, before adding earnestly, 'But yes, please. That would be incredibly generous.'

They'd walked no more than thirty minutes when a loud crack of thunder rang out high above them. Strangely, there were no clouds in the sky.

'Curious,' said Marius.

'Very much so.' Almost everything was curious to Sawwse. The canopy within the Blue Forest was so thick and full that she hadn't ever really seen the sky before. It was amazing. 'That's been up there the whole time?'

Marius walked them to a nearby clearing and set down his backpack. Sawwse hopped out and stretched her arms wide. 'Wow. That last day or two really dragged. This Rhyddinas? Bit smaller than I imagined.'

'We've only been walking for half an hour.'

'Gotcha. About halfway there?'

Suddenly, an icy gust of wind cut through the clearing, chilling Sawwse to her boots. It blew through the clearing and travelled up a nearby hill.

'Don't move.' Marius' demeanour instantly changed from amiable to alert, fierce almost.

'Are you sure?' asked Sawwse. There was panic in her eyes, but not in the direction of the wind. She was looking straight ahead at the other side of the clearing. 'Because my instinct would be to run.'

Marius slowly turned to see what had caught her attention. An enormous beast pushed through the trees at the edge of the clearing, knocking them down in the process. Its eyes were red. Drool poured from its jaw. And it had a hungry look about it.

'That shouldn't be here,' said Marius quietly.

Aaaaawoooooooarrrggghhhh!

The beast howled. It was a cry of pain, fear, frenzy, and several other things that made Sawwse glad she'd stumbled across an ogre the size of a small house.

'Can I run now?'

'No. I'll deal with this. Do not move.'

Marius ran full tilt at the beast, colliding with it at force and rolling back out of the clearing, and out of Sawwse's sight.

Sawwse waited approximately two seconds before pegging it in the opposite direction, which just happened to be up the same hill the icy wind had travelled. She half ran, half scrambled, through the thickets that blanketed the hill.

Only once she reached the top did she afford herself a glance back down at the clearing at the foot of the hill. Sawwse walked backwards, keeping an eye out for any movement below. She took a few steps and then felt the heel of her boot press down on something squishy.

Squelch.

Sawwse hopped on one foot and lifted her other foot to her waist. There was a tiny, squashed frog stuck to the underside of her boot. It wore a tiny, gold crown – now crushed.

'Sorry, King Frog!'

Sawwse peeled the frog from the sole of her boot and laid it down on the ground in front of her. She put her right arm at her breast and bowed in her traditional manner. When she raised her head, she let out a gasp. There was a creature lumbering towards her, arms outstretched. Its long black hair fell across its ghostly pale face. It was a creature she'd hoped never to encounter: a sorrow-wraith.

'Well, crimp.'

Sawwse bolted it back down the hill and decided that she'd almost certainly do whatever Marius told her to in the future.

Chapter 3:
King Frog

A short while before Sawwse encountered a sorrow-wraith, a royal carriage stopped atop the same hill. It was a nice carriage. Not just nice, in fact, but luxurious. It had the comfiest seats, leg room for days, and even an in-built entertainment system – which was just a small goblin tied to a chair delivering stories upon request. The carriage was capable of twelve horsepower. Less if any of the horses were feeling lazy. If you were to see this carriage at the local trader, it'd probably be listed as "the fancy boy." But you'd be very unlikely to come across it in a shop, because this carriage belonged to King Poht of Dorienne: The Reflective King. He'd brought it here to show his daughter the extent of their kingdom.

'All this will be yours, Eugenie.' King Poht shifted in his seat and drew back the carriage window's thin red curtain.

'Oh, papa. It's so vast!' Princess Eugenie leant forward and peered out of the window.

The scene was perfect. Dappling sunlight filtered through a row of beech trees, and between two of the trees, the path opened to a wide vista showing plains, valleys, settlements, towns, and far away, large blue mountains. Distance was subordinate to the gaze of those who held this view. Most views were subordinate to King Poht's gaze, who only really had eyes for himself, hence the nickname. Mirrors were propped up all over the inside of the carriage. He was currently attempting to hold one out of sight of his daughter.

'Did you bring me here merely to look at yourself?' Eugenie rolled her eyes and then pulled at her father's sleeve. About a dozen tiny mirrors clattered to the floor of the carriage.

'Ahem. I brought you here, because it is time you learnt the ways of governance.' King Poht played with the curls of his luscious dark hair. 'I will not look this fair forever, after all.'

'I am ready, papa. I am the sword that will protect Dorienne.'

'Pfft. There is no sense in ruling with an iron fist.[8] There is also no need. All the hard work has been done already.' King Poht raised his head to the roof of the carriage and smiled at the reflection beaming down at him. 'Peace with our closest neighbours. No pesky foreign wars to contend with. And a home populace content with their lot.'

'That is something I have always wondered about,' began Princess Eugenie, casually taking the mirror from the roof down and tucking it under her seat. 'Why are the people content with their lot? Should we not do more for them?'

---

[8] Just ask Iron Fist McGraw whose diplomacy and negotiations were always scuppered by his unyielding handshakes.

'Ha! Spoken with all the naivete of an eighteen year old. More, she says.' King Poht doubled over with pretend laughter. He retrieved a mirror from within his trouser leg.

'Well, why not?' Princess Eugenie held out her hand until her father begrudgingly placed the mirror into it.

'You cannot give the people too much, because it would never be enough. The secret is balance. We take a small proportion of the population and give them more than the others, and they in turn protect us from the rabble. As long as we wave from the carriage or balcony every once in a while, they are kept happy.' King Poht held his hand out in front of him to check his cuticles. 'That's why we should always look our best, my dear. We are public servants after all.'

Father and daughter shared a look before both burst out laughing. 'Oh father, you are devilish.'

'*Us* serving *them*! Could you imagine?'

Their entertainment system – the small goblin who had thus far been patiently listening to the conversation – suddenly spoke up in a gruff voice. 'There was a princess in times of yore, who made it her mission to serve the poor. She'd walk the streets, giving the homeless new sheets, and her generosity passed into lore. Whence she chanced upon–'

'No,' interrupted King Poht.

'Whence she chanced upon some glühwein, her heart–'

'I said no!' King Poht threw a grape at the goblin.

'Seems relevant is all.'

'I don't care how relevant it is!'

'She was very popular. Just saying.'

'He makes a point, papa.' Princess Eugenie frowned. 'What if they don't like me as much as they like you?'

'That wasn't my point,' muttered the goblin.

'Oh darling, they will adore you. Besides, we will take our time. You will accompany me more often in public. We will get you some less… militaristic attire. Over time the people will see you as the one best placed to lead them. So long as we work slowly and steadily, all will be well–'

A loud crack rang out high above the carriage.

Princess Eugenie's hand snapped to her scabbard resting against the carriage door. She leant her head out of the window and asked the nearest guard to investigate.

'I am sure it is nothing.' King Poht shared none of his daughter's concern. He clapped his hands together and addressed the goblin. 'A story.'

'I really wish you wouldn't clap at me,' said the goblin under his breath.

'A story, you cretin!'

'Okay, okay. Blimey O'Reilly.' The goblin cleared his throat. 'How about the one with the little guys who have to throw a ring into a big fire?'

'Too long!'

'There's the one with the boy wizard who fights the bad guy whose name you can't say?'

'Too nerdy!'

'Perhaps the ice queen who struggles to let things go?'

'Too catchy!'

'What about the warrior princess who tries to turn back time?'

King Poht considered this. 'I do not think I know that one.'

'Marvellous. It begins with a princess unexpectedly bereaved. She gathers counsel from a dangerous source who tells her about an ancient machine capable of controlling time.'

Princess Eugenie wasn't listening. Her focus was drawn to the icy wind that had just permeated through the carriage. King Poht merely pulled his velvet blankie over his legs, but Eugenie sensed this was something more sinister than a mere chill. She drew her long blade and pushed open the door.

What she found outside was like something from a dream, and a bad one at that. Her eight-strong team of powerful knights were gone, replaced by a who's who of woodland animals: badgers, foxes, cramble knadgers.[9] They wore miniature versions of the Dorienne armour. Had it not been for the worrying implication of transmogrification magic, it would have been incredibly cute.[10]

Impossible, thought Princess Eugenie. The amount of magic it would take to launch an attack like this on eight of her best knights was unthinkable.

Without warning, the royal carriage rocked violently from side to side, and she heard her father's high-pitched squeal.

'Papa!' Princess Eugenie turned on her heel and launched herself into the carriage, but it was too late.

---

[9] "Cramble knadgers: these curious beasts have the ability to walk on two legs but choose to scurry around in the dirt and mud. This tells you a lot about cramble knadgers. Mostly, that they know how to have a good time. There are rumours that they hold the same mental faculties as humans but choose to keep them hidden. To that we say: if only humans did the same." (Gnomeopedia, p. 171)

[10] Even *with* the implication, a dormouse wielding a tiny sword and shield will always be incredibly cute.

There was a tiny snail sitting where the in-built entertainment system should have been. It even had a tiny earring. Her father's seat was empty.

'Papa, where are you?' Back outside, she threw a couple of foxes and mice out of the way, searching for whatever her father had been turned into. And then she saw it. A little gold crown glittered in the light. It rested atop the head of a frog, currently hopping around like crazy towards a thicket. 'Wait! Let me catch you!'

Princess Eugenie froze in horror as she watched the heel of a boot crush her transformed father. It was a gnome of all things. Princess Eugenie let out a gasp as the murderer spoke in a scornful tone: 'Sorry, King Frog,' before mocking her father further by bowing elaborately.

The gnome saw her and ran away.

A thousand thoughts flashed through Princess Eugenie's head as she cradled her father's slimy body in her hands. But one thought kept rising to the top. Revenge. Now, if only there was a way to turn back time…

Chapter 4:
Terror Incognita

An even shorter while before Sawwse encountered what was not in fact a sorrow-wraith, a crack appeared in the sky and a wizard fell out of it.

Wheeeeeeeeeeeeeeeeee!

Since we last met Mirrah, she figured out that she had been set up by one of her own. The trap could only have been set by another member of The Twelve. Mirrah had already alerted her closest colleague about the double agent.

Wheeeeeeeeeeeeeeeeee!

Since we last met Mirrah, she understood that she could do nothing about the Ancient Device, which was probably already calling to the dark forces in the world. She'd also realised that the curse affecting her mind was too powerful to unpick, and therefore, she was doomed.

Wheeeeeeeeeeeeeeeeee!

Since we last met Mirrah, she had gone quite mad.

Mirrah fell through the air like a lead balloon, albeit a lead balloon that flapped its arms like a bird and thoroughly enjoyed itself. Her sanity returned moments before she hit the forest floor, which she would have done had she not been one of the most powerful wizards across the Four Continents.

'Right,' said Mirrah, hovering an inch above the earth.

This had become a habit. She'd lose control of her mind and when she wrested it back, she'd be somewhere she didn't recognise. Mirrah dropped the remaining inch to the ground and heard a squelch. Fox poo.

'Typical,' she said, using a simple spell to clean her robe. 'Another fine mess you've gotten us into.'

This had also become a habit. Talking to herself. She'd never wanted to be one of those stereotypical mad old wizards that talked to themselves, and to be fair, she wasn't old. She wasn't really talking to herself either. It was more that her rational self had begun chastising the self that had gone a bit loopy.

You see, losing one's mind isn't as simple as a switch being flicked. It's a drawn-out process, taking away faculties piece by piece over time, like, for example, her sense of place.

'Where have you brought me this time?'

A gentle breeze blew through the trees surrounding Mirrah. She closed her eyes and took in the rich scents of the forest floating on the air, and before she could stop it, she was floating along with them. Losing control of her magic had become yet another habit. Her body turned to wind, and she drifted through the forest, through a clearing, through thickets to a hilltop. There was a carriage parked atop the hill.

Mirrah's body rematerialised. Several knights guarded the carriage. One of the knights approached her. She was relieved. Someone to give her answers.

'Hello there. Could you tell me what realm this is?' These were the words that Mirrah had intended to say.

Unfortunately, what left her mouth was quite different. She'd actually spoken the arcane language of magic.

In an instant, the knight was transformed into a little squirrel, armour and all.

'Oops.'

The other knights immediately rounded on Mirrah, ready to attack.

'Ah, no. That was an accident. Look, I'll change her back now.' Mirrah focused on the squirrel-knight and gestured with her hands, muttering more magic words under her breath while she did so. When she looked up, all the other knights had been turned into woodland animals. 'Oh, for goodness' sake.'

Mirrah ran to the carriage door, just as Princess Eugenie stepped out of the other one. She poked her head in and frightened King Poht and his goblin storyteller half to death.

'There's been a bit of a misunderstanding. I'm trying to figure out where I am.'

It happened again. This time Mirrah saw the fear in King Poht's eyes as the spell she hadn't meant to cast left her mouth and bounced around the carriage, ricocheting off the mirrors attached to each surface, and rocking the wagon in the process. Mirrah didn't wait to see King Poht turned into a frog. She ducked out of the carriage and ran, as far away as she could before she did any more damage. Once she was sure there was no one else around, she took cover under a large tree and hoped she'd keep control of her mind long enough to plot her next move. If only she could go back to before any of this began.

'That's it!'

Inspiration struck. So did lightning. A huge bolt of forked lightning struck the tree that Mirrah was resting on. Another accidental bout of magic. But Mirrah took no notice. She was thinking of the Ancient Device.

'I can simply use the Device and turn back time before I discovered it. No more curse, and no more danger of the Device falling into the wrong hands. Why hadn't I thought of that before?'

Mirrah had seemingly forgotten that the Ancient Device was only capable of controlling time for evil purposes, hence why it had been hidden in the first place. She suddenly seemed to notice the tree's bushy leaves above her were ablaze. Casually waving her hand, the fire froze in place. She shrugged. 'Close enough.'

Mirrah walked away from the tree and picked a random direction. 'Now, if I could only remember where the Ancient Device was…'

Chapter 5:
Upsetting an Ogre

Sawwse Bohge skidded back down the hill, tumbling through the bushes and brambles until she reached the clearing where Marius had told her to wait. The sorrow-wraith had not followed her, thank the gods, but her troubles were far from over, for there was Marius sitting with the very beast he had supposedly chased away. The worst part was, they appeared to be getting on.

'Gra! Gra! Gra!' The beast slapped its thigh. 'Grood one.'

'I just assumed the mushrooms would grow back,' said Marius.

'Mushrooms!' The beast growled its approval, wiping tears from its red eyes as it laughed. 'Back!'

'Er, Marius?' Sawwse stood cautiously at the perimeter of the clearing.

'Ah, there you are,' said Marius, acknowledging Sawwse with his wide grin. He patted a spot on the picnic blanket between himself and the beast.

Sawwse didn't move. Her gaze was transfixed on the incredibly terrifying beast and the way in which it was currently devouring a crumpet. It was devouring it in the way only a fifty-eyed, five-hundred-toothed, hairy, scary, hulking, shulking monstrosity could do. Wetly.

'Oh, sorry.' Marius shook his head. 'I forgot to introduce you. This is Johan.'

'His name is, "Johan?"'

The beast spoke up in its gruff voice. 'Well, that's the closest I can get in the crommon tongue. My actual name is–' The noise that left the beast's mouth was so horrifying that Sawwse immediately threw up and keeled over. The beast rushed over to her side. 'Aprologies. That can happen.' He pointed to the pool of vomit. 'Are you finished with that?'

Sawwse nodded meekly.

Before the beast had fully unfurled its tongue to lick up Sawwse's vom, Marius placed a gentle hand on its shoulder. 'Let's get you home.'

The beast slowly retracted its tongue and nodded. It turned to Sawwse and said, 'Nice to meet rou.'

'Charmed,' muttered Sawwse.

Then, the most peculiar thing happened. With a faint popping sound, the beast vanished.

'What on Esh?' Sawwse jumped to her feet in astonishment. She felt the air where the beast had been, carefully stepping over her own puke.

'I sent him home.' Marius chuckled.

'You mean to say that you know…' Sawwse dropped her voice to a whisper '…magic?'

'A little.' Marius smiled his warm-hearted grin and gestured for Sawwse to return to his backpack.

Sawwse was dumbfounded. Magic! Actual full-blown magic! This was incredible. The only magic she'd seen in the Blue Forest was the old magic that kept it secret. But that was *old* and *boring*. Nothing like being able to vanish something… some*one* out of thin air. 'Yer a wizard, Marius?'

'I'm a gardener.'

'Have you ever turned anyone into a chicken?' Sawwse hopped into Marius' backpack. 'How about cheese? Have you ever made cheese?'

'You don't need magic to make cheese.' Marius grinned, picked up his backpack and strode off.

'Have you ever made any imps dance the fandango?'

'No.'

'Have you ever ridden a tornado?'

'No.'

'Have you ever flown in the air like a bird?'

Marius raised his eyebrows. 'Perhaps some music?'

That's not a no, thought Sawwse. But she decided not to press it. After the excitement of the sorrow-wraith and the beast, it would be nice to relax with some music.

Clearing her mind, Sawwse focused on the landscape around them. A beck gently flowed over, under and through a bed of rusty coloured rocks. On their left, the ground rose to a beech grove, while on their right, the path led them steadily downhill. Large fern bushes and brambles bordered the path, and large pyramidal trees with strange pink fruits hung over them. Sawwse played an appropriately slow, meandering melody.

After walking in this way for some time, the land levelled out and Sawwse spotted a large congregation of trees: their branches and trunks twisting around each other. It wasn't possible to see through their tight netting, but in the centre was a small thatch hut. With some effort, Marius pulled open its heavy stone door and gestured for Sawwse to enter.

Inside was a very modest home. There wasn't much in terms of furnishings, just a simple straw bed, a few shelves, and a wooden desk.

'Ah, so *this* is Rhyddinas?' asked Sawwse, somewhat disheartened.

Marius bore his big toothy grin. 'I have a few matters to attend to before we get to Rhyddinas.'

'Oh, you did say that.' Sawwse picked at the straw of Marius' bed. 'So, this is your home?'

'Yes. And through here is my garden, Garmish.' Marius pointed to a large plank of wood that covered a circular hole in the wall.

'Huh?' It was weird. Sawwse knew that Garmish meant 'safe haven,' but she didn't know how she knew. She didn't speak Ogreic after all. She began to say as much when she suddenly became aware of the thick grunts coming out of her mouth. 'Wait a minute, have we been speaking Ogreic this whole time?'

Marius simply tousled the gnome's hair and gently motioned her outside. Sawwse was about to argue when she was struck by an incredible sight. A garden unlike any other, filled with lush, verdant plants, flowers and fruits from across the world. Even the most ardent of nature-haters would find it difficult to be unimpressed with the scale, variety and beauty of Garmish.

The amiable ogre led Sawwse through his grounds, gesturing at this plant and that, occasionally taking seeds from his pocket to scatter in the wildflower sections. Sawwse, stupefied, followed close behind, awed by the garden's beauty, and, in part, awed by Marius too.

After they had walked for a while, the day's adventure took its toll on Sawwse, who couldn't stop herself from yawning. Marius placed a large gentle hand on her shoulder and led her back inside the hut to a tiny, gnome-sized bed. Her eyes drifted closed as she watched Marius return to pottering around in his garden.

--

The next few days passed in a similar pattern. First, the sun would softly peel back the night until the hut was too bright for sleep. Then, Marius would busy himself at his desk. It was too tall for Sawwse to see what "matters" he was attending to, so instead, she set about exploring the vast gardens, taking inspiration from beautiful and bizarre trees and flowers to create new melodies with her lute. As the evenings drew in, Marius would find Sawwse in the garden and prepare for her a feast of roasted nuts, berries, and the freshest fruit imaginable. It was pure, uncomplicated bliss. Though, Sawwse did begin to wonder whether they'd ever set off for Rhyddinas.

It came as a shock then, when Sawwse awoke one morning to find Marius gone. She climbed to the top of the tallest tree she could find, but there was no sign of the ogre anywhere.

It was weird. And though she'd only known him for a few days, she knew it wasn't like him to leave without saying anything.[11]

Sawwse slinked back into the hut and froze. There on Marius' straw bed was the Gnomeopedia, open about a quarter of the way through. Her eyes widened as she read the entry:

---

[11] He wasn't like those other ogres who say they're nipping out for cigarettes and never come back.

> Ogres: generally dim-witted creatures that spend much of their time clubbing each other over the head. There are worse ways to spend an evening than sojourning to a village tavern and informing the nearest ogre that someone has called them a 'kradak adahr' - a moth eater. This really sets their ear flaps itching. Take pleasure in the ensuing chaos - preferably with a cold beer to hand.

There was an incredibly insulting depiction of an ogre underneath.

'Crimp!'

Sawwse grabbed the offending book, swept her things into her bag and ran out through the crack in the stone door.

'Marius! Marius! I didn't write that. You have to believe me.' Sawwse inhaled deeply, readying herself to project a louder shout throughout the woods, until she considered where she was: an unfamiliar woodland where sorrow-wraiths and scary beasts appeared around every corner. 'Er, best not.'

The ground was cushioned with old, soft pine needles. Sawwse slumped onto it, deflated. She took out the Gnomeopedia and placed it in front of her. Thinking back to Marius' kindly face and the care with which he had looked after her, Sawwse violently scribbled out the entry on ogres and in the space below wrote: 'Ogres: kind and generous lovers of seeds, mushrooms, music, and people.'

That doesn't really do him justice at all, she thought glumly.

Even worse than losing her friend, Sawwse had lost her lift to Rhyddinas, and she had no idea which way it was.[12] She scurried up the nearest tree and looked out past the woodland. There was a well-travelled road leading to a village.

'Seems as good a place to start as any,' muttered Sawwse.

'Do you reckon?'

The unfamiliar voice came from beside Sawwse's ear, startling her so much that she lost her footing and tumbled down the tree, colliding with, what felt like, every single branch along the way.

'Oof.' Sawwse rubbed her bum.

'I'm so sorry! That was an accident!'

There was the voice again, but its owner was nowhere to be seen. Sawwse spun around. 'Who's there?' There was no reply. 'Friend or foe?' She was doing her best not to sound scared. Though, the fact that she hadn't been eaten yet was a good sign.

'I don't have any friends.' A pause. 'Also, what's a foe?'

'I think it's some kind of noodle dish. Anyway, never mind that. Perhaps we could become friends?'

'I think I'd like that.' A white butterfly fluttered in front of Sawwse, settling on her nose. 'My name is Ruby Schap. It's pleasurable to greet you.'

Always one to respect manners, Sawwse introduced herself. She was going cross-eyed looking at the

---

[12] There were maps in the Gnomeopedia, but they were the equivalent of directions from 'that bloke' in the pub who scrawls the way to 'the best chippy' on some slightly damp bog roll.

butterfly, so she offered it her finger and the butterfly gingerly moved across.

'I don't suppose you know the way to Rhyddinas?'

'There's a road up ahead leading to a village. Seems as good a place to start as any.'

'You're just repeating what I said? Up in the tree?'

'No, I don't think it'd be up in the tree,' said Ruby, unironically.

'Right… well, I'm going to head over there if you fancy joining me?'

'Oh. Wait. I should–'

All of a sudden, Sawwse felt her hand growing heavier. The butterfly's wings began to thicken and grow, morphing into arms and legs, and the white silkiness of the body changed into a robed woman, all of which was suspended on Sawwse's right hand. There was a moment where this new form seemed to defy gravity. It was brief.

Sawwse dropped her hand to the ground, leaving Ruby heels-over-head. 'Sorry, sorry!' squeaked Ruby, apologetically. 'I knew I'd get that wrong. My head's still aflutter.'

'Not a bother.' Sawwse helped her up, amused and curious. 'You're human?'

'Currently? Yes.' They were of a similar size and stature, but Ruby had the features of a human. Personal space was clearly not an issue for Ruby who stood a few inches away from Sawwse's face.

Sawwse stepped back to get a better look at her: between the bangles and the multicoloured pendant, she looked a bit like a new age hippie. She had a youthful face, but it was in contrast with her unkempt sandy grey hair.

Ruby stepped forward once more, just ever so slightly too close. A nervous look was cast on her face. She looked like an anxious dog tossed aside countless times, yet desperate to be accepted. Ruby held out her hand and Sawwse gripped it firmly. 'Sorry about that.'

'Don't worry.' Sawwse smiled playfully. 'We have a saying in the Blue Forest: shake a hand twice, and… save your… lice. Or something.'

'But I don't have any lice. At least, I don't think I do.' Ruby sat on the floor and scratched the back of her neck with a foot, just like a dog. 'What's in Rhyddinas?'

'It's the musical conservatoire. I'm going to study there and become the greatest musician in the world!' Sawwse beamed her infectious smile.

Ruby smiled back. It was hard not to. The sheer confidence of the little gnome was intoxicating.

'So, fancy coming?'

It had taken Ruby a lot to strike up the conversation in the first place. She'd lived as a hermit for many years up until this point, but there was something about Sawwse that brought out an adventurous spirit in her that she didn't know she had. Ruby's anxious mind fired off a million reasons not to go, but instead she opened her mouth and said: 'I think my legs could do with a stretch.'

'That's the spirit.' Sawwse clapped Ruby on her shoulder and set off toward the open road.

'No, I mean literally.' Ruby called after her, walking with a strange gait. 'I was a butterfly for bloomin' ages.'

Chapter 6:
Eugenie's Return

While Sawwse spent her days pleasantly wandering around a beautiful garden with a very friendly ogre, Princess Eugenie was afforded a different luxury. And by luxury, I mean ordeal. Her father had just been murdered, her royal guard turned into woodland animals, and the horses that had driven her carriage had been turned into a fleet of lemmings. Instead of riding home in the posh carriage, she'd had to walk, all the while carrying her father's squashed frog body, and corralling her disobedient animal knights.

Having walked through forests, plains, villages and towns, Princess Eugenie arrived in Doriana, capital of the Dorienne Kingdom. It had taken three days and three nights on her feet without stopping, except to scold the knights for trying to eat one another, but she was finally home. Grief and shock paralysed her mind, while exhaustion wracked her body. She stumbled through the outskirts of the city and collapsed into a bundle of hay.

'Everyfink alright?'

It was a young turnip seller called Cribbins. He parted from his cart and crouched over Eugenie, instantly recoiling at the sight of a badger who bounced out of the hay and snapped at him.

'Er, I was just going to offer a nice crunchy turnip.' Cribbins turned one round in his hands. 'Might make her feel better.'

The badger barked and Cribbins dropped the turnip. He backed away as several foxes, mice, and cramble knadgers crept out of the hay and began hacking away at the turnip. Cribbins was about to run away when he felt a little tug at his trouser leg. A tiny dormouse looked up at him with tears swelling in its big round eyes. It gestured to Eugenie.

Cribbins cautiously stepped around the other animals and leant over the woman in the hay. Her feet were calloused and filthy, her uniform was tattered, and she appeared to be clutching a squashed frog. But wasn't that the royal crest? He turned her over and let out a quiet gasp. 'P-princess Eugenie!'

Without wasting a second, he tipped out the turnips from his cart and hauled Eugenie into it. After a fraught negotiation involving returning some of the turnips into the cart, he persuaded the animal knights to get in as well, and then covered them all with hay. With his makeshift rickshaw ready to roll, he burst from the market street as if his life depended on it, drawing the ire of fellow hawkers as he knocked into this stall and that, cabbages and potatoes cascading to the ground.

Two guards blocked the entrance to the short path which ran to the palace. They signalled for Cribbins to pull over. This was bad news. If they spotted the princess in his cart, he'd lose out on his reward, *and* he'd probably get in trouble.

'Halt. What's in the cart?'

'Turnips.'

The cart began to jostle as the animal knights fought within the hay. The guards gave Cribbins a dubious look.

'They're very fresh.'

One of the animals barked.

'And vocal.'

'Whatever, just leave the cart. We'll send for staff to collect it.'

Cribbins didn't move.

'Didn't you hear her? She said leave the cart.' The guard looked down his nose at Cribbins. He scoffed. 'You didn't think you'd be allowed in, did you?'

'Sorry, it's just that they need to use these turnips to help look for the princess, and I'm the only one practiced in… turnipmancy.'

The guard gave Cribbins an incredulous look. He was about to reprimand him again, when the other guard put a hand on his shoulder. 'The power of turnips is nothing to be sneezed at. I say let him through.'

With some reluctance and scepticism, the other guard waved Cribbins through. He forced himself to walk ten paces before breaking into a sprint. The huge stone dome sat atop the Palace and the large imposing spire rose high above it into the sky.

'Stop.'

Eugenie's faint voice came from within the hay.

Cribbins stopped instantly and started throwing off the hay. It turned out one of the badgers had fallen asleep on Eugenie's face and was suffocating her. He gingerly prised the badger away from the princess and set it down on the ground, before helping Eugenie out of the cart.

They walked the rest of the way to the palace gates together. Cribbins supported her frail body with his arm. He noticed that she still clutched the squashed frog to her chest.

Cribbins knocked on the large doors protecting the palace. After a pause, several guards appeared. They immediately dropped to one knee upon seeing Princess Eugenie's face.

'Your Majesty,' they said at once.

'Take me to the Council. At once.' Eugenie spoke with a quiet resilience. 'Invite this gentleman into the palace. I am to confer upon him the title of Lord Protector of Turnips.'

'Er…' Cribbins wasn't sure about this at all. He'd have much preferred a simple reward. 'Is it mandatory?'

The guards looked bemused. But what could they say? She was Princess Eugenie after all. 'Of course, your Majesty.'

'Find a wizard to turn this lot back into humans.' Eugenie gestured at the rabble of woodland animals in the cart. 'And then have them locked up for failing their job so spectacularly.'

Princess Eugenie laughed in that bleak way where the boundary between laughing and crying is completely obscured. There were tears anyway. Floods of them.

One of the palace guards placed an arm around the princess and led her into the castle. Cribbins slowly backed away, but only until he felt one of the guards prod him. There was no choice. Apparently, you can't turn down royalty, even if they're quite obviously mad.

'The bedchamber, Your Majesty?'

'No,' said Eugenie, through her sobs. 'Take me to the Council.'

Once inside the Council's Chamber of Secret – the one secret being what work the Council actually did – the room gasped, and then launched a barrage of questions.

'Your Majesty!'

'We assumed the worst!'

'Where is King Poht?'

Princess Eugenie stepped forward to the circular table and delicately placed the squashed frog down. The Council looked dubiously at one another. One of the braver councillors tried her luck.

'I thought it was your cousin that kissed a frog and–'

'This is my dear papa.' Eugenie wiped away a stream of snotty gunk from her nose. The expression in her eyes changed from deepest grief to harshest anger. 'He was callously transformed and killed by a powerful gnome wizard.'

'Our intelligence reports no such rogue wizardry in Dorienne,' said one of the councillors.

'We're not suggesting that you're making things up,' said another.

'Goodness no!' said a third. 'We're just saying that sometimes all you need is a cup of tea and a biscuit.'

Princess Eugenie took out her father's shrunken crushed crown from her pocket and threw it at the councillor. He turned it over in his hands and then nodded at the rest of the Council. The crown bore the royal insignia, which was impossible to replicate.

'We will send for the royal sketch artist at once. You must describe to him this wicked gnome.'

'We'll stick it on wanted posters across every inch of the kingdom.'

'My honourable friend means queendom, I'm sure.'

'No,' said Eugenie abruptly. 'We are a kingdom.'

The councillors looked askance at each other. One of them spoke up cautiously. 'I know it is awkward and difficult, but a quick coronation is usually best to quell the public mood.'

'There will be no coronation. Not yet.' Princess Eugenie paced back and forth. 'What does the Council know of temporal magic?'

This caused a hubbub among the Council. Surely, she wasn't serious.

'Surely, you're not serious?'

Eugenie pointed at the councillor who spoke and gestured for the guards to take him away. 'Lock him up.' She pointed at Cribbins, who had thus far been quaking at the very edge of the room, and told him to sit in the councillors place. 'This is the Lord Protector of Turnips. Your new colleague on the Council. What do you know of temporal magic?'

'Well, if I had it at my disposal, I'd increase my turnip yield a hundred-fold.'

Princess Eugenie smiled. 'Exactly. It isn't to be feared. It is to be utilised.'

One of the councillors who wasn't a turnip-seller spoke in a gentle voice. 'Your Majesty, I would love to see King Poht return, probably more than anyone else on the Council–' The other councillors grumbled at this '–but temporal magic is the purview of only the most powerful wizards. I don't know if even The Twelve have access to that kind of magic.'

'There's something else.' Eugenie tapped the side of her head. 'Something buried here. A memory of some kind of ancient magic. Do none of you sense it?'

The Council watched Eugenie cautiously.

'It's waiting for us. Somewhere. Once we find it, we will bring my dearest papa back to life.' Princess Eugenie turned away from the Council. 'I am going to bathe now. Then, I will sleep, and dream of murdering my papa's killer in a million different ways. When I return, I expect you to have found the ancient magic thing that I'm talking about.'

After Eugenie had stormed out of the room, the Council sat in a bewildered silence. The squashed froggy body of the former King Poht, stared lifelessly at them from the centre of the circular table.

One of the councillors spoke in an incredulous tone. '"The ancient magic thing?" Really?'

This got a laugh from the rest of the Council. Princess Eugenie had clearly lost her marbles, but what could they do about it? With no other heirs to the throne, they were going to have to follow her whims. Once the laughter died down, the councillors sat awkwardly in their places.

Finally, a lone voice at the table spoke, and it said: 'Turnip anyone?'

Chapter 7:
Wanted

Out in the countryside, the sun hid behind a tower of thick clouds, and the light turned blue as dusk approached. Squint and you'd see herds of micro cows and flocks of spherisheep[13] grazing in the lush fields that bordered the open road. Squint harder and you'd see a tiny gnome and her new companion skipping along said road, oblivious to the machinations in Doriana Palace.

'Woah. Look at that.' Sawwse pointed to a large tree in the middle of the road. Its bark was a shock of white, while its bushy green leaves were seemingly ablaze as they caught the sun's rays. Except, the sun's rays weren't touching the tree. 'It's on fire! Kind of.'

---

[13] "Spherisheep are perfectly round sheep that roll from one field to the next. They look pretty but are difficult to herd. Farmers will train their dogs at snooker for years before they are allowed to herd the spherisheep. Of course, the risk is that the dogs will train so well that they enter the pro snooker circuit and never return to the farm, focusing on their maximum breaks instead. Spherisheep wool is delightful. Good all year round. Best for balaclavas." (Gnomeopedia, pp. 690-691)

As she walked closer, she noticed that the fire wasn't spreading. Or moving at all. It was completely frozen. Sawwse wanted to reach out and touch it but wasn't sure she wanted to know what an ice-fire burn would feel like.

Sawwse spun on her heels toward Ruby but was instead accosted by a bird bursting from the ground into the air. As she righted herself, she became aware of a strange, squat man with an ugly hat addressing her with some urgency.

'Eert taht morf yawa teg!' shouted the man.

'Er… what?'

'Eert taht morf yawa teg!' shouted the man again. He gestured for Sawwse to come towards him. Sensing her reluctance, he pointed at the tree and then imitated an explosion, before calling her over to him once more.

'Oh, I get it.' Sawwse casually walked towards him. 'But I don't think you have to worry. It's frozen in–'

The tree exploded.

Sawwse was flung forward through the air and landed in a heap on the ground. The man quickly ran to her and helped her up.

'Yako ouy era?' he asked.

'Sorry, I don't understand.' Sawwse brushed herself down. 'Do you speak the common tongue?'

'Sey.' The man looked at Sawwse like this was obvious. 'Eugnot nommoc eht kaeps *uoy* od?'

Sawwse wasn't sure what to do. But then she remembered some advice from the Gnomeopedia. Sawwse spoke very slowly, very loudly, and very gesturingly. 'HELLO. MY NAME IS SAWWSE BOHGE. WHAT IS YOUR NAME?'[14]

The man folded his arms across his chest. He seemed annoyed. In response, he said: 'OLLEH. BERG SI EMAN YM.'

'Oh!' It suddenly dawned on Sawwse. 'You're speaking backwards.'

'Ton m'I on.'

'You are too! We used to play backchat loads when I was growing up. I'll prove it. Pick any word.'

'Kayak.'

'Not that one.'

'Madam.'

'Or that one!'

'Racecar.'

'What even is that?' Sawwse sighed.

The man chuckled. 'Esroh tuoba woh, yako?'

'Right. Horse. Now, how do you spell it?'

The man looked sceptical. 'H. O. R… ho. Ees I.'

'Exactly. You can spell it forwards, but only say it backwards.'

'Won tahw?'

Sawwse took an unreasonably long time to decipher. 'Oh! What now? Gods. No idea. I just wanted to prove I wasn't going mad.'

---

[14] "Some travel advice: In the unfortunately common instance wherein you, a gnome of the common tongue, might happen upon an individual of a different tongue, it is vital that you speak slowly, enunciate every syllable, and gesture wildly with your arms. This alleviates any difficulty that may arise from the conversation, as if you speak in this way, it's likely the individual won't want to speak to you at all." (Gnomeopedia, p. 1356)

'I might have–' Ruby's voice sounded from next to Sawwse's ear, scaring her half to death.

'For the love of crimp! When did you come back?'

'Oh. Straight away. I heard him telling you to get away from the tree in backchat, so I knew he wasn't bad.'

'You knew he was speaking backchat the whole time.' Sawwse pinched the bridge of her nose. 'Right.'

'I was just going to suggest a potion.' Ruby opened her sack-like bag, the contents of which looked purposefully packed as haphazardly as possible. While she scrummaged through the bag, she pulled a torn piece of parchment from her pocket and handed it to Sawwse who read it aloud.

'"Ruby Schap: an apothecary for all."'

'Ykcul s'taht,' said the man.

'Aha!' Ruby sprang up with a small, corked vial in her hand. The liquid inside was murky and mucky, like a storm cloud had been rolling around in the mud. She handed the vial to the man. 'This should be the one.'

The man uncorked the vial and, with some trepidation, poured the liquid into his mouth.

Ruby furrowed her brow like she'd just remembered something. 'It was either backchat or constipation. I really need a better labelling system.'

'Pah!' The man coughed and spluttered. 'That was absolutely vile!' Ruby sank her head and looked so disheartened at this that the man quickly clarified. 'Vial. I meant, that was absolutely a vial. It's something we say round here.'

'Never mind that, the potion worked!' Sawwse clapped the man on his shoulder. She worked her way back through their conversation. 'Your name is Greb?'

'That's right.'

Sawwse took out the Gnomeopedia. She flicked to a page with the title 'Human Names' and scanned it. Circling the name Craig, she wrote Greb next to it and added a question mark. 'I'm Sawwse and this is Ruby.'

'Nice to make your acquaintance.' Greb smiled kindly. Then, without even a hint of awkwardness about it, he drew out a sword. 'I'm going to have to ask you to turn around.'

Sawwse turned round in a circle.

'I meant you're going to have to leave.'

Sawwse exchanged a look with Ruby and then picked up a handful of burnt leaves from the ground, offering them to Greb.

'Gnomes,' muttered Greb. He narrowed his eyes. 'I cannot let you into Pettibeck. It's locked down for everyone's safety. You'll have to turn away.'

'Safety?' Ruby shuffled behind Sawwse.

'Haven't you heard?' Greb dropped his voice to a whisper. 'There's a fallen wizard on the loose causing mayhem everywhere they go. Hence the backchat.'

'Should someone not help them up?' asked Sawwse.

'No, *fallen*. As in, fallen from grace.'[15]

'That's not good, Sawwse. Not good at all.' Ruby tugged at the sleeve of Sawwse's tunic, her eyes wide with fear. 'We should probably head back.'

---

[15] "All wizards who study at the Magical Academy in No'areth take an oath upon completing their studies. I can't remember how it goes, but it's something boring like blah blah blah only use magic and wizardry for good purposes. Fallen wizards are those that break the oath. The more powerful the wizard, the more dangerous it is that the oath is broken, hence the phrase: the bigger they are, the harder they fall." (Gnomeopedia, p. 209)

'No chance! I can't leave yet. How else will I get to Rhyddinas?' Sawwse turned back to Greb. 'Look, you'll have to let us through. You'll hardly notice we're there. A quick bite to eat in one of your human pubes and then we'll be on our way.'

Ruby couldn't help noticing Sawwse's use of the collective pronoun.

Greb looked conflicted but shook his head. 'I'm sorry.'

'Okay.' Sawwse let out a big sigh. 'Let me sing you a song before we turn back. It's a custom where I'm from.'

Greb looked uncertain. After a pause he relented. He could hardly refuse a song after barring the poor sod's entry. 'Go on.'

Sawwse sat cross-legged on the ground. She checked her pitch with a series of gentle hums, and then softly, she began to sing a lullaby about a young boy. Standing by the edge of a lake, the boy gazed in wonder at the reflection of the moon. It was so still that he couldn't believe it wasn't actually in the lake itself. He went to jump in the lake, but then thought better of it: he didn't want to disturb its stillness. Instead, he sat down facing the moon-lit lake and breathed in and out, slower and slower, until he was as still as the moon.

'What did you think?' Sawwse sprang to her feet only to find Greb curled up on the ground, fast asleep. She didn't know it yet, but this was her very first foray into *music magic*. 'I guess it was a little slow, eh Ruby? Ruby? Where's she gone this time?'

Sawwse searched the ground by her feet. There, nestled in between the grass, was a tiny, sleeping rabbit with sandy grey fur. Sawwse gently picked up rabbit-Ruby, placing her at the top of her rucksack.

With a shrug, she made her way past the exploded tree and followed the dry-stone walls into the village. Pettibeck was a small settlement comprising three rows of houses, a little church in a square, and a pub. At the opposite end of the village from Sawwse, a post-badger[16] dropped the week's mail off, including a bunch of expedited wanted posters direct from Doriana Palace. Sawwse didn't notice. She was too excited about entering her first human pub: The Quaint Partridge.

The Partridge was one of those country pubs that would have been lovely were it not for the bad food, tacky design, and hostile environment. Sawwse walked past a crowd of old men, who stared at her as she made her way to an iron bar. She'd read that you "ordered at the bar" and yet even after a series of taps and prods, she couldn't figure out how it worked.

A cough from above roused Sawwse from her tinkering.

'Oh, hello,' said Sawwse.

There was a large man looming over the counter. His lack of notable features was compensated by his unpleasant personality. He pointed to several high stools propped up by the counter. 'Order round here.'

Sawwse hopped up onto one of the stools. She cleared her throat. 'The finest grub you have, sir!'

The landlord scoffed and then walked into the back.

The Gnomeopedia had been pretty clear on pub etiquette, but perhaps she'd misconstrued the advice. It

---

[16] "It wasn't entirely clear how badgers had got postal contracts across Esh'areth. They were short tempered, didn't speak the common tongue, and would occasionally eat the mail, but for some reason their contracts were always renewed." (Gnomeopedia, p. 7)

was far from the warm reception she had been promised. A quick glance around the room told her that they weren't used to seeing gnomes in these parts, as most of the locals were still staring at her. Either that or the fallen wizard was more of a concern than she'd first thought.

Sawwse turned around in her chair to face the other side of the pub. A woman sat alone in the furthest seat along the bar. The woman looked back at her and smiled. She was the only person in the pub to meet her eye with something other than barely disguised antipathy. There was something else too. Something magnetic. Sawwse was immediately drawn to her, but before she could say anything the landlord returned and dropped a dish on the counter in front of her.

'Your food.'

It was some kind of indiscernible meat covered in a dark gravy with the consistency of slime. Sawwse prodded it with a spoon. 'What is it?'

'Rabbit stew.'

Sawwse gasped and checked her backpack. It was fine. Ruby was still fast asleep curled up at the top. 'I thought you'd cooked my friend!'

The landlord shook his head. He looked between Sawwse and the other woman at the bar, who held her hands open like she was reading an invisible book. He wondered what in the hells Greb was playing at letting strangers into the village in these troubling times.

After poking at the bowl of stew a little more, Sawwse pushed it to one side and took a crumpet out of her pocket. It had been there for a few days, but she decided to err on the side of stale and chewy over mouldy and gooey.

'You're going to have to pay for that.'

'Eh?'

'The stew.' The landlord stared down his nose at Sawwse and held out an open palm. 'It's a fiver.'

'Oh-kay.' Sawwse reached over the counter and slapped his hand.

'Very funny.'

'It wasn't a joke.' The Blue Forest had no currency and therefore Sawwse had no concept of money. The Gnomeopedia was unhelpful on the issue, only stating that it was "trouble," and that it "must be funny, in a rich man's world." 'I'd gladly sing a song for you instead.'

'The only notes we accept are those with the king's face drawn on them.'

'I'd gladly draw you one. What does he look like?'

The landlord nodded to two burly-looking chaps sat near the door. They approached the bar grunting, cracking their knuckles, their necks, and their pecans, which they wolfed down in a brutish manner befitting of a 'heavy'. 'Our friend seems to have misplaced her wallet.'

'I should really be on my way,' said Sawwse.

Suddenly, the door swung open. It was a guard who held a stack of papers. She casually walked to the landlord and put one of the papers down on the bar. Sawwse was struck. It was her face on the poster! And below it, a single word in bold lettering: WANTED.

'I'm in demand already!'

But before Sawwse could rejoice, the guard shouted: 'Get her!'

She dived backwards off the stool, dodging the grasping hands of the heavies, and then slid underneath the guard's legs. A bolt of strange blue light bounced around the room just as she reached the door. Sawwse didn't look back. Instead, she bolted out of the pub and ran down a ginnel tucked behind the houses on the main street.

Once she was sure she wasn't being pursued, Sawwse rested behind a bush in someone's backyard. The light had gone from the sky – the moon playing coy behind a set of clouds. Although the square's tall lanterns had been lit, the ginnel was almost pitch black, and it was also almost completely silent. The only noise was a growing disquiet coming from the main square.

'Best wake up, Ruby.' Sawwse placed her backpack in front of her. She gently felt for rabbit-Ruby, but her hand only made contact with her trumpet. 'Unbelievable. I've lost her again.'

A light breeze played with the strands of hair relaxing on Sawwse's neck. She shivered. It was unnaturally cold, just like the wind she'd felt when she was with Marius. She was about to set off searching for Ruby, when she felt the cold, sharp blade of a knife against her throat.

Chapter 8:

Sawwse and Mirrah

Well, she thought it was a knife at first. It turned out it was a banana. In many ways it's more terrifying to be held up with a banana than a knife, because the owner of said banana is quite clearly cuckoo.

'Look here, I'll get the crimping money! I'll just need a bit of assistance figuring out what that means.'

'I don't care about money,' said a voice at her ear. It didn't sound like the voice of a killer. It was low and velvety. If anything, it sounded rather sultry. 'And I'm not holding you up.'

'But… the banana?'

'I was just taking some measurements.'

Sawwse felt the banana move from her neck. She cautiously turned around. A dark figure stood over her. After a moment, the moon shifted from behind the clouds revealing the figure to be the woman from the bar. She was looking at the banana and nodding.

'That all checks out. It is, in fact, a banana.' The woman burst out laughing.

Sawwse laughed too. The woman was clearly a little mad. But Sawwse was well used to mad. She'd grown up surrounded by mad in the Blue Forest. Mad. 'I'm Sawwse.'

'Mirrah.'

'Oh, like mirror, mirror on the wall?'

'I suppose I could be on the wall.' Mirrah suddenly jumped backwards and stuck to the side of one of the houses. 'This kind of thing?'

'Wow! How'd you do that?'

'I'm... not sure to be honest.' With some effort, Mirrah unstuck her arms and back from the wall and jumped down. 'There are lots of things I'm not sure about these days. Like my name for instance.'

'You just said your name was Mirrah.'

'Aha! That's the one.' Mirrah clapped her hands together and smiled at the gnome. She waved her hand and a small sphere of light appeared in the air between them. 'Now, let's take a look at you.'

While Mirrah looked Sawwse up and down, Sawwse saw her clearly for the first time. She was a human like the villagers, tall, with sharp, angular features. Her golden blonde hair had turned silver in the magical light. Beneath her cloak, Mirrah wore a knee length green dress and big brown boots. Sawwse stared at her blue, blue, electric blue eyes. They seemed to be charged with power, or magnetism, or gravity, or some other force that she didn't understand. Whatever it was, it drew her in.

Sawwse suddenly remembered all the caution about the fallen wizard. She wasn't sure of the best way to broach the subject. 'You're not evil, are you?'

'Evil? Me?' Mirrah looked shocked. 'Gods, I don't think so.'

'I think it's usually a yes or no kind of question.'

'Hm.' Mirrah thought about this for a moment and then began twirling her hands around in an arcane gesture. 'If I was evil, would I do this?' She released her hands in the air with a flourish and a purple, skull-like ghost smoked into existence and hissed: 'Ssssarasilliousssss mussssst dieeeee,' before disappearing into the ether. Mirrah scratched her chin. 'Okay, bad example. But I don't think I'm evil.'

'Er…' Sawwse blinked. 'Who's Sarasillious?'

'Not sure.' Mirrah shrugged. 'Who are you?'

'Gods, where are my manners.' Sawwse bowed in her traditional manner. In response, Mirrah lowered her head and squatted, placing a hand flat on the ground in front of the gnome. 'Is that how they bow where you're from?'

'Yes. No. Maybe… I don't know.' Mirrah began spinning round on the spot. Her cloak whirled and whirled. 'Can you repeat the question?'

'It wasn't important.' Sawwse grinned and began twirling alongside Mirrah. 'How fast can you go?'

Mirrah laughed and then spun faster and faster, until she was spinning so fast that Sawwse could no longer see her face. In fact, her whole body blurred until a swirling vortex took her place. Sawwse watched as the bush alongside them began to buckle and pull towards the wizard whirlwind. She tried to back away, but it was too late: her body was whisked through the air into the maelstrom.

Inside Sawwse didn't feel like she was going round and round at an impossible speed. It was the opposite. Everything had slowed right down. Mirrah took Sawwse's hands. Her eyes were closed, and she was beaming. Sawwse was stunned. A thought suddenly crossed her mind. Something she'd never really considered about anyone before. 'You're gorgeous.'

'Oh.' Slowly, Mirrah opened her eyes. Just as quickly as the vortex had begun, it stopped. And they were left holding hands in the silence of the ginnel. 'You feel it too?'

'Feel what?'

'This...' Mirrah gestured between the two of them. '...attraction.'

Sawwse gulped.

Mirrah reached over and gently wiped a tiny bit of banana peel from Sawwse's neck, and then let her hand linger softly by her face. It was a tender moment that sent the gnome's pulse racing.

This was new territory for Sawwse. These sorts of things happened differently in the Blue Forest.[17] It left her completely clueless as to the right thing to say. 'Banana to meet you. Crimp!'

Mirrah chuckled. She let go of Sawwse's hand and then walked further into the ginnel.

'Blew it.' Sawwse didn't really understand what she'd blown, but she felt like she'd blown something. She followed Mirrah. 'Wait up!'

The ginnel extended behind one full row of houses, but then a path curved back to the main street. Sawwse hadn't really paid attention at first, but now she noticed a stream which seemed to run through the centre of Pettibeck. There was some kind of commotion happening at the other end of the village, but she paid it no attention. Instead, she followed Mirrah to the edge of

---

[17] It mostly involved making offers you hoped the other gnome couldn't refuse e.g. hobby-horse head in the bed.

the stream and sat down alongside her. Had Sawwse known that a curse was spreading through Mirrah's mind, eradicating her memories, her logic, her knowledge, her sense of place, her sense of time, her sense of smell, and her control over her powers, perhaps she would have been less blasé in her approach. As it was, Sawwse just saw her as a slightly nutty new friend who happened to be incredibly attractive.

'Are they… fish?' asked Mirrah staring into the stream.

'Not sure.' Sawwse dunked her head under the water and looked around. She whipped her head back up, now sopping wet. 'Yep. They're fish alright.'

Mirrah beamed. It was one of those smiles that has its own gravitational pull. Dangerous in the wrong hands. Even more dangerous in the wrong face. 'Can you do something for me?'

'Yes.' It was weird, but Sawwse felt like she'd do almost anything for Mirrah, despite having only just met her.

'Can you pull my finger?' Mirrah held out her pinky finger.

'Oh.' Sawwse was disappointed. This was one of the most basic pranks in the Blue Forest that even the little gnomelings did. She obliged, but rather than anything crude, Sawwse pulled Mirrah's finger and fireworks exploded in the sky far above them. 'Ha! You're a bit magic, aren't you?'

The smile faded from Mirrah's face. She turned to stare at the stream. 'Something like that.'

Sawwse couldn't help feeling she'd said the wrong thing again. She made to say something else, faltered, and then just watched the stream alongside Mirrah.

The moon emerged from the clouds once more, illuminating the pale blue stream with a pink hue. The occasional carp troubled the water, causing lilacky reflections to dance upon their faces. On this side of the village, everything was still apart from the gently flowing stream. The pair sat like this for some time, bathing in the calm.

'Thank you,' said Mirrah.

'You're welcome. Though, I don't know what for.'

'For this.' Mirrah gestured around them. 'There aren't many moments of peace left for me anymore. I keep losing myself.'

'Whenever I lost my grobble stick, it was always in the last place I looked.[18] Can you remember where you last found yourself?'

'Well, that's the rub-a-dub-dub. I can't remember much of anything.'

'My friend is an apothecary! I'm sure she'd have a memory potion of some sort. She's probably around here somewhere. In fact…' Sawwse dunked her head back into the stream and waved at the fish, which all promptly swam away. She raised her head and spat out a mouthful of water. 'Thought she was a fish.'

'I fear a potion would not be strong enough.' Mirrah smiled gently. 'But thank you for your concern.'

'So, what are you going to do?' asked Sawwse.

---

[18] Grobble was invented when the gnomes of the Blue Forest decided they needed a national sport. Although they took inspiration from sports around the world that the Gnehsehgs had reported back on, they couldn't settle on anything. Therefore, Grobble ended up a mixture of nets, balls, bats, sticks, pucks, hoops, disco, wickets, pockets, and, most importantly of all, grobbles.

'Well, that's the rub-a-dub-dub. I can't remember much of anything.'

Sawwse grimaced.

'I'm joking! I'm not that far gone yet.' Mirrah playfully punched Sawwse's arm. 'I don't know what I'll do next. I felt like I was looking for something, but I…' She trailed off, gathering her thoughts up like so many loose threads. 'Perhaps I will pick a direction and see where I end up.'

The gnome looked at her with admiration. 'That's just like Emmeline Flowerdew. She set off without a clear direction and wandered the world, wherever her heart took her.'

Mirrah looked down at Sawwse with curiosity. 'An aimless, travelling life is nothing to be jealous of.'

Sawwse shrugged. 'I could give you a clear purpose, if you'd like?'

Mirrah raised her eyebrows, sceptically.

'Maybe someone stole your doughnuts? Yeah! I think someone stole your doughnuts! The very idea.'

A slow smile crept over Mirrah's face, dimpling each cheek.

'They were your true favourites. Crunchy on the outside, with a divine rose jam running right through the centre. Or else… I've got it. Your neighbour borrowed a shovel and it's coming to the end of onion planting season!'

Mirrah laughed. It was a hearty laugh, and it had been some time since she'd had one. Catching her breath with a hiccup, Mirrah wiped tears from her eyes. 'There is something interesting about you.'

They gazed into each other's eyes, and in that moment a connection was forged. It electrified Sawwse's body. The excitement of this spark between them left both Sawwse and Mirrah momentarily breathless. But then, once the connection was established, Mirrah felt herself being pulled away from this special moment. She wanted to stay with Sawwse so dearly, but she could already feel her mind going elsewhere. 'Now, dear Sawwse. I should really be going.'

'Oh.' Sawwse couldn't hide her disappointment.

Mirrah stood and brushed some dust from her dress. She reached inside her cloak and pulled out a small spherical object. 'I want you to have this.'

Sawwse examined it. It was a glass sphere, full of red sand. 'Thank you. What is it?'

'It's a… something or other.' Mirrah shrugged. 'I don't know, but I think it's special in some way.'

Sawwse was touched by this offering. 'I will keep it for you until you have retrieved your doughnuts. Will I see you again?' The little gnome couldn't believe the words coming out of her mouth. She sounded desperate. Desperate for what, she didn't really understand. Also, this was the woman that had begun their meeting with a banana to her throat. And yet… and yet. Sawwse couldn't deny the connection between them.

'I'd like that.' Mirrah answered without hesitation. She dropped a small, heavy bag down next to the gnome. A few shiny coins fell out as it hit the ground. 'And you might find this useful.'

'I have something for you too. A song.'

Mirrah felt like running before Sawwse got caught up in her next magical accident, but she nodded.

Sawwse breathed in deeply, and then began singing. It was one of Flowerdew's songs that she'd picked up from *Walken Musike*. A slow, melancholy song about a transient connection the bard had made with a dwarven cobbler.

Something in the song cleared the fog from Mirrah's mind for the first time since arriving in Pettibeck. The Ancient Device. That was her goal. Get to it and turn back time to before the curse. She'd forget Sawwse. But then she'd have the pleasure of meeting her all over again. Mirrah wiped a tear from her eye. She unsheathed her banana and raised it into the air. 'Until we meet again.'

Sawwse raised her clenched fist, before bowing to her again. When she looked back up, Mirrah had already gone.

She took the ball of red sand out of her pocket and gazed at it. It was beautiful and caught the bright moonlight in a striking way. Looking at the glass sphere closely, Sawwse caught the reflection of her own sapphire-green eyes staring back at her. She was startled when Ruby appeared next to her, completely out of breath.

'There you are!' Ruby's tone was all panic. 'Come on, we've got to go right away.'

Sawwse would learn that panic was Ruby's default state. But in this instance, she sensed the panic was justified. She followed her back into the ginnel and walked with her to the far side of the village. 'What's going on?'

'Something to do with that fallen wizard.'

'I was just with her. Really lovely. Not evil… she doesn't think.'

'What?'

'She's called Mirrah. A bit nuts, but aren't we all?'

Ruby looked stricken.

'And her eyes, Ruby. Her eyes!'

'Did you not see what she did at the pub?'

Sawwse shook her head.

'She…'

'What? What did she do?'

'She turned everyone inside out.'

'You mean, she roughed them up? Weird. She said she wasn't interested in money.'

'No, Sawwse.' Ruby's face was pale, like she'd seen something she couldn't unsee. 'I mean literally inside out. I don't really want to talk about it, but it turns out skin does a lot of heavy lifting aesthetically. Half-digested pecans everywhere…' She shuddered. 'The worst part was that they weren't even dead. They were just shuffling around talking about how sensitive everything felt.'

'It must be a mistake.'

'There's something else too.' Ruby took out a piece of parchment. It was the wanted poster Sawwse had seen in the pub. 'Look at this.'

'Yes, I saw it. Can you believe someone wants me for a gig already!'

Ruby tapped the parchment. It was a phrase Sawwse had missed. It said: "Dead or Alive."

'How am I supposed to play if I'm– Ohhh. Wait, why do they want me? What've I done?'

'I don't know, but we have to leave.'

As they emerged from the ginnel, panic was running through the village: raised voices, people running around, carriage horses bucking and whinnying. News of what happened in The Quaint Partridge had clearly spread. Ruby guided Sawwse to a big, broad-shouldered man hurryingly loading various suitcases and bags onto a wagon.

'Here's my friend,' said Ruby, tapping the man on the back. 'Are we still okay to travel with you to Rhyddinas?'

'Rhyddinas,' repeated Sawwse, her eyes lighting up at the name.

'If you can find a space back there, you're welcome to join me.' The big man looked Sawwse up and down while continuing his packing. When he spoke, he wasn't unfriendly. But nor was he thrilled at their presence. 'It's the next realm over though, so it'll cost you dearly.'

'Money means nothing to me,' said Sawwse.

The driver didn't realise he was to take this quite so literally. He placed the last bag in the wagon. 'Right you are. Get in.'

Sawwse and Ruby jumped into the back of the wagon. It was packed to the brim with suitcases, crates, and loose clothes. They found a seat next to each other on a couple of travelling bags.

Moving quickly, the driver gave a signal to his horses, and they galloped off into the night, leaving the chaos of the village behind them.

Chapter 9:
Bandits

An excerpt from the Gnomeopedia

The route between Doriana and Rhyddinas is beautiful. Stunning. Gorgeous. It's all wildflower meadows, lush plains, and pristine lakes, and the breathtaking *Slaepan Wiga* mountain range overlooks it all. The scenery is so breathtaking that occasionally birds will collide with trees because they're too engrossed. This only serves to further underpin the wonderful aesthetics of the region as colourful feathers cascade tenderly through the air every time it happens. Even the border crossing out of the Dorienne Kingdom and into Pāx is attractive: a long, wide river of pure blue separates the two regions. In the past, people would relocate from one region to the next purely for the views. What I'm saying is that if you miss the opportunity to see this, you're a big, stupid poo poo head.

Sawwse was asleep. To be fair, it was night-time for most of the journey, so there wasn't much to see anyway (apart from the occasional Glowing Marimba). Sawwse was curled up in the back of the wagon – her head wedged between a suitcase and a dresser – and her sleep was disturbed by every tiny bump on the road (had she been in a fancy boy carriage, she'd have been offered more suspension).

Ruby's sleep was also restless, but for very different reasons. She was memory-dreaming again, as she did most nights. It was always the same memory: the day she left home. Unlike the poshos heading off on gap yahs to go swimming with dauphines in Spüdland or partying on the Islands of Inebriation, Ruby did not choose to leave home. It was a decision forced upon her by circumstance. And that circumstance was eating her parents…

…The dream began as it always did, with Ruby entering her house and immediately feeling tense. Her shoulders hunched and her arms tightened to her sides. Taking a deep breath, she walked into the dining room and sat opposite her father at the table. A bowl of dust-coloured, too-thin soup was laid out in Ruby's place.

'Where have you been?' Her father did not look up from his paper.

'I was in school,' said Ruby. Not technically a lie.

Her father picked his bulbous nose and flicked a ball of snot at Ruby. 'I meant afterwards, dumb-oh.'

Ruby's appetite diminished. She stared into the grey soup in front of her and sighed.

'What's the matter? *Cat* got your tongue? Hah!' Ruby's father smacked his hand down hard on the table causing her to jump.

As if it wasn't obvious, Ruby's father was an idiot. Some people act aggressively because they are too stupid to think of any other way to act. It's scary, but less so than someone who acts aggressively despite their obvious intelligence. Not that Ruby would know, because her mother was an idiot too.

'Hur hur! Good one, Mitchell.' Ruby's mother appeared at the door. 'Now tell your father where you were, you little *rat*.'

'Hah!' Her father clapped his hands together emphatically.

'I was spending time with friends after school.' Ruby spoke almost under her breath. She knew where this kind of thing led, and she was scared.

'Speak up,' said her mother.

'Yeah, you're being as quiet as a *mouse*.'

'Hur hur!'

'I was with friends,' said Ruby. Thick, dark hair spurted from the back of Ruby's hand, and the palm became padded, leathery. She whipped it out of view.

'Friends?' Her mother repeated the word as though it was distasteful. She spat on the floor. 'Who would want to be friends with you?'

'Are these friends… human?' Her father stood, letting his chair hit the ground. 'You better not have been talking to the livestock again!'

'We've told you about this before. Do you not care what people think of you? They think you're weird! It reflects badly on us.'

Ruby bowed her head. The anxious thoughts whipped round her mind. She tried to focus on skin. Normal human skin. The shapes of her knuckles and the length of her nails. *I am normal, I am normal, I am normal.*

'Answer your mother!' Her father smacked Ruby's bowl and sent the soup splashing against the floor. 'Unless you want us to treat you like a bad *dog* again?'

'No!' Ruby instinctively raised her hands up. A dire mistake.

'Ew!' Her mother gagged. 'What is that?'

Ruby looked at her hands. They'd turned into tentacles. Her ears burned red. They were guenon ears.

'Urgh. I think I'm going to be sick.' Ruby's father held his stomach exaggeratedly.

'*Normal* humans do not shapeshift. It isn't natural.' Her mother pointed to the cellar door. 'Time for after-school club.'

'Please don't.' Ruby's eyes began to swell with warm tears.

'Hurry up, you *sloth*.' Her father pushed her towards the cellar.

'Hur h– what's a sloth?'

'It's a… kind of…' Her father shrugged and then kicked Ruby down the remaining steps of the cellar. 'Dunno.'

Ruby fell through the door of the cellar. It was cold and damp. There was a large desk with a few masonry tools scattered on it, but other than that the place was unused. So, it was a cellar. Ruby took her usual seat facing the dank wall and placed her tentacle-hands flat on the desk in front of her.

'Look, she's remembered something.' Her father reached for the long cane. 'I guess you can teach a young *dog* new tricks.'

'Hur!' Ruby's mother walked down the cellar steps and placed a cold, wiry hand on her shoulder. 'You need to know that we're doing this out of love. All you have to do is stay normal and stop being as mad as a March *hare*.'

Smack! Her father smacked the cane across Ruby's tentacle-hands.

Ruby's hands turned human, but a howl of pain burst from Ruby's lips. Not the scream of a young child, but a cacophony of anguish.

'Silly *goose*, what did your mother just say. Be normal!' Her father raised the cane again and brought it down hard. *Smack*!

The same growl-screech-yell-roar from Ruby. She frantically repeated a mantra in her head: *I am normal, I am normal, I am normal.*

Smack! This time the cane smacked against desk instead of flesh as Ruby removed her hands. She curled her injured fingers into her chest as she sobbed and pleaded with her parents. 'I'm sorry, I'm sorry. Please don't do it again. I'm not sure I can control it–'

'Bad *doggy*.' Her father's rough calloused hands grabbed her arms and forced them onto the desk, and her mother held them there. He raised the cane above his head once more and once more Ruby moved her hands out of the way. This time she shoved them both away.

'I said, don't!'

Ruby's body shifted out of her control. It tripled in size. Striped, purple fur coated her body. Drool poured from the fangs hanging out of her mouth, and claws lengthened to the size of daggers. Ruby screamed a scream that would haunt her parents for the rest of their lives, which happened to end approximately two seconds later.

They were as dead as a *dodo*…

…Somewhere else, the Ancient Device stirred. If it spoke, it would have said: 'Excellent. A victim full of regret, ripe for the taking. Yummy.' Instead, it kind of burped an incomprehensible mechanical chord…

…Somewhere close, Sawwse shook Ruby awake.

Ruby opened her eyes. Sawwse was leaning over her wearing extra thick oven gloves. 'What's with the…' She trailed off, suddenly realising that she was in the form of a hedgehog. Ruby immediately shifted back to her human form. 'Sorry!'

'I don't mind.' Sawwse smiled warmly, taking off the gloves. 'Bad dream?'

'Yes,' said Ruby quietly.

'You're awake now. No night monsters can hurt you out here!' Sawwse squeezed Ruby's shoulder and then suddenly remembered something. 'Oh, that's right. The driver wanted me to let you know that there are bandits outside.'

'Bandits!?'

'You've heard of them too, huh?'

'Of course I've heard of bandits! They're going to take all our stuff!'

'They can't take any of my instruments. Well, I suppose they can have the triangle.'

'I'm not sure you'll have a choice in the matter.' Ruby stared at Sawwse blankly, unsure how anyone could be that naïve. There was a thump from outside the wagon. 'Oh gods, we'll be lucky if we're not killed!'

Sawwse patted Ruby's leg reassuringly. 'Relax, I'm sure it's all just a misunderstanding.'

'Get out of the wagon or we'll eat your hearts,' called a voice from outside the wagon.

Sawwse and Ruby cautiously pulled back the canvas enveloping the wagon and stepped outside. They were stopped in front of a shabby building. Three bandits were facing them: two human men who wore wide brimmed hats, bandanas, dusty boots and stirrups, and an old, unkempt dwarf with a large, battle worn axe strapped to his back that matched his weathered features. White scraggly hair covered the dwarf's head and most of his scar-pocked face.

'"Eat your hearts," Francesco?' asked the taller of the two men.

'Got 'em out of the wagon, didn't it?' said the other man. He was smoking a cigarette and blowing out clouds of purple smoke into the air. Sawwse held her scarf up to her mouth to block the sickly-sweet scent. 'Did you think it was a bit much, Mauro?'

'I usually only make threats I intend on carrying out,' said Mauro.

'Oh, but I do intend to.' Francesco ran his tongue along his lips while staring at Sawwse and Ruby.

'Stop it.' It was the dwarf. He spoke very quietly, almost under his breath. 'There's no need to harm them.'

'Thought you left your principles behind?' Francesco spat on the ground. 'This isn't the time for noble deeds. This is the era of getting what you can get.'

'What's the matter, Osrik?' Mauro stepped alongside the dwarf and put an arm around his shoulder. 'Nothing wrong with a bit of fun while we're on route to Dorienne.'

'I'm not going.' Osrik shifted uncomfortably on his feet. 'It's not right.'

Francesco and Mauro exchanged a nasty grin. Francesco took a drag of his cigarette and blew out a plume of green smoke before he spoke. 'You didn't have a problem with it before.'

'This is different.'

'Not sure it is,' said Francesco. 'We're just after money. Same as you.'

'You're talking about toppling a regime,' said Osrik.

'King Poht is dead. The regime is already toppling.' Mauro held one of his arms up vertically, swaying it slightly like a tower teetering. 'We're just giving it a helping hand.' He dropped his arm and mimicked the sound of an explosion, breaking into a wide grin.

'I've no interest in chaos.' Osrik folded his arms across his chest.

'We can leave you guys to it, if you'd prefer,' said Sawwse. 'Sounds like a private discussion.'

Francesco gestured for Sawwse and Ruby to move away from the wagon, and then began unloading it. 'You've gone soft, Osrik. Come with us and reap the rewards of collective anxiety.'

'Look, most people hate change.' Mauro continued trying to persuade the dwarf. 'They want security, safety, and reliability. People like us embrace change. Relish it. Take advantage of it. That's all we're doing.'

Francesco blew out a vibrant pink cloud and spoke over his shoulder. 'Things get shaken up and our opportunities grow. Thought you needed the money?'

'I'll wait,' said Osrik.

'Don't waste any more time on him.' A woman's voice sounded from the roof of the building above Sawwse. Looking up she saw a tall figure silhouetted against the sky. 'I told you that our time with this one would be short-lived.' The red cloak surrounding the figure billowed as she jumped off the roof and floated slowly to the ground.

'That was a very cool, floaty magic trick,' said Sawwse.

'Shush!' Ruby nudged her in the ribs.

'It's true! I wish I could do that. It'd make life easier getting down to the forest floor from my house in the mornings.'

'I mean it, Sawwse,' whispered Ruby. 'She's a fallen wizard.'

'How can you tell?'

'See that glowing light behind her?' Ruby gestured to a trail of glowing embers that floated behind the wizard. 'That's her oath. All wizards have them, but they're invisible unless you break it. Then they follow after you so that everyone can see you're bad.'

'Are you sure fallen wizards are bad, because even that sounds incredibly cool!?'

'Right, that's the wagon cleared.' Francesco stood with his foot on one of the suitcases. He gestured to Sawwse and Ruby. 'What should we do with these two, Alla'fyr?'

The red-cloaked wizard didn't even look at them. 'What you will.'

'Better not to leave any loose ends.' Mauro brushed open his long jacket to reveal the hilt of a sword resting within an indigo scabbard. He drew the long sword from its sheath. It was milky white and looked more like a tooth than a sword.

'We are so far from loose ends,' said Sawwse. 'We're tight ends. And I'm not talking about my position on the grobble pitch.'

Francesco took out his own sword: a long, curved blade with arcane symbols etched onto the steel.

'Wait! What if we promise not to say anything about any of this to anyone? Oh! I know. I can play you a song. I'm very talented.'

A harsh laugh fell out of Francesco. He tossed his cigarette on the ground and then nodded to Mauro. They burst from the spot and launched themselves at Sawwse and Ruby.

Clang!

Steel clashed with steel as Osrik met their strike with one of his own, knocking both Francesco and Mauro backwards. He slowly turned his gaze to Alla'fyr, who was clearly in charge. 'There's no need for this.'

'Suit yourself.' Alla'fyr's red cloak swung around and Sawwse found herself locking eyes with the woman underneath it. Her sunken cheeks and large, dark eyes gave the impression of a skull. Wavy auburn hair was hidden beneath the crimson fabric of her hood. Whereas everything about Mirrah's gaze was attractive, Alla'fyr's stare was repellent, forcing Sawwse to look away. 'It'll be a shame to lose your power, Osrik.'

'We can take him,' said Mauro.

'I'd relish the fight,' said Francesco.

'Best to leave insignificant matters to insignificant creatures.' Alla'fyr began walking away. She wore a mocking grin. 'Subterfuge never was one of Osrik's strong points. Infiltrating Doriana will be easier without him.'

Osrik growled.

Alla'fyr casually walked onto the wagon. 'Let's go.'

Mauro and Francesco gave a last reproachful look at Osrik, before sheathing their swords. They mounted the horses at the front of the carriage.

Alla'fyr stared at Osrik from the wagon. 'Before I go, you should know that if we ever cross paths again–' Before Alla'fyr had a chance to finish speaking, the wagon shot off down the road. In the distance, Sawwse, Ruby and Osrik watched the fallen wizard throw up her hands in frustration.

'Thank you so much.' Sawwse made to bow, but Osrik held up a hand to stop her.

'It's no bother.' A smile wrinkled his pale grey-blue eyes. 'And there's no need for any of that. A simple nod will suffice for me.'

'Fair do's.' Sawwse followed his lead and dipped her head in a short nod. 'You certainly have strange friends.'

'They're not my friends.'

'Then, you're not a bandit?'

'A mercenary. It's different.' The smile faded from his eyes as he looked down at his feet. 'Kind of.'

'We're not bandits either,' said Sawwse, gesturing between herself and Ruby. She gave Osrik a big thumbs up. 'But we *are* friends.'

'Must be nice,' mumbled Osrik. He strapped his axe onto his back and began walking towards the shabby building.

'So, your mercenary… colleagues, have deprived us of our lift to Rhyddinas. It's very important I get there. I don't suppose you know where we can get another lift from?'

Osrik scratched his scraggly beard and then pointed to the building. A big sign hanging outside said: Stables. He carried on walking.

'Of course. Stables. Makes sense. Totally.'

'It's a place where you hire horses,' offered Ruby.

'And they give you directions or what?'

'I think the idea is that you give the horse directions.'

Sawwse looked puzzled. 'You hire the horse in order to tell it where to go? I don't know anything about money, but that feels like a confusing system.'

Ruby scratched her head. 'It *is* confusing now that you say it.'

Osrik paused at the door to the stables. 'I'll show you what to do.'

As they walked over, Ruby tugged at Sawwse's sleeve and whispered to her. 'Are you sure about this? He is a mercenary.'

'I'm sure it's fine.'

'But he was travelling with that fallen wizard! She was so obviously evil. Her face looked like a skull for goodness' sake!'

'True, but he's not with her now. Plus, he has kind eyes.' They paused in front of Osrik by the door of the stables. Sawwse grinned. 'You're not going to kill us, are you?'

'No,' Osrik answered glumly. His wrinkled face creased even further into a frown. Then a look of disappointment flashed across his eyes. He moved his lips as if to say something more, but then turned and walked into the stables.

Inside, Sawwse and Ruby watched as Osrik haggled with the owner of the stable, who disappeared and brought out two dusky grey horses. Osrik paid and then walked the horses out of the wide opening at the back.

Osrik looked at Sawwse for a long moment as if mulling something over. 'I'll take you to Rhyddinas.'

'Really? That's amazing!' Sawwse jumped up and down gleefully.

Osrik rubbed his tired eyes. Babysitting a pair of hapless travellers was not on his list of priorities, so what was he thinking? He didn't know it, but Sawwse had this effect on people. She was charming in a disarming kind of way. People wanted to help her without really knowing why.

'Are you joining the musical conservatoire too?'

'No,' grunted Osrik. 'I'll look for work.'

'What kind of work?'

Osrik sighed. He was already regretting this. 'There's talk of a new adventuring guild. No entry fees.'

'Ooh that sounds exciting, doesn't it Rubes?'

Ruby wasn't listening. She was busy gossiping with the horses about the new mulch feed they had been given.

'Listen,' said Osrik. 'Adventuring guilds aren't for…'

Sawwse looked up at him with big eyes. 'Aren't for what?'

Osrik considered the best way to phrase it, but soon gave up. Words weren't his thing. 'Never mind.' He lifted Sawwse and Ruby onto one of the horses and then mounted the other one. He took hold of the reins of both horses. 'I'll take you to Rhyddinas, but that's it.' Osrik made a few clicking sounds with his tongue and the horses set off down the long, dusty road towards Rhyddinas.

Chapter 10: Rhyddinas

'Great Gnomelord up in Groma-tundhi,' gasped Sawwse. She'd never seen a proper city before, and the Free City of Rhyddinas was quite the city. It was almost too much of a city. It had six theatres, five universities, four cathedrals, three competing crunkball teams, two city councils, and a partridge in a pear tree, which by way of an archaic law technically owned half the property in Rhyddinas. There were rows and rows of houses and shops all stacked backwards on top of one another, and a vast stone wall that encircled the whole city. It was all rather overwhelming.

As Sawwse, Ruby, and Osrik dismounted the horses at the side of the road, they were immediately accosted by an elf wearing a traffic warden uniform who presented them with a fine. Like most 'free cities' it was very expensive.

'Would this cover it?' Sawwse was about to hand over the bag of coins that Mirrah had given her when Osrik intervened.

'Let me see that.' The dwarf looked in the bag and his eyes widened. He took out a relatively small coin and gave it to the warden. 'On your way.'

After the warden had left, Osrik looked down at Sawwse and Ruby. He held the bag up to them. 'How did you get this?'

'My friend Mirrah gave it to me,' said Sawwse. 'Why, do you want it?'

'What? No. I can't take it.' Osrik handed the bag back. 'You must be careful. People will do dark things for that kind of money.'

'I know people hate traffic wardens, but "dark things" is a bit of an exaggeration.'

'There are lots of people here,' said Ruby, wide-eyed.

It was true that even though it was evening, the streets were still bustling with city folk: shopping, chatting, drinking, eating. There was great variety in the people here too. Elves and dwarves, humans and goblins, ogres and goo-faced pohs all chatted freely with one another. It looked exactly like the kind of place that would have brittle right-winged trolls frothing at the mouth.

'So, which way to the conservatoire?' asked Sawwse with a big grin.

'I'm not sure it'll be open,' said Ruby.

'But that guy's open.' Sawwse pointed to a shop selling cheese-flavoured potions.[19]

'I know. I think some shops stay open late, but schools and museums and things don't.'

---

[19] The most popular of these were potions of 'feta fall' and 'grater healing.'

'Oh, never mind.' Sawwse was slightly disappointed, but then she smiled again and patted Osrik on the back. 'We'll tag along with you for a bit longer then.'

'I really don't think that's a good…' Osrik trailed off. Sawwse had already clambered up onto his shoulders in a piggy-back position. He let out a long, weary sigh, and then walked on, resigned.

They snaked their way along one of the narrow streets, until gradually, several other paths converged, and they found themselves on a wide boulevard lined with large everpink trees. At the end of the boulevard stood a breathtakingly beautiful monastery, which seemed to glisten under the moonlight. A large circular stained-glass window danced with many colours, bouncing from the torches surrounding the building. Choral music floated from behind the thick stone doors.

'Woah.' Sawwse was blown away. 'This is the adventuring guild?'

'The adventure is singing?' asked Ruby.

'Now that's a guild I can get behind!' Sawwse clapped her hands together and began vocalising.

Osrik grunted. He trudged over to a decrepit lot behind the monastery and set Sawwse down on the ground. There was a crowd gathered around a figure who was standing on a platform of detritus: old crates, packaging, broken furniture. The man was mid-speech, and talking with a passion that was hard to ignore.

'And spare a thought for those who have freedom but choose not to use it. What a peculiar choice! The freedom of this city was hard-fought for. A reward for the centuries of subjugation that came before. Would it not be an insult to victory if we ignore the chance to put our spoils to use?'

'Psst. Osrik.' Sawwse tapped the dwarf's arm. 'What's he on about?'

Osrik put a finger to his lips.

'It's about mouths? That's creepy.'

'No,' growled Osrik. 'It's a… recruitment drive.'

'*This* is the guild?' asked Sawwse incredulously.

'Yes.'

'It's literally in a rubbish heap. No wonder there's no entry fee!'

Osrik grunted.

Ruby shuffled behind Sawwse. 'He looks a bit sinister.'

She wasn't wrong. The speaker was a heavily built man covered by a black cloak, which glittered in the torch light like a beetle's carapace. A glowing, white-horned mask floated an inch from his face, veiling his expressions in secrecy, and further deepening the beetle-like resemblance.

'Our time is finite and precious. We walk this land for only as long as we are given, and that's true… whether you have received a boon of longevity or not.' He pointed to a pair of elves exchanging sceptical looks. 'Let us use these grains of sand to pursue lives we can be proud of. Let us eschew the dull, the safe, the staid. Let us embrace adventure.'

'Stop stirring trouble!' shouted someone in the crowd.

'Yeah! What's wrong with safe?' added another.

'It's boring, that's what,' said Sawwse. She hadn't meant to speak so loudly, but several people in the crowd turned to face her.

'And what's wrong with boring?' said one of them, boringly.

'Oh! Well, it's, er, kind of…' Sawwse tried to think of a reason but came up short.

'It leads to complacency.' The beetle-like man at the front of the crowd came to her rescue. He was looking directly at Sawwse. The mouth of his white-horned mask curled into a slight smile. 'There are dangers rising in the world and we are numb to them.'

'You're talking out of your bum, mate,' said a bored-looking goblin.

'None safer than Esh'areth!' heckled an elf. This got a murmur of approval from the crowd.

'Yes, we've been safe for a little while, but I'm afraid trouble is knocking on our door too. What of the monsters that return to our lands?'

'Probably just someone in a costume,' said the goblin, yawing.

'No, it's true! I saw a beast right outside my home,' said Sawwse. 'He was called Johan. He ate a crumpet.'

'That sounds *exactly* like someone in a costume.'

The beetle-like man continued. 'You can choose to ignore what is obvious. You can choose to look inwards like our politicians and so-called leaders. Or you can choose to face up to the realities of what is happening and help to combat them.'

'Ah, bugger off!' A tall woman threw her apple core at the speaker. It flew straight towards the white-horned mask, but before it made contact it instantly turned to ash, which drifted towards the ground. Despite the gasps this drew from the crowd, the tall woman was not deterred. 'Go back to where you came from.'

The beetle-like man was unconcerned. He paused as many of the crowd dispersed, and then continued speaking to those that remained. 'Danger is coming whether we want to believe in it or not. Please join me and we will build a guild together. It will be called Actum Tempus for it will be a guild that recognises it is the time for action.' He finished speaking, and took a long, deep breath. He looked at the smaller group of twenty-or-so people facing him, and a smile crept slowly across the white-horned mask. The eyes within the mask glowed bright blue and then he vanished on the spot. He popped back a second later, quickly said, 'Terms and conditions apply,' and then disappeared again.

Sawwse suddenly experienced a strange sensation in her head. It felt like someone had just flicked her brain. She rubbed her head and then noticed Ruby was doing the same. Meanwhile, Osrik was grumbling about something.

'What was that all about?' asked Sawwse.

'Mental projection,' muttered Osrik.

Sawwse and Ruby shared a confused look, but then the flicking sensation happened again, followed by a clear image of a golden hourglass set against a steel shield. The words Actum Tempus appeared clearly in their heads.

'The guild's first meeting is tomorrow evening?' said Sawwse.

'In The Happy Hearth…' added Ruby.

'Damned magic.' Osrik shook his head from side to side as if to dislodge a piece of earwax. 'Mental intrusion.'

Sawwse wasn't sure it was that big of a deal. In fact, she thought it was kind of a cool trick to put an image into her head like that. Though, she didn't say anything in case Osrik got offended.

'Right, I'll walk you to your lodgings and then it's best we go our separate ways.' Osrik folded his arms across his chest. He was done being soft.

'Ah, lodgings.' Sawwse stuck her finger up in the air. 'That's a great idea.'

'We could sleep here, I suppose.' Ruby was moving some of the wooden crates that the beetle-like man had been standing on. 'I have a potion of comfort in my bag, which could turn that old rug into a duvet?'

'Mm.' Osrik held onto the back of Sawwse's bag as she began happily strolling over to the rubbish heap. He grabbed Ruby too and then carried them one under each arm. 'I'll take you to the nearest youth hostel and *then* we'll go our separate ways.'

'I'm one hundred and thirty-eight – am I not a bit old for a youth hostel? Also, we can split up, but then we'll see you tomorrow evening at the guild meet. Big day tomorrow, now that I think of it. Joining the musical conservatoire in the morning and an adventuring guild in the evening! Dannse would be so proud…'

As Sawwse continued to witter on under Osrik's arm, the dwarf did his best to ignore her. She'd hopefully get settled in the conservatoire and give up the notion of joining the guild. Then, his babysitting duties would be over.

Osrik deposited Sawwse and Ruby in the youth hostel. He paid for their room, bid them farewell, and then left to find lodgings of his own.

--

Sawwse woke early the next morning, wrote a note for Ruby, and then headed out. Ruby had explained that just like closing early, the conservatoire might not open first thing in the morning, so Sawwse stopped herself from running all the way there by strumming her lute while she walked. This method worked for approximately two minutes until she saw a signpost with directions to the conservatoire, at which point all her patience evaporated and she took off in a sprint. She ran down one street, then the next, and the next, until she was well and truly lost. Fortunately, a nice man in a trilby pointed her in the right direction, almost making up for his choice of hat.

Finally, Sawwse stood before the long, curved building, which she instantly recognised from the Gnomeopedia. The conservatoire was built in the shape of a gigantic stringed instrument.[20] The sign in front read:

Musical Conservatoire of Rhyddinas:
where music flows as freely as the city.

A tingle spread through Sawwse's belly, and an airiness spread through her lungs. She took a deep breath and entered the building. Expecting to be greeted by melodies and harmonies, basses and trebles, soaring strings and crashing drums, she was shocked to hear… nothing. Nowt. Nada. There was complete silence.

Silencing magic? thought Sawwse, assuming they used such things to let everyone practice in peace. She walked through a reception area into a wide hall.

Boxes and crates filled the hall. Reams of parchment spilled over their sides. Sawwse followed a narrow path between the boxes until she found a little man sitting on the floor, surrounded by stacks of paper. The man seemed to be trying to make sense of the notes in front of him. As Sawwse approached, he did not look up from his notes.

---

[20] Adopting the Lutalist architecture style.

She coughed. Not too loudly, but loud enough to be heard.

No response.

Sawwse wondered whether the man was slightly deaf and adjusted her speaking volume accordingly. 'HIYAAAA!'

'Flaming djinn!' The man shot up, sending a huge stack of paper into the air. He clutched tightly to his chest as the papers gently floated back down.

'I'm sorry, I didn't mean to scare you,' said Sawwse.

Spinning around, the man's shocked expression came face-to-face with Sawwse. He had two sections of short, white hair either side of his otherwise bald head, and two oval patches of deep navy patterned around a pair of startlingly sky-blue eyes. With his black and white kaftan, and the small bamboo pencil tucked behind his left ear, Sawwse thought he looked exactly like a panda.

'No matter,' said the man, catching his breath. He turned and began picking up the scattered notes.

'I'm here for the conservatoire.' Sawwse smiled and played a simple chord on her lute.

'Humph. It's all very well being here for the conservatoire now…' He trailed off, mumbling.

'I have a modest set of skills, but I'd love to learn more.'

'You're late. Oh, so late.' He shuffled the papers he had finished collecting and placed them in a seemingly random crate before turning his attention to an enormous wooden box. 'There'll be no more learning. Oh no, no, no. We can't have that.'

'Is there no way I can enrol?'

Half submerged within the box, the man thrust a bit of parchment behind him and asked Sawwse to sign it. Looking it over, she could see that it was covered by musical notation. She read the notes and played out the tune in her head: a waltz of some kind. Sawwse wasn't sure of the significance of the paper but signed it nonetheless and handed it back to the man.

'There. You're enrolled. Congratulations.' He dived back into the box. There was a scuffling noise that sounded like wood shavings being vigorously moved around.

'But all I signed was that piece of parchment.'

'Correct.' The man jumped out of the box and picked up a nearby double bass that almost completely eclipsed him. Struggling, he lifted it into the box, falling in after it and creating a plume of sawdust.

Sawwse had been desperate to get here, but now what?

Reappearing from inside the box, and now covered in sawdust, the man rested his arms on the side of it and looked Sawwse in the eye. 'Look, the conservatoire is closing. Closed. Our esteemed colleagues at the Rhyddinian City Council have decided that there's no money for "frivolous activities" anymore. Unfortunately,' he held up the parchment that Sawwse had signed, 'this means that we will have to reject your application, strong though it was.' As he surveyed Sawwse's crestfallen face, his own softened slightly for a moment. 'My name is Con Duco and–'

'I'm Sawwse Bohge.' She bowed.

'Yes. Well, it's nice to meet you, but I'm afraid you'll have to excuse me. I have to sort through… *this*.' He gestured to the hall in general, before turning his back on the gnome.

'Oh dear. Thank you anyway.'

Fully defeated, Sawwse turned on her heel and began to walk dejectedly back to the entrance, when a golden gleam in her peripheral vision caught her attention. The gleam was coming from a musical instrument she had never seen before. It was triangular in shape, much taller than she was, with a golden frame leading out from a column. Attached to the frame were various dials and between the top and bottom parts of the frame were taut strings. It was a harp. I'm describing a harp.

Curiosity got the better of her. Sawwse tentatively plucked one of the strings and was delighted with the result. The resonation created a gorgeous sound. She plucked further strings, noting the pitch of each note played, and then created a simple melody. Beaming, she carried on, developing more and more elaborate music as she did so.

'Did I say you could play that?'

'Crimp!' Sawwse jumped away from the instrument and saw Con Duco's frowning face. 'I'm sorry, I completely forgot to ask.'

'That harp is priceless.'

'A harp. That's a nice name for it.' She sounded it out a few times. 'A harp. Harp. Harrrp.'

'Yes, and it was made for none other than Queen Hlysnan.'

'Did she not want it or something?'

'You've evidently been neglecting your musical history. Quite common with youngsters these days. It's all about hands-on practice and never enough about theory. Well, I suppose it's not about very much at all currently.' He looked downcast before remembering his company once again. 'Anyway, you play quite well. Where did you learn?'

'The harrrp? Nowhere.'

'Well then, who are your parents?'

'Excuse me?'

'Your parents. I might know them, who are they?'

'I don't know. They're nobody, I think. I'm not sure they passed any skills on, other than my charming personality.' She smiled disarmingly. 'Depending on the whole nature versus nurture thing. I never met them.'

Con Duco apologised under his breath.

'That's okay, I've had almost a hundred and thirty-nine years to get over it.'

'A hundred and thirty-nine!' he wheezed. 'You're a messer.' Walking over to a crate behind Sawwse, he reached in and pulled out a long, curved metal tube. 'Mess around with this.'

Sawwse took the object and looked it over. The tube curved round on itself twice, ending in a larger opening that reminded the gnome of a flower. She rested the flower on her shoulder, letting the tube extend out away from her, holding it up with her hand. Then she put her mouth to the smaller end, inhaled deeply through her nose and blew out into the tube. A deep, intense vibration of sound resonated from the instrument. Sawwse instinctively rested her other hand further down the tube. The instrument telescoped as she slid the tube away back and forth, changing the pitch. It was a Kalsnatchian death trumpet. I'm describing a Kalsnatchian death trumpet.

Just as she was getting familiar with the instrument, it was snatched out of her hands and replaced with a violin.

'Ah, I know this one.' Sawwse recognised the curvy shape from the books in the Blue Forest, though she had never had the opportunity to play one. She flipped it around, resting her chin on the base and Con Duco handed her a bow. 'Now, how did Flowerdew describe it?' Sawwse slowly drew the bow to and fro, ushering a mournful tune.

Con Duco watched as the light around them seemed to dim. His eyes widened and he grabbed the instrument back.

'Did I get that one wrong?' asked Sawwse.

Con Duco ignored her. He placed a hand on Sawwse's back and proceeded to push her from box to crate; each time taking out a different instrument and handing it to the gnome.

Some of the items were more familiar to Sawwse: a silver flute, a guitar, a double bass. However, some of the items were missing from Emmeline Flowerdew's work: a spidery object, with eight smaller shells connected to a central drum, an enormous horn, which had to be stepped inside of in order to play, and a piece of fabric that created a high-pitched squealing sound when scratched. Why anyone would choose to play that last one, she did not know.

Con Duco did not say anything while thrusting Sawwse toward the instruments. He merely raised his eyebrows from time to time, or let out an abrupt noise. It was unclear in each case whether this was approval or discontent. Finally, he took his palm from Sawwse's back and spun her around to face him. 'And can you sing?'

Sawwse cleared her throat and began softly singing the lullaby about the moon in the lake.

Con Duco quickly muttered something under his breath, causing a faint glimmer of light to glow at his edges. 'Yes, yes. I thought as much. Okay, that's enough, thank you.'

Sawwse stopped singing right away and stared at the panda-faced man. She was exhausted, but exhilarated.

'Well then, there's nothing for it. I'll have to tutor you myself. You'll start–'

'But you said the conservatoire had closed?'

'Djinn's luck! I got carried away and forgot for a moment.'

'I thought it was too good to be–'

'Still though. Yes, well, it'll have to be private tuition then. I demand it. Not ideal to study without a cohort or an orchestra, but with your innate ability you should be fine.'

'That's brilliant–'

'Now that my source of income has gone,' he said, gesturing around them. 'I'll need to be paid per session.'

'Yes, paid. Payment. Money. Moonay. Right.'

'Shall we say fifty aur?

'Sure, we can *say* it.'

'At four o'clock in the afternoon? Three weeks today?'

'I definitely know what some of that means.'

Con Duco picked up a random parchment from a nearby box and scribbled his address on it. 'You'll find me here.'

Sawwse looked it over and hummed out the musical notation on the parchment: a jaunty little ditty this time. When she raised her head, she saw Con Duco holding a bassoon.

'I will see you in three weeks' time Ms. Bohge. For now, I must get back to clearing up this hall.'

He blew into the bassoon and Sawwse felt herself flying backwards through the air. Rather than crashing into the boxes and crates behind her, as she imagined she would, the fabric of the room peeled away around her as if shedding her from itself, leaving her stood outside the entrance once more.

Disoriented, Sawwse took a few moments to regain her coordination. Once she had it, she grinned as wide as she'd ever grinned before. Okay, so she wasn't studying at the conservatoire, but she had the next best thing: private tuition from the head of the conservatoire. Well, she presumed Con Duco was the head of the conservatoire. Either way, private tuition! It felt like a proper step towards being the greatest musician in the world.

'Pardon. Can I squeeze past you?'

Sawwse looked down to see a short and stout goblin holding a set of extendable ladders under one arm. With her other hand, she was holding a glass box with a flame inside. The goblin pointed at an unlit torch high above them.

'It's evening already?' Sawwse was stunned. It was only now she realised that the sun had drawn in again. She moved out of the goblin's way. 'How long was I in the conservatoire for?'

'Couldn't say, miss. I just light the torches.'

The Actum Tempus symbol of the golden hourglass atop a steel shield flashed once again into Sawwse's head. She gasped. 'The guild meeting!' Without wasting another second, Sawwse dashed from the conservatoire and went looking for Ruby.

Part way along her search, Sawwse realised she was being followed by a large, shaggy dog. It didn't look dangerous per se, but it barked and then seemed to be chasing her with determination. To be on the safe side, she ran as fast as she could, darting through arcades, down small side streets, and skidding round corners until she was free of it. She bent over to catch her breath.

'Finally, I thought I'd never catch you.' The dog rubbed up against Sawwse's legs, before shifting into a human form. Ruby smiled at the gnome.

Sawwse blinked. 'Could you not have said it was you?'

'I did! Oh. Sorry. I've just realised that I was speaking in Dog.'

'Right… Let's go and find that guild meeting!'

'I'm not sure.' Ruby looked nervous. 'It sounds scary.'

'Nonsense! It sounds fun.'

'What about the "trouble" he said was knocking on our door?'

'I'm pretty sure he said "bubble." "Bubbles" were knocking on our door.'

Ruby held up her finger to the air as though she'd just come up with a very good idea. 'Here's a thought, what if we didn't go to the guild?'

'That's the exact opposite of what I want to do.' Sawwse put her arm around Ruby. 'It'll be great. Trust me. Now we just need to find it.'

Ruby pointed to a tall, thin inn sat at the end of a cobbled road filled with crooked buildings that looked in danger of collapsing, leering as they did into the centre. The inn may have been cosy at one point, but now the white paint on the walls was chipped and falling off. A sign hung from the inn at an angle. Its faded surface depicted a man, woman and child, smiling while warming their hands by a fire. It read: The Happy Hearth.

'Oh.' Sawwse's grin widened. 'We're here.'

Chapter 11:
A Wolf at The Door

Across the river and over the other side of the Blue Mountains, in the Western belly of Esh'areth lay Doriana, capital of the Dorienne Kingdom. The last time we were here, Princess Eugenie had just returned, and people let out a collective sigh of relief. For those in Doriana, a king or queen missing from the throne was akin to going to the toilet without the lights on i.e. a chaotic mess. Little did they know that Eugenie's return would result in more chaos than less. It was exactly this chaos that Alla'fyr was here to exploit.

'Your princess seeks a wizard?' asked Alla'fyr.

The guards facing her were shaking in their boots. The trail of fragmented symbols identified her as a fallen wizard. 'W-we c-can't let you p-pass.'

'Oh, this?' Alla'fyr pointed to the broken oath. 'That's just a silly misunderstanding.[21] I'm in the process of having it looked at by the relevant wizarding authorities.'

---

[21] The roomful of peers at the Academy misunderstood her when she said, "I will burn you alive unless you stop singing that infuriating song."

She smiled as sweetly as someone who looked like a skull could smile.

The guards exchanged a glance. This was a little above their pay grade. They lifted the barrier and nodded her towards the palace, and then watched her drift away, feet floating an inch above the ground. 'Probably fine.'

It wasn't. They'd just let a wolf in wolf's clothing into their kingdom's inner sanctum. A couple of *charming* spells later and Alla'fyr was being chaperoned by royal guards into the palace. This was all too easy. Had she been a hero, something would have gone wrong quickly enough. But she wasn't. She was a villain through and through. Hence Alla'fyr's arrival in the Council's Chamber of Secret without any trouble at all.

The Council were in the middle of making excuses.

'The thing is,' began a councillor wearing a feather boa. 'I was going to research the "ancient temporal magic thing" you spoke of, but a big boy pushed me and ran away.'

'Yes. I was there too.' A snout-nosed councillor piggy-backed on this idea. 'He pushed me too.'

Princess Eugenie held her head in her hands. 'None of you have found out *anything* useful?' She turned to her Lord Protector of Turnips. 'What do the turnips say?'

Cribbins – now wearing a large, hollowed out turnip on his head like a kind of crown – rolled several turnips across the Council's round table. He cleared his throat nervily. 'Er… they say that, er, the turnip never falls far from the tree?'

Eugenie shook her head and smiled. 'At least I can always rely on your wisdom.'

Another councillor was about to point out that turnips don't even grow on bloody trees, when an unfamiliar voice spoke up.

'Perhaps I could offer assistance?'

Eugenie spun around to find Alla'fyr at the door to the room. The Council were shocked. Shouts of: 'A fallen wizard!' 'How did she get in?' and, 'That's a lovely red robe,' erupted around the table. Finally, one of the councillors spoke above the din. 'Guards, what is the meaning of this? No one unauthorised is allowed to enter this chamber.'

'Wait.' Eugenie held up her hand to quiet the Council. 'What do you mean offer assistance?'

'Apologies, I couldn't help overhearing your conversation.' Alla'fyr put on her best impression of innocence. It wasn't very convincing. Especially because the royal guards either side of her were obviously hypnotised with literal stars in their eyes. 'I believe you seek the Ancient Device?'

Eugenie pointed to the side of her head. 'That's it. That's what I have been talking about.'

'To be fair, you said "ancient magic thingy,"' said one of the councillors. 'All this "Ancient Device" business is news to us.'

Eugenie nodded at a guard who immediately took the councillor away. 'As luck would have it, a spot on our council has just opened up.'

Alla'fyr smirked. This was going to be easier than she thought.

A murmur spread around the table before a couple of the more confident councillors spoke up. 'Are you sure we should be inviting a fallen wizard to the Council?'

'We don't know anything about her! No background checks. No nothing. What if she's just here to sow chaos, take over the kingdom by stealth, and then run it into the ground all on behalf of some shady organisation that lurks in the shadows?'

Alla'fyr flinched. This was unbelievably close to the mark. Luckily for her, Eugenie was too blinded by her mention of the Device.

'It matters not,' said Eugenie. 'If she assists us with the Ancient Device, all else is irrelevant.' She turned to Alla'fyr. 'Where is it?'

'It will take a little time to find. A location spell won't work. It is too powerful, too ancient, and too well hidden.'

'Then what?'

'We need to find it the old-fashioned way, by searching in the old world: tombs, temples, crypts, and forgotten lands. There will be a trace of a map somewhere, and once we have that, we will find the Device. *And then I will seize the Device for myself, ready to manipulate time for my Agents of Chaos, and destroy peace across the Four Continents.*' Alla'fyr stared into the middle distance, a malevolent smile playing upon her lips.

The Council looked at Eugenie pleadingly, having heard everything that Alla'fyr had tried to think internally.

Eugenie shook her head. She'd deal with the fallen wizard when it was time, but not before she got as much out of her as she could. 'You'll start south of Rhyddinas in the Tomb of Tombombaboobybobbalus.'

'Me?' asked Alla'fyr.

'Perhaps I misunderstood your offer of assistance?'

Alla'fyr's smirk faltered for a moment, but then returned. She covered her mouth. '*What does it matter to me? I don't appreciate the princess' tone, but the sooner I find the Ancient Device, the sooner I'll take control of Doriana.*'

Uncovering her mouth, she added. 'I will get ready to depart.'

Chapter 12:
Guild Meet

The Happy Hearth had seen better days. When? It wasn't clear. Perhaps back when it was built. What *was* clear was that it currently looked like balls. The furniture was falling apart, the paint peeling from the walls, and there was one of those generic, unplaceable smells permeating the whole place. A large stone-lined hearth was positioned as a centrepiece in the room, but it'd been a long time since the fire was last lit. The Hearth was also sparsely attended: an old couple who barely looked up from their pints, and a surly-looking goblin working on a cross word.[22]

Sawwse and Ruby made their way towards the bar, where the landlord, a miserable man known as Grimiser, was drying tankards with a dirty rag. He looked the newcomers up and down, snorted, and then nodded his head towards a nearby door. 'They've already started.'

---

[22] It was reserved for the apothecary who'd sold him cream for his eczema, which had only exacerbated the issue. If he'd read the tube carefully, he would have spotted that it was for excessema.

'We're late!' Sawwse rushed through the door and entered a small room. There was a step down, which she missed, so she ended up tripping head over heels into the room. She used the forward momentum to turn the fall into a kind of awkward dance and ended with a low bow. 'Nailed it.' Looking up, she saw Osrik grimacing. She waved at him frantically and spoke a mile a minute. 'Hiya! I thought we were going to be late, but we hurried as quickly as we could. Oh! I found the conservatoire and the guy in charge said the place was closing, but that he'd tutor me privately. What a result! Anyway, did you have a good day? Is the guild everything you hoped it would be?'

Sawwse took in a huge breath and finally realised that everyone in the room was staring at her. Osrik gestured with his eyes for her and Ruby to take a seat quickly.

A large oak table dominated the room. The figures sitting around it glared at Sawwse with a mixture of curiosity, amusement and annoyance.

'Welcome.' The beetle-like man who had addressed the crowd the previous evening sat at the centre of the table, hidden by the same, white-horned mask and glittery black cloak. However, he spoke with none of the passion from the previous night. 'Now we're an even ten.'

A portly man with a bulging red nose slowly rose as if to make a pronouncement, but slumped over instead, knocking his head on the table and passing out on the floor.

'That's fine, we can start a guild with nine.'

A pair of elves at the back of the room shared a look with one another, before one of them spoke. 'Er, Guild? Is this not the Cosmo Card Collecting Club?'

'I think that's in The Hoppy Hearth,' said an affable dwarf with rosy-red cheeks sitting on top of a cask of beer. Beneath his bushy beard were youthful features framing a kind face.

The elves shuffled out and carried the unconscious man with them.

The beetle waited for them to leave before he spoke again. 'Seven. Seven is perfect.'

'Seven new friends!' offered Sawwse.

'We're not here to make friends,' said a nasally voice. Across the room from Sawwse stood a tall rogue with a penetrating stare. He wore rogue's gear and lurked in a corner roguishly.

A small cough came from a wizard at the other end of the table. She wore deep blue, hooded robes that had globes of various sizes stitched into their folds. The peak of the hood hung out over cloudy unseeing eyes, casting them in shadow. 'We may not be here to make friends, but team cohesion is incredibly important. Perhaps an ice breaker would be appropriate at this juncture?'

'We've broken enough ice.' This time it was an elf directly to Sawwse's left who spoke. She had long, tight curls of fiery red hair. It was said that there was something cosmic about elves. That their eyes were a portal to other worlds. True enough, but the galaxy seen in these elven eyes had been tempered by a hot rage: vengeance simmered just below the surface. It looked incredibly painful. She turned her intense gaze to Sawwse and Ruby. 'This isn't a place for children.'

Sawwse opened her mouth to reply, but Osrik came to her defence before she'd had a chance to speak. 'They've as much right to be here as you or I.'

The rogue scoffed. 'So, this adventuring guild welcomes old age pensioners as well as children?'

'Say that again,' growled Osrik.

'So, this adventuring guild welcomes old age pensioners as well as children?'

'I don't think he meant it literally,' said the wizard.

'Yes, it was a metaphor,' said the rosy-cheeked dwarf.

'Well, no.' The wizard stroked her chin. 'I think it may have been rhetorical, rather than a metaphor.'

'It doesn't matter what it was. I was calling him old.' The lurking rogue emerged from the corner of the room wearing a smug grin. 'I'd rather not fight alongside someone too frail to lift a battle-axe.'

Osrik's chair hit the ground as he took hold of a small hand axe at his waist. 'Stop your yapping or I'll slice you a new mouth as wide as the Vordinian delta.'

'*That* was a metaphor,' said the rosy-cheeked dwarf.

'Hm.' The wizard looked confused. 'I think that was a simile.'

'Is that simile to a metaphor?'

'Oh, shut up!' The rogue whirled round and grabbed at the rapier in his scabbard. Strange. It was missing.

Osrik seized the opportunity and made to throw his axe. His intention was to hit a shoulder or finger, just to make a point. But as soon as he'd let loose the axe, it disappeared.

'Let's settle down.' The beetle-like man's calm, firm voice cut through the already-strained atmosphere. 'A guild is built on mutual trust and understanding between guild mates. And if it isn't built on that, it's built on putting up with people you may not like. Sit down.' The masked figure clicked his fingers: the hand axe reappeared at Osrik's waist and the rapier to the rogue's scabbard. They scowled at each other but sat back down without another word.

'Awkwaaard,' mouthed Sawwse.

The masked man at the centre of the table opened a heavy, leather-bound ledger set in front of him. 'I am pleased that you have all chosen to be here today. I expect that you all have different reasons for getting involved with this new guild, but together I believe we can build something strong and prosperous, whether you get along or not.' He turned his face to Osrik and then to the rogue. It was impossible to read his expression past the impassive mask, but one could assume he was peeved. 'Firstly, some business. I will act as the convener for our adventurer's guild, and you can call me Convener.'

'Not much of a name,' said Sawwse. 'How about we call you Beetle Face instead? Or Beetle-o? With the Beetles? Or how about Mask-o? Maskington? Masque of the Red Death?'

'Sawwse,' said Osrik softly. He placed a finger to his lips.

'Gotcha. Sorry.' Sawwse held her hands up in apology. She pointed to her head. 'I'll keep stewing on it.'

But she didn't keep stewing on it. As Convener began to describe the rules of guild membership, the fees involved, the ethos of the guild etc., Sawwse had already zoned out. It wasn't that she was bored. Well, she was a little bored. It was mostly that she was too excited to concentrate. She thought of all the stories Dannse Gan had told her about travelling across the Four Continents, and wondered whether she would end up as a grandgnome telling her own stories of adventure, heroism, music, and… itchy feelings at the back of her neck?

Sawwse looked at Ruby, who was scratching the back of her own neck with her foot, and then at Osrik who leaned his crinkled face on his fist. A moment later, Osrik slammed his fist down on the table and shouted: 'Stay out of my mind!'

The rest of the would-be guild mates looked to Convener for an explanation. He did not offer one. 'If you have nothing to hide, you have nothing to worry about, Osrik Bitterforge. It is a simple background check. There's less paperwork this way.'

Sawwse and Ruby exchanged perplexed glances.

'No.' The rogue with the penetrating stare shook his head, turning his ire toward Convener. 'Unacceptable.'

'It is necessary,' said Convener. 'It is important for us to know your intentions regarding this guild. We have had some difficulties in the past.'

'You and who else?' The fierce-looking elf crossed her arms over her chest.

'Excuse me?'

'You said "we." Who else is there?'

'A slip of the tongue,' offered Convener, but explained no further. 'Do not be alarmed. Anyway, I have already completed the checks.'

The wizard cleared her throat. 'As someone recently engaged in employment within a Human Resources department, this does seem a somewhat,' she took her time finding the right word, 'unorthodox way of doing things. I'm not sure this method would pass a preliminary committee session, truth be told.' She chuckled to herself, shaking her head in disbelief, as though following the rules was the most straightforward thing in the world. 'Also, paperwork gets such a bad rap, but it needn't be a chore if it is completed promptly and effectively.'

'I'm not sensing any bad vibes from him to be honest,' said Sawwse. She wasn't thrilled about someone rooting around in her head uninvited, but it was true that she sensed no ill will from Convener.

'And we should trust your "vibes"?' The rogue scoffed.

'He's r-right, Sawwse,' stuttered Ruby. This was the first time she'd spoken in the room, and she was very nervous. She seemed to shrink deeper into her seat with each word. 'H-how can you t-trust someone who d-doesn't even show their f-face?'

'I had to ensure that there were no bad apples in our midst,' continued Convener without addressing Ruby's point.

'And *he* passed that test?' Sawwse pointed at the rogue.

'You may withdraw from the guild at any point if you are not happy. The early exit fees are all laid out clearly in the contract.' Convener flipped to the back of the ledger, retrieved a crisp piece of parchment and placed it in the centre of the table. 'This contract ensures that you will adhere to the rules of the guild.' He placed a thin, wire frame over the top of a candle on the table. Retrieving a small tub from within his cloak, he placed it on the frame above the candle, where it slowly began to give off thin blue smoke and the smell of dying flowers. 'Please read it through and place your mark.'

The wizard picked up the contract. 'As a former HR administrator, perhaps it would be appropriate if I were to study the contract first–'

'I am a scholar. I will assess this contract.' The rogue snatched the contract from the woman. His eyes darted around, scrutinising the page. When he reached the bottom, he furrowed his brow. 'How do you know our names? More mental intrusions?'

The rest of the room stared at Convener.

'A simple trick. Nothing sinister.' The mouth of the white-horned mask curled ever so slightly into a smile, but it was so plain that it was impossible to read. 'As you are all surrounded by unfamiliar faces, your names are at the forefront of your thoughts. I simply borrowed them while performing the background check.'

Sawwse tapped her head again. 'So long as you don't look too closely at the tightly-sealed box marked teenage years, I'm happy.'

Osrik muttered something under his breath.

'No one is forcing you to sign the contract. If you would prefer to return to your mercenary ways, you may do so. There may be better money in it, but at what cost to your morality?'

Osrik growled. He plunged his thumb into the hot wax, grabbed the contract and then marked it. 'I Osrik Bitterforge, son of no one, hereby agree to the terms and conditions of this guild. And you know nothing of my morality.' He pushed the contract and wax to his left, in front of Ruby. He leant closer to her and spoke quietly. 'You don't have to do this.'

Ruby looked down at the contract and gulped. She felt as though a lump the size of a particularly large chew toy was stopping her throat.

'Poo or get off the pot,' said the rogue, to death stares from Sawwse and Osrik.

'Right. Yes. Sorry.' Ruby shrunk a little in her seat. Literally. The goal had been to set herself up as an apothecary in a sleepy backwater village somewhere. Instead, she was on the verge of joining an adventurer's guild in a city that was very much a wakeful frontwater. How had she gotten herself into this situation again? Ruby turned to look at Sawwse who was beaming at her, nodding encouragingly and giving her a double thumbs up. Of course. That's how. She sighed and dipped her thumb into the wax. 'I Ruby Schap, daughter of… no one, hereby agree to the terms and conditions of this guild.' She marked the contract and then moved it over to her friend.

Now everyone turned their eyes toward Sawwse. Picking up the parchment, she read it over two or three times without taking a single word in, excitement halting her hand. Signing this contract felt like embarking on an adventure in and of itself. Leaving the Blue Forest was one thing, but joining an adventurer's guild was something she'd never even countenanced.

'Just mark the infernal contract!' It was the rogue again.

'Crimping heck, give me a minute.' Sawwse looked around the table for support, but everyone stared back at her impatiently.

'To be fair, you have been staring at the contract for about ten minutes,' said Ruby.

'Is that a long time?' Sawwse scratched her head and then met eyes with Convener, as much as one could meet eyes with an impenetrable mask. *If a guild is built on trust, should we not have a guild leader that seems even remotely trustworthy? Perhaps he's listening to my thoughts right now. Big bums!* Convener continued to stare at Sawwse, impassive. *Perhaps not.*

'I Sawwse Bohge, daughter of… I don't know, hereby agree to the terms and conditions of this guild.' Sawwse grinned broadly, dipped her thumb in the wax and marked the contract. 'This thumbprint might be worth a lot someday.' But rather than leaving an imprint on the contract, the parchment absorbed the wax into itself, leaving no trace of the thumbprint. 'Or not.'

Sitting back in her seat, Sawwse felt a familiar thrill run through her. It started as a tingle in the tips of her fingers and toes, and rose up through her body to the nose. As it passed through her lungs, she inhaled deeply, filling her chest with air. Sawwse stood on her chair. She opened her mouth to burst into song… when she was interrupted by the elf to her left.

'I Vadania Avindico, daughter of a sacked god, hereby agree to the terms and conditions of this guild.'

'Probably not the right moment,' muttered Sawwse, slowly sinking into her chair.

Vadania took up the contract and moved it across the table along with the wax. The rosy-cheeked young dwarf gave his name as Rangrim, and the former HR administrator as Corinne. They both marked the contract in turn. Finally, the tall, intense, and somewhat rude rogue signed as well, giving his name as Larn.

After collecting the completed parchment, Convener sat very still for a few moments. He placed his fingertips together in front of him and his mask glowed a bright white. 'Welcome, all of you, to Actum Tempus, our humble guild. The road ahead may be lined with dangers, but overcoming these obstacles may lead to great rewards, interesting stories and mutual honour. Perhaps dishonour too. Your adventures may call for you to cross borders into many different lands, provinces, kingdoms. Where terror rises, this guild seeks to quell it. We will not change the world, not yet at least, but together we can make a difference.'

Sawwse listened to Convener's speech and wondered how many other Blue Forest gnomes had been in this position before her. She began picturing herself alongside Emmeline Flowerdew: prancing about on stage in duet. She thought also of the Gnehsehgs and

Dannse Gan, and the fact that she was now finally following in their footsteps, exploring the world beyond the Blue Forest, meeting new people and having adventures. It was scary. But good scary.

'I have covered our board here for the foreseeable future and you will find your lodgings upstairs.' Convener flashed his unreadable smile once again. 'However, don't get too comfortable. You will need to be up early for your first quest.'

'Bagsy the quest!' snapped Larn quickly.

'I'm not sure that is an appropriate way to request ownership over a particular quest or mission,' said Corinne, frowning.

'I can think of a better way,' said Osrik, patting his axe.

'Foolish machismo.' Vadania stared across the table at the others. And then proceeded to take out her twin short swords. 'But if it is a competition of strength, then I will win.'

'Don't be so sure of that,' said Rangrim. He retrieved an absolutely humongous sword from his back.

'Honestly, this is worse than working in a nursery.' Sawwse rolled her eyes. 'The simple thing would be to play a game of Rock, Parchment, Glockenspiel.'

'Maybe none of us need to go on the quest?' offered Ruby. 'We could all just sit down with a nice cup of herbal tea.'

'Enough.' Convener spoke, but his voice was different. It resonated through the room, vibrating the floorboards underneath their feet, and shaking the candles on the table. It commanded attention. 'This quest requires all of you to work together.'

Larn was about to protest, but Corinne put a gentle hand on his shoulder. He shrugged it off but remained silent.

'You will travel to the Tomb of Tombombaboobybobbalus,' said Convener.

'That's it's actual name?' asked Sawwse.

'There is something buried deep within. A fragment of something that could lead to a great source of power.'

'Vague.'

'You will need to be quick, lest the item falls into evil hands.' The eyes of Convener's white-horned mask narrowed. 'You will also need to work well together. What is a guild if its members do not look out for one another?'

'How do you know about this source of power?' asked Vadania.

'I have my… sources.' With that, Convener left the room. He could have teleported but chose to awkwardly shuffle and squeeze past Vadania and Sawwse to reach the door, the horns of his mask getting temporarily tangled in their hair.

Then there were seven. They each sat still, exchanging awkward glances and saying nothing. The pause extended for a while. Then a while longer. And then an even longer while. Eventually, when Sawwse couldn't take it any longer, she took out her lute and began to fingerpick a pleasant meandering of notes. Almost instantly, the atmosphere in the room became a little less oppressive.

'You play well.' Vadania looked down at Sawwse. She had attempted to soften her gaze, but it was still only a few notches down the intensity scale from a gorgon.

'Thanks!' Sawwse grinned from ear to ear. She still wasn't used to being complimented for her lute-playing after so many years of insults from the other gnomes back home. She began to sing nonsense lyrics: 'The blue monk swam into the bell tower; the red monkey ate a beetle to fly higher.'

While Sawwse continued to play, Rangrim searched the stacks of barrels at the back of the room for a drop of ale. He tore off the lids one by one and peered inside each of them in turn. After the tenth barrel, his face lit up and he shouted excitedly: 'I've struck gold!'

'Haha I get it, like in the mines?' asked Sawwse. The silence that followed her comment was enough to alert her that this was a faux pas. Even Larn looked somewhat offended.

'Not all dwarves are miners, Sawwse,' whispered Ruby.

Fortunately, Rangrim either didn't care or hadn't heard. He was too busy searching the shelves for something to drink from. Wiping dust off a collection of discarded bowls, he picked the cleanest one and dipped it in the barrel before raising it to his lips. 'Delicious!' he said, beer dripping through his beard. He filled each bowl with ale and passed them round the table.

Seven bowls were raised in the air, and seven voices proclaimed seven toasts revealing seven wishes for the future.

'To knowledge!' said Corinne.

'To heroism!' said Rangrim.

'To redemption!' said Larn.

'To honour!' said Osrik.

'To acceptance!' said Ruby.

'To music!' said Sawwse.

'To vengeance,' said Vadania, quieter than the others.

The low gravel of Osrik and Rangrim's Dwarvish was counterbalanced by the melodic chime of Sawwse's

Gnomish, the beautiful earthiness of Vadania's Elvish mixed with three different dialects of the human tongue from Larn, Corinne and Ruby. Each language wrapped around the other, creating a beautifully diverse chord that rang out around the room.[23]

There was another long pause. This time the silence was broken by Osrik. 'I remember once crossing the winter fells of Svaalind. Our provisions were running low, but our pursuit of the Orc commander Kagn Dramrs was almost complete…'

The others sat and listened, enraptured by Osrik's thrilling stories from his mercenary past. Then, after each story, Sawwse played another tune, with accompanying clapping from the others.

It was in this way that the adventurers of the Actum Tempus guild spent their first night together, sat in a dingy, poorly lit storage room swapping stories, drinking too much ale and enjoying Sawwse's music. But there was someone sat round that table who was not participating as much as the others. It wasn't Larn, who was clearly a lightweight and got drunk on the second round, but rather Vadania, whose mind was elsewhere.

Behind the intense glare of her eyes played a memory-scene that she kept close to the surface. It was something she couldn't forget if she tried. As it happened, she didn't want to. Remembering kept her anger at no less than a simmer, but she'd need that anger when the time came. The memory began the same as always with…

…pale moonlight filtering through a grove of ash trees, a gentle stream running softly into a pool, and a

---

[23] The right-winged trolls threw up a little in their mouths.

weird bird making an irritating hooting noise. Peacefully, Vadania sat with her bucket, filling it up with water. The triangular symbol of Soldi, the god of geometry, was painted on her forehead. After soaking a piece of cloth and wringing it out, it felt cold, refreshing on her face.

Vadania was fond of this spot. Even though it was the furthest pool from the temple, the water was so fresh and clear that she believed it was well worth the long walk. It also occasionally got her out of clean-up duty, much like a well-timed toilet break. It was during her walk back to the temple that she became aware of a large, menacing shadow moving slowly overhead. It blocked out the light and filled the forest with dread. The shadow trembled through the trees as it passed overhead. She began to run and run and run, but the shadow effortlessly outpaced her. The trees hampered her vision, but as the shadow turned in the sky, she saw a dragon's huge scales glistening green and black in the moonlight. An ear-splitting roar rang out across the night sky. By the time she got there, the village was ash…

…Far away, the Ancient Device stirred once more. If it spoke, it would have said: 'A mind obsessed with vengeance is tasty indeed! She will almost certainly be mine.' Instead, it made a sort of mechanical clicking noise that sounded like a small bird knocking its beak against a wall…

…Nearby, Vadania awoke with a start, hot rage filling her lungs. The meeting room was empty. The other guild mates long since departed for bed. It was still night as she walked into the moonlit backyard of The Happy Hearth. She grabbed her twin short swords and began training while her new guild mates slept soundly in their rooms above.

Chapter 13:
A Hero's Sword

A lot has been written about the *morning after the night before*, but most of it written by those fighting off fuggy-brained, bleary-eyed, tired-limbed hangovers, and therefore most of it centred on philosophical quandaries like, "Did I really show Tina my Sugrubian nostril tattoo?" or "How many dragonfire cannonballs did I end up drinking last night?" The writers never seemed to focus on how brilliant the night was, how interesting and engaging the people were, or how warm and fuzzy it had made them feel. That's because they weren't Sawwse Bohge. Tucked up in bed and still wearing her jammys,[24] Sawwse wrote a letter to Dannse Gan. She'd just gotten onto how lovely her guild mates were when a boot kicked the side of her bed.

'Get dressed.' Larn loomed over her. 'It's time to leave.'

'Already?' Sawwse looked at an imaginary watch on her arm. 'But it's only two hairs past a freckle.'

---

[24] "Jammys [jah-meez] *n.* Pyjamas covered in jam." (Gnomeopedia, 'Definitions and Schmefinitions,' p. 203)

'Grow up.'

Sawwse shrugged. 'Well, at least it was nice that you came to get me.'

Larn snorted. 'We drew lots.'

'Same!' Sawwse held up a piece of parchment crammed with pictures of her guild mates drawn on it. She pointed to a crude sketch of Larn. His arms were folded across his chest and his eyebrows frowned excessively. A speech bubble next to him read: "We drew lots."

'How did you know? Never mind.' Larn turned on his heel and left the room. He paused at the door and pointed to one of the other beds. 'Get him up too.'

Rangrim lay horizontally across a bed opposite Sawwse with his mouth wide open, every third intake of breath a loud rasping snore. He wore nothing but a pair of tight white long johns, which was somehow worse than if he'd been naked.

Sawwse quickly got dressed, and then, shielding her eyes, walked over to Rangrim. She leant down beside his ear and whispered: 'Hops.'

'*Where*?' Rangrim shot upright, rolled off the bed and onto the floor. The move could not have been described as graceful, but there was a certain practised rhythm to it. He jumped to his feet with his bag in his hand. 'I'm awake.' The dark grey, sleep-encrusted bags under his eyes betrayed another truth.

'I decided to wear clothes, but I guess it's up to you,' said Sawwse, still shielding her eyes.

'Gods! Sorry!'

'I'll leave you to it,' said Sawwse, leaving Rangrim to scramble around his bed. Stepping out of their dorm room, Sawwse walked down a long corridor. Wooden beams crossed in a triangular shape overhead. There were myriad rooms, multiple staircases and branching pathways to the inn, far more space than the outside might have suggested.[25]

Partway down a winding staircase, Sawwse thought she spotted something in her peripheral vision. But it was gone when she turned her head. She carried on walking only to see it again. Again, it disappeared when she tried to focus on it. Sawwse ran her hands through her hair and then brought them in front of her face. A tiny spider hung from a little silk thread attached to her pinky finger. It said: 'Morning Sawwse!'

'Argh!' Sawwse reeled backwards and the spider flew up above her, gathered mass, and shifted into Ruby, who winded Sawwse on impact and sent them both rolling down the stairs. As added icing on the slapstick cake, Sawwse and Ruby knocked heads as they attempted to stand up. 'How long had you been in my hair?'

'You walked through my web.' Ruby picked bits of cobweb from Sawwse's hair. 'I didn't know you were afraid of spiders.'

'I'm not! I just don't expect them to speak to me before I've had my breakfast.'

'What, spiders? Oh, they're chatty little beggars, honestly. They'll spin a yarn any time of day or night.'

'That's not really what I meant… oh. Hello everyone.'

Vadania, Osrik, Corinne and Larn stood in the Hearth's main room near the bottom of the stairs, staring at Sawwse and Ruby with disdain.

---

[25] But there wasn't literally more space inside than out, because that was impossible outside of a pocket dimension, a vortex snail's shell, or a blue police box.

'Amateurs,' said Larn. He quickly added: 'Bagsy not babysitting them.'

'Bagsy not–' Osrik began to say the same, but Vadania's death stare was enough to warn him off landing Sawwse and Ruby in her care. He turned to Corinne, but he had a natural mistrust of wizards. Osrik let out a huge sigh and then gestured to the hapless pair. 'Grab some breakfast. We need to depart.'

Vadania, Larn and Corinne left the inn without another word. Osrik left the inn with several words, all of which were muttered and grumbled, laced with scorn and aimed directly at Larn's back.

'Not much of a choice, is it?' Sawwse pointed to the table where breakfast had been laid out. There were three options: discoloured melon, stale bread, or mouldy cereal. 'How does cereal even get mouldy?'

Before they'd had much of a chance to contemplate this important question, Rangrim thundered down the stairs and barrelled into the room. He ran up to the breakfast table, shovelled the mouldy cereal into his gob and then dashed outside the Hearth. Sawwse and Ruby each stuffed a stale bread roll into their travel packs and then wandered outside where they found the others, including Rangrim who was currently retching into a bush.

'So, who's giving the pep talk?' asked Sawwse.

The guild mates looked at each other awkwardly.

'Surely, we've got to have some kind of speech.' Sawwse appealed to them. 'We're about to set off on our very first adventure!'

'Sawwse is right, you know,' said Corinne. 'An inspiring speech at the front end of a project can really drive team morale, motivation *and* productivity.'

Sawwse elbowed Osrik. He cleared his throat, stared at his feet and then began muttering so quietly that none of the others could make out a word he was saying. Osrik raised his fist in the air.

'Oh-kay, not quite the rallying cry I was hoping for,' said Sawwse. 'Anyone else?'

'I can think of something motivating.' Larn stormed away from the group. 'I'm going to get to the tomb first and claim all the loot for myself.'

'That's the wrong way,' said Vadania.

'I knew that.' Larn folded his arms across his chest and then sulkily waited for someone else to take the lead. 'I was just checking that the coast was clear for your benefit.'

Vadania glared at the group. She had no desire to lead, but between the dwarf throwing up into a hydrangea and Corinne scribbling reports onto a clipboard, there was no other choice. She strode away from the Happy Hearth. 'Follow me.'

The guild mates did what they were told. From their perspective, it made sense to follow the woman who looked like two wrong words would result in her kicking seven shades of sandwiches out of you. Larn followed too, but mostly because directions weren't his thing.

They headed south and had been walking for roughly ten minutes when Sawwse complained.

'Are we nearly there yet?'

Osrik put his hands on Sawwse's shoulders and turned her around. He pointed behind them at a sign that read: 'Welcome to Rhyddinas.' 'As I have already said, try and at least wait until you can no longer see the city before you ask again.'

'Okay, okay.' Sawwse began walking backwards keeping her eyes on the city. 'I wouldn't have to keep asking if someone told me how far away the tomb is.'

'It's half a day's trek,' said Osrik, as patiently as he could manage. 'And I have told you. Seven times already.'

'Yes, but I still don't know what that means.'

'It's half as much as a day, and twice as much as a quarter,' said Ruby.

'Helpful.' Sawwse spun back around. 'Could we not have ridden horsies to the tomb?'

'I'd love a catch-up nap if we're taking a horse and carriage.' Rangrim trudged along miserably behind the others.

'Take that up with Convener,' grumbled Osrik.

'Too stingy,' said Larn.

'Well, to be fair, there are a lot of overheads in setting up a guild,' began Corinne. 'He's paid for bed *and* board, and only asked for a cut of any rewards we take in. Having looked at the market rates before deciding to join this guild, it is one of the more reasonable offerings out there. So, not hiring horses for a short trek seems entirely justified to me.'

No one really knew what to say to that.

'A song.' Vadania stopped walking. Music was the one thing she didn't have when she travelled alone. 'A song would be pleasant.'

Needing no further encouragement, Sawwse whipped out her lute and began picking out a tune while they walked. She sang simple lyrics describing the plains, the coppices, the settlements that they passed. Before she knew it, they were stopping for a rest. 'We're breaking up the journey already?'

'We've been walking for three hours,' said Osrik, using a tinderbox to relight an old campfire in the shadow of a large hill with a peaked top.

Sawwse gave up. She was never going to get to grips with this whole "time" thing.

Had Sawwse had the ability to process it, she'd have known that it'd been nearly an hour since the members of Actum Tempus had taken their well-deserved break. Instead, she parsed it only in musical terms: two folk medleys, a power ballad, and a lengthy solo on the lute.

The guild mates had just about finished with their rations when they heard a hissing sound, a bit like a punctured bike tyre except more aggressive. It was a bandit group. They climbed over the peak of the hill and made their way toward the guild mates. The hissing was coming from an enormous, blood-thirsty orange reptile. The lizard was tied to a leash, but it took three of the bandits to hold it in place. As they drew nearer to the campfire, the reptile snapped, spit and gnashed.[26]

'Sorry 'bout Zigmund,' said the goblin leading the bandit group. She had a tattoo of a rose running down the side of her neck. The orange reptile continued to hiss, so she turned to the reptile and barked. 'Down, Ziggy! Bee'ave.'

The giant lizard sunk its head sullenly and let out a quiet, almost sassy hiss.

'Any room at the inn?' said the goblin pointing to the campfire.

The adventurers within Actum Tempus looked at the bandits with caution, subtle hands closing around the

---

[26] Snap, Spit, and Gnash were the mascots for a very popular off-brand cereal in Las Orcas.

hilts of their concealed weapons, and, for Sawwse and Ruby, easy hiding spaces clocked and ready to leap into. It was possible to avoid this fight, but it'd require all the sensitivity, tactfulness, and diplomacy that they could summon up.

Larn stepped forward.

'Er, perhaps someone else should–' Sawwse was interrupted by Larn, who held up his hand and smiled. His expression suggested that it was fine. He'd "got" this.

Larn walked over to the goblin and put his arm around her. 'You and all your bum friends and your stupid bum lizard, are the biggest pack of bums I've ever seen in my entire life.'

There followed an awkward silence where the bandits tried to work out exactly how offended to be. It turned out it was very, very offended. The goblin flicked her arm forward and a little knife appeared in her hand. 'Say that again.'

Larn took out his rapier and made his way back to the others.

'Oh-kay, I don't believe this needs to escalate any further,' said Corinne. 'I ran several workshops on deescalating conflict within the workplace. Let me see, now. I always start by saying, let's communicate clearly.'

One of the bandits gasped. 'She's baking bun of my beech imbediment!'

'How could she?' asked Sawwse. 'This is the first time you've said anything!'

Corinne held up her hands in apology. 'It was sincerely not inbentional. Intentional!'

The giant orange reptile hissed loudly, clawing at the earth and yanking at its chains to get closer to the guild mates. 'I think Ziggy likes you. Per'aps we should let 'im 'ave a closer look.'

'There is no need for you to lose your pet today.' Vadania unsheathed her short swords and the *shing* of metal on metal hung in the air.

With a nod from their leader, the three bandits holding Zigmund's chains released them, and the ravenous beast came half-scurrying, half-sliding towards the guild mates, snapping its jaws and hissing. Vadania walked calmly towards the reptile. As Ziggy leaped, so did Vadania, up and over the lizard, slicing through its neck on either side as she landed. The pitiful creature began a headless dance, scampering away before stopping dead.

'Z-Ziggy!' One of the bandits dropped to his knees and began to cry.

What happened next was pure chaos. Corinne tried to settle matters early on with a 'spell of calming,' but accidentally created a minor earthquake. Larn set upon two of the bandits with his rapier but lost his balance at the tremors and all three of them landed in a pit. The goblin leader barrelled towards Vadania, slipped on reptile blood and nutted Osrik in the delicates. Sawwse and Ruby clung together, hiding behind a rock alongside Rangrim, who was quietly feeling awful *before* Corinne's spell, and much worse afterwards.

'Stop this damned quake!' shouted Larn, scrambling out of the pit.

'Er, I'm trying.' Corinne was rifling through a little pocketbook of spells she always kept with her. Her finger stopped on a page. 'Ah. This might work.' Corinne made an arcane gesture with her hands and the ground stopped shaking. Unfortunately, the shaking was replaced by wobbling, as the ground became jelly. 'Oh dear.'

Peering over the rock, Sawwse saw little glimpses of what was happening. Osrik held two bandits in a headlock, one under each arm. Larn lost his balance again and then spun around to make sure no one saw. Vadania seemed to be entirely unphased by Corinne's misspells, striking down three bandits without much effort.

'I should help.' Rangrim staggered up to his feet, belched and then shouted. 'Get ready to meet *Slaepan Gigas!*' The dwarf reached behind him as he spoke, but his hand grasped at an empty scabbard strapped to his back. 'Corinne! For the love of all the Dwarven gods, return my sword at once!'

'I didn't realise I'd…' Corinne rapidly rifled through her book.

'Come on! Quickly!'

'Er… Rangrim?' Sawwse tapped him on the elbow.

'Not now, Sawwse.' Rangrim leant down and tousled Sawwse's hair. 'I'm about to save the team. This is my hero moment. I just need Corinne to unhide my sword.'

'That's the thing.' Sawwse reached up and tousled Rangrim's beard. 'Corinne didn't hide your sword. You left it back at the inn.'

Rangrim blinked, once, twice, and then his face crumpled in shame. He *had* left it at the inn. 'Oh no.'

Thunk.

Something hard connected with the back of Rangrim's neck and he collapsed to the floor. It would be easy to blame the chaos of the brawl, but it would be accurate to blame Vadania who had purposefully cudgelled Rangrim with the hilt of her sword. As his consciousness faded, he heard Sawwse shout, 'What did you do that for?'

'Now he won't get in the way,' said Vadania, while chucking a knife at a bandit ready to strike Larn.

'I was handling that,' snapped Larn.

'He could've just sat out of the way,' said Sawwse.

Rangrim was vaguely aware of the squabble continuing, but his mind had already turned elsewhere. The sword. How could he have forgotten the sword? What was he even doing playing at being a hero? It didn't take long for his mind to close to the waking world altogether, and to drift into a fitful sleep, full of bad dreams and even worse memories…

…Head in a fug, eyes bagged and crusty, Rangrim gradually became aware of a heavy shoe kicking his bum. He lay slumped on Hero's Point, the grassy mound that overlooked his mountain village.

'Mhmph.' He tried to speak, but his mouth felt glued together.

'Wake up, you lump.'

Rangrim slowly wiped the sleep from his eyes. The daylight stung as he opened them. 'What's going on?'

The large crowd he saw around him appeared as silhouettes, backlit by the overwhelming brightness of the sun. One silhouette was larger than the others. It was the village elder, Thrimbald, recognisable even in outline due to the cucumber-shaped protrusion jutting out from his head. No one was quite sure whether it was a concerning growth or what, but it didn't stop the kids calling him cucu-head behind his back. 'Get up, you stupid oaf. Look at what you've done.'

Rangrim raised himself up with some effort, rocked unsteadily, and then stumbled back onto one knee. The world spun wildly around him. He raised a finger in the air, and, after a brief pause, vomited up all the previous night's ale onto Thrimbald's shoes.

'Oh, Rangrim.' His mother's voice could be heard above the crowd. She stood arm in arm with his father, disapproval radiating from them both.

Rangrim was yanked to his feet by the surprisingly strong elder. 'Anything missing?' The elder shook him. 'Do. You. See. Anything. Missing?'

It was a struggle for Rangrim to focus while the world continued to spin, but after a few moments it clicked. 'The sword! It's been lifted.'

'Yes. Yes, it has, hasn't it.'

Thrimbald thrust Rangrim forward and he fell to his knees once more. An extremely large sword lay flat on the ground in front of an ancient stone block.

'Rollo and Khanan's stores were both raided last night. Do you think that's a coincidence?'

'But… the legend?'

Rangrim was taken aback. The sword was known amongst the mountain dwarves as *Slaepan Gigas* or Sleeping Giant. It was supposed to watch over the village until a hero worthy of waking its true power retrieved it. The fact that it had been removed was shocking enough, but Rangrim couldn't countenance that *he* might be the legendary hero, especially since he couldn't remember anything of the past night, beyond a hazy memory of leaving The Rugged Pony as it closed and stumbling off in search of food and company.

Seemingly reading his mind, Thrimbald spoke again. 'I'd rather the sword lay dormant for twelve more centuries than for you to be the hero.'

Rangrim sunk his head in shame. He glanced up to look for his parents, but they had already begun to walk away, shaking their heads in disappointment…

…In its secret chamber, the Ancient Device whirred. If it spoke, it would have said: 'Another one! Its mind is full of regret and shame. Yummy scrummy in my tummy!' But it couldn't speak, so it simply buzzed like a high-spirited bee having a party for one inside a tulip…

…In a secluded chamber, Sawwse gently rocked Rangrim until he opened his bleary eyes.

'What happened?' he asked, groggily.

'There's probably no need to go into specifics.' Sawwse scowled at Vadania. 'But the bandits are no longer an issue.'

'My sword!' Rangrim sat bolt upright and immediately regretted it as his head collided with a rock jutting out of the low ceiling. They were in some kind of dark cave. 'Where are we?'

'Long story short – we're a bit lost.'

'It turns out elves don't always have the best sense of direction.' Larn was sitting with his back against a wall. He spoke with an unjustified air of superiority. 'Perhaps we should have followed me after all.'

'You literally led us into quicksand,' said Sawwse.

'I didn't see the elf leading us at the time.'

'Elves are allowed a loo break as well.'

'I'd rather you didn't advertise that,' said Vadania sternly.

'I let everyone down,' said Rangrim quietly.

Osrik was slumped on the floor with his arms folded. 'You've plenty of time to prove yourself, son.'

'Oh. My. God. Are you father and son?' Sawwse squealed. 'Twist!'

'No, Sawwse.' Ruby whispered in Sawwse's ear. 'Do you have a thing with dwarves or something? They're not all related.'

'He said "son!"'

'It's a turn of phrase.'

'It's a turn of stupid, is what it is.' Sawwse spoke quickly and defensively in the way that everyone does when they say something accidentally offensive. 'Why say "son" if you don't mean it?'

'I should have been prepared.' Rangrim continued to wallow in self-pity like a shamefaced hippo. 'If I had been ready, no one would've been injured.' He gestured to a fresh nick on Larn's cheek.

Larn flushed angrily. 'Had I been on my–'

'*Had I been on my own*,' said Sawwse, putting on a silly voice. 'Perhaps then you'd have missed the goblin's slingshot.'

'I didn't see much of a contribution from you out there!'

'She thought you could handle them on your own,' growled Osrik.

With a look of thunder, Larn turned his back on the others and shouted into a small passageway in the cave. 'What's taking you so long?'

Rangrim looked around the cave in confusion, counting out the guild mates.

'That's right,' said Sawwse drily. 'We've sent the one member of our team who can't see to look for the entrance to the tomb.'

'Found it!' called Corinne, a moment later.

'Finally.' Larn slunk out of the cave.

Vadania followed next.

Rangrim made to leave the cave after her, but Osrik put his hand on the younger dwarf's shoulder. 'Best stick at the back. Without your sword, you know.'

'I still have my fists.'

Osrik smiled sympathetically and then left the cave.

Rangrim turned around. Sawwse and Ruby were playing slapsies. It felt very much like being relegated to the children's table at Cronksmas. He sunk his head and shepherded them after the adults.

Outside the cave, there were more caves. The landscape was hollowed out, creating a path which descended into a large pit in the earth, and was buffered by small caves on either side. Sawwse and Ruby spent most of their descent trying not to look over the edge into the pit, as it wasn't possible to see how far down the path led. It was two wells deep, meaning it was the depths of two wells stacked together, and also that it was deep enough for a passer-by to exclaim, 'Well, well, well, that there hole is at least two wells deep.'

Finally, finally, finally they reached the bottom of the path. In the centre of the pit was a large stone tablet. Something was written on the tablet in an ancient script. Larn traced a finger over the lettering.

'Can you read it?' asked Sawwse.

'Yes.'

'Well, go on then. What does it say?'

'It says, "Tomb of Tombombaboobybobbalus."'

Sawwse was disappointed. She'd assumed it would say something like, "all ye who enter will lose their hair," or, "turn back lest ye hair goes frizzy," or, "seven hair-based curses upon those who enter this tomb." She was having a bad hair day. 'At least we're in the right place.'

'But it appears we are not alone.' Vadania pointed with one of her swords. The join between the edge of the tablet and the ground was slightly discoloured, like it had been burnt.

'Please don't tell me there are skeletons down there,' said Ruby, clutching onto Sawwse's backpack.

'It's a tomb,' said Larn. 'Of course there'll be skeletons.'

'Yeah, but dead ones, right?' Ruby quivered. 'Not… *un*dead ones.'

'Aren't we all technically undead?' asked Sawwse.

While this conversation went on around him, Osrik quietly seethed. Unlike the others, he'd seen burn marks like those on the tablet before. He spoke under his breath. 'Alla'fyr.'

'What?' asked Vadania.

Roused from his seething, Osrik took up his battle worn battle-axe. 'Be on your guard.'

Vadania dug her fingers under the thick tablet and hauled it to one side. Underneath was a dark stone chute: the entrance to the tomb.

Corinne cleared her throat. 'Perhaps now would be a good time to formulate our strategic goals ahead of entering the–'

'Geronimoooooooooooooooo!' Sawwse jumped in.

'Gods!' shouted Osrik.

The others traced Sawwse's yell down the length of the chute until they heard a quiet thud. It was followed by a quiet scuffling sound, and then a very unquiet scream.

Osrik instantly dived into the chute. Ruby shifted quickly into a small bird and flew in after him. Osrik landed and swung his axe in front of him, while Ruby swiftly found a perch in an upper corner of the room. 'Where is she? Where's the fiend?'

'There!' Sawwse jumped past Osrik's axe into his arms. She pointed at a tiny spider dangling on a thread in front of them.

Ruby flew down from the ceiling and shifted back to her human form. 'So, you *are* scared of spiders.'

'Nothing should have that many legs!'

Osrik dropped Sawwse onto the ground. He shouted up to the others. 'It's clear.'

Once the others had all reached the bottom, they found themselves in a dusty, square stone room. A patch of the floor had been cordoned off with pegs, and there were rows of racks standing against the wall, all of which were covered with huge grey sheets. There was a space with a patterned archway above it leading to a small corridor. A thin band of hieroglyphs ran underneath the cornicing at the top of each of the walls.

'Can you read them?' Sawwse tapped Larn on his elbow.

Larn revolved slowly to examine all the symbols. His eyes were alight with excitement. 'This is fascinating. It appears to be an ancient pictorial language, but I haven't encountered it before.'

Vadania approached him. 'What might they mean?'

He was silent for a few moments, turning and deciphering in his head. 'I am conjecturing, but it appears to be an old ward.'

'An old hospital ward? That's a relief!' Sawwse wiped her brow. 'Better the unwell than the undead.'

'No, you dolt. Many ancient cultures left magical wards on their tombs to protect their dead for perpetuity.'

'Oh, magic. I should…' Corinne rifled through her little spell book and began raising her arms.

'No!' Larn spoke with the urgency of someone whose fingernails had fallen off earlier due to one of Corinne's misspells. He adjusted his tone. 'I meant, there's no need. The ward has long since passed. However, these symbols might tell us more about what's buried here. I'll look ahead for more information.' He nodded to himself, before walking through the patterned archway out of the room.

The others watched Larn exit the room.

'Wow,' said Ruby. 'That's the first non-selfish thing I've seen him do.'

Sawwse gestured at the hieroglyphs. 'Turns out badly drawn pictures of eyes, reeds, and horsies are all we needed to stop Larn being an arse.'

This got a laugh from the others. It was cut short by a loud crash from down the corridor. Rushing through it, they found Larn repeatedly smashing a man against a wall with one hand, while his other held his rapier to the man's throat.

'Talk,' snarled Larn.

Chapter 14:
Tombs and Temples

...**Somewhen in the past**, a ring of light encircled Larn as he knelt on the floor of his academic office. Forbidden books lay open, sprawled across almost every surface of the room. He'd analysed and synthesised all of the knowledge in each book and had prepared everything he'd need for the ritual: a fourteen-pointed circle of chalk, a pot of gold, an armadillo skull, a tepid glass of water, and five odd socks. He stole the money from the university. He'd have felt worse about this if his application for promotion hadn't been denied. But that didn't matter anymore. Soon he wouldn't need money, because he'd have power. And money can't buy this kind of power.

Reading from his notes, Larn recited an exiled language. It was forbidden, almost forgotten, and sounded a bit like a frog playing a harmonica.

A light breeze began to blow, turning the pages of the books.

Larn raised a pendant towards the centre of the circle. Little flakes of light began to peel away from the circle and collect within the pendant. *It's working*!

But something went quickly wrong. There was a loud sucking noise, like a drain capturing water or a troll eating spaghetti. The breeze turned into a sharp wind, which whipped at Larn's clothes and bit at his head, shoulders, knees and toes (knees and toes). Larn held onto his notes with one hand and steadied himself with the other. He couldn't catch his breath. Then, an ear-splitting pop and a horribly evil laugh.

The force with which the demon arrived seemed impossible. The office was filled with pages upon pages ripped from Larn's books. Shelves snapped, the tepid water boiled, and the armadillo skull shattered. And the demon's grinning white face continued to laugh.

Larn was knocked over by the force. He held the pendant above him. 'I am offered protection by the energy collected within the pendant of Zay-Nmal-Ik.'

A phantom hand appeared and tapped the pendant with a single finger. It smashed into a thousand pieces. The demon clicked its fingers and a contract appeared on a gold leaf page.

'W-what is it?' asked Larn.

You seek power, hissed the demon.

Larn nodded.

Then sign.

'Er, well, I definitely want power. It's just I'd usually have the university lawyers look at a contract before I–'

Then I will destroy you and find another host to bestow my power upon.

'No! No. I'll do it.' Larn signed it. 'There.'

The demon cackled, crackled and boomed,[27] and the wind began sucking in to form a vortex. Larn held on to

---

[27] Yet another set of cereal mascots in Las Orcas.

the legs of his heavy oak desk as he felt his own legs being torn apart. Sinews snapped, muscles melted, bones smashed, and his legs were ripped off into the ether. Out of the vortex came machinery, the likes of which he had never seen before. Thin copper wires coiled around reinforced steel pipes, which then connected to various shapes and sizes of metal. The metal separated into two prosthetic legs that jutted forcibly into the scholar's newly formed stumps. A pair of tiny Alan keys tightened everything.[28] Larn howled in agony.

The contract floated towards Larn, reducing in size as it did so until it was but a speck of gold dust resting on his forehead where it vanished.

Another explosion and the demon vanished from the room, setting it ablaze. As Larn cowered and whimpered, he heard a voice inside his head and realised he'd just made a huge mistake.

Hi there, bunk buddy. You might want to move. We've got a lot of work to do…

…Somewhere in the present, the Ancient Device rattled within its hidden cavern. If it could speak, it would have said: 'This one pretends he does not wish to return to his prior life, but I sense it underneath the surface. I will ravage him along with the rest. Yay!' But it couldn't speak. Instead, it clicked a little, clanked a little, and clunked a little, and then, unusually, it clecked…

…Somewhere else in the present, Larn pressed his rapier against the trembling skin of a man's neck. 'Talk!'

---

[28] The world was grateful to Alan for designing such useful keys. There was even an 'Alan day' celebrated in most kingdoms across the Four Continents to mark his achievements in hexagonal key making.

The others bolted into the room and quickly surveyed the scene. The man being accosted by Larn was clearly an archaeologist, complete with khakis, leather jacket, and fedora - only the whip was missing. There were pegged off excavations on the ground. He was even clutching a brush and trowel. 'Help!' he gasped.

'Larn!' shouted Sawwse.

Larn pulled the man in close. 'I don't like you.' He reluctantly let the man go and then slowly backed away. Larn pointed at Rangrim. 'He doesn't like you either.'

'That's not true.' Rangrim scratched his beard. 'Honestly, I don't know why he'd say that.'

The archaeologist took out a handkerchief and wiped his sweaty brow. 'Ahem. I knew they would send someone tough, but I didn't expect to be roughhoused like that.' He began to relocate some of the artefacts that had fallen from the shelf. 'You got here very quickly, I must say.'

Sawwse shared a confused look with the others.

'You were expecting us?' asked Rangrim.

The man narrowed his eyes. 'Well, I thought so.'

'Oh, don't worry about my colleague.' Sawwse placed a reassuring hand on the man's forearm, which was as high up as she could reach. 'He just placed the stress on the wrong word. He meant: you *were* expecting us.'

'That's still quite a weird thing to say–'

'*Anyway*, why don't you describe the situation for us in detail? They're a bit lax back up at the, er, head office.' Sawwse jovially elbowed him in the side, making a 'what are they like?' kind of expression.

The archaeologist frowned. 'I did already explain all this to your other colleague. The nice woman with a red hood who arrived here not long before you and did *not* put me in a chokehold.'

Osrik clenched his jaw. So, she *was* here. He let out a deep, guttural growl.

The archaeologist thought Osrik's tension was aimed at him, so he quickly described the situation again. 'I'm conducting research for the University of Qllarniquolp, investigating religious iconography from the Messylithic era. This tomb was unsealed just last week and even the first floor is full of interesting artefacts.' The archaeologist held out a broken pot enthusiastically for the party to see.

'Ooh! What's in it?' Sawwse stood on her tiptoes, trying to peek inside the pot. 'Sweets? Biscuits? Dannse Gan's famous apple biscotti?'

'No, the pot. The pot is worthwhile.'

'Oh.' Sawwse sighed. This was one of the most significant heartbreaks of the journey so far.

'They suspect there's even greater treasure to be found deeper inside the tomb, but unfortunately there are monsters lurking down there, endangering potentially very significant discoveries.'

'So, the university sent us to clear the tomb?' said Rangrim, speaking aloud as he worked it out.

The archaeologist frowned, looking questioningly at the adventurers. 'Again, I had assumed so.'

Sawwse burst out in her best fake laugh. 'Rangrim just placed the emphasis on the wrong word. Again! He actually meant: So! The university *sent* us to *clear* the *tomb*.'

'Right.'

'This colleague of ours,' said Osrik in his low gravelly voice. He was passing his battle-axe back and forth between his hands. 'Where is she now?'

'She went on ahead.' The archaeologist stared at Osrik's well-used axe. 'Are you concerned about her?'

'You could say that.'

Rangrim turned to Vadania and attempted subtlety. 'The "treasure" is probably the same thing that Convener was on about.' Unfortunately, Rangrim couldn't whisper. Vadania flicked him on the shoulder.

'The treasure?' The archaeologist lowered his voice and spoke in a conspiratorial tone. 'You didn't hear it from me, but we believe there's the potential to find incredibly well-preserved corpses.'

'I knew this was going to be an undead thing,' murmured Ruby. She burrowed her head into Osrik's travel pack and chattered her beak nervously. This was particularly weird because she'd already shifted back into her human form.

'Huh,' said Rangrim. 'I think Convener implied it was some kind of map that would lead us to–argh!' Vadania stamped on Rangrim's foot.

Before the archaeologist had a chance to speak, Sawwse clapped her hands together. 'Right, we'll clear the monsters from the tomb for you and definitely not steal any of the artefacts while we're down there.' She winked exaggeratedly at the others. 'Let's goooo–oh no. Where's Larn?'

Vadania swept across the room quickly toward a stone staircase. 'The man's a liability.' The others followed her. Down the stairs, another corridor opened ahead of them before turning sharply to the right. Vadania signalled for the rest of the team to wait while she scouted ahead.

'Okay, before we action this, let's assess our situation going forward and see if we can synergise our ideas.' Corinne crouched alongside Sawwse at the front of the group and spoke in hushed but extremely business-like tones. 'Sawwse, perhaps you'd like to give us a steer on that.'

'Er…'

'Actually, before you get started, just one or two health and safety things we should go over.'

Osrik grunted. There wasn't enough room for him to squeeze past the pencil-pushing wizard, and he didn't fancy being turned into a marsupial again.

Fortunately for Sawwse, she was slight enough to creep forward as the impromptu health and safety briefing began. She peered around the corner to see Vadania and Larn in an alcove whispering in a heated discussion. Sawwse made her way over to them quietly.

'I don't need permission,' said Larn.

'In this instance, yes. You do.' Vadania placed a hand on Larn's shoulder and forced him to stay kneeling as he tried to stand. 'You have forced us into an unnecessary encounter once already today.'

'Take your hand off me.' Larn tried unsuccessfully to shrug off Vadania's hand. 'And that encounter was inevitable. I merely speeded things up.'

'It is a poor adventurer who causes needless bloodshed.' Vadania tightened her grip. 'We will tie them up and question them.'

Sawwse looked past the pair into the torchlit room beyond. The light bounced off the sandstone causing the room to pulsate in daffodil yellow bursts. Three goblins dressed in white smocks stood by a set of shelves at the back of the room, ransacking said shelves for anything that looked valuable, which they piled into brown sacks with "swag" written on the side. They were wholly unaware that they were the source of some contention amongst the two most furious Actum Tempus guild mates.

'They are in my way.' Larn pushed back against Vadania's firm grip. There was a metallic whirring sound and Larn's legs emitted steam. He rose until he was facing Vadania eye-to-eye. 'I do not like it when things are in my way.'

Vadania's fingers wrapped around the hilt of her sword. The tension was palpable. Had it been tangible, Sawwse would have smashed right through it when she brushed past them, strolled into the room, and shouted, 'Hiya!'

The goblins turned around and let out various high-pitched shrieks. This was not without reason. They weren't expecting anyone else in this part of the tomb. They especially weren't expecting an overly friendly gnome flanked by perhaps the least friendly pair of adventurers any of them had ever seen.

'Talk,' said Larn.

'Is that honestly your opening gambit every time?' Sawwse threw up her arms in despair.

'It's effective.'

'It really isn't.'

'Is too.'

'Is not.'

The goblins exchanged an awkward glance with Vadania, whose stern demeanour had melted a little into embarrassment. She cleared her throat.

'Right, yes. Sorry. I'm Sawwse Bohge.' She shot Larn a dirty look. 'This is a normal way to start a conversation.'

One of the goblins pointed between them in turn. 'Grobnak. Broknuk. Nuttkrak.'

'Charmed.' Sawwse gave the goblins a quick curtsy. 'How did you get in here?'

'We snuck in when the tomb was opened.'

'What's with the smocks?'

'There's a kind of cult down below.'

'What about the monsters?'

'Mm they are running the cult.'

'Can you guide us down there?'

The goblins formed a huddle and spoke to each other in Goblinese.

Larn pointed the tip of his rapier at them. 'They're planning to kill us.'

The lead goblin scoffed. 'You don't know mud from mud.'

Gears turned and weight shifted instantaneously. In the blink of an eye, three hands full of chubby goblin fingers flew into the air and a howl filled the chamber. In several further blinks of several more eyes, Sawwse and Vadania rounded on Larn, the rest of the guild mates rushed past Corinne's HR spiel into the room, and the goblins dropped their swag bags and bolted from the room.

'What's happened?' asked Osrik.

'What do you think?' said Sawwse. She folded her arms across her chest and faced Larn. 'Anger issues over here just cut those goblins' harp careers unfairly short.'

Larn casually wiped the blood from his rapier with a handkerchief. He returned the stares of his guild mates. 'I cleared the room, didn't I?'

'Technically, guild procedures dictate that we question those that do not immediately seek to cause us harm.' Corinne flicked through the pages of her clipboard. 'Yes. It's right here. Section 15: Tombs and Temples, paragraph 4, section 16, clause 3 (ii).'

'Let's keep moving.' Osrik gave Larn a sour look. His patience was wearing thin. He'd been part of too many mercenary companies not to recognise a loose cannon.

The problem with loose cannons was that they often fired randomly without warning. Sure, they were powerful, but what's the point in power if it will sink your own ship? Much better to have a sturdy, reliable cannon on a ship. One which can be depended upon time and again. Ah, ships. The open sea. Some of Osrik's fondest memories had been while carrying out work at sea. At least if a crew mate is irritating you there, you can face the sea and let your thoughts drift away on the salty breeze.

'Er, Osrik?' Sawwse tugged at the dwarf's arm.

'What's that?'

'You were kind of staring into space.' Sawwse gestured to the empty chamber. 'We should follow the others.'

'Or we could turn back,' said Ruby who'd built herself a nest of sorts within Osrik's backpack. 'Just saying.'

Osrik proceeded through several similar chambers. They had mostly been excavated, with lightweight shelves placed alongside the walls and sconces lit above them. However, after several more chambers there came a much longer, larger space. The only lights within the room were the torches being held by the other teammates, who were spread out across a grid-like tiled floor.

Sawwse made to step into the room, but Osrik yanked her back behind him just in time.

'Traps.' He pointed to Vadania, Larn and Rangrim. The flickering light of their torches illuminated the beads of tension-sweat rolling along their faces, and the hangover sweats that Rangrim was suffering from. One such bead of sweat fell to the floor, splashing on the tile next to Rangrim. Upon impact, a huge stake drove out of the ceiling and crushed the tile.

'Crimp,' said Sawwse.

'Look. Across the other side of the room,' said Ruby. 'It's Corinne.'

'How did you make it across?' shouted Osrik.

'I floated.' Corinne smiled. She was stood at the farthest end of the room, beyond the gridded section. 'It seemed like a fair use of magic. I did offer to help the others float across, but they declined for some reason. I suppose there's no harm in conserving some magical energy for whatever may lay beyond us, farther into the tomb. That is why it's so important to factor in various elements in strategic planning…'

While Corinne wittered on, Vadania began to move. She leaped from her tile onto another one. It was safe. Two more leaps. A strand of hair dropped onto a tile behind her. Another stake drove straight through the tile. The force of it knocked Vadania off balance, but she quickly found her footing again, jumped onto the next tile, and then off the grid altogether, landing safely next to the wizard.

'Woah!' Sawwse and Ruby began clapping.

'Impressive,' said Osrik quietly.

'Do you have a focus?' Vadania handed her torch to Corinne and explained her plan.

Corinne nodded and rummaged in her robe pockets for a minute before retrieving a glass prism. She muttered a spell and a powerful beam of light shone from the prism.

'The darker shaded ones are trapped.' Vadania used the prism to guide Rangrim's steps through the trapped room. Once he was safely across, Vadania guided Osrik, Sawwse and Ruby over too.

'Yay!' whispered Sawwse, silently high-fiving Ruby.

Osrik and Vadania turned to leave.

'Wait, what about Larn?' asked Sawwse.

'What about him?' asked Osrik.

'We can't just leave him.'

Vadania stared at Larn impassively. 'When we entered this chamber, he said that "he alone would reach the other side" and that "we were foolish if we ever thought we could match his prowess." He then mooned us, jumped onto that tile, and has been stranded there ever since.'

'I get it, he's hard work,' said Sawwse. 'But what if underneath the surface there's a gooey caramel centre? Man, I'd love some chocolate.'

'He will lead us to ruin,' said Vadania coldly. 'If not now, then at some point in the future. Better to have done with him sooner rather than later.' She turned and walked on toward the next chamber.

'There are better hills to die on,' mumbled Osrik. He looked at Sawwse with his sad kindly eyes, and then followed after Vadania.

Rangrim shrugged and shuffled into the next chamber.

'We're not even on a hill,' said Sawwse. She turned to Corinne. 'How about you? Surely there's something in guild protocol about leaving no Larn behind?'

'Indeed, there is.' Corinne shuffled through the notes on her clipboard. 'But it all depends on consent. I can use magic, but only if Larn allows me to. Of course, I'd have special dispensation to use spontaneous magic if the situation required it. That said, in extreme cases–'

'Corinne?'

'Yes.'

'Stop talking.'

'Ah. I was rabbiting on again.'

'I do that sometimes,' said Ruby.

Sawwse turned to Larn. 'You need to ask Corinne for help.'

'What?' snapped Larn. 'And be turned into a balloon or something?'

'She'll cast a quick spell, and you'll float over to us. You don't need to admit you're wrong. You don't need to say thank you. All you need to do is ask her to–'

'Just cast the infernal spell already!'

Corinne smiled and retrieved her pocket spell book. She flicked through the pages and ran her finger over the raised lines and dots of the floating spell. She'd used it only a moment ago, but magic could be finicky. Spells were different for personal use and for general use. The wrong conjugation and you could go from casting a floating spell to turning someone into a balloon.

Corinne cast the spell.

Larn turned into a balloon.

'Ah. Sorry about that. I said, "floati*us*" whereas I should have said "floati*mus*."'

Balloon-Larn drifted over towards Corinne and the others. Even in this inflated format, Sawwse could tell that he was absolutely fuming. Sawwse and Ruby jumped up and grabbed hold of his cloak to hold him in place.

'One moment,' said Corinne. 'I'll just figure out how to deflate you.'

With one hand on Larn, Sawwse used her other hand to slip her bag off her shoulder and rummage around in it. A moment later, she retrieved a needle. Sawwse held it up in the air, delighted with herself.

'Mnmnmnmnhhh,' said Larn. It was very hard to talk when your face was that swollen. It was also hard to shake your head or move your arms or signal in literally any way that this was a very bad idea.

'Sharp scratch.' Sawwse pricked him.

Instantly, Larn whizzed through the air deflating at pace. Unable to let go of his cloak in time, Sawwse and Ruby dangled behind him. They shot into the middle of the chamber and touched off the ground, one of the giant stakes drove out of the ceiling and smashed a tile, missing Sawwse by inches. As Larn deflated further, he rebounded from one tile to another at random, releasing so many stakes from the ceiling that the ground was almost entirely smashed to bits. Sawwse and Ruby did their best to duck and weave, but mostly held onto Larn's cloak for dear life and prayed that the stakes missed them.

Eventually, after destroying much of the room, Larn landed on the ground beside Corinne. He was back to his normal size, albeit hunched over and wheezing heavily.

'Right,' said Corinne. 'I think I've got it.'

'I almost died, you clown!' said Larn.

'Ah. You appear to be back to your normal self. Jolly good.' Corinne pocketed her book of spells. 'Shall we find the others?'

'Useless party members and their half-cocked wizardry…' muttered Larn. He made to move out of the room quickly only to find a dead weight yanked him backwards. It was Sawwse and Ruby. They were clung to his cloak in a catatonic state: eyes wide, pupils small, teeth chattering. This was known to happen to adventurers after their first near death experience. Larn yanked his cloak from their grasp and stormed out of the room.

Corinne knelt beside Sawwse and Ruby. 'Are you okay?'

'S-so m-many s-spikes,' muttered Ruby.

'I am become death, the destroyer of gnomes,' said Sawwse, as if in a trance.

'Come on.' Corinne chuckled and led them out of the room.

Once they had caught up with the others, they continued their descent through the tomb. There were more rooms chock-full of traps, but as soon as Corinne had a firmer grip on her 'Trap Locator' spell, these rooms weren't much of an issue.

'I feel a bit sorry for the guys who trapped this place.' Sawwse watched as Corinne waved her hand and a large statue of an owl glowed blue, rocked a little from side to side, and then fell on its side spilling poison-tipped arrows from its beak. 'They went to all this effort.' A huge stone rock began rolling towards them but fell into a pit some distance away. 'And we're just strolling past it all. It feels like cheating.'

'What about almost dying back there?' asked Ruby.

'I dunno. It was kind of fun.'

'Shush. There's something up ahead,' whispered Vadania.

There were noises coming from the next chamber. It sounded a bit like speaking. But it wasn't a language any of them had ever heard. It was… wet-sounding, like someone paddling their finger between their lips as if pretending to speak underwater. Though, it didn't really matter how it sounded, because a second later it screamed, and screams were universal.[29]

'Come on.' Vadania moved with purpose toward the next room.

The next chamber didn't look like it belonged in the same tomb. It was long, narrow, and pockmarked with deep, water-filled holes. At the far end of the room was a black robed cowering figure with four creatures surrounding it. The creatures had amphibian heads, with sharp teeth and long claws.

'Frupgoans,' muttered Larn.

'Help!' shouted the cowering figure.

The Frupgoans instantly dove into the pools of water, out of sight. But not before Sawwse registered a look of confused fear on their faces. Or at least that's what she thought it was. It was hard to tell with the whole frog head of it all. The guild mates began cautiously moving along the room towards the shivering figure, peering into the deep pools as they went.

'There's something not right here,' said Sawwse.

'What makes you say that?' asked Ruby.

'Osrik's grumble metre is off the scale.' Sawwse pointed at the old dwarf.

Osrik was growling as they approached the figure. His furrowed brow did not mask his tension, nor did the ever-tightening grip on his battle-axe, which had turned

---

[29] Except in Hell where tormented souls use an amazing variety of nuanced screams to communicate with one another. 'Aaaarrggghhhh' can mean, 'My feet are being chewed by an Antaxallion Saw-toothed Devil,' whereas, 'Aaargghaaggh' can mean, 'If the blue pixie demon asks you to listen to his violin recital, do yourself a favour and say no!'

his knuckles white. 'Didn't think I'd see you again so soon.'

The black robed figure instantly stopped shaking. Instead, she slowly stood and drew herself up to her full height. She tapped her robe and it turned red. Whirling around, Alla'fyr faced the guild mates with a sickening smile. Her dark, hollow eyes gleamed in her skull-like face.

'That… was a rubbish disguise,' said Sawwse. 'You just turned your robe black. Bit of a low effort.'

There was a pause as Alla'fyr registered Sawwse for the first time. She was the one on the wanted posters in Dorienne. '*Eugenie thought that* this *gnome had been the one to kill her father? What a hilarious notion. In fact*: Ahahaha.'

'Oh-kay. I can see why you left her,' said Sawwse to Osrik, who was gritting his teeth as if bracing for something that was about to happen.

Alla'fyr stopped laughing and turned her attention back to Osrik. 'So, you've joined a poxy adventurer's guild? To be fair, you clearly know someone with good intel. I'm assuming you've come for the map fragment?'

'So, it *is* a map fragment,' said Rangrim. 'Convener wasn't sure.'

'Convener…' said Alla'fyr.

'It's a terrible name, isn't it?' said Sawwse. 'I suggested Maskington.'

'Rangrim, could you stop blurting things like that out?' asked Vadania.

'Remember when I said we could just turn back and go home?' said Ruby. 'Still an option.'

Corinne cleared her throat. 'I'm afraid guild protocol dictates that we have to finish the job unless there are exceptional mitigating circumstances.'

While the others wittered on, Osrik's gaze had not left Alla'fyr. He was the only one who knew how much of a threat she really was. That was until a moment later when Alla'fyr clicked her fingers, and it dawned on the rest of them too.

'Get back,' roared Osrik, tackling Sawwse and Ruby to the ground.

A wall of fire erupted in front of the guild mates. The heat distorted her vision, but Sawwse saw Alla'fyr staring straight at her, grinning. 'The chaos you've caused is magnificent, and you don't even know it.' Alla'fyr turned her back on the guild mates and left them to suffer the inferno. 'Ciao for now.'

Chapter 15:
Terror Seeks the Infirm

The inferno roared in front of the guild mates and scorched the sandstone around them. Osrik held Sawwse and Ruby down to protect them from the worst of the blaze, while Vadania and Larn dived into a nearby pool of water. Inside, they found what appeared to be an extensive network of waterways: narrow underground passages that connected and then split off into myriad directions. Vadania grabbed Larn's arm and pointed to a passageway. They swam up through the passage only to find it blocked at the other end. They tried a different pass, but it only led further down. Larn clutched at his mouth. He'd held his breath for just about as long as was possible.

Sawwse and the others looked through the inferno nervously, waiting for Vadania and Larn to resurface. There was a long pause. Then suddenly, Vadania burst through one of the pools of water and dragged Larn with her. She threw him to the ground and thumped his chest. Larn gobbed out a lungful of water and then gasped for breath.

There was another long pause.

'Did she really just say "ciao for now?"' asked Sawwse.

'Irritating, right?' grumbled Osrik, despite his supposed distaste for gossip. He turned to face Corinne. 'Can you do anything about this fire?' With his heavy armour on, there was no way Osrik would be able to swim through the tunnels below. As much as it left a bad taste in his mouth, the solution would have to be magic. 'A spell or something.'

'Indeed. I believe that under the new regulations, this too should fall under the category of "fair use" as it were,' said Corinne, retrieving her small, leather-bound spell book again.

'Which bozo came up with all these regulations anyway?' asked Sawwse.

'That would be me.' Corinne leafed through her book. 'I thought it would be appropriate for the guild's magic users to have a set of regulations and procedures to follow.'

'But aren't you the only wizard in Actum Tempus?'

'Well, to say I am a wizard may be overstating it. I haven't received, what you might call, formal training.'

'And yet you've devised a set of rules purely for you to follow?'

'It's important to start the way you mean to go on,' stated Corinne, matter-of-factly. 'As and when Actum Tempus grows, the regulations will be there.'

'You can have this conversation later,' growled Osrik.

Corinne gave a little cough and then began mumbling an incantation under her breath.

Magic seemed wild and unpredictable to Sawwse. Alla'fyr had created the inferno with a click of her fingers. It boggled her mind seeing someone with such mastery over it. *Shame she wasn't on our side*, thought

Sawwse, watching Corinne with barely suppressed scepticism. However, her doubts turned to awe as a mist gathered within the chamber, whirling around and gathering within itself until it became a thick, dark cloud… and then her doubts returned as the storm cloud floated directly over Rangrim's head, nowhere near the inferno. Sawwse took a step back. So did Osrik. So did Ruby.

'Er, Corinne?' Rangrim raised his weary head to look at the storm cloud above him. He tried to step away, but the cloud followed his movements.

'Don't worry, I'm almost finished.' Corinne continued the incantation until the heavy rain cloud was rumbling with thunder and ready to burst.

'I think you may have got the positioning slightly wrong,' said Sawwse.

Too late. The storm cloud sprayed water all over Rangrim.

'Aha. So, my water creation spell works!' Corinne smiled. She looked proud of herself.

'It's certainly created water,' said Sawwse. Her and Ruby were trying very hard not to laugh as Rangrim's tunic began to go see-through.

'Hm. This should fix it.' Corinne waved her hands. The rain immediately intensified, pouring a torrent of water over Rangrim's head. 'That any better?'

'If by "better," you mean, "Rangrim is now piss wet through," then yes. It's better.' Sawwse and Ruby rolled about laughing on the floor of the tomb.

'Oh dear.' Corinne scratched her head. She walked over to Rangrim and physically grabbed the cloud from above his head and then hurled it over the blazing wall as though it was an inflatable ball. The fire hissed as it was hammered into submission by the rain, creating a fire-free channel in the centre of the wall.

Osrik, Sawwse, Ruby, and Corinne took it in turns to run through to the other side. Rangrim sighed and trudged across in his sopping clothes. At least he could dry himself with what remained of the inferno.

Through the other side, Vadania and Larn were knelt beside another deep pool of water. A Frupgoan bobbed lifelessly atop the water. Osrik carefully took up the amphibian creature and laid it gently on the ground. Despite not knowing the ins and outs of amphibian-humanoid biology, they could tell that it had died in a particularly gruesome way. There were blisters running across the inside of its slimy skin.

'Burned from the inside out.' Osrik folded the creature's arms across its body. He placed a coin on each of its eyes.

'Sweet bread beer.' Rangrim stopped feeling sorry for himself pretty quickly. Much better to be wet than burnt. 'Who was that wizard?'

'Alla'fyr. A dangerous, evil and extremely capable wizard.'

'And she signs off with "ciao for now,"' added Sawwse.

'How powerful?' Larn gave Osrik a sceptical look. 'Did she flunk out of the No'arethian Magical Academy, or fall from The Twelve?'

'She's a disgraced wizard turned mercenary. It's not good that she's here, but it means that Convener was right to send us.' Osrik took a weight from his bag and tied it securely to the creature before setting the body down again in the water. The Frupgoan body sank out of sight. 'And I don't know her full history, but she often made grandiose claims about falling from up high.'

'A load of claptrap if you ask me!' Rangrim laughed heartily and clapped Sawwse on the back. 'There's no way in a million years one of us will ever meet a member of The Twelve. They're far too highfalutin to rub shoulders with us.'

'I learnt to play the falute when I was one hundred and two,' said Sawwse, blissfully unaware that she had, mere days ago, met a member of The Twelve in Mirrah. 'Who are The Twelve, anyway? They sound like a boy band with too many members.'

The others stared at her blankly.

'How clueless are you?' Larn tutted.

'The Twelve keep the world in balance,' said Corinne.

'So they say,' said Osrik.

'They're an order of powerful wizards,' said Ruby.

'But Alla'fyr couldn't be one of The Twelve, right?' Sawwse laughed nervously.

There was an awkward pause.

'Enough.' Vadania strode to the staircase at the end of the chamber. 'Whether she is a member of The Twelve or not, she is ahead of us. We need to move.'

'Go ahead.' Corinne had turned back to the inferno and was wafting her hands to move the rain cloud over it. 'I'll finish dampening the flames and meet you down there. Of course, I'll need to write a quick report justifying my use of such a powerful spell. I think the mitigating circs will easily cover it… you've already left, haven't you?'

They had.

Corinne hummed a tune to herself while she put out the fire. Her mind began to drift and she thought back to her previous life, which was so very different from adventuring. As often happened when she recollected, the one memory she tried to repress crept into view like an obese ginger cat sliding in on a skateboard. Once you'd thought of it, there was no going back…

…The courtroom in which Corinne Brightwood sat was beige in both colour and atmosphere. It had to be one of the most unremarkable rooms in the whole world. From the jury box to the judge's bench, everything in this room was so plain as to be almost 2D. Even the judge was dull. He had one of those faces that was like… well, it was rather like… a bit like… nothing. It was so uninteresting that it was impossible to even describe it.

Despite its lack of interesting features or personnel, important things got decided in this room. This was HR Office B6-2 after all. It was the office used for all disciplinary hearings.

The judge spoke in a monotone. 'We have taken into account your long-standing service to this island, the quality of your work here, and the detailed report you delivered in your defence. Please stand to hear my verdict.'

Corinne stood and faced the judge. These disciplinary proceedings had not taken her by surprise. She had bypassed a regulation, and she was being reprimanded. It was fair. Hadn't she spent years ensuring regulations were upheld? It was only right that she be held to the same standard.

'The Regularis Section VI District Court with Responsibility for Magical Misdemeanours, Unlicensed Transmogrification, and Unsanctioned Grape Eating finds the defendant guilty.'

It was difficult to pay attention, even for someone as conscientious as Corinne. Perhaps that was why it took her a moment to realise the judge had *mis*judged her. He had surely meant to say, "guilty of a misdemeanour," meaning that as the offence itself was only minor according to the statutes, it merely warranted a formal warning and a slap on the wrist. "Guilty" without the caveat meant something else entirely. 'Pardon?'

'We therefore decree that you are expelled from office permanently and with immediate effect.'

This sent Corinne reeling. Her job was everything. 'Surely there's been a mistake.'

'It was you who made a mistake, Ms Brightwood. It is our right to determine the correct punishment.'

'All I did was transmute a loaf of bread.'

'Unsanctioned use of magic carries heavy consequences, as you well know.'

'She was homeless. I took the ingredients from my own supply. I'm certain this should be counted as a misdemeanour. I have clerked on several cases whose outcomes have all been the same.'

'We have already heard your defence, Ms Brightwood. Verdict so ordered.' The judge banged his gavel in the least dynamic way possible. 'You can hand in your lanyard, clipboards, badge, and gun at the door. And by gun, I mean retractable pencil.'

'My whole collection of clipboards?'

'Indeed.'

And that was it. Corinne couldn't argue against the verdict, so she had to accept that her lifelong career was over without fireworks, pomp or ceremony, and with no special retirement pencil. It was a moment completely and utterly devoid of magic…

…At a different, more current moment, the Ancient Device crackled with powerful arcane magic. If it had lips, it would've licked them like it had just had a mouth-watering meal placed in front of it: a regret pot pie, with steamed remorse and melancholy gravy. A bit salty, but otherwise delicious. It didn't have lips – thank the gods – so it just turned its cogs and continued to bide its time…

…A moment later, Corinne sighed. The inferno was dealt with, and she'd just finished jotting down her reports (plural because she'd also written a retrospective one regarding Larn's accidental ballooning). She tried to locate the others. It wasn't difficult. Firstly, everyone had an energy trail and for wizards these were very easy to follow. Secondly, they were being very loud.

'Ew! What's all this sticky stuff?'

'Talk a little louder and let everyone know we're here.'

'I think it's algae.'

'What's that then?'

'Er, pond scum?'

'Gross! Tell me that before I put my hands all over it.'

'Algae has no place in a dusty old tomb.'

Corinne descended a staircase, and found the floor was indeed sticky and wet. The walls were gummy too. 'It appears the Frupgoans have made themselves a home here.'

'Somewhere down here must connect to a waterway,' said Vadania. 'The Frupgoans might have accidentally found their way in and stayed. Either way, we cannot lose focus from our mission.'

'Which was what exactly?' asked Sawwse.

The others stared at Sawwse blankly. Corinne cleared her throat. 'Our principal mission is to find the fragment of magical power that Convener sensed somewhere in this tomb. It seems Osrik's associate–'

'Ex-associate.'

'–is after the same thing. Therefore, our secondary objective is to neutralise her threat. We should, of course, also be watchful of the Frupgoans. It isn't clear what purpose they have for being here.'

'Their purpose doesn't matter.' Larn paced back and forth, reviewing the runes that decorated the room. 'If they get in my way, I shall destroy them.'

'Oh dear,' said a quiet, muffled voice.

'You can moan all you like. I will not let you suppress my spirit!'

'It wasn't us this time,' said Sawwse. 'It came from over there.'

It was a wall cladded with the same thick, moist webbing. However, the webbing here had been twisted into strange shapes that looked almost like runes.

'Fascinating.' Larn stared at the patterns on the wall. 'I thought the Frupgoans were too primitive for this.'

'I can still hear you,' said the muffled voice.

'What is it?' asked Rangrim.

'It's a runic lock.' Larn's eyes lit up. He used to love solving these kinds of puzzles back at the university. He began tracing the arcane symbols in the air, and then he twisted the mesh cladding to create new shapes. 'Find the right connection and it should…' There was a loud squelching noise and then the wall began to rumble and shake. A moment later the bricks shunted backwards and slowly moved to one side to reveal a hidden room.

'You freed me.' It was a young Frupgoan girl trapped within an iron cage. She spoke with the common tongue. 'Thank you.'

Larn stared at the girl and then began closing the space over again.

'What are you doing?' Osrik elbowed Larn out of the way, who simply shrugged and moved to the back of the chamber. After he'd finished glaring at Larn, Osrik turned back to the cage. He shuddered in spite of himself. Despite the years since the incident, he could still feel the rusty metal bars against his bare hands, still smell the despair and terror, and still hear the clamouring voices pleading. Osrik shook his head violently and seized his axe. 'Stand back.'

Osrik launched his axe at the cage's lock. It broke with a smash and he prised open the door, offering his hand to the girl. She hesitated, but then stepped out of the cage with Osrik's help. She pointed to Larn but was interrupted by a grunt from Osrik. 'Don't ask.'

'Talk.' Sawwse appeared between Osrik's legs. 'Only joking! Just my impression of Larn. I'm Sawwse Bohge. It's a pleasure.'

'I'm Kali.' She returned the guild mates' surprised looks with an incredulous one. 'What? We can speak the common tongue, you know. We're not completely uncivilised.'

'We'd been told to expect monsters,' said Sawwse.

'Oh right, so now everyone descended from frogs is an abomination?'

'Not at all. I had a great granduncle that was descended from frogs. He was one of my favourite uncles before he croaked.'

'Oh, I'm sorry. He died?'

'What? No.'

'Right…' Kali sighed. 'I'm sorry. I'm just stressed. Probably something to do with being locked in a cage for trying to stop a ritual from happening, which, you know, will probably end up in tears.'

'What's this ritual you speak of?' asked Vadania.

'Tjark. He thinks he found a Lung-dor.' Kali raised her brow as if the others should know how ridiculous this is. They stared back at her blankly. 'There's no such thing as a Lung-dor.'

'Ohhh,' said Sawwse.

'The ritual,' said Vadania.

Kali opened her mouth to speak but was interrupted by Larn. He was stood several feet away with his back to the others. 'Lung-dors are usually incredibly powerful magical artefacts that fall into the hands of primitive cultures by chance. They are then used in primitive rituals to summon gods. Of course, it is all primitive nonsense.' A familiar phantom itch climbed Larn's legs as he spoke. 'I have read of primitive tribes wiped out by those foolish enough to accidentally summon a demon.'

'Did you *have* to say primitive that many times?' said Kali, exasperated.

'Ignore him,' said Sawwse. 'He's a wind-up merchant.'

'He sells clockwork toys?'

'The ritual!' Vadania struck the wall with her fist. There was a damp squelch as her fist was subsumed into the moist cladding. 'The Lung-dor is probably the very same thing Convener has sent us here to find.'

'Where is the ritual taking place?' asked Osrik

Kali looked at the guild mates. Then she looked at the guild mates' weapons. 'You won't hurt them? My family?'

'I thought you wanted to stop the ritual?' asked Rangrim.

'Well, Tjark could go die in a ditch for all I care. It's just that he's put my family under a kind of spell. It's like they're blinded by Tjark's promises of religious salvation. But please don't "destroy them."' She gave Larn a dirty look.

'We'll keep him on a tight leash.' Osrik knelt beside Kali and looked at her with his kind eyes. 'Which way?'

--

'I was a member of a church once.' Ruby spoke from her hiding spot behind Corinne's robes while they followed Kali all the way down to the very bottom of the tomb. 'You'd never think of pigs as being super religious, but they went in for it in a big way.'

'Whole hog?' suggested Sawwse.

No one laughed. It was mostly down to bad timing. Their attention was taken by a loud bass-y vibration that reverberated around the tomb. It came from a passageway at the far end of their current room. This was clearly an unsanctioned extension to the tomb, without the proper planning permission. It was essentially a large hole in the stonework. Vadania led the others towards the noise.

Through the hole was a much larger chamber. It looked more like a cavern than a tomb because that's what it was. There had been a structure here once, but the Frupgoans had eroded and beaten the sandstone down so that it blended with the natural rock underneath. There was a massive pool of water where the Frupgoans must have originally surfaced, but attached to the walls were gilded coffins. The most intricately designed tomb was positioned centrally at the back of the room. The symbols lining this particular coffin said: *xrgouahergoaie*, which presumably translated as Tombombaboobybobbalus. Standing over the tomb was a large Frupgoan wearing various dyed webbings, which were fashioned into ceremonial gear.

'Tjark,' murmured Kali.

He was using the ornate coffin as a kind of pulpit and altar. In front of him floated what could only have been the Lung-dor, which could only have been the magical something-or-other that Convener had sent them to find. Even at the other end of the room, Sawwse could see its brilliance. It shone bright like a star. Its power was as dense as one too.

'Alla'fyr's near,' snarled Osrik. 'I can smell her.'

'We need to stay focused,' said Vadania. 'It doesn't matter if she gets to the power source first. She will not get past me.'

'There is a slight issue with that,' said Corinne. 'The surge in magical energy coming from that altar is significant. If I'm not mistaken, it is dangerously unstable. It could explode to devastating effect.'

'Out of curiosity, how long until that happens?' asked Sawwse.

A magical orb surrounded the Lung-dor. Every few minutes the orb shrunk inwards, creating the deep vibration they had felt outside. Tjark was chanting alongside two other Frupgoan priests. Between the clergy and the guild mates were the congregation: a hundred or more Frupgoans, provoked into cultish frenzy. They rocked back and forth, bowed, and repeated recitations.

'That fool's going to blow this place apart,' spat Larn.

'Corinne literally just said that,' said Sawwse.

'*Corinne literally just said that.*' Larn mimicked Sawwse's voice.

'Perhaps intraguild civility is advised as we approach a mission critical encounter,' said Corinne. She pulled out her clipboard. 'The next step is to action our action points from the report, if you will. Ha ha.'

They ignored her.

Osrik pointed at the mad priest and then at Vadania, Rangrim and Larn. 'You three, stop him. I'll stop Alla'fyr.' Vadania and Larn moved quickly. They pushed through the crowd either side of the cavern and ran where they could. Rangrim moved slower. Osrik placed a hand on Corinne's shoulder. 'Stay here and look after the others.'

Corinne muttered to herself. 'If you'd read the report, you'd know that was already the plan…'

Osrik shrugged and then charged into the fray. Alla'fyr was likely to have made herself invisible, but that didn't mean she was impossible to find. His eyes were alert for anything amiss: a misshapen shimmer, an uncanny blur, a peculiar penumbra. *I'm going to take a grim satisfaction in crushing her skull underfoot*, thought Osrik, grinning ear to ear.

'I'm assuming you forgot I was up here.' Sawwse was sitting atop Osrik's shoulders.

He stopped grinning. 'What the hells are you doing? You're going to get yourself killed!'

'It was you who charged away!'

'You could've said something.'

'I did. Repeatedly. You kept running.'

'Bad ears,' grumbled Osrik. He placed Sawwse on the ground. 'Never mind. Go back to the others.'

A Frupgoan acolyte behind them shook with religious fervour and let out a wet, throaty screech. Sawwse looked at Osrik deadpan.

'Fine. Stay. But keep your eyes peeled. This isn't the time for jokes.'

'How about a witty comment about how absolutely disgusting peeled eyes sounds?' Sawwse placed a finger to her nose and then pointed at Osrik, giving him a 'you know you want to laugh' look.

He really didn't.

He could smell Alla'fyr. That acrid, burnt and bitter scent that always trailed behind her.

She was close.

The air bent around a silhouette.

There!

'Come on. It was funny.'

'Not now, Sawwse!'

Too slow. A powerful force knocked Osrik and Sawwse to the ground. Sawwse sprang back to her feet and raised her fists into an old-fashioned boxing position. 'Come on then, if you think you're hard enough! I was the junior Blue Forest bounce-boxing champion for three years running!'

Osrik was slower to get up. This was increasingly becoming the norm. He slammed his fist into the ground and then turned to Sawwse. 'Bounce-boxing is made up, right?'

Sawwse nodded. She lowered her fists. 'Is she still nearby?'

'Must be. Though I've lost her scent.' Osrik dragged the head of his axe against the ground. Raising it up, he pointed it past the congregation to the magical energy glowing at the mad priest's altar. 'We mustn't let her get a hold of the Lung-dor.'

Nearest the altar was Larn. His motorised legs blurred as he ran with impossible speed, smashing through the congregation without a second thought. He used one of the praying Frupgoans as a springboard, launching himself from their back towards Tjark. He'd calculated everything perfectly: the trajectory of his jump, the angle of his rapier, the force with which to pierce the priest's heart. But something stopped him. It wasn't his conscience. It was an invisible forcefield. His rapier bounced off the air. He was sent hurtling backwards into the grasping webbed hands of the congregation below.

Further back, Vadania watched as Larn's attack was brushed to one side and he disappeared into an angry mob of amphibian-headed religious nutjobs. She tried not to smile.

'There… you are,' wheezed Rangrim, appearing at her side. 'Ran… as fast as… I could.'

'Why?' Vadania stared at Rangrim coolly. Not in a sunglasses way. It was more of a 'couldn't give two tosses if you dropped dead' kind of way.

'Er…' Rangrim felt behind him in the vain hope that his sword had somehow magically reappeared at his back. It hadn't. 'Moral support?'

Vadania turned away from the dwarf and notched an arrow to her bow. She pointed it towards the altar, but not at Tjark. There were two more priests stood at the back. They chanted and channelled energy into the forcefield surrounding the altar. Vadania loosed the arrow. It stayed true to its target and one of the priests collapsed to the ground.

Before she'd had a chance to notch another arrow, she was seized upon by the congregation. There were too many of them. They smothered her.

Rangrim grabbed at the Frupgoans, jerking them away from Vadania and throwing them to the ground. But there was a zombie-like relentlessness about them.

'I will handle this,' shouted Vadania through the crowd. 'Take out the other priest.'

Rangrim nodded and barrelled past the crowd. He edged past the altar and ran towards the other Frupgoan priest, whose eyes swivelled to focus on the young dwarf. Rangrim had never actually been in a fist fight before, especially not with a priest, but now was not the moment to back down. This was definitely a hero moment. And besides, Vadania might see. Now, what was it that heroes said?

'Time to say your prayers, because soon you'll meet your maker and–ooohhsonofa…'

The priest kneed him in the intimates.

Rangrim doubled over. He recovered and struck the priest with an uppercut, which sent him staggering backwards. He prepared to punch the priest again, but before he'd had a chance, two arrows struck the priest's chest and knocked him to the ground. Rangrim turned to see Vadania standing strong amongst a heap of unconscious Frupgoans.

'Out of interest, how much of that did you see?' asked Rangrim, readjusting his trousers.

Vadania gave nothing away apart from the tiniest sly smile. She had another arrow notched and aimed at the mad priest's head. Without a moment's hesitation, she fired.

At the other end of the chamber Kali panicked. 'You said you wouldn't harm them!'

Corinne placed a reassuring hand on her shoulder. 'I'm sure my guild mates are taking every precaution to undertake their duties to the best of their abilities while maintaining the strict 'no civilian casualties' policy remains intact.'

Kali looked blankly at Corinne.

'She means they're doing their best,' said Ruby, nodding encouragingly. 'Except Larn. He's a law unto himself.'

'Well, no. He should be following the same "law" as the rest of us.' Corinne shook her head. 'I've been wondering how he might respond to a performance review.'

'I think I have an idea,' said Ruby. She looked toward the altar, where Larn seemed to be arguing with Vadania.

'What on Esh are you doing?' Vadania stared daggers at Larn. She also held a pair of daggers at Larn.

'Ha. I won't let you take the glory for yourself.' Larn's boot rested on the arrow he'd just knocked out of the air.

'I don't care about glory.' Vadania drew her bow once more. It wasn't immediately obvious whether she was aiming at the mad priest or at Larn. 'But I do care when someone gets between me and my quarry.'

'Guys?' Rangrim watched as Tjark continued murmuring in his amphibian language and the bubble surrounding the fragment of magical energy was now shimmering, vibrating, and almost certainly about ready to blow up.

Vadania and Larn continued staring each other down.

Then, within an instant, Vadania flicked a knife from her sleeve and Larn lunged forward with his rapier. The knife and rapier struck Tjark simultaneously, either side of his large, slimy neck. Tjark screamed a throaty, gargling cry of anguish as he fell away from the altar.

'I won!' shouted Larn, leaping down from the altar towards Vadania.

'You fool! Grab the fragment!'

No longer bound by the mad priest's spell, the fragment of magical energy gently dropped to rest on the altar's surface. Then, two webbed hands appeared either side of it. Tjark hopped atop the altar and raised his hands in the air. He screamed: 'Glurrg ugaarggl uggrll!' A giant wave as tall as the cavern materialised out of thin air and crashed down in front of the altar.

Larn, Vadania, and Rangrim were all washed away.

Further back, Sawwse and Osrik were knocked back too.

Even Corinne, Ruby and Kali were buffeted by the wave.

Vadania was first to her feet. She sprinted to the altar, but she was too late once again. Tjark's blistered body lay on the floor behind the altar, burned from the inside out. Without the mad priest to guide them, the Frupgoan congregation began to run amok: crying, screeching, and flailing around wetly. Vadania span around at the altar. The fragment was gone.

'The fallen wizard has it!' shouted Vadania.

'For now,' muttered Osrik, his weathered battle-axe held firmly in his hands. He stood facing a near-invisible Alla'fyr. Only the air melting away from her outline gave her away. Osrik had worked alongside Alla'fyr long enough to sense her presence even when he couldn't fully see her. He signalled where she was to Vadania and Larn, who positioned themselves appropriately. Not that this seemed to worry Alla'fyr.

'I've always despised that term. "Fallen wizard."' The air around Alla'fyr sizzled as she slowly dropped her veil of invisibility. 'It implies wizards are somehow called to a higher purpose. It's rot.' She spat on the floor and then smiled. 'Some of us are just born this way.'

Osrik pointed to the fragment of magical energy in Alla'fyr's hand. 'What are you going to do with that?' he said, through gritted teeth.

'I'm going to get paid.' Alla'fyr held the sparkling object between her forefinger and thumb. 'As if I would reveal my master plan to you. *No, by the time they find out about the Ancient Device, it will be far too late. I'll already have turned back time and plunged the world into chaos.'* Alla'fyr laughed in a way only maniacal villains can.

Osrik blinked.

'What? Why are you looking at me like that?'

'No reason.'

'I did the thing again, didn't I? Where I think out loud?'

'So… the Ancient Device?'

'Damnit!'

Alla'fyr suddenly thrust her hands forward releasing a stream of fire directly at Osrik. He quickly rolled out of the way and then brought his axe down in a great arch across her chest. She effortlessly swerved away. Vadania drove her twin short swords towards Alla'fyr, but the wizard easily spun around them, firing a blast of flame at Larn as she did so. Larn slid forward, dodging Alla'fyr's attack and rebutting with his rapier. Alla'fyr was too quick. She dropped a ball of fire to the ground and used the momentum to propel herself backwards. Unbeknown to her, she landed in front of Sawwse.

Sawwse watched with wide-eyed horror as Alla'fyr flung fire all around the cavern with no regard to the Frupgoan congregation. The fire spread to the coffins lining the walls and dark, choking smoke filled the chamber. Alla'fyr was using the flames to keep the others at a distance. Sawwse was desperate to help, but what could she do? The magical fragment twinkled tantalisingly in Alla'fyr's hand. The wizard's back was to Sawwse, and she was distracted. Surely there was an opportunity here.

Sawwse crept forward until the red glow of Alla'fyr's flames flickered on her face. She leapt as high as she could and clutched Alla'fyr's hand.

'No!' screamed Osrik.

But yet again, it was just too damn late.

Sawwse's excitement instantly turned to fear as Alla'fyr suddenly dragged her through the air to the top of the cavernous chamber. Floating there, Alla'fyr turned her skeletal face towards the gnome. An awful smile spread across her thin lips and hollow cheeks. The wizard's red robe opened and grew as wide as a tent. It enveloped Sawwse. The sights, sounds and smells of the room vanished.

'There is a saying where I come from,' said Alla'fyr.

'Fallen wizards are secretly nice and let curious gnomes go free?' Sawwse smiled weakly.

'"Terror seeks the infirm and out of place."'

'Different.'

'I am the terror.'

'Yep. I got it.'

'I could kill you now with the click of my fingers.'

Sawwse opened her mouth to speak but breathed in a lungful of smoke instead.

'However, your reputation in the Dorienne kingdom amuses me.' Alla'fyr laughed. 'A worthless piece of nothing like you, causing a kingdom's meltdown. What fools! Remember that you are small and have no place here.'

'To clarify. Do you mean here in this chamber? Or here in–' Sawwse coughed and spluttered as she breathed in more of the black smoke. 'If you clear the smoke, I could sing you a song! I've got a lovely voice.'

Alla'fyr sighed. Her smile faded and she dispelled the darkness from Sawwse. 'I *detest* music.'

'What?' Sawwse looked up at Alla'fyr with puppy dog eyes. 'Surely not. No one *hates* music!' She cleared her throat.

'I swear to all the gods and all the devils, if you sing so much as a note, I will make your death as painful as humanly possible.'

'But I'm a gnome.'

'*As gnomishly possible then*,' said Alla'fyr through gritted teeth. What an irritating gnome. But it didn't matter. She had the map fragment after all. 'I'm feeling generous. You created the chaos that allowed me a foothold in Doriana. For that I shall let you go.'

'Thank you! Thank you! Yes, please.' Smoke stung Sawwse's eyes. She looked up and realised she was clinging to Alla'fyr's leg fifty feet above the ground. The look in Alla'fyr's eyes told Sawwse all she needed to know. 'Oh. You meant literally.'

With the snap of her fingers and an unnecessarily extravagant explosion of fire, Alla'fyr disappeared in a haze of smoke. Sawwse grasped at the air but found no purchase. She fell like lead.

Chapter 16:
Imbuement

It was often said that your life flashed in front of your eyes before you died. Quite who was living to explain this was unclear.[30] Either way, it wasn't true for gnomes of the Blue Forest. When you passed away in the Blue Forest, you were likely to be in your home surrounded by the community. It was a calm and peaceful time, during which the dying gnome could talk through their memories at length with family, friends, and, depending on the gnome, frenemies. Their life didn't so much 'flash,' as it spanned several days, playing out like a godsawful piece of durational Dwarven theatre. Blue Forest gnomes were blessed to still have one of the most kind and beautiful death cultures across the Four Continents…

Sawwse Bohge was finding out that in certain circumstances, you don't really have much chance to curate your memories. One of those circumstances was

---

[30] Except it was clear and it was ghosts. If a ghost is still knocking about with their unfinished business, odds on they'll tell you *all* about how they died.

suddenly falling fifty feet through the air. Her mind bounced from Dannse Gan, to coming last in the fun run; from Marius' big friendly face, to the strangely intoxicating Mirrah; from the first time she played her lute, to that time she accidentally schnarked her pants in front of the whole school… *why has that popped in there*? A question that dawned on her now and at the time of her schnarking.

Sawwse wouldn't have a chance to find out the answer.

An immense force suddenly pierced the cavern. It sent the weirdest sound reverberating off the walls, like a goose breaking the sound barrier. There was a blinding blue light and it shone directly in front of her. And then there was Mirrah, shining brilliantly like a star. She held Sawwse in her arms and began to slowly float down towards the ground.

'Oh, hello,' said Mirrah.

A choir of angels sang a radiant, heavenly chord. Just the kind of nonsense you hallucinate when you've got severe carbon monoxide poisoning.

'Helbo… bolbow… bwilp…' was all Sawwse managed to say.

'Well, helbo bolbow and bwilp to you too!'

'Is this the real life?'

'Who could say?' Mirrah laughed. And what a laugh it was. It energised her entire face. In that moment she was both stunningly beautiful and world-shatteringly insane. She booped Sawwse on the nose. 'You feel real.'

'But how are you here? I mean, what are the chances?'

'It's the damnedest thing. I was humming your song and then all of a sudden. WHOOSH! I'm here.' Mirrah frowned. 'It's curious. I keep forgetting things, but I can't forget you.'

'You say it like it's a bad thing.'

'Oh no. It's marvellous.'

Sawwse and Mirrah locked eyes. Not just in the casual way where you spot a friend at a socially awkward party. They properly locked eyes. Everything around them vanished. Nothing else mattered, because in that moment there was nothing else. No quest, no tomb, no fire. Nothing apart from each other's gaze.

But then, Mirrah's feet touched the ground.

In the same instant, Mirrah disappeared and everything else reappeared. It was chaos. Fire now encircled the cavern, and the air was thick with foul, black smoke. Not only that, but the battered sandstone walls of the cavern shook, crumbled, and grew less stable with every passing second. As if that wasn't bad enough, a giant chunk of rock hurtled from the ceiling straight towards Sawwse.

'Sawwse!' Osrik knocked her out of the way. The rock smashed onto the ground exactly where she'd been standing. 'We need to go.'

'But Mirrah… she was just here.'

'Who?'

'She literally just saved me.' Sawwse spun in circles trying to catch any sign that Mirrah had been there. Nothing. Had she dreamt it?

'Hm.' Osrik quickly checked Sawwse's head for injury, before dragging her behind him. 'The others are up ahead.'

The clamour of the Frupgoan congregation was deafening as their home disintegrated around them. Many dived back into the giant pools of water, while others scrambled to escape from the smoke and flames.

Some of the Frupgoans ran in circles or cowered or prayed to their failed god.

'What about them?' asked Sawwse, staring at the Frupgoans as Osrik charged ahead.

'There's no time.'

'But they'll die down here!'

'Do you want to die with them?'

'No, but…' Surely there was something she could do. Sawwse saw one of the Frupgoans clinging to a rock half submerged in the water, calling out to another with a throaty gurgling call. Wait, hadn't she read about something similar in the Gnomeopedia? Sirens. They called out to sailors at sea with their alluring voices and got them to come over to their rock for a cup of tea or something. She hadn't read the whole entry. But that was it! It was worth a try anyway.

Sawwse took in a lungful of air. Strangely, since Mirrah appeared, she was able to breathe clearly despite the smoke surrounding the chamber. And then, she sang.

Come with me,
and you'll be,
In a world of purer inhalation
Watch out, duck!
then you're free,
From the fire and flame annihilation.

Instantly, she got the attention of a large group of Frupgoans. Once they stopped, others stopped too. The cavern shook even more violently, crumbling all around them. The coffins that lined the walls were bursting apart because of the fire, spraying flaming stakes in their path.

Osrik ran out of the cavern, diving this way and that to avoid the falling debris. Finally, the Frupgoans began running after him, drawn in by Sawwse's siren song.

Let's begin, with a win
And escape this tomb of pure damnation
Once you're free you'll receive
Salvation.

They climbed back through the sticky chambers that the Frupgoans had made their own and into the unaltered tomb. Fortunately, the wave of energy that started the tomb crumbling had also rendered the traps useless. The floors were wrecked, and the walls were falling down, but at least there were no poison darts up the wazoo.

If you want to view paradise…

'Then bloody run!' shouted Osrik.

Not without reason. The whole tomb was now falling to pieces around them. The Frupgoans bolted ahead to the tomb's entrance. A huge pile of rubble now created a ramp to the much-wider opening. The sunlight was stark and bitter after spending so long in the tomb, but it was also liberty.

Osrik and Sawwse got swept up by the wave of Frupgoans who threw themselves onto the impromptu ramp and scrambled up to safety. Once they were out, the structure holding the tomb together finally gave way. The limestone rocks crumbled and caved in, destroying all traces of the ancient burial place. The rockfall's rumble reverberated for some time. The ensuing silence was only undercut by the marshy-throated calls of the

Frupgoans, blinded by the sun and bewildered in the world above the ground.

Out of breath, out of sweat, and almost out of everything, Sawwse and Osrik collapsed on their backs. Their guild mates ran over to check on them. Not Larn.

Between breathless breaths, Sawwse smiled and turned to Corinne. 'How'd we do?'

Corinne slowly moved her clipboard out of sight. The words 'NEEDS IMPROVEMENT' were written in bold.

--

After a long, tiring walk, they were back in the small dimly lit room at The Happy Hearth, de facto HQ of the Actum Tempus adventuring guild. Although, Sawwse felt it was more like being back at school. There didn't seem to be any custard pies positioned menacingly around the room in case anyone failed their trigonometry test, but you could smell the same overbearing sense of disappointment in the air. Though, that could've just been Rangrim's feet.

Convener sat at the back of the room. He placed one finger to either temple and listened as Corinne detailed their failings in full.

'...although we executed the key deliverable – which was to investigate the source of power you had identified – we should still count our mission as ultimately unsuccessful. We did not stop the tomb from being destroyed, our actions were partly responsible for the displacement of a whole clan of Frupgoans, and, crucially, we lost the map fragment.'

Convener was silent for some time. As always, his expression was impassive. The white-horned mask hid his true emotions, if he had any, from view. 'A fragment of a map leading to the Ancient Device…'

The others waited for him to speak again, but he did not.

'Had you not forced us to work together against our will, this would not have happened.' Larn leant back in his chair with his feet propped up on the table. 'I could have delved into the tomb and retrieved the map fragment on my own. The others slowed me down and the gnome cost me the fragment.'

Sawwse's stomach lurched with shame. She caught Ruby's eye, who looked at her consolingly.

'It is not Sawwse's fault.' Osrik sighed, deeply. 'Alla'fyr got the better of us all.'

'She is certainly formidable,' said Vadania.

'Even you have to admit that!' Rangrim clapped Larn on the shoulder, causing him to lose his balance on the chair and fall over. 'Sorry.'

Once Larn had recovered, he made to speak but found himself at a loss for words. Not quite able to boast that he was stronger than Alla'fyr, but also unable to admit to the others – or himself – that she would have swatted him away as easily as a Garthrupian time monster knocking a minute into the middle of next week.

'Allow me to clarify something.' Convener placed his hands flat on the oak table. 'Whatever bombastic rumours circulate about this wizard, she has certainly not fallen from The Twelve. If you're ever unfortunate enough to cross paths with one of The Twelve, you'll know about it.'

'Sounds like you have experience in the matter,' said Sawwse.

Convener stared at Sawwse for a moment but did not respond to her comment. He pivoted back to Alla'fyr. 'However, she is clearly very powerful, and someone who will only be defeated with a concerted effort from all of you. It is disappointing that you worked so poorly together on this quest. I had expected much more.'

An awkward silence descended, the same stench of failure hanging in the air. Rangrim put his shoes back on. While he was down there, he noticed something odd. 'Hey, why's your bag so bulky?' Rangrim suddenly yanked Larn's bag from under the table.

'Imbecile,' gasped Larn.

Rangrim tossed the bag away from Larn. It clanked as it hit the centre of the table. Before Larn could grab it, Vadania sliced through the cloth with her long knife and spilled the contents. Ritual gold, shiny metals, a few gummy drops, and several jewels spread in front of the team. Larn sat back in his chair and folded his arms.

A look of mild annoyance flickered across Corinne's face. 'Correct me if I am wrong, but this wouldn't happen to be the treasure that belonged to the Frupgoans, would it?'

'We need it more than they do.'

'When did you even get a hold of this?'

'I traded with them for information.'

'Information?'

'They wanted directions to a place of safety. I wanted their treasure. It was simple.'

Corinne pinched the bridge of her nose. 'Where did you send them?'

Larn paused. 'The Burning Sea.'

The others threw their hands up in despair.

'They're obviously going to die!' said Sawwse.

'You could've just sent them to Rhyddinas,' growled Osrik.

'This shows a complete disregard of morals!' Corinne's cheeks were flushed red with agitation. 'I'm going to have to write this up!'

While the group chastised Larn, Convener surveyed the haul and organised the various treasures into categories. 'This should keep our boarding here for some time.'

'Sh-shouldn't we return it?' asked Ruby.

'No. We cannot afford to.' He waved his hands over the piles of treasure. It melted and then remoulded into a solid block of gold. Convener's horned mask furrowed at the brow. 'Far more difficult choices lie ahead.' He caught Vadania's own furrowed brow. 'Of course, if someone light on their feet could catch up with the Frupgoans before they reach the Burning Sea that would be great.'

Vadania nodded.

Sawwse suddenly spoke up. 'Can we circle back to the "Ancient Device" you subtly namedropped earlier? Mainly to discuss what on Esh it is!' She looked around the table at the others, assuming it would be yet another thing missing from the Gnomeopedia that everyone else already knew about. But she was met with shrugs and ignorance.

Except that somewhere, within each of the other guild mates there was a sense of… something. A niggling feeling at the back of their mind that they *did* know what the Ancient Device was, and the immense power it was capable of. This was the Ancient Device's magic. Since Mirrah had awoken it, it had already planted the seed of its own existence inside each of them. In time, that seed would grow, until it became an insatiable and uncontrollable desire to use the Ancient Device. And using the Ancient Device probably meant the end of everything.

'Er… anyone?' Sawwse tried again. The room had grown silent and the mood gloomy.

'It is dangerous, and it is complicated,' said Convener. 'I will explain more in time. For now, I must settle our board with our hospitable landlord.' Convener took up the gold in his hands and began shuffling awkwardly out of the room, squeezing behind the others and unsnagging his glittery black cloak as it got caught on their chairs.

Once he'd gone, Larn tried to sneak out of the room unnoticed. Even if it wasn't such a small room, it still would've been impossible. Corinne was primed. She followed him out of the room, giving him an absolute earful. 'The Burning Sea for goodness' sake!

A few moments later, Vadania left saying she'd keep the Frupgoans from harm. Rangrim waited approximately 0.25 seconds before chasing after her.

Sawwse and Ruby watched as Osrik sat unmoving. The moment of introspection that had passed quickly for the others, lingered for the old dwarf. He sat head bowed and shoulders hunched like he was folding in on himself.

'Fancy a game of gin rummy?' asked Sawwse.

Osrik didn't look up. He didn't even move. He was like a sleeping elderly relative who you want to hug just to check they're still alive.

'I think we should leave,' said Ruby quietly.

Sawwse was reluctant, but wasn't sure what else to do, and didn't know how to play gin rummy anyway, so they left the room. Glancing over her shoulder at the door, Sawwse thought she heard Osrik whisper something. It sounded like 'rosebud.' But it wasn't 'rosebud,' it was indiscernible.

--

It was a fitful night. Sawwse's dreams were plagued by images of doom, dark clouds and fiery storms. She normally dreamt lucidly, but in these dreams she felt completely out of control. It was like the night before her anti-geography exam all over again.[31]

A little gang of skeletons had just pushed her into a fiery pit when she woke with a start. It was early. There wasn't even a hint of light. Her throat felt as dry as a dessert (an overbaked one). She wandered downstairs with a glass of water and found an armchair to settle into with the Gnomeopedia. Sawwse trawled the pages for any mention of Ancient Devices, Lung-dors, or fallen wizards, but found nothing that seemed to be of any use. There was a small section on Frupgoans, but it described them as a peaceful people that lived in a grand, pink-hued lagoon. Sawwse couldn't concentrate. She read the same sentence over and over until she woke herself up with a loud, muffled, 'Hngmmph.'

Sawwse snapped her head awake and wiped the drool from her chin. She was curled up on a wingback chair opposite the unlit hearth. How long had she been asleep? Jumping to her feet, she saw Ruby sitting alone at a table. Sawwse rushed over to her.

---

[31] Anti-geography was the inward-looking Blue Forest Council's way of instilling geographical ignorance at a young age. It was essentially a large list of geographical features and places, which absolutely, unquestionably, one hundred per cent, did not exist.

'Ruby, what time is it?'

'Oh, I'm not sure,' said Ruby. 'About half–'

'Crimp! I'm late!'

'Late for what?'

'My music tuition!' Sawwse dashed out of the inn.

'I didn't think that was for another couple of…' Ruby stared at the vacant door. She'd been hoping to talk to Sawwse about something, but it'd have to wait. '…weeks.'

Despite having no sense of direction, Sawwse ran as quickly as she could towards Con Duco's house. Osrik had very helpfully drawn directions on the parchment containing Con Duco's address, and then Corinne had animated it with magic so that it emitted a little beep if she went the wrong way. It beeped a lot. But eventually, she got there.

Wheezing and sweating, Sawwse stood outside a tall and thin house patterned with deep green tiles. A large ornate knocker shaped like a lyre was attached to a simple wooden door. Sawwse wasn't sure whether to play it or knock it.

Sawwse was about to grab the lyre when the door swung inwards. A small boy, holding a recorder and flanked by his parents, stood crying in the doorway. The parents shot Sawwse a sour look, before thrusting their son out onto the lane and stomping past themselves. There was no one there to greet Sawwse, so she tentatively stepped forward into the house.

'Hello?'

It seemed that most of the items from the Conservatoire had ended up back in Con Duco's residence. The dark wooden antique furniture and most of the floor were buried under piles of notes and boxes, and musical instruments of all major categories: brass, percussion, woodwind, strings, strangs.

Sawwse heard a voice coming from the top of a steep thin staircase. Con Duco leant his mostly bald head out, finishing his grumbling train of thought. '...hundreds and hundreds of instruments, but no, let's all choose the recorder. Could at least have the decency to play it well. Ah, Ms. Bohge, I didn't think I'd see you again so soon.'

'But we arranged tuition.'

'Yes, in two and a half weeks.'

Sawwse looked at her wrist as though that might somehow clarify the situation. 'Has it not been two and a half weeks?'

'No. It was only the day before yesterday.'

'And how long does "yesterday" last?' *Because it felt like it went on forever*, she thought.

Con Duco sighed. 'Well, you're keen. Nothing wrong with that. I'll just bump the next recorder lesson.' He shuddered. 'Okay, come on. Upstairs.'

The staircase led to a spacious room. A grand piano sat underneath a huge window, which took up most of the space on the opposite wall. Sawwse wandered over and saw that it overlooked a large pretty square lined with bijou cafés.

Noticing her gazing out of the window, Con Duco stood alongside her. 'I am sometimes obliged to give concerts from this room. Some of my more talented students have also performed here.'

The gnome smiled absent-mindedly, now picturing herself performing Elven operas and Dwarven symphonies to a crowd of thousands.

'I'll fetch the tea.'

'There was a kitchen under all those papers?'

'Well, I haven't quite gotten around to organising…' Con Duco scratched his chin, as if his train of thought had switched tracks and was heading in a completely different direction. He spotted Sawwse and smiled. 'Take a seat.'

As Con Duco walked downstairs, Sawwse looked around the room for a seat. There was a piano stool, but that didn't seem quite right. Nothing else. She shrugged and sat cross-legged on the dark herringbone floor.

When Con Duco returned, he carried a little lime teapot with two mugs, and set them in front of Sawwse. He sat down opposite her and poured the tea. 'This is Shi'arethian tea, a fine tea from the Southern continent.'

Sawwse brought the mug to her lips but was halted before she'd taken a sip.

'Bring it to your nose, not your lips.' Con Duco flared his nostrils and wafted the scent of the tea to his nose.

Sawwse lifted the mug to her nose. Instantly, she was hit by a strange mixture of fruits and flowers: there were roses and lavender, oranges and lemons, peaches and fuchsia. The scents kept changing and were somehow distinct from one another. After a few moments, the smell of peaches lingered as the others faded away. Con Duco nodded approvingly.

'Ah peach, a tasty choice.' Upon seeing Sawwse's bemused expression, he added: 'Shi'areth tea reacts to your nasal receptors. Whichever flavour your nose responds to, the tea brews accordingly.'

Sawwse took a sip of the tea and felt as though she had just bitten into a particularly juicy peach. 'Oh my giddy uncle. That's delicious!'

'Indeed. There is much power in reflexivity.' Con Duco took a sip of his tea. 'Mmm, lemon rose. There are many delicious teas, but that is not enough in Shi'areth.

The same is true of music. One could be the most talented musician in the world, but that is as nothing without the ability to respond to an audience, a feeling, an atmosphere. Too many students believe they can become great by rote-learning. Yes, they will know the syntax, but what great art needs is semantics.'

Smile and nod. Just smile and nod. Sawwse smiled. She also nodded.

'To make music without reflexivity is merely an exercise. Playing in response to an audience is something else entirely. It's when music comes alive.'

Sawwse quickly took out a piece of parchment and a pencil. She'd imagined the first lesson would be going back over the basics she'd learnt from the Flowerdew texts, but she already felt a little out of her depth.

Con Duco held up his hand before she'd had a chance to write anything. 'You do not need to make notes.'

'I brought my lute, but perhaps I won't need it?'

'It's unlikely. First, I'd like you to focus.' Con Duco stood and walked to the piano. He opened the lid and sat down. 'Close your eyes, Ms. Bohge, and try to clear your mind.'

Sawwse shut her eyes. Her mind was immediately crowded with images, all vying for attention. There was the skull-like visage of Alla'fyr, the map fragment in her grasp. There were the other gnomes back in the Blue Forest, taunting her for her music. Marius' upset face was there, or at least, how she imagined Marius to look after finding the insulting entry in the Gnomeopedia.

DUNNNNNNNNN.

Sawwse's eyes sprang open at the sound. She sat bolt upright.

'Did I not say to clear your mind?' Con Duco's fingers were resting on the central keys of the piano.

'You said to try to,' muttered Sawwse under her breath.

'Again.'

Sawwse closed her eyes again. This time her mind meandered away from the room and back to the first time she had played music for anyone. Within a little grove, she had gathered a few fellow gnomelings and asked their guardians to join them. Playing the lute that she had inherited from the parents she'd never met, she had performed a wistful song about a gnome who fell in love with a ghost. The whole group burst into laughter, thinking it was an elaborate prank. She'd been so upset by the ordeal that she hadn't touched the lute again for a long time.

DUN DUNNNNNNNNN.

'You are not trying.' Con Duco lightly brushed the piano's keys with the top side of his fingers, a practised habit which had led to the slightly worn look of the ivory. 'Perhaps you need a little assistance. Focus on the note.'

Con Duco played the same note again, quieter.

Dunnnnn.

Sawwse tried to keep her mind attuned to the note.

Dunnnnn.

Con Duco repeated the note again and again while Sawwse focused.

Dunnnnn. Dunnnnn. Dunnnnn.

She pictured a clear black lake. The repeated note formed a series of ripples on the water. Now detached from the room, she heard the disembodied voice of Con Duco.

'Good. I'm going to channel an emotion and I want you to feel it.'

Sawwse didn't understand but didn't question it either. She kept focusing on the ripples, while the note continued to play.

Dunnnnn. Dunnnnn. Dunnnnn.

The subtlest change showed itself in the ripples. The expanding circles became tinged with something that wasn't a colour or another shape. It was something beyond materiality. Sawwse didn't know how, but she felt sadness within the notes. 'You're upset about something.'

'Very good,' replied Con Duco. 'Now you sing the note, and we'll try something similar.' He continued to play the note as a guide for Sawwse, until she was ready to take over.

Dunnnnn. Dunnnnn.

She breathed in deeply and then sang at the same pitch as the note. The tutor closed the lid of his piano. In her mind, she continued to see the ripples on the black lake. This time, she was in control of them.

'I'm channelling emotion again. Feel it and respond accordingly.'

The black lake and the ripples did not alter physically, but Sawwse felt a kind of happiness emanating from them. She changed her pitch and began thinking of a happy memory. Sawwse was practising her singing alone in a secluded part of the Blue Forest one evening, when Dannse Gan passed by. She was unaware that Dannse was there and continued to sing. Dannse, who was much wiser than the average gnome, gave Sawwse warm words of encouragement, the first that she had ever received for her music. It inspired her to keep practising and to take back up the lute.

In the room, Con Duco sat on his piano stool smiling. *Raw talent and she learns quickly*, he thought. His mind bounced frenetically between music methods and theories that he might inscribe on Sawwse.

Sawwse beamed. She was lost in pleasant memories and just the pure joy of singing.

'Very well Ms. Bohge, you may stop singing.'

The gnome stopped and opened her eyes to find Con Duco sat opposite her on the floor once again. 'I think I felt your happiness. The tune began to melt, so I just tried to follow the change.'

'*Imbuement.*'

'Bless you.'

'No, *imbuement.* It's a musical skill.'

Sawwse looked at her tutor blankly.

Con Duco sighed. 'We covered two skills today: *Reception* and *Imbuement.* I think you may have some experience already.' Con Duco gently rubbed his temples with his forefingers. 'Or your nascent abilities are more advanced than I previously thought.'

'I don't know what nascent is, but it's probably that one, because I haven't got a clue what you're on about. Is this…' Sawwse checked over her shoulder as if someone might pop out and catch her talking about something forbidden. 'Is this magic?'

'Hm. Some people call it magic, magicke, magique, the hidden art, the secret skill, the invisible trick, the untold story, or many other things, but we're engaging with something far more ancient than magic and even more powerful too: *music.* Music transcends everything. It was there long before we picked up a rock and bashed it against another rock, and it'll be there long after we're returned to dust. It's all around us, all the time. A musician merely hopes to momentarily tune into its ethereal beauty.'

Sawwse sat there wide-eyed and stunned. It was happening. It was actually happening! She was being given the tools she'd been craving. It was a tangible step towards becoming the greatest musician in the world.

'Practice *reception* ahead of our next session. Please be careful with this skill and only practise responding to emotions. Do not *imbue* until we have had a chance to cover this in more detail.'

'Can I not *imbue* just a little bit?'

Con Duco shook his head.

'I'm sure a tiny bit of *imbuing* would be fine though,' said Sawwse. 'Like a cat. I could practice on a cat.'

'No.' Con Duco began walking Sawwse down the stairs to the door. 'There are numerous things that can go wrong when *imbuing*. Exhibiting control is as important as the skill itself.'

'Yeah, but I'd just be making a cat happy. Imagine. It's little cat legs dancing a happy jig.'

Con Duco was unamused. 'Promise me.'

Sawwse sighed. It was like being given a new toy and being told not to play with it. 'Okay. I promise.' But Sawwse had crossed her fingers behind her back in the arbitrary but universally recognised symbol for 'promises don't mean crimp.'

Sawwse hadn't realised quite how much effort the lesson had taken. Out the door, she dragged her feet all the way back to the Hearth, immediately retired to the dorm room and collapsed into bed. This time, there were no dreams of flaming pits or imps. Instead, Sawwse closed her eyes and entered a deep, dreamless sleep.

Chapter 17:
Rhinoholm

The next morning, there was an old cork noticeboard in the front room of the inn. It sat beneath the window, which beamed dustmotes into the room. Messages scrawled on parchment were pinned to it, detailing quests (e.g. retrieving a powerful sapphire deep within a minotaur's lair), pleas for help (e.g. shutting down a bandit encampment near a peaceful village), and odd jobs (e.g. a man called Maurice was stuck in a bush). Variously coloured threads were strung between the different notices in a completely incomprehensible way. It looked a bit of a mess. Larn stood beside the noticeboard. He looked a bit of a mess too. His hair was sticking up at odd angles and there were dark bags under his eyes. He was also radiating the kind of nervous energy you only get from working on something all night and accomplishing nothing except a misplaced conviction that you *have* accomplished something.

The rest of the guild mates stood opposite, arms folded across their chest. Sawwse asked what they were all thinking. 'What exactly does any of this have to do with the Ancient Device thingy?'

Larn scoffed. 'You mean you can't tell?'

'Well, no.'

'It's blindingly obvious!'

Sawwse pointed to one of the notices. 'So, the "unstoppable dance party in Frijsia" is relevant?'

'Well…' Larn gesticulated wildly at the noticeboard. 'See how the red thread takes in everything within a ten-mile radius of Rhyddinas, the blue thread connects between all the quests whose messages start with the letter 'A', the yellow thread symbolises…'

The others exchanged an awkward look.

'What's the green thread?' asked Rangrim.

'Let's see…' Larn took the thread between his forefinger and thumb and followed it around the noticeboard. 'Aha! When the green thread connects between the messages, it creates a pattern that looks a bit like a koala bear.'

'Er, excuse me,' said Ruby quietly. She'd just about gotten used to the incredibly intense elf and the grizzled dwarf, but Larn still made her very nervous. 'Is now a bad time to tell you that I spoke to Convener when he brought the noticeboard in, and he said these were jobs to keep us occupied while he investigated the Ancient Device?'

Larn's face dropped. 'What?'

'N-nothing,' squeaked Ruby.

'Can I just clarify something?' Anyone else and Sawwse would have let it go, but this was Larn. You had to take these opportunities when they arose. 'You think that there's some kind of koala-based conspiracy underpinning the legendary Ancient Device?'

Larn's face reddened.

'Are koalas totemic for you in some way?'

Larn snatched a quest at random from the board and stormed out of the room, returning a moment later to grab a different one and mutter something under his breath about dance parties.

Once he was gone, the others approached the board and took their turn choosing quests. Vadania set out to take down a Soupy Beast in the Forests of Broth, Rangrim sought a wizard who needed help excavating a ruin, and Osrik left to save the village from the bandit encampment.

'Looks like it's just the three of us,' said Sawwse. Corinne would not have been her first choice of companion, but Ruby would make it fun.

'Actually…' Ruby looked down at her feet. 'I think I'm going to stay here.'

'Oh. O-kay.'

Ruby shuffled back towards the dorm room. Meanwhile, Corinne waved her hand over the messages on the noticeboard. Some of the parchment curled at the edges as Corinne's hand passed by, as if drawn in by a magnetic pull. And then one message ripped from its pin and flew straight into Corinne's hand.

'I believe this one will be the most appropriate.' Corinne tapped the first word of the message and a voice with the plummiest accent Sawwse had ever heard read it aloud. "A local chief has requested assistance after their village began walking away. They have promised a significant financial reward."

'Sounds ideal.' Sawwse slung her rucksack over her shoulders. 'We should set off now if we're to catch up with it.'

'Indeed. But perhaps first we could run through the adventuring protocol a few times.' Corinne began rooting around in her bag.

Sawwse had already left. Selective hearing could be incredibly useful at times when one wanted to focus on one thing at a time. Sawwse didn't have selective hearing, she was just very good at ignoring things she knew would be boring.

Corinne sighed. She'd whip this guild into fine administrative shape eventually. For now, she'd have to be content with some on-the-fly health and safety reporting.[32]

Once Corinne had caught up with Sawwse, they took transport out of the city to the north and then hiked a few miles through pleasant countryside. After a few hours they stopped for a break on a shallow ridge overlooking three hills in the distance.

'I had hoped that we'd have reached the village by now.' Corinne's stomach made a loud rumbling noise. 'I fear I was counting on it for my lunch.'

'I've got your back.' Sawwse pulled out some barm cakes from her bag and handed one to the wizard.

Corinne felt the bap and lifted it to her face, sniffing it. 'Where did you get these?'

'Back at the inn,' said Sawwse, breadily.

'I don't think these were out at the breakfast buffet.'

'Nah, I had to go rooting around the kitchen.'

'I'm not sure they were intended for us.'

'Ah, relax. I just pilfered a few spares.'

Corinne grabbed Sawwse's bag and felt inside. It was stocked full of bread rolls. 'I'm not even sure when you had the time to–'

'It's fine! They were going to be thrown away.'

'Were they?'

---

[32] Flies absolutely hated this kind of reporting.

'Sweet blessed Gnomelord!'

'Look. I know it's not 'cool' to be concerned about this stuff, but it is important–'

'No, not that. The middle hill up ahead. Is it…? It is! It's moving!'

Corinne placed her palms flat on the ground. Distant vibrations flowed into her mind's eye. 'Oh dear.'

'What is it?'

'The "hill" is heading straight towards another village. It's going to get crushed if we don't hurry.'

'Then let's go!' Sawwse grabbed Corinne's robe, and with surprising strength, pulled her along as they ran towards the hill.

It turned out the scare quotes were accurate. This wasn't a hill at all, but rather a Rhinoholm: a gigantic, moss-covered rhinoceros, woken from a centuries-long slumber. With every step that the Rhinoholm took, the earth under Sawwse and Corinne's feet shook relentlessly.

Vrrrrrrrrrr

'Look! Up there!'

Vrrrrrrrrrr

Atop the Rhinoholm they could see an otherwise very normal-looking village: houses, a small chapel, doughnut shop. Sawwse could even make out small, scared faces in some of the houses. Beneath the Rhinoholm, the other settlement was visible in the distance, although distance was becoming an increasingly inappropriate word.

Vrrrrrrrrrr

'What shall we do?'

'This is where–' started Corinne.

Vrrrrrrrrrr

'–effective planning is vital, because–'

Vrrrrrrrrrr

'–otherwise, you end up a bit stuffed.'

Sawwse rolled her eyes. 'There's no time for one of your speeches. Sure, we could've prepared before we got here. But now we're here, we need to do something… now!'

Vrrrrrrrrrr

'If you'd let me finish, I was about to say that–'

Vrrrrrrrrrr

'–this is why I planned a jumping spell for us.'

Corinne gestured to one of the Rhinoholm's hooves that had just landed in front of them. It was pockmarked, but the rough, ancient skin of the leg looked to be covered by foliage further up.

'When you're ready, I'll boost us up to the moss.'

Vrrrrrrrrrr

'And you're sure you've prepared the right spell?' asked Sawwse more than a little bit nervous.

Vrrrrrrrrrr

'…' The pause from Corinne was telling.

Vrrrrrrrrrr

'Fine, just do it!'

Corinne placed a hand on Sawwse's back and muttered something incomprehensible. They shot up together fifty feet into the air and grabbed hold of the moss, just above the back of the rhino's knee.

'It worked!' shouted Corinne.

'It's really the surprised tone that fills me with confidence.'

Vrrrrrrrrrr. The hoof came down hard, loosening their grip on the moss and almost throwing them back down to the ground. They fixed their hold and then scaled the Rhinoholm. Climbing came naturally to Sawwse, so she scurried up the hind leg like she would one of the trees in the Blue Forest. When she reached the hip, she turned around and grabbed hold of Corinne's hand, hoisting her up.

On top of the Rhinoholm they were no longer hampered by the vibrations they'd felt on the ground. In fact, the 'ground' up here was surprisingly stable.

'We should speak to the villagers,' said Sawwse.

'Good plan. That way we'll find out how this started.'

'Oh, sure. I was thinking they might have doughnuts. But both plans are good.'

They ran through the village, but it was deserted.

'Perhaps they are too scared to leave their homes,' said Corinne.

They made their way to the head of the Rhinoholm and watched as the settlement below grew closer. Sawwse said nothing for a couple of minutes and waited for Corinne to stop the Rhinoholm with magic. When she made no immediate motions to stop, Sawwse leant in close. 'So, what spell are you going to use? A spell of halting? *Slowicus Minimus*? That kind of thing?'

Corinne chuckled to herself. 'No, no. I fear the Rhinoholm is far too big for that kind of magic. Perhaps if I was more powerful, I could manage it, but as it is, I'm afraid I would barely get its attention.'

'Right.' Sawwse waited for the back-up plan. 'So…'

'I'm a bit stumped actually.' Corinne scratched her head. 'Treating it like a big rock is wrong. It's a living thing. We need to tap into its head somehow and persuade it to stop. It's very unusual that it's awake. The local Rhinoholmologists didn't predict this one would wake up for another thousand years–'

'Corinne!' interrupted Sawwse, before Corinne's spiel had time to gather momentum.

'Yes, right. Sorry.' Corinne smiled awkwardly. 'Know any songs that might make a rhinoceros stop?'

Hm. She did know a pretty soporific nursery rhyme that used to put the gnomelings to sleep in the nursery's toddler room. Well, it put them to sleep eventually, because toddlers of all stripes are messers.[33] The only problem was that there was a big difference between a roomful of gnomelings and a Rhinoholm. About 40,000 kilograms. It was impossible. Unless… she could *imbue* the song. Okay, so technically Con Duco made her promise not to use it, because there were blah blah dangerous blah blah implications. On the other hand, she really really wanted to. If anything, Con Duco ought to be pleased with her initiative! She'd made up her mind.

Sawwse whispered her idea in Corinne's ear.

'Are you sure?'

Sawwse nodded that she was.

Corinne rifled through the pages of her spell book until she found the correct charm. It was called *Loudicus Maximus*. She took a few moments to familiarise herself with it and then pocketed the book. Corinne traced circles around her eyes with her index fingers: a faint blue glow shimmered around her. Then, holding her hands together, she began to incant.

Meanwhile, Sawwse cleared her mind like Con Duco had taught her. She took several deep breaths and paused. In her mind's eye, there was the still black lake. The Rhinoholm's hoofsteps caused the water in the lake

---

[33] You know the drill: half an hour of singing, ten minutes reading, twenty minutes of flicking a switch on and off with their right toe, thirty seconds of pinching, five minutes of telling you to get out, fifteen minutes upset because you left, a big hug with each of their teddies and they're out.

to ripple like mad, but Sawwse focused on what it felt like.

She's grumpy, thought Sawwse. *Because she's woken up too soon from her nap. It's exactly like the toddlers*!

Now it was just a case of changing that grumpiness into sleepiness. Sawwse nodded at Corinne. The wizard placed her palms flat against Sawwse's chest and tilted her head down to concentrate on the amplification magic.

When Sawwse took in a breath, it was so loud that it was like she was sucking in all the sound around them. And then she sang. It was a beautiful Elven song about… trees or something. She'd never bothered to learn the meaning of the song, but that didn't matter because it was working!

The Rhinoholm made weary, grunting noises before groaning so loudly it was like thunder had fallen from the sky. Once it could no longer lift its feet, it gradually folded itself back down to the ground and lowered its head, fast asleep to finish its nap.

But it wasn't just the Rhinoholm who'd heard Sawwse's soporific song. The villagers hidden in their homes or seeking solace in the chapel, had fallen into a deep slumber too. Sawwse's song had even reached the settlement below. The stonemason slumped over her gargoyle, a teacher and pupils dropped their parchment and quills, a shopkeeper dozed off on a pile of flour sacks, and the large crowd that had gathered to watch in wonder as the behemoth approached, now lay in a pile of pleasant dreams.

Sawwse and Corinne smiled at one another.

'That was beautiful,' said Corinne. 'But tell me, how did you ensure that it was only the Rhinoholm that fell asleep and not all the villagers?'

'That's just the, er, skill of a great musician.'

'All the villagers are asleep, aren't they?' Corinne sighed.

'Er, well…'

Suddenly, they heard the manic, attention-grabbing coos of a strange man down below them. Sawwse was grateful for the distraction. She led Corinne off the edge of the Rhinoholm's head, sliding down the huge horn, which was now half-buried in the earth.

Sure enough, when they reached the bottom, there was a tiny moustachioed man with an enormous hat who'd just arrived on a donkey. He was out of breath. So was the donkey. It harrumphed and bucked the man onto the earth in front of Corinne and Sawwse. Corinne offered him her hand. 'Are you the chief of this village?'

'Correct,' he answered curtly. The chief dusted himself off, picked up his elaborate headgear, and looked up at the village atop the Rhinoholm. 'What's the village doing all the way up there?'

'I presume the Rhinoholm was sunk into marshy earth when you settled your village, giving the illusion that there was no elevation. Now that the Rhinoholm has settled into its natural position flat against firmer *terra firma* if you will, hoho, there will be a bit of a climb to get to the village.'

'That's completely unacceptable!'

'That is simply the situation.'

The chief harrumphed and his donkey mimicked the sound. Then, he began to climb the Rhinoholm.

'Now now, the general procedure indicates that we should settle up first.' Corinne pulled the chief back down by the end of his robes. It was done with the perfect amount of force: enough to know she was serious, but not too much as to be threatening.

'My village is in completely the wrong place!' The chief harrumphed. His donkey mimicked again.

Sawwse looked to the village atop the hill and then pointed across to the settlement now a very short walk away. 'I think it's in a better place. It's got a lake view, and as for convenience, look at how much closer you are to the nearby town. That'll do a lot for property prices, that will.'

'I don't care about property prices! My village was established–'

'On the back of an ancient beast? Yes, we know. We stopped it from walking into a lake and sinking the entire village. You're welcome, by the way.'

'I'd rather it was where I left it.'

Corinne cleared her throat. She held up a contract, signed both by the chief and by Convener. 'Feel free to read the conditions you agreed to again, but we have satisfied our requirements, and require you to do the same.'

This time the chief and his donkey harrumphed in unison. He looked up at the Rhinoholm, now slumbering as peacefully as a block of granite, and back to the adventurers. 'Fine.' He fished in one of the panniers strapped to the side of the donkey, retrieved a coin purse and handed it to Corinne. The chief raised the brim of his enormous hat in begrudged acknowledgement and then began ungracefully climbing to his home.

Sawwse clapped Corinne on the back. 'Right! All's well that ends well. Shall we?'

Corinne frowned. 'You put everyone in the village to sleep. I need to stay behind and fix it.'

'So, I put a village and town to sleep. What's the big deal?'

'You put the town to sleep as well! Who knows how long they'll sleep for if I don't intervene?'

'They could probably use a break from the hustle and bustle of their… quaint life in a quiet town?'

Corinne gave her a withering look. She took out her clipboard and wrote something down. Never a good sign. After telling Sawwse to head back to the Happy Hearth, Corinne began walking hastily towards the nearby town to wake it up.

It took until nightfall for Sawwse to get back to the guild. There had been a large build-up of traffic on the M Fifty-Moo.[34] Once she was there, she immediately sought out Convener. He was sat alone by the empty hearth. It seemed like he was gazing into it intently, but with the ever-present mask it was hard to tell.

'Er, hello?' ventured Sawwse quietly, not wanting to interrupt… whatever it was Convener was doing.

'Welcome back, friend.' Convener took the contract and coin purse that Sawwse handed to him. He turned away from the hearth to face her. 'You stopped the Rhinoholm. Well done.'

Sawwse quickly recounted the day's work. She even admitted to accidentally putting the village and town to sleep, but Convener didn't seem too bothered.

'I must admit, Elven songs tend to put me to sleep as well.' Convener's mask shifted ever so slightly into a smile.

Corinne walked through the door of the inn. 'It was a well-executed plan from Sawwse, despite the wide-reaching power of her song.' She smiled at the gnome, who looked at her bemusedly.

---

[34] Cattle farming was big in this part of the world.

'How on Esh did you get back here so quickly?'

'I flew. Beats the traffic.'

'But… you made me walk?'

'I don't have a permit for passengers.'

'Right.'

Convener took several coins from the purse and handed it back to Sawwse. 'I've taken a cut for the guild. The rest can be divided evenly between you.' Without another word, he turned back to gaze at the empty hearth.

Sawwse and Corinne wandered to another table and divided up the coins between them. Sawwse was pleased about completing the mission but distracted by Convener's preoccupied air. She spoke in a whisper. 'What do you imagine he's thinking about?'

Corinne considered the question carefully. 'Perhaps the Ancient Device? Perhaps Alla'fyr? Perhaps motions and motives beyond our comprehension. It is hard to tell what's going on behind that mask, but perhaps it is best we don't know. What I do know is that we have earnt some dinner.'

Not that it was clear what dinner was going to be. The smells that came wafting in from the kitchen were hardly appetising: burnt garlic, charcoal and liquorice. When the food arrived, it did nothing to overturn their low expectations. It was a very tiny and very bony fish, sat atop a little pile of overcooked vegetables. A purple jus of some kind had been squirted over the top, though even the colour did nothing to stop it looking like flem.

'I think this is maybe an attempt at haute cuisine,' said Corinne, prodding the fish with her fork.

'Yeah. Whoever made this definitely hates food.' Sawwse pushed her dish to one side.

‘Pardon me, but I must see someone about this.’ Corinne stood and took her dish in the direction of the kitchen.

Sawwse shrugged. She wasn’t that hungry anyway. Instead of eating, she retrieved the Gnomeopedia. Heaving the tome out of her bag, she dropped it onto the table with a big thunk.

The Blue Forest gnomes’ compendium of knowledge was written in a friendly tone but organised in a typically Gnomish way: chaotically. Sawwse flicked past pages on Frimbledops and Frimpledeeps, the cabbage-y smell of (Northern) Brastos, to the ear-melting sounds of the Sao bird, until she found what she was looking for: Magic. It was one of the longer entries in the Gnomeopedia. The Gnehsehgs who had put together the book described their experience of magic, the many uses they had encountered, and how dangerous it could be. Sawwse found one section particularly interesting:

> The Twelve have, apparently, been chosen to bring balance to the world, but this changes depending on whom you ask. Having encountered several instances of magic used for nefarious purposes, even in such peaceful times as these, I now somewhat question the function of The Twelve. According to some people we have spoken with, it has been a hundred or so years since any of The Twelve have been seen. Worrying, if these are our protectors, no? (See further notes in the separate section on The Twelve).

There was no further section on The Twelve.

Reading about the dangers of magic had put Alla'fyr back in her mind. *Shouldn't The Twelve put a stop to a fallen wizard as quickly as possible?* She shrugged. *Perhaps they had already done so.*

Sawwse shut the Gnomeopedia. She was about to head upstairs when she thought she heard Convener whispering something. He was hunched over, head in his hands.

'Everything alright?' asked Sawwse, taking a step closer.

He spoke again, but it was inaudible.

She crept a little closer. 'You okay, Mask-o?'

Convener paid no attention to Sawwse. His attention was not in this room. It was possibly not even on this plain.

'Maskington?' Sawwse reached forward to place a hand on his shoulder, but suddenly he sat bolt upright.

'That's not good,' said Convener. 'That's not good at all.'

Chapter 18:
Beetle on the Wall

'So, tell me again how the turnip helmet–'

'Crown.'

'Apologies. How the turnip crown aids with the… what was it that you called it?'

'Turnipmancy.'

'Yes, the turnipmancy.'

Beads of sweat rolled down Cribbins' head. Not only was having to wear a hollowed-out turnip crown in public uncomfortably warm, but he was also incredibly nervous. It felt like the Dorienne Council were always two seconds away from discovering how much of a fraud he was.

'Well, er, the thing with turnips, right. The thing with turnips is that they, er, contain raw energy from the earth. Yes, the earth, that's good. They're pulled from the earth, so they are sort of, er, tapped into earthen energy. That's what the, er, helmet does.'

'I thought you said it was a crown?' The councillor stared at Cribbins with a look of pure scepticism. She wasn't the only one.

'Er... right. Yes. It *is* a crown.' More sweat collected at the point where the bottom of Cribbins' turnip crown-helmet met his brow. 'I mean, er, technically it is a helmet. Crown is just what we say in the turnip trade.'

'But you corrected me when I called it a helmet?'

Oh well. It was a good run, thought Cribbins. He was bound to be figured out as a fraud sooner or later. It was, in fact, a good thing. He never wanted a seat on the Council. A little extra money would've been welcome, sure. But he had been happy selling his turnips. There'd been much less stress, anyway. He wasn't having to constantly look over his shoulder. Or, if he had been, it was only related to the japes they used to play in the RVC (Root Vegetable Community).

The trick now was to admit that he was an imposter, but in a way that wouldn't end up with him being thrown in gaol. It was best to do this before Princess Eugenie came back. Otherwise, she'd probably order him to stay. Cribbins stood up to address the Council. 'Okay. The, er, thing is. I'm actually just a lowly turnip–'

The doors to the Council chamber swung open dramatically. It was Eugenie. She was wearing her military uniform: plated metal and a blood red cloak. The uniform was only ever supposed to be worn in times of war, but Eugenie had taken to wearing it all the time. She stormed into the room and spotted her Lord Protector of Turnips. 'Cribbins? Do the turnips speak to you?'

Cribbins smiled weakly. 'Er, yes. They say, "the sun rises in the east and sets in the west," so...' He was also running out of aphorisms.

Eugenie gave his comment serious thought. 'Very wise. Very wise and very appropriate...'

The sound of the councillors rolling their eyes was audible.

'…for there is something in the east that we need.'

Cribbins slowly sat back down. Looks like he was staying put for another while.

'It is another fragment of a map leading to the Ancient Device. Alla'fyr believes she knows where to find it.'

A murmur circulated around the Dorienne Council. None of them were particularly keen to speak out against their leader, but someone had to say something.

'Ahem.' There was a polite cough from a councillor with a goatee. 'We were all saying earlier how impressed we were with your initiative in hiring the mercenary.' A murmur of agreement from the table. 'The only small thing, and it is a small thing, is that we're not sure–' another polite cough '–we're not sure how much we trust her.'

A silence followed, partially in respect of the goateed councillor whom the rest of the council assumed was for the chop.

'I see,' said Eugenie.

Another few brave souls spoke up.

'We think she might take your money and run!'

'It's probably for the best, too. Getting someone like that mixed up in matters of the state is perhaps not in our interests.'

'And her smell was revolting!'

'I told you they wouldn't understand.' The voice came from inside the chamber. It was instantly recognisable. Alla'fyr slowly emerged from within her veil of invisibility, peeling it back like a peapod made of pure fire. She was standing next to Eugenie.

'I meant, take your money and run to the bank to invest it wisely!'

'And I meant, not just in our interests, but in our *best* interests!'

'Er, the smell thing was a joke.'

'Sycophants,' spat Eugenie.

Another murmur rippled around the table. This bad attitude of Eugenie's was becoming the norm of late. They thought it so obvious that she was being twisted by the evil of Alla'fyr. What they didn't realise is that the mercenary had little to do with it. Eugenie's mind was being twisted, that much was true. But it was being perverted by the Ancient Device. Its magic had burrowed deeper into her mind than anyone else's.

A councillor wearing a blue silken scarf spoke up. Thefania was the longest-serving member of the Council and had been King Poht's most trusted advisor. Perhaps because of this, she felt more able to challenge Eugenie. 'How do we know this "fragment of power" is even a map? It may not even have anything to do with the Ancient Device. Perhaps Alla'fyr is having you on.'

Eugenie looked at Thefania. Her gaze softened, but then Alla'fyr leaned in close to Eugenie's ear. 'Shall I show them what I found?' She nodded.

Alla'fyr held out her left hand in a fist and slowly unfurled her fingers. And there it was. The fragment of power taken from deep within the Tomb of Tombombaboobybobbalus. It was tiny, but it shone as bright as the most brilliant diamond. Well, it didn't. But it was pretty bloody bright.

With her right hand, Alla'fyr made a circular motion over the fragment. She moved her hand faster and faster before stopping dead. The bright speck lifted from her hand and floated in mid-air. Alla'fyr drew complex patterns around it, until finally, with a huge strain, she clapped her hands together. There was a massive burst of fire and the circular table erupted in flames.

The Dorienne Council jumped from their seats, falling backwards to get out of the way of the crimson fire. The flames licked at Eugenie's plated armour, but she remained completely still until the last of the fire had died away.

Returning to the table, the councillors saw the trace of something burned into the wood. It was quite clearly a map. In fact, to the untrained observer it was a comprehensive map leading directly to the Ancient Device. There might as well have been a big arrow and a sign reading: "Ancient Device this way." But of course, it wasn't so simple.

'Alla'fyr showed me earlier. This is just the first layer of the map,' said Eugenie.

'You've already done this to another table?' A solitary tear ran down the cheek of the Royal Table Acquirer.

'If we followed this map, we would be sent on a wild goose chase,' said Eugenie. 'Alla'fyr thinks we need two other pieces to make a complete map. Once all three maps are layered together, it will unlock our path to the Ancient Device.' She waited for another loud murmur to quiet before continuing. 'In alarming news, Alla'fyr has alerted me that my father's killer has put together a dangerous adventurer's guild and that they are also searching for the map fragments. Sawwse Bohge…' Eugenie whispered the name with the same embittered reverence you would show a dragon or a dinner lady.

Alla'fyr tried hard to stop her smirk from showing, but it was too amusing watching the shocked faces of the Council.

'Of course, we cannot let them find the Device. Fortunately, we know where the next fragment is. But you will divert all effort to searching for the final one.' After a pause, she turned from the table and began to leave the room.

Thefania stood quickly. 'My Queen, please wait–'

'You know my feelings about titles.' Eugenie turned around, furious. 'There has been no coronation, no ceremony in which I magically became the queen. There is a king in Doriana and he will serve again.'

Thefania felt deeply uncomfortable. She had been there at Eugenie's birth. She had watched her grow from a baby to an incredibly talented and fierce young woman. It was upsetting to see her so drastically altered by grief and by… something else. King Poht had been the reflective king. Yes, he'd been obsessed with his image. But he'd also been rational. Complete disregard of reason was not something the Council were used to, and it had caught them unawares.

'Eugenie, please wait. We haven't yet debriefed you on the affairs of state.'

'There is only one affair of state and that is the Ancient Device.'

'But we are receiving worrying reports from both Magnarra and Ishgari, on our western borders. It seems the alliances your father worked so hard to negotiate are beginning to falter. These "allies" somehow know you are preoccupied. They're testing us to see how much they can get away with.[35] I strongly recommend we

---

[35] The similarities between sabre-rattling states and toddlers has not been made often enough.

divert some of our strongest troops to these borders to make a really strong statement. Strong.'

Eugenie paused for a long time. Looking at Thefania's earnest face brought back memories of her father. She willed herself not to cry. Not now. Not here.

'Please, Eugenie,' pleaded Thefania.

But something now deep inside Eugenie's mind clicked and her resolve hardened. 'No. Concentrate on the task at hand. Now that we have one of the map fragments, we need the troops here more than ever to protect it. Especially now that we know the powerful wizard, Sawwse Bohge, is after it too.'

Thefania sat back down, defeated.

Alla'fyr smirked to herself. *The gnome is probably already dead, but I mustn't say anything. It's too much fun hearing that pathetic gnome's name hold so much power in this room. Perhaps I should offer to kill her and collect a little extra income on the way? No, that's silly. I won't need income once I have the Device. Wait, why are they all looking at me?* Alla'fyr cleared her throat. 'Was I thinking out loud again?'

'No.' Eugenie looked at her with scorn. The Council weren't wrong about Alla'fyr, and she disliked her too. Unfortunately, she had no choice but to keep working with her. She was the only one bringing the Ancient Device within reach. 'I asked you where the next map fragment was.'

'Zell.'

'A pretty city. I visited with papa when I was younger. Why would it be there?'

'I'm only conjecturing, of course, but I expect the "shiny, secret, magic-y thing" that the monks keep in the cathedral is probably another of the fragments.' Alla'fyr began to casually stroll towards the door. 'I'll set out at once to retrieve it.'

'No,' said Eugenie firmly.

This took Alla'fyr aback. 'Er, what?'

'This map fragment is too important.' Eugenie furrowed her brow. 'I need you to stay with it. We cannot afford to lose it.'

Alla'fyr seethed. She hated being given orders, but if she could just keep her head things would work out rather well for her in the long run. 'Of course. I will send an associate of mine. He can get to Zell quicker than any of us. *And I will remain here to babysit a table, which is such an excellent use of my skills*.'

'Sarcasm isn't just the lowest form of wit, it's also the ugliest,' said Eugenie, almost cutting Alla'fyr with a sharp look. 'Send your associate. I will send five of our knights to accompany him. The rest of you get to work on finding out where the final fragment may be.' With her cape sweeping behind her, Eugenie left the room.

There was a pause while the councillors looked uneasily at Alla'fyr who was staring at the door muttering obscenities. She left the room too, albeit in a puff of smoke rather than the door.

The council members began shifting in their seats. Some set straight to work on gathering intelligence. Others tried to make conversation about brighter things. Cribbins took a bite out of a turnip. But there was one councillor who remained seated, unmoving. He was an unremarkable man with grey hair and brown eyes. Malthus Hulther had often remained quiet in these meetings, observing more than taking part. He was almost a fly on the wall. Except fly isn't quite the right word. Beetle. Beetle would be more accurate. And that was because in the right light, at the right moment, if you looked very, very closely, and you looked directly into Malthus Hulther's right pupil, you would see the faint reflection of a tiny, glowing, white-horned mask and a glittering, beetle-like cloak.

Chapter 19: Touch Gydi, Get Dizzy

'What's not good?'

'Hm?' The eyes of Convener's mask glowed as he tuned back into his surroundings within the Happy Hearth. It was Sawwse Bohge. She looked concerned. 'Apologies. I was… miles away.'

'You just said "that's not good" in a way that hasn't terrified me in the slightest.'

The lips of Convener's mask curled into a slight smile. 'Unfortunately, we live in increasingly terrifying times. Please call the others. There is something we need to discuss.'

'It's quite late though,' said Sawwse, stifling a yawn. 'Are you sure you want me to disturb them? They're probably just getting cosy in bed. Well, as cosy as you can get sleeping in a dorm room with Rangrim. Sir Snoresalot, am I right?'

Convener stared blankly at Sawwse. He gestured to a large horn on the table beside him. It looked to have been made from some kind of animal tusk. 'Use the Meeting Horn.'

Sawwse turned the horn over in her hands a couple of times. It was milky white and definitely magical. She looked into the fat end and then blew into the thin end. No sound came out of it. Curious. She tried again and again, blowing harder and harder, but nothing happened. At least, nothing seemed to happen. What was actually happening was that a piercingly loud siren was going off in the dorm room above. The floorboards creaked and cracked as the guild mates stormed out of the room and thundered downstairs.

Vadania ran towards Sawwse and knocked the horn out of her hands.

'What the hells are you playing at?' snapped Osrik.

'I didn't know!'

'So loud.' Rangrim wiggled his finger in his ear to try and dislodge the last of the reverberations.

'Convener repeatedly told us about the horn,' said Corinne.

'Well, I'm sorry if I didn't pay close attention to the horn briefings, but… is that a nightie?' Sawwse stared at Osrik who was in fact wearing a white nightdress.

He shuffled on his feet awkwardly pulling at the hem. 'So?'

'It doesn't leave much to the imagination.'

'It's perfectly normal night wear.'

'Why is it so short?'

'My knees get hot!'

'Enough.' Vadania scowled at Sawwse and Osrik. She wasn't wearing a nightdress or pyjamas, because she was never not fully dressed in her adventuring gear. Obviously, it wasn't easy to sleep with swords, daggers, and traps about her person, but she didn't tend to sleep much anyway. 'Why did you call us here?'

Convener rose from his seat by the unlit hearth. With a wave of his hands, the whole room seemed to rotate and whirl around them until they were in the familiar meeting room with the large oak table. He gave them a moment to recover from the sudden transportation and then spoke. 'I have received some worrying news.'

'Osrik's nightwear?' said Sawwse.

'I am now clear on why Alla'fyr was seeking the map fragments.' Convener's white-horned mask settled on a look of grim severity. 'She is working for the Dorienne Kingdom.'

'They have no need of a mercenary like her,' grumbled Osrik.

'Though he is vain, King Poht is respected across the continent,' said Corinne. 'This seems like the most unusual course of action. Why would Poht hire a fallen wizard?'

'King Poht was murdered. Princess Eugenie is in charge.'

The guild mates looked at each other in shock. Except Sawwse, who didn't have a clue who Princess Eugenie or King Poht were, despite her significance in their life and death respectively, and was still thinking about Osrik's nightie.

Convener continued. 'She wants to use the Ancient Device to reverse time and bring her father back, but it gets worse.' He placed his hands together and then opened them again. Energy spread between his hands like putty or glue or a sticky pasta dough. Then the energy turned into forms, which danced into life before playing out the scene that Malthus Hulther had witnessed within the Dorienne Council. 'The Ancient Device must not be used under any circumstances.'

'You still haven't told us what's so scary about this old machine thingy,' said Sawwse.

'Is there anything you have done that you regret in life?'

'You should be asking Osrik.' Sawwse punched the dwarf playfully on the arm. 'You know… because of the nightdress.' No one was amused. In fact, Osrik and the others had already withdrawn into themselves. Sawwse caught the glowing eyes of Convener's mask, which now focused solely on her.

Let me stress the severity of the situation. Convener spoke directly into Sawwse's mind.

Woah. Ever heard of consent?

I don't want the others to hear.

We could've just used a breakout room. Sawwse tried to mutter this thought under her breath, but judged from Convener's burning gaze that that was basically impossible to do within your own mind. *Sorry, I'll listen. Why don't you want the others to hear?*

The Ancient Device's magic has already burrowed within them. Deeper within some than others. Convener briefly glanced at Osrik, and then returned his gaze to the gnome. *It has pinpointed the memory they regret the most and seeks to exploit it. It will make that feeling of regret so profound, that it will gnaw away at them until there is nothing else in the world that matters to them apart from rectifying that moment.*

Sawwse nodded.

But I'm curious. I can sense that you are not affected. Is there nothing you regret?

There was that time I stole Findon Umlock's plums. Am I proud of it? No. Do I regret it? Still no. They were delicious! Sawwse grinned and then looked around the room at the others. They looked so pitiful. Especially Osrik.

Especially because of the nightdress. *Can you not help them? Stop their regret?*

Convener shook his head. *The Device's magic is too ancient, too powerful. There will come a point where you and you alone will need to keep the others in check. You are the only one who can.*

Sawwse was stunned. She was important. It wasn't something she was used to feeling. It made her want to stand up on the table and sing! Though, now that she thought about it, that seemed like a lot of responsibility. *What happens if the Ancient Device is used?*

Are you familiar with the butterfly effect?

Sure. Step on a butterfly in the past and something something sports almanack?

Think of every single decision or even micro-decision you make throughout a day. You blink. You walk down the stairs one second rather than the second before or after. You scratch your arm. Now think of every other single person or animal or demon making similarly minute decisions across all Four Continents. Enter a change into this scenario and watch as time ripples uncontrollably, fragments as all those micro decisions now become potential pathways. It would be like opening up a multiverse. It sounds interesting on paper, but it is completely overwhelming. Oh, and eventually the world would be ripped inside out.

So, the Ancient Device wants to be found? It's trying to be used?

Indeed. It was released from its cage of obscurity–

Excellent band name.

–and now it is seeking out those compelled to use it.

Sawwse observed her guild mates. They looked a miserable bunch. Who would laugh at her jokes if they were so caught up in their own regret? And where was Ruby? She looked around the room, but there were no squirrels squirrelled away or mice miced away listening into the conversation. Perhaps she was still in the dorm room. Sawwse turned her back to Convener. 'What would you like us to do?'

'At first light, Corinne, Sawwse and Vadania will travel east to Zell. That is where Alla'fyr believes the next map fragment to be.'

'Her?' asked Vadania. 'Are you sure?'

'Yes. I believe you will reach Zell before whoever Eugenie sends. And Zell is a civilised city. I think this map fragment will be kept under lock and key, rather than buried within a tomb. It will take diplomacy in order to retrieve it.'

'And you think Sawwse will be helpful in that regard?' Vadania looked dubious.

'I'm very diplomatic! Corinne, tell her.'

'Hm. Which bit? The bit where you called the man in the stables an assclown?'

'He looked like a clown, and he sold donkeys. It was wordplay. We got to where we needed to go in the end, didn't we?'

'Yes. We walked.'

'Osrik and Rangrim,' began Convener, choosing to ignore Vadania's pleading look, 'I'd like you to travel north to Brastos. There is a dwarven temple there that may hold another of the fragments or at least information about it. Larn is currently investigating something deep within the Decay. I cannot overstate how important this mission is. This is our chance to put ourselves firmly on the map as Esh'areth's protector, and to save the world from chaos beyond measure.' Convener bowed his head slightly and placed his fingertips together. 'Get some rest. You will need it.'

Sawwse wanted to ask how Convener knew all that stuff about Dorienne, but there didn't seem to be any point. Firstly, he'd just been speaking directly into her mind, so he was clearly capable of a great many things that Sawwse would probably never understand. Secondly, he'd already started shuffling awkwardly out of the room, accidentally knocking a few candles to the floor on the way.

After a few minutes in quiet contemplation, the guild mates left the meeting room and walked together in silence to their dorm room. Sawwse knew they were each battling something deep inside. This didn't stop her from making jokes about Osrik's nightdress again once they were tucked up in bed, but Osrik merely snuffed out her candle and plugged his ears with wax.

At first light the next morning, Sawwse and Corinne awoke to find Vadania had already left. They quickly scooped up their breakfast – today it was muesli, which, by the taste, could have been a cardboard recreation of muesli – and ran out of the inn.

Because of where the Happy Hearth was located, they had to move south first before they could leave the city to the east. There were fewer of the large stone buildings and monuments in South Rhyddinas than in the northern part of the city. It was what the middle classes referred to as "real" or "authentic" or "untrammelled by gentrification," and therefore they spent absolutely zero time there. It was in the outskirts of the south that they just about caught up with Vadania.

'Remind me why you are here.' Vadania spoke tersely and didn't break her stride nor slow her pace. To her, the city was a necessary inconvenience. She'd prefer to spend as little time here as possible, but she needed the adventuring guild to help hunt the dragons.

Sawwse panted breathlessly. 'We are… going with you… to Zell.'

'Convener said as much in last night's meeting.' Corinne wasn't quite as winded as the gnome. Probably something to do with the cheeky floating spell she'd allowed herself to cast while they were running.

'I'm aware of what he said.' Vadania glanced around at the residential sprawl. This was also something foreign to her. She'd assumed so many houses this close together to be a human thing. Not willing to live off the land, instead relying on others to produce their food. Classic human stuff. But no. There were elves here too. And dwarves. And all sorts. She glanced back at Sawwse. It was taking all the gnome's effort to barely keep up with her. 'If you cannot even keep pace with me, we cannot hope to work together.'

'What are you… talking about. We're… completely fine.' Sawwse clasped a hand to her mouth to stop her from throwing up.

Vadania effortlessly hopped up onto a short brick wall. She bounced from there to a veranda and then to a roof. Vadania continued her pace, leaping roof to roof like a grasshopper or something much cooler. 'Can you not just work with the dwarves in Brastos?'

'No way… José. Brastos… smells like… cabbages.'

'Convener asked us to work together, and I have never willingly disobeyed an order,' said Corinne proudly. 'Furthermore, he implied this was a priority. So, explain why you are dressed for a hunt.'

This stopped Vadania in her tracks. She looked down at Sawwse and Corinne from the top of a nearby disused market building. It was true that Vadania was wearing her hunter's gear, but this wasn't a surprise. She slept in it after all. However, alongside her recognisable twin blades was a pike, a huge net, and what must have been the biggest beartrap in the world.

'We can help you hunt,' said Sawwse, quite bravely considering the implications of a trap that big. 'But we must go to Zell. Convener–'

Vadania leapt from the roof and landed in front of Sawwse and Corinne. She looked down at Sawwse, bent over double to get her breath back. 'You do not know what I hunt or why.'

'Dragons?' said Corinne.

'Yeah, gotta be dragons,' added Sawwse.

'Well, yes. Okay. But you do not know why.'

'A grudge?' asked Sawwse.

'I had also assumed some kind of deep-seated grudge of some kind,' said Corinne.

Vadania sighed. 'I advise you to turn back now, but somehow, I know you will not. If you get into danger, I may not be able to save you.'

With every hunt Vadania took on, she felt herself drawing closer to her goal. It was the only way to keep herself going. Vadania didn't want anything to jeopardise her chance at revenge, and yet… the Ancient Device did feel consequential. Vadania began walking again but slowed her pace. She pulled one of the noticeboard's quest advertisements out of the top of her armour and consulted it. 'We'll leave the city here and walk to the Forest of Zell. In the centre of the forest is a dilapidated chapel where I will lay a trap for my quarry. As it is the people of Zell who have requested that this beast be felled, we will head there afterwards to search for the map fragment.'

Corinne wasn't particularly pleased about deviating from Convener's instructions, but as the forest was technically on the way, she decided not to raise a complaint. Obviously, she'd be marking it down on

Vadania's PDR (Performance and Development Review) form, but that was a matter for later.

It was a lengthy trek through unremarkable suburbs and remarkable overburbs before the guild mates reached the forest. Once inside, Sawwse and Corinne kept close behind Vadania, who seemed to know each and every twisting turn that the forest presented to them. Vadania said no more than a few words along the way. It was all 'this way,' 'those are poisonous,' and 'stop singing Sawwse so help me gods.'

'Wait here,' said Vadania, before manoeuvring through a dense thicket of trees into a clearing.

After she had gone, Sawwse watched as what looked like a giant dandelion seed floated past her and Corinne. Except, she could've sworn it had a face. And wasn't it… was it smiling? Yes. It was smiling. She chuckled and walked further through the thicket.

A few more of the giant seeds floated harmlessly towards Sawwse. She stretched out her cheeks and blew raspberries with her tongue, mimicking the weird faces that appeared on their surface.

'What exactly are you doing?' asked Corinne.

'I'm playing with these seeds.' She wafted her hands around causing the seeds to dance through the air. 'They're so weird!'

A look of concern spread across Corinne's face. 'Sawwse, what do these seeds look like?'

'Well, they're big, white, and kind of fuzzy. Like a big furball. But they're also very happy. Haha there's one coming this way now actually and it has got the most hilariously fun expression on its face.'

'Oh dear. That's unfortunate.'

'What is?' Sawwse smiled as the goofy-looking fuzzy seed aimlessly floated towards her.

'Gydi seeds. I cannot hear them, so I believe I'll need your help. We need to move. Now. Do not let them touch us.'

Sawwse ducked out of the way of the gydi seed just in time and grabbed Corinne's sleeve, dragging her through the trees. They emerged from the thicket and into the clearing that stretched ahead to another part of the forest. Vadania was in the centre of the clearing, undertaking an extraordinary range of acrobatic feats: dodging, flipping, and flinging herself every which way, all to avoid these giant friendly seeds.

Vadania's eyes flared angrily. 'You fools! Get behind cover!'

Sawwse pulled Corinne toward a thick bush near the edge of clearing, ducking and weaving as required to ensure they both avoided the seeds. 'Couple of questions. What the hell are gydi seeds? And why are we running away from them?'

'You know how nettles sting? It's like that except they fill you full of giddiness.'

'That doesn't sound so bad–'

'So much so that you can't contain the giddiness and usually end up with some combination of keeling over, throwing up, and blacking out.'

'But they look so cute.'

'Do not touch them, Sawwse!'

Unfortunately for Sawwse, she didn't have much of a choice. The gydi seeds were suddenly whipped into a frenzy by a sharp gust of wind. Sawwse just about managed to push Corinne behind the bush, but before she had a chance to dive to the ground herself, a seed bumped into her arm.

Sawwse immediately felt violently sick. The earth moved beneath her feet, lurching her to the right and then to the left. She tried to take a step forward but ended up moving backwards. Everything was the wrong way round. Intending to run for cover, she ran straight out into the open space of the clearing. More gydi seeds pelted against her arms and chest and legs. Sawwse turned around, but her world turned the opposite way. More seeds exploded against her back, her hands, her head. A huge, winged shadow passed over the ground, but Sawwse didn't notice. That's because she had just achieved the triple threat of keeling over, throwing up, and blacking out.

When Sawwse came to, the world was still spinning. Her head lolled forward. But wasn't she lying down? No, she was now sat with her back resting against a tree stump. She wearily raised her head again. There were two blurry figures standing in front of her. She squinted and tilted her head. 'Marius?'

The larger of the two figures spoke in a gruff voice. 'Can you not use magic?'

'No, Article Fifteen prevents it,' said the slighter figure. Even though her vision was blurry, and her hearing was muffled, Sawwse knew it was only Corinne that spoke like this. 'Her life isn't in danger, she's just very uncomfortable.'

'But you made up Article Fifteen?' said the gruff voice, though it was beginning to soften. 'Surely you can bypass it if you're the one who wrote it?'

'Rules are rules.' Corinne crossed her arms. 'However, you are an apothecary. Surely, you have something helpful?'

'I'll have a look.' The large ogre-sized shape shrank in stature until it was Ruby-sized. The little shapeshifter rooted around in her bag before producing a vial. The liquid inside shone with a silver glow. 'This might help?'

'What is it?' asked Corinne.

Sawwse could just about make out Ruby's shoulders shrugging, before the strange vial was placed to her lips. She drank down the viscous substance, immediately feeling a harsh burning feeling in her throat. Sawwse gasped for water as her cheeks flushed bright red.

Corinne handed over her flask, and listened, disappointedly, as the gnome drank it all up.

'Crimping heck, that was disgusting!' Sawwse closed her eyes firmly, took a deep breath, and then opened them again to a stable world. 'Oh, thank goodness.' She paused and then realised someone was missing. 'Vadania! Is she okay?'

'She seems to have run on ahead,' said Corinne. She knelt on the leaves and began to prepare a location incantation.

'Not before chastising you both for slowing her down,' said Ruby with a grin.

Sawwse smiled too. It was good to see Ruby. It'd only been a couple of days, but she'd missed her. 'You weren't at the guild meet?'

'No, I was here.' Ruby shuffled awkwardly from one foot to the other. She wanted to tell Sawwse that she'd left the guild. Ancient Devices and fallen wizards? It was all a bit too much. And what could little old her actually contribute anyway? This whole journey was just a silly idea, and she should just hole up again somewhere far away from all this adventure.

'I was…' Ruby looked at Sawwse's beaming, joy-filled, enthusiasm-sharing smile. 'Gathering supplies. I was gathering supplies.' She gestured to a stuffed bag over her shoulder. 'I thought having a few gydi seeds would be useful for a gremlin lotion idea that I had the other day. And then I saw you struggling out in the clearing. My bear form isn't affected by the seeds, so I dragged you out of harm's way. The only difficulty was resisting the temptation to eat you.' She laughed nervously.

'Hah!' Sawwse slapped Ruby's back, but then judged from her expression that this might not actually have been a joke. 'Er… good one.'

'Found her.' Corinne was knelt in a patch of fallen leaves. She rubbed them gently between her thumb and forefinger, and then suddenly flung her other hand forward. A curving beam of warm, glowing light shot out through the forest. 'This way.'

'Hang on. You can do that, but you couldn't help Sawwse,' said Ruby.

'Lazy,' added Sawwse.

'Look here. Have either of you even read the Actum Tempus Rules and Regulations on the Use of Magic?'

'Obviously not,' said Sawwse.

'It's not a slight book, is it?' said Ruby.

Corinne frowned and then followed her guiding light deeper into the forest. Sawwse and Ruby shared a conspiratorial grin before quickly catching up.

It didn't take long to find Vadania. Unusually, they heard her before they saw her. That was because she was screaming. Not in a bad way.[36] It was her battle cry. And it was followed by a harsh, bone-rattling screech.

Sawwse, Corinne and Ruby rushed through the trees until they emerged into another break from the forest's canopy. There stood the dilapidated chapel that Vadania

---

[36] This very much depended on whether Vadania was screaming at you or on your behalf. If you were draconic, reptilian, or even just wore a lot of green, it probably *was* a bad thing.

had described. It looked pretty much abandoned: vines growing up all its sides, stonework in disrepair, and a sign outside that read, "Abandoned Chapel."

Up on the roof stood Vadania, keen-edged blades raised and ready to pounce. Opposite her was the source of the marginally scarier scream: a giant, winged, reptilian creature with cerulean scales, and it was snapping at Vadania, continuing to screech.

'Is that a dr-dragon?' Sawwse and Ruby spoke in unison. They were dumbfounded. Dragons were not a common occurrence.[37]

'I think not,' said Corrine. 'The sound is not quite as powerful, its aura not as majestic.'

'It's dragonesque though,' said Sawwse. 'Dragon adjacent? Dragon-like?'

'I believe it is a drake. Let us strategise.'

'Should we strategise when we get there? Our friend may be eaten by the dragon thing before we can help.'

'It's not a dragon. And I'm sure Vadania can handle things until we have come up with a POA. That's plan of–'

'–action, yes, I know. You've said multiple times. But what good is a plan if the dragon kills V before we can get over there!'

'It's a drake.'

'I am not going anywhere near that thing!' shouted Ruby, a little too loudly.

---

[37] In fact, they were a Tier 1 legendary creature in *Fobleman and Fogelschmitt's Bestiary of Legendary Creatures Across the Four Continents.* There was a Tier 0, but this only consisted of gods and border collies.

Up on the roof, the drake cocked its head, instantly turning its attention to the guild mates down on the ground. Vadania used the opportunity to slice at one of the claws that gripped the chapel's crumbling towers. The drake screeched and lunged at the elf faster than she was anticipating. Vadania narrowly avoided its jaw but was rammed against the opposite tower. She had to duck swiftly to avoid a swiping claw.

'That's it, Ruby! You've cracked it. We'll get its attention.'

This was the opposite of Ruby's intention. She noticed Sawwse breathing in a deep lungful of air ready to shout. Ruby poked her in the stomach.

'Ooof.' Sawwse clutched her tummy. 'What'd you do that for?'

'I really don't think you should call it over here!' said Ruby in a kind of shout-whisper.

'O-kay. But can't you just turn into a bear again? That'd be awesome. You'd be all like "Rarw!" and "Graaaw!" and "I'm a bloody bear!"'

Shame flooded through Ruby. 'It's not that simple.'

'Ruby, can I ask you something?' said Corinne suddenly. 'Are those ginkgo berries I can smell in your bag?'

'Yes, I collected them earlier. Why?'

'Corinne, not now with berry regulations,' said Sawwse impatiently. 'I thought you were "strategising." We're a bit short on time here.'

'I did come up with a plan, thank you very much. I just think that we may have to adjust it due to unforeseen circumstances.' Corinne pointed behind them to the chapel.

The drake's nostrils flared as its head peered over the side of the church. It slid its body over the brickwork.

Stone flaked off the chapel's bricks as the drake's scales brushed against them. The drake sniffed the ground before its gaze settled on Ruby.

In an instant, Ruby turned into a tawny sparrow-like bird and shot into the trees nearby, leaving her bag to fall open on the ground.

'Seemed pretty simple,' muttered Sawwse. She began slowly pacing backwards alongside Corinne without taking her eyes off the beast.

Jumping from the roof of the chapel, Vadania's short swords caught a ray of sunlight causing them to look as though they were glowing. It wasn't really Vadania's style to pay much attention to her feelings, but in this moment, it was hard to avoid feeling like an absolute badass. She landed on the drake's back, piercing its scales with all the force she could muster. The monster howled a harsh cry. Vadania mustered all her strength and drew the swords down the drake's spine, carving a 'V' shape with her blades.

The drake rocked back and forth furiously, eventually bucking Vadania from its back. As she fell, its tail whipped against her side, shattering three of her ribs and launching her inside the chapel. The screeching drake was too large to enter the church. It thrashed around trying to reach Vadania who lay just out of reach.

Sawwse knew it was only a matter of time before the drake broke through the chapel walls. But what could she do? There wasn't enough time for a song! Besides, her throat was still aching from Ruby's de-gydifying potion. 'That's it!'

She whispered her plan to Corinne, who nodded in agreement. Slowly, the gnome retraced her steps back to Ruby's bag.

Fortunately, the drake was still focused on Vadania. It had begun ramming its shoulders into the gate of the chapel, unfixing the bricks from one another.

Reaching into the bag, Sawwse felt all manner of textures: rough, soft, coarse, slimy, wriggly, bite-y. She tried not to think about it. After a few moments she found what she was searching for: a glass jar containing a bunch of gydi seeds squashed against one another. They still had that goofy smile and looked so cute that she almost forgave them for knocking her unconscious. Sawwse loosened the lid and hurried silently towards the cerulean drake.

The walls of the chapel looked increasingly less stable as they approached. With her spell book to hand, Corinne quickly began channelling the air around them into a gentle breeze: not powerful enough to attract the drake's attention, but strong enough to blow the seeds on their way. Taking off the lid of the jar, Sawwse shook them out into Corinne's magical current of air.

The gydi seeds floated placidly through the air towards the drake.

'Oi! Big stupid dragon thing!'

'It's a drake…'

The drake spun around quickly and caught the gydi seeds in its snout. It flared its nostrils and breathed in the seeds. There was an instant effect. The drake stumbled one way and then the next. It screeched its wrenching howl again before shaking its head, trying to shake out the dizziness.

'It worked!' Sawwse jumped up and down with joy. But then she realised the drake was stumbling directly towards them, so she jumped up and down with sorrow.[38]

Sawwse and Corinne quickly scrambled backwards, but the drake had locked onto their scent despite its nausea and disorientation and distraction at how cute the gydi seeds were. It craned its neck and snapped its large, sharp teeth at them. They jumped out of the way, once, twice and then BOOM! a cosmic-sounding explosion.

The sound knocked both Sawwse and Corinne to their backs, as the earth vibrated underneath them. Fortunately, the drake was knocked off balance too. Spinning around in confusion and fear, it hardly felt the two clean swipes to the neck that ended its life.

Vadania stood over the drake's body as its deep red blood spooled out of its neck. She felt like a badass again. 'You may not be a dragon–'

'Aww.'

'–but you are dragon-kin, and that is crime enough.' Vadania walked over to Sawwse and Corinne, helping them to their feet. 'I owe you an apology.' She knelt on one knee, eye-level with the gnome. 'You both helped greatly, thank you.'

'It was nothing, really.' Sawwse mock-brushed dust from her shoulder. Though secretly it felt a bit like a huge rock star had given her a compliment.

'The biggest assistance came from that explosion,' said Corinne. It was clear that she was still recovering from the sound, hunched over as she was, hands over her ears.

Vadania stood again and looked over in the sound's direction. 'Hm.'

---

[38] Smaller, sadder jumps.

'Is it safe to come out yet?' said a quiet, chirpy voice from the branches of the trees above them.

'Does a dead dragon shed its scales?' said Sawwse, as though it was obvious. 'No, seriously. I'd like to know.'

'Yes, it's safe,' said Vadania, who was busy carving up parts of the felled beast.

'It was… a drake,' managed Corinne, who was still struggling.

Ruby hopped down from the tree and bounced onto the ground in front of her bag. Her arms grew from the sparrow's wings and hooked around her bag's straps, then her legs extended out and a sandy-haired head popped up inside her hood. 'Phew, that was a close one.'

'Imagine how we feel,' said Sawwse.

Ruby scooped a few things back into her bag. 'Any idea what that noise was? It almost stripped my feathers off.'

'It sounded a bit like how I imagine the end of the world sounds.'

'It was laced with magic.' Corinne held out her hands for them to see. There was a thin layer of translucent film running over them, which shimmered with the rainbow tie-dye patterns you'd see in an oil slip.

'Whatever it was, it was not good.' Vadania called back to them as she wrapped the enormous head of the drake inside a net, and then lugged it over her shoulder. She began walking away. 'We must hope it has nothing to do with the map fragment.'

'Indeed,' said Corinne, following behind. 'Especially because we should assume that Alla'fyr's "associate" is as strong as she is.'

Ruby didn't like where this was going. Hadn't she been leaving the guild? It was going well before Sawwse and Corinne showed up. She looked at Sawwse who was skipping alongside the others. It was certainly less lonely with Sawwse around. More dangerous, sure. But definitely less lonely.

'Come on, slowcoach!' Sawwse called out over her shoulder, a big grin on her face.

Perhaps danger was the price she'd have to pay to stay friends with Sawwse. Oh well. Nothing for it. Ruby gathered her bag and ran to catch up.

They walked in silence. Tension building with every step closer to the origin of the explosion. Fortunately, Sawwse was there, and her opinion was that tension shouldn't exist. Sawwse and tension were like oil and water: oily and wet, but separately. 'V, when the job asked you to bring back a "trophy" from the dragon, do you think they had something smaller in mind?'

Vadania rolled her eyes and continued to drag the drake's head across the forest floor behind her.

'I'm sure an eye would have sufficed,' said Sawwse.

'Or a tooth,' suggested Ruby.

'Or a claw.'

'Or its jaw.'

'Or a tongue.'

'Or its don–'

'There is a talented blacksmith in Zell,' said Vadania, interrupting their game. Well, she attempted to interrupt the game.

'Oh! That sounds like the beginning of a rhyme!' shouted Sawwse. 'There's a talented blacksmith in Zell.'

'Who creates armour to make you excel,' sang Ruby.

'She hits metal by day.'

'Very well, some would say.'

'But when speaking, sounds just like a bell! Ding! Dong! Ding! Dong!'

Sawwse and Ruby fell about laughing. They rolled in the leaves on the floor in front of Vadania, who instinctively made to chastise them. But the more they continued shaking with laughter and the more they added rhymes to their song, the more Vadania found herself beginning to smile. Personal quests for vengeance didn't have much space in them for amusements, but really, where was the harm? In a moment of reckless and unguarded folly, she decided to join in.

'There's a talented blacksmith in Ze–'

A large five-pronged leaf suddenly smacked her in the mouth.

This made Sawwse and Ruby laugh even more. The kind of silent laugh that physically hurts. But then, two more leaves shot up from the ground and sealed around their mouths.

'Shhh,' whispered Corinne, holding a finger up to her lips. 'There's something nearby.'

Vadania was understandably furious. But then she too noticed something awry up ahead. She slipped her arms out of the straps holding the drake and drew her twin blades. They had been dulled a bit by the drake's tough skin, but there wasn't time to sharpen them. 'Who goes there?'

There was no response, so the guild mates cautiously moved closer. The atmosphere changed. There was an aura of power greater than any of them had ever experienced before. Except Sawwse… she thought it seemed somehow familiar. There was electricity in the air.

'We seek safe passage to Zell,' said Vadania. This was on the off chance that the aura belonged to an unusually powerful forest troll from whom they needed to request entry.

Again, no response.

And then, just ahead: *thunk*.

The guild mates moved forward to investigate. There was someone there, unconscious and slumped against a tree.

'M-Mirrah!' shouted Sawwse. Her heart suddenly leaped and fluttered uncontrollably.

Mirrah's clothes were tattered and covered in dust. A large, bloody gash in her side soaked through her green dress. The gnome ran to her. She placed a hand against Mirrah's cheek but recoiled as a shock trembled through her body. First in the tomb, and now here. This was too strange to be a coincidence. What on Esh was going on?

'Who is this?' demanded Vadania.

'She's a sort of friend, I think. I met her in Pettibeck. And then she saved my life in the tomb. Corinne, can you do something?'

Corinne knelt beside Mirrah and raised her palms above Mirrah's body. 'I will do my best, but the power here is… immense.'

'Er, guys?' squeaked Ruby, in hamster form on Corinne's shoulder. 'What's that incredibly shiny thing in her hand?'

The others stared at Mirrah's hand. Clutched within was something as bright as a star. They'd only ever seen something that shiny once before.

'Another map fragment.' Sawwse faltered. 'Why would Mirrah have one of these?'

'That's not the only thing.' Vadania had walked on ahead. She was standing at a large city gate, bent out of twisted tree branches. Beyond the gate was Zell. Except that it wasn't there. 'It's… gone.'

Chapter 20:
Tempus Incognita

What to do when you've just accidentally insulted an Orc battalion on the eve of a great battle? Run would be the obvious answer. But what if the way you've insulted them is by giving their knees mouths that keep using the very worst Orc curse words? Well, then you'd probably feel some obligation to sort it out. Especially because you know that the great battle they're preparing for already took place fifty years ago and there was no mention of potty-mouthed Orc knees in the history books.

Yes. Not content with stripping Mirrah's sense of place, the curse was now destroying her sense of time. For a wizard, that meant time travel. Not in a time paradox-y "I'm my own grandson" kind of way. That level of time manipulation only happened with the Ancient Device. No, when wizards travel in time, any changes tend to change back before the effects ripple down the line and kangaroos end up bouncing around in suits.

'I didn't even know I knew that spell,' said Mirrah, ducking out of the way of an axe blow and a particularly nasty knee-mouthed insult at the same time. 'But if you stop attacking me, I might be able to sort it out.'

'Thars whart yous said the larst time,' said a large Orc who spoke in a weird way. 'And loork whart harppened.' She pointed to several Orcs in one corner of the tent who had been half-turned into trees.

'Clearly an accident!'

There was a flurry of blows from axes, swords, halberds, spears, knives, shuriken, and everything else the Orc battalion had at their disposal. Mirrah ducked, dodged, and dived out of the way until she backed into a wall.

It wasn't that she was scared of the Orcs. She was one of The Twelve after all. It was that she didn't want to make things any worse than they already were. Control over her magic was slipping with every passing moment.

'Wait! Wait. Give me one more chance to fix things.'

This particular Orc battalion wasn't known for its patience. However, it was either kill the wizard and definitely have mouths for knees for the rest of their lives, or give her a chance to fix it, potentially get normal knees back, and then kill the wizard.

'Orkay, yous harve one minurtte.'

Focus, Mirrah. Focus. Just reverse the flow of magic. It's simple. Feel the energy in the air, take a breath, and then… VWOOMSH! She disappeared.

'Borllorcks,' said the Orc's knee.

Unmoored from time and space, Mirrah meandered through both. She saw empires come and go, tectonic plates shift, continents drift, cosmic entities appear at the boundaries of the world and think "Nah." It was all rather overwhelming. Mirrah hummed a tune in her head, something to anchor her. It was weird, but she felt herself getting teary. *What was this song again?* That's when she remembered Sawwse Bohge. When all else was falling from her memory, there she remained. VWOOMSH!

And then there she was.

'Helbo… bolbow… bwilp…' said Sawwse.

'Well, helbo bolbow and bwilp to you too!' said Mirrah.

'Is this the real life?' asked the little gnome.

'Who could say?' Mirrah laughed. What a joy it was to see her again. What a joy it was to recognise someone, anyone, but also not just someone, anyone. Specifically, her. Specifically, Sawwse Bohge. Mirrah wasn't sure what to do with her emotions. She booped Sawwse on the nose. 'You feel real.'

'But how are you here? I mean, what are the chances?'

'It's the damnedest thing. I was humming your song and then all of a sudden. WHOOSH! I'm here.' Mirrah frowned. She'd really like to stay here with Sawwse. Wherever "here" was. 'It's curious. I keep forgetting things, but I can't forget you.'

'You say it like it's a bad thing.'

'Oh no. It's marvellous.'

Mirrah locked eyes with Sawwse. In that moment, everything around them was completely irrelevant. Nothing else mattered, because in that moment there was nothing else. No madness, no curse, no Ancient Device. Nothing apart from each other's gaze.

But then, Mirrah's feet touched the ground.

VWOOMSH!

'I just had to think of that bloody Device, didn't I?' Mirrah stomped her feet on the ground like a spoiled little badger. 'I was enjoying that, you know!' The 'not quite but absolutely definitely talking to herself' had continued and was getting worse. So was her grip on magic. It now seemed to flow out of her without her realising, which explains why she'd landed next to a turtle that was walking upright, eating pizza and wearing sunglasses.[39]

'Yo,' said the turtle.

'Bums. This is because of that business with the Orcs?'

'Sounds gnarly, dude.'

'Gross.' Mirrah looked around her. It was dark. Grim. Sewer-y. 'Where am I?'

'You mean you don't know?' The turtle looked shocked almost to the point of dropping its pizza. 'You're only in the best city in the world! New Yor–'[40]

VWOOMSH!

She was gone again.

It was difficult to keep a handle on things when your sense of location had been destroyed. She did her best. And by that, I mean she stuck her fingers in her ears and said, 'This isn't happening,' over and over again.

It didn't work.

Mirrah was flung this way and that, hurtling through space like a horse on a travelator, and falling through time like a grandfather clock thrown from a five-storey building through a transdimensional portal.

It was Sawwse Bohge who had brought her stability before, maybe she could do so again? Mirrah tried to

---

[39] Everyone knows turtles wear bandanas, not sunglasses.

[40] "New Yorg City is often called the "best city in the world," but only by people who live there and have grown accustomed to the smell of the sewers, the rudeness of the people, and the ceaseless busyness. The pizzas are very, very good." (Gnomeopedia, p. 335)

hum the melody Sawwse had sung for her, but this time she couldn't remember it. She couldn't focus. Things were moving too fast.

This was incredibly bad news. A wizard falling through space and time builds up dangerous levels of momentum, increasing their velocity with each teleportation until they crash and release a massive explosion of magic: enough to destroy a large cathedral, make a whole market square levitate, or give all the animals in a zoo a ponytail.

If a wizard of Mirrah's calibre were to stop, it would release a level of magical energy hitherto unheard of.

Had she not been under the effects of a curse, Mirrah would have at least been able to mitigate the collateral damage of her crash by landing in the middle of the ocean.[41] But she was not in control. It was some primal part of her now in charge. A part of her under the growing influence of the Ancient Device. A part of her that somehow knew where a map fragment was hidden.

Boing.

Mirrah bounced as she landed in the centre of Zell, and then skidded along the ground headfirst into a lamppost. The lamppost turned into a giraffe.

'That wasn't so bad.'

And then it happened. An explosion of magic so powerful it could be heard for miles around. And with that explosion, Zell was plucked out of the air.

'Well, balls.' The only thing that remained behind was something very shiny floating in the air. Mirrah let it

---

[41] Because who would honestly care if a dozen whales suddenly got the ability to plait each other's hair?

gently fall into her hand. 'A map? That's right. Once I find the Device, I can go back to before all this began.'

Mirrah stumbled out of – what was until several seconds ago – Zell, and into a nearby forest. But her legs felt like jellybeans, and she had a banging headache. She stopped by a tree to get her bearings but collapsed instead.

Chapter 21:
Zell

'What do you mean, "gone"?' asked Corinne.

'It's just… gone,' repeated Vadania.

'Cities don't just vanish.'

The evidence was stacked against her and Vadania explained as much. 'Where there was once a school, there was now nothing. Where there were once children playing on the street, there was now nix. Where the trees lining the broad boulevards had once rung out with birdsong, there was now not even a dicky bird.'[42]

'Yes, that's enough, thank you.' Corinne knelt beside the perimeter to the city where a curved line in the earth clearly delineated what had been removed. She placed her palm to the ground and took a magical reading. 'What I don't understand is how it happened. It would require an unfathomable amount of magic.'

'There's nothing in Esh that powerful,' said Vadania.

'And yet…'

'And yet.'

---

[42] Which was just as well because everyone hated dicky birds. For obvious reasons.

The words hung in the air as they both turned back towards the woman slumped against the tree. They felt a growing sense of unease.

'She needs a cleric,' said Sawwse, walking over to the others. 'A proper one.' She turned to Corinne. 'No offence.'

'None taken. The irony of course is that Zell was renowned for its clerics.' Corinne still had her palm on the ground. She was nervously thumbing through her spell book with her other hand. 'I daresay it's quite impossible for me to bring the city back. I'm struggling to even read its teleportation signature.'

'Who did you say she was?' asked Vadania, eyeing Sawwse suspiciously.

'Ha! You think Mirrah did this? Pfft. I doubt it. Sure, she's magic. And yes, she didn't seem like she had the best control over it. But it's not like she just made a city vanish for fun!'

'Then explain how she is here and no one else is.'

'I guess I don't know her that well.'

They turned back to where they'd left Mirrah and found that she was no longer alone. There was now a portly man bent over her wearing some kind of religious clothing.

'A cleric! What are the chances?' Sawwse ran back to the spot, flanked by Vadania who drew her swords and pointed them at the man.

'Oh! Goodness graaaacious! Don't hurt me. I'm merely aaaa monk.' The man was wearing a religious habit: a clay-coloured tunic with a pointed hood and a heavy set of beads hung around his neck. But he also didn't look like a monk. Something to do with his eyes.

'What were you doing?' growled Vadania.

'Well, I was merely seeing if this woman needed any aaaassistance, of course!' His voice was plummy, sickly sweet, almost perfumed. 'Is she aaaa friend of yours?'

'Yes,' replied Sawwse instantly. 'And yeah, she desperately needs a cleric's help.'

'Aaaah I'm afraid I am not that kind of cleric,' said the monk, flashing an apologetic smile. 'I meant, er, spiritual aaaassistance.'

'Nah. She's not a ghost,' said Sawwse. 'I guess you could say she ghosted me?'

'Where did you come from?' asked Vadania.

'Where did you go?'

'No. Just where did you come from?'

'Cotton-eyed–'

'Sawwse! This is important.' Vadania glared at the monk. He should not have been able to slip by them unnoticed. And he couldn't have been in Zell or else he'd have vanished too. Something wasn't right here. 'Did you witness what happened?'

'Well, I was returning from my monk's meditaaaation in the forest, and I had just reached the edge of the woods when I saw aaaa blinding flaaaash of light. It seemed to cut through the aaaair. I was so confused, but I didn't realise aaaanything was wrong until that huge BOOM! The force knocked me baaaack into the woods. I must have hit my head on something and paaaassed out.' The monk rubbed the back of his head. 'When I came to, I waaaas stupefied. Staring at the utter scaaaale of it.'

'Do you really call it a "monk's meditation"?' asked Ruby, popping up as a squirrel on a nearby tree branch. 'Is that not like calling a fiddling stick a *priest's* fiddling stick?'

'A talking squirrel. How curious.' The monk looked at Ruby with amusement. This was the thing about shapeshifters, they could always recognise one of their own. Unfortunately, Ruby hadn't been around her own kind long enough to reciprocate. 'Your wizard over there. Is she aaaable to return my city? I'd be ever so graaaateful.'

Corinne got up from the ground and slowly walked over. 'It's far beyond the scope of my power. I can't even tell where the city has gone! One thing I did ascertain, is that the energy signature matches.'

'Matches what?' asked Sawwse.

The others looked at Mirrah.

Of course, thought Sawwse. *The one who makes my heart feel like this is the one who causes whole cities to disappear. Typical. Unless… there was some mistake?* 'Mirrah's not a bad person. Slightly deranged, but not bad.'

Vadania hung her head and breathed out a long, slow sigh. 'Perhaps Convener will know what to make of this.' She tied Mirrah's body to the drake's head and began dragging them back toward the forest proper.

'Leaving aaaalready?' asked the monk. This was a shame. He'd be leaving empty handed and his boss wouldn't be happy, but the elf was strong and the wizard unpredictable. Part of being a survivor was knowing when to fight and when to not get chopped up into tiny pieces by a woman who's just brought down a drake.

'We should get back,' said Sawwse. 'Convener will want to know about the map–' A leaf flew up and spread flat against her mouth.

'That's quite enough,' said Corinne.

'I don't know why you always see the worst in people.' Sawwse spat out the last remaining vestiges of leaf mulch. 'This monk might be able to help us. You know, get some divine inspiration as to where we can find the Ancient–'

'You're as bad as Rangrim!' shouted Vadania, as another leaf sealed Sawwse's mouth shut.

'Come on, Sawwse,' said Ruby quietly, kneading the gnome's hair. 'Let's just go. There's something strange about this guy.'

The monk looked down at them and smiled. It was an easy smile. Casual. Not the kind of smile one wore after a whole city had been displaced. There was something else about him too that had Sawwse suddenly nervous. It was his smell. It was both smoky and sweet, like candy cigarettes. The strangest part was that it was… familiar.

'Have we met?' asked Sawwse, taking a step backwards as she spoke.

'Perhaps.' The monk's easy smile was now more like a smirk.

'Sawwse, come on,' hissed Ruby.

'I wish Zell a speedy recovery.' Sawwse quickly bowed her head and then hastened after the others alongside Ruby.

'Well, isn't that so sweet.' The monk waited until they were out of earshot. He took out a cigarette and match from within a pocket of his habit. His frame began to narrow, and his round stomach shrank, and then his face morphed into that of the mercenary Francesco. He lit the cigarette and breathed in the sickly-sweet perfume it produced, savouring it. Tilting back his head, he let out a cloud of cyan smoke into the air and watched it dissipate.

'Well, back to the boss I go.'

Francesco grinned. He squatted before rocketing up into the air. The monk's habit and human flesh fell away, leaving a magnificent bird of prey streaking through the sky as Alla'fyr's loyal lieutenant returned to his captain…

…After a long, silent, slog in miserable weather, Sawwse and the others made it back to the cold embrace of the Happy Hearth. Grimiser the landlord wasn't thrilled about the enormous drake head forced through the front door, but he had let a guild into his pub, so what else could he expect? He wondered how he'd been convinced of the arrangement in the first place, but then his eyes found the white masked man sitting by the unlit hearth. Right. *Him.* Grimiser seemed to agree to all sorts of things when *he* was around that normally he'd turn his nose up at. It didn't bear thinking about, and that suited Convener just right. Grimiser shook his head and let the guild convene in the lounge.

It didn't take a genius to recognise that Convener was particularly gifted with magic, particularly the mental magics like telepathy, telekinesis and telephantics.[43] But even he couldn't believe the power radiating from Mirrah. She was unconscious and still had this much power flowing around her! The eyes of his mask widened as Vadania explained all that had happened.

'The power to relocate a city.' Osrik sighed. His eyes took on a bewildered look as he spoke. 'I've seen a lot in my time, but never power on that scale. Might she be one of the–?'

'You love saying people are one of The Twelve, old dwarf!' Rangrim slapped him on the back. 'It's ridiculous. Tell him Convener.'

[43] See: creating tiny mental elephants. Self-explanatory really…

Convener stared at Rangrim. He pulled down the collar at Mirrah's neck to reveal a number 12 on her skin.

Rangrim looked embarrassed. 'Okay, anyone can have a slightly misjudged tattoo! Osrik, show them your rollerblading crab.'

'We're going to need to circle back to that later,' said Sawwse. But then she stared at Mirrah's face. It was obvious that she was one of The Twelve now that she properly considered it. Sawwse knew this meant bad things for their mission, but what did it mean for how she felt? She was surprised to learn that it meant nothing. It didn't change how she felt in the slightest. Some connections transcend everything: status, class, stench. 'I'm certain she didn't do it on purpose. Zell, I mean. She saved my life in the tomb of tombob… that tomb.'

'No, she hasn't fallen. There is no broken oath around her. However, her entry into this race for the Ancient Device is unexpected and unwelcome.' Convener held his hands together, pressing his fingers lightly against the lips of his mask. The group sat in silence for some time while they waited for his next response. 'One good piece of news. Once I have prised the map fragment from her hand, we will be ahead of our counterparts in Doriana.' Convener pulled out a scroll and unfurled it. On it was drawn an intricate design, clearly depicting a landscape. 'I drew the map based on the memory of my vassal in the Dorienne inner chamber. I believe if we combine the maps, we will begin to pinpoint the Ancient Device's location.'

'What do you mean by vassal?' asked Ruby.

'Don't worry, it is consensual.'

'That's somehow even more worrying.'

Without explaining anything further, Convener turned his attention back to Mirrah. He knelt in front of her and lifted her head into his lap. As he placed a finger on either side of Mirrah's face he fell into a trance. After a few moments, a shimmering light appeared above her body. The others watched the golden light turn grey and diseased. Convener suddenly began to jerk and twitch, and was finally flung backwards, smacking into the wall.

'Are you okay?' Corinne rushed forward to help, but Convener waved her away.

'A curse.' Convener spoke quietly. He adjusted his cloak and reclaimed his seat in the wingback chair. 'You did the right thing in seeking a Zellean cleric to tend to her, but the wound is unimportant now. The curse is severe and…'

'She's going to die!?' shouted Sawwse.

'The curse isn't killing her.'

'Phew! That's a relief.'

'It's just slowly eroding her mind until it's nothing but an empty husk. An empty husk that contains the most powerful magic in the world.'

'That's worse. That's much worse.'

'Once the curse claims even more of Mirrah's mind, what happened with Zell will become a best-case scenario. That city was simply relocated. Such is the extent of her power that she has the potential to herald an apocalypse.'

'Bloody Dwarven Hell,' gasped Rangrim.

The guild mates stared quietly at Mirrah. A thought appeared in Vadania's head. Had Larn been there, it would've almost certainly occurred to him first. But he wasn't, and so it fell to Vadania to say: 'We should kill her.'

'I'd assume you're joking,' began Sawwse, furrowing her brow, 'only I know never to assume that about you. You can't kill her!'

'The thought crossed my mind too,' said Osrik.

'You can't be serious?'

'If it means stopping an apocalypse…' muttered Rangrim sheepishly.

'You too?' Sawwse shook her head and turned to Ruby, who was at that moment shrinking into her hedgehog form. 'At least I can rely on you, eh Rubes?'

'Chrrk,' chittered Ruby in hedgehog-speak.

Sawwse could tell by the look in her eyes what that meant. 'This is ridiculous. And I'm simply not going to let it happen.' Sawwse stood over Mirrah's body. 'You'll have to go through me first.'

The guild mates looked at one another awkwardly.

'No one is going to kill Mirrah. She is more useful to us alive.' Convener stood and placed a hand on Sawwse's shoulder, gesturing for her to move away from Mirrah. 'I will see what I can do to slow the curse, but first I will take the map fragment. Once we complete the map, we will be able to find the Ancient Device and shut down its evil forever.' With a surprisingly tender motion, he picked up Mirrah's body and began carrying it from the room. 'For now, try to relax. Take on some more local quests. Continue your music lessons. Do whatever it is that you find restorative. I will send Grimiser over with a round of something celebratory. You have done well.'

The guild mates watched him leave.

Rangrim scratched his bushy beard. 'I don't know about anyone else, but I might struggle to relax knowing that someone nearby could cause the apocalypse.'

There was a murmur of agreement. A moment later Grimiser entered the lounge holding a large pitcher of ale and half a dozen dirty mugs. A soggy cocktail umbrella was floating limply in the pitcher.

After he'd left, Corinne tutted. 'Is this what passes for celebratory? Perhaps it's time I had yet another word with the landlord.'

'Well, at least we're alive at the moment.' Ruby spoke quietly. She hadn't even meant to speak out loud, but that happened sometimes when she shifted back to human. However, it was clearly the right thing to say. Osrik poured a round of drinks from the pitcher and then raised a mug. 'To being alive at the moment. Can't say fairer than that.'

Osrik and Rangrim shared stories from their trip to Brastos. There'd been a large rock snake that Rangrim had taken down, a corrupt chieftain that Osrik had forced from power, and the ever-present smell of cabbages. It had been eventful. But Sawwse wasn't really listening. Her thoughts had stayed with Mirrah. Convener must have been mistaken. There'd be some way to remove the curse completely. There had to be.

'Play us a tune, Sawwse.' Rangrim beamed behind a beard covered in ale-y froth.

This roused Sawwse from her thoughts. She looked at the group who stared back at her keenly. Well, there was no sense staying miserable when there was an audience to play for. Sawwse took out her lute and began thumping the side, creating a beat while she strummed. And then she was fine. Because she'd always be fine if she had music.

While the guild mates let off steam, Convener retired to the Happy Hearth's cellar. He waved his hands to a blank wall and the bricks fell away, reforming again once he had stepped into the secret room. The walls were bare, and the only object of any kind was a simple wooden bed. If Convener slept, this was presumably where he did so. He placed Mirrah gently on the bed and stood over her, staring at the map fragment in her hand. He placed his hands either side of her head. 'Now, let's try that again…'

…Meanwhile, beyond the Blue Mountains, night had settled in, in Doriana. The palace dome's magnificent glass spire glistened in the moonlight, its refractions dancing upon the surrounding stone like a kaleidoscopic light show. Unbeknownst to most Dorienne city folk, there was a little gap at the cusp of the dome. Through the gap, there was a viewing platform perfectly positioned to admire the beautiful frescos that adorned the inside of the dome: they depicted famous battles and ugly monarchs from Dorienne history. However, the stairs leading up there had never been finished, so the platform was almost completely inaccessible. You'd have to fly to reach it. Hence why Francesco stood there and no one else. He blew out his colourful clouds of perfumed smoke and looked at the paintings with faint amusement.

Francesco only had to wait a minute or two before the empty space next to him began to shift, the air to blur. The warped space erupted in flames. You could say a lot about Alla'fyr – she was evil, powerful, dangerous, nasty – but at least she was punctual. She walked through the fire.

'Boss.' Francesco tipped his wide-brimmed hat.

Alla'fyr waved one hand casually to close the portal behind her and held the other out in front of her. 'The map fragment.'

'I come with something better than the fragment.' Francesco blew out a cloud of green smoke and paused for dramatic effect. 'Information.'

'That… is not better.' Alla'fyr stared at him blankly. 'Why don't you have it?'

'There was an extremely powerful wizard.'

Alla'fyr looked Francesco up and down. 'You don't look like you've been in a scrap with a wizard. All your limbs are still attached and you're not a frog.'

'Well, no.' Francesco took another long drag on his cigarette. 'The wizard was unconscious by the time I got there.'

'Unconscious.'

'Er, yes. And just as well really, because moments earlier she'd made the whole city of Zell disappear!'

'But you didn't take the map fragment while she was unconscious?'

'A third party got there before I had a chance.'

'A third party?' repeated Alla'fyr. It couldn't be who she thought it was. Surely.

Francesco chuckled. 'Weirdly, it was that gnome we met the other day. Remember when we ditched Osrik? *That* gnome. Sawwse, I think her name was.'

'Sawwse. Bohge.' Alla'fyr spoke through gritted teeth.

'Ah, you do know her!' said Francesco, failing to see just how angry Alla'fyr was. 'She has a lovely singing voice.'

Alla'fyr seethed and her anger radiated outward. Literally. The end of Francesco's cigarette burst into flames. He quickly spat it out. 'That pathetic little wastrel of a gnome is your reason for not retrieving the map fragment?'

'Well, no.' Francesco suddenly felt incredibly hot under the collar. And under the sleeves, the trousers, the underpants. Alla'fyr was heating the air around them to about 109-degrees Darrenheight.[44] 'She was with a hunter. An elf. She looked nails!'

'Nails?'

'She'd just taken down a drake. I was hardly going to fight her!'

'And the self-titled "master spy" couldn't inveigle his way into their trust?'

Sweat dripped from Francesco's forehead, down his neck, armpits, nips, and everywhere sweat tended to collect. 'I followed them. To their guild's base. A grotty little pub in Rhyddinas.'

Alla'fyr sneered at Francesco. With a wave of her hand the temperature dropped. 'Whatever. I shouldn't let the gnome enrage me. *Just remember what Dr Payneawey told me: "Let go of what no longer serves you."*'

'Er, sure,' said Francesco, breathing in the cooler air.

Alla'fyr paused to consider her next move. She was framed by a huge painting depicting a great Dorienne king of yore, framed by two huge waterfalls, framed by the Blue Mountain range, framed by the picture frame. 'At the very least, they'll never complete the map so long as the map fragment here is under my protection.'

'About that.' Francesco explained that he got the feeling the guild somehow had access to their map.

'A spy on the council.' Alla'fyr's eyes burned with tiny flames. 'That turnip nonce is going to fry.'

---

[44] The unit of measurement discovered by Darren, which represented the average temperature of the air at his height of 5'9" (though his dating profile stated 6').

Francesco assumed this was another thing Alla'fyr hadn't meant to say out loud. But she made no further mention of it.

'I need to strategise.' Alla'fyr began pacing the viewing platform. She hated being on the back foot. And if she could say one thing about the current situation, it was that it was absolutely rubbish. Alla'fyr stopped pacing. 'Any suggestions would be welcome. It's your fault we're in this mess.'

Francesco didn't think that was entirely fair, but he also didn't want to be burnt alive. A little flattery was necessary. 'How about we wait until they're not expecting it and then destroy them, taking the map fragments for ourselves? With your power, they wouldn't have a chance.'

'That's the worst plan I've ever heard in my life. But it has given me a great idea. We'll wait for an opportunity to strike and then we'll dispose of them and steal the map fragments for ourselves.'

'Great plan, boss.' Francesco tried very hard not to roll his eyes. He lit another cigarette instead and blew out a perfumed cloud of red smoke.

'Head back to Magnarra and continue your work there. We'll have this continent before long, and once we get the Device we'll have the world.' Alla'fyr smiled cruelly. 'But before all that, I'll deal with the gnome personally.' She summoned another fiery portal and vanished through it without another word.

'Still not as bad as that micromanager I had,' said Francesco, thinking about his time working for pixies in Wed'areth. He faced a mural depicting a symbol of unity: a king holding hands with people from many different places. One of the figures in the painting was a smiling, rosy-haired Magnarrian cleric.

'It's always bloody priests.' Francesco stood closer until he was almost nose to nose with the figure in the mural. 'You look too happy. I'm gonna see if I can do something about that.' The hair under his hat turned from sooty black to rose, and then his body morphed back into an eagle. He shot out of the dome and screeched into the night air.

Chapter 22: *Fortitude*

Sawwse stood outside Con Duco's green-tiled house staring at the ornate lyre-knocker. Convener had said to do something restorative, and what could be more restorative than music? Corinne had suggested a spa resort in No'areth, which would've been a more attractive proposition had she not been using it to practice teleportation. No, Sawwse was sure she'd made the right choice.

She was about to grab the knocker, when the door burst open, and an inconsolable young girl was marched past Sawwse by a very angry-looking father. He turned around and shouted into the house. 'This is an outrage, Duco. I pay you to teach my daughter how to play the piano, not to torment her!'

Con Duco shouted back from somewhere inside the house. 'If she could play one sequence without making me want to tear my ears off, maybe she'd not be so upset!'

'I hardly think Ploum's "Rondo for the End of the World" is appropriate for her level!'

'Well, then maybe she should make more effort to improve!'

'She's five!'

'Bah! Excuses, excuses.'

'You won't be seeing us again!' The father dragged the still sobbing girl away from the house.

Once again, Sawwse stepped tentatively into the house. It was still full of instruments and stacks of papers.

'Back again so soon, Ms. Bohge?' Con Duco appeared from behind a huge stack of musical scores. He handed one to Sawwse. 'What do you make of this?'

Sawwse reviewed it. It was Ploum's Rondo. It was without exception the most complex piece of music Sawwse had ever seen. It was designed for five hands. 'It's… quite advanced.'

'I did give her the reduced edition. But perhaps I was a little harsh. Never mind, never mind. Come now, follow me. We'll start today's lesson in the kitchen.' Con Duco led Sawwse to a small door tucked away behind a double bass.

In the kitchen, Con Duco rooted around inside a cupboard. The room was baffling to the gnome. It was long and thin, with a similarly long and thin island worktop taking up most of the space. The surfaces were no less cluttered than the hallway: a percussion section over the hob, a barrel organ in one corner, and eleven violins sticking out of the wine rack.

'Ah, here we go.' Con Duco retrieved a lime green tea set.

'Ooh are we going to drink Shi'arethian tea again?' Sawwse licked her lips in anticipation.

Con Duco shoved the notes cluttering the kitchen island to one side and placed the teapot and mugs down in their place. 'Indeed.' He delicately moved the percussion instruments from the hob and brought a pan of water to heat.

Sawwse rubbed her hands together. 'Good. I asked for it back at the inn, but they didn't have any.'

'Unsurprising. Recently, Shi'arethian exports have been getting pricier. I'm not sure what's going on down there, but it certainly makes getting hold of tea more difficult. This supply will have to keep me going for now.' The panda-faced man opened a drawer next to Sawwse and pulled out a small cloth bag. 'Right. While the water boils, come here.'

Sawwse shuffled along the limited floor space until she was next to Con Duco at the dining table. He opened the cloth bag and offered it for her to smell. 'Sniff gently,' he warned.

She followed his suggestion and breathed in the aroma from the bag. It was incredibly faint. 'I can't smell anything.'

Con Duco smiled mischievously. 'Not yet, no.' He added two spoonfuls of tea to the pot. It looked like a fine powder of many different colours. Tying string around the bag, Con Duco placed it back in the drawer. The pan of water had begun to boil, so he took it to the teapot and slowly filled it. 'Now, I want you to pour a sup of tea every eight bars of four beats.'

Sawwse was unsure what her tutor was getting at, but she nodded.

They stood in silence while Con Duco counted each beat with a tap on the counter. At eight bars, the gnome poured a tiny amount of tea into one of the mugs. Con Duco gestured for her to drink it, while he kept the beat going.

Sawwse sipped the tea. Again, there was not much of an aroma, and no discernible taste other than hot water.

At the next two intervals, she felt much the same way. But after thirty-two bars, the tea took on an increasingly bitter and sour mixture of flavours. It was like the occasional unripe apple that Ruby had pilfered from the woods.

The smells and tastes became sweeter, richer, deeper after sixty-four bars, and after counting out precisely eighty bars, Con Duco asked Sawwse to pour two full mugs of tea.

The gnome raised the tea to her nose and breathed in deeply. 'Ahh, blueberries and honey.'

'Apple and mint. Delicious. Thank you for preparing the tea.'

Sawwse performed a short bow. Then, she raised her head, and said, 'This isn't the whole lesson, is it?'

'Patience.' Con Duco rummaged through the notes on the table and pulled out a small metal thimble. He held it up to Sawwse, before pausing and counting out a further sixteen bars. Taking up the teapot, he poured the last sup of tea into the thimble and offered it to the gnome.

'Squibal!' Sawwse raised the thimble up in the air. She drank from the thimble and then immediately spat it out. 'Eurgh!' The gnome tried hard not to gag. 'It tastes like rotten fruit.'

Amusement played across Con Duco's eyes. He handed her the blueberry and honey tea, which she used to rinse her mouth. 'You see, Shi'areth knows the power of *imbuement.* Too little, and the taste doesn't carry through, too much, and you overload the senses. The same is true of music. When *imbued* and shaped properly, it can communicate feelings and emotions to even the most heavy-hearted or closed-minded.'

'Right.' Sawwse tried to rub the taste out of her gums with her index finger. 'Tell me next time.'

'You'd deprive an old man his fun?'

'You could coo at babies and shout at cyclists like other old men.'

Con Duco and Sawwse shared a smile. But then Sawwse's faded. 'I need to admit something. I know you told me not to *imbue* anything before the next lesson, but there was this Rhinoholm, and we had to stop it from crushing a village, so I kind of, sort of, *imbued* my voice and put it to sleep.'

'A Rhinoholm?' Con Duco's eyes widened. 'You put it to sleep with your voice alone?'

'And the surrounding village.' Sawwse explained that Corinne had amplified her lungs.

'Intriguing. Yes, the issue is whether you *imbued* too much or too little. Not enough, and the Rhinoholm has a quick snooze before stomping ahead once more. Too much and the villagers never wake up.'

'What?' Sawwse clutched her heart and hoped this wasn't true. 'No wonder Corinne was so annoyed.'

'This is the power of *imbuement* and why it is essential that it is used correctly. Picture singing in an opera. You'll need to hold sway over hundreds of people, twisting their emotions to follow the narrative throughout. It is not unheard of for riots to start at operas. All you need is a particularly unskilled *prima donna* or *primo uomo* to send the audience's emotions out of control.' Con Duco took up his mug of tea and drew in a deep breath, before supping it blissfully. 'But when *imbued* correctly, there is nothing quite like it.'

Sawwse and Con Duco finished their drinks, before heading upstairs to the clutter-free room with the piano. This single room in the house was an oasis from the claustrophobic mess downstairs. They sat cross-legged opposite each other in the centre of the room.

'Now, let's see.' Con Duco stroked his chin. 'Sing me a note, and channel what I am feeling.'

Sawwse closed her eyes and imagined a pool of still water. As she sang, the water rippled, and she focused on its shapes and colours. Sensing consternation and frustration, she varied the pitch of her singing. The notes she sang became shorter, sharper, attacking the air. A few moments more and the frustration seemed to fade, dissolving into melancholy. She softened her voice and slowed the pace, switching to a minor key. When she opened her eyes again, Sawwse saw that Con Duco's hand was raised.

'Very well. It looks like you have practised…' began Con Duco. Sawwse's smug grin faded as her tutor continued. 'To an extent. However, you have a ways to go. You have the power to be *receptive*, but you lack subtlety. Still, there is enough of a baseline for you to begin learning *imbuement* properly.'

'Oh, I'm definitely ready. I *did* put a Rhinoholm to sleep after all.'

'Hm. Let's see.' Con Duco furrowed his brow. 'The first and perhaps most important feeling that you will wish to invoke is: satisfaction. This underlines every other emotion when performing as an artist. The audience should be as satisfied with the music as they are when they finish a delicious three-course meal.'

'Emmeline Flowerdew said, "Always leave them wanting more."'

'Flowerdew?' Con Duco hesitated before responding. 'Alternative schools of thought exist, of course.' He didn't elaborate. Instead, he stood and walked over to the piano. He lifted the lid and brushed the backs of his fingers against the keys. 'I'm going to play a melody. Sing it back to me as best you can.'

Con Duco quickly played a simple tune, a childish theme. A beat, and Sawwse sang the melody back with perfect pitch.

'Remember your method of *reception*.'

The gnome pictured the still pool of water again.

'Sing the melody back to me once more, but this time shape the notes with happiness.'

With her eyes shut and the pool of water focused in her mind's eye, Sawwse began to sing the melody. The water rippled as she sang. The ripples shimmered a warm, hazy glow. At the end of the line, she opened her eyes.

'Not quite.' Con Duco was stony-faced.

Shutting her eyes once again, she conjured the water. The rippling began as she sang, but this time she stopped the waves in their place. Instead, the notes became shimmering bubbles, and each bubble contained a happy memory. She imagined these bubbles spraying from her mouth and popping happiness everywhere they touched.

'Hah! You've got it.' Con Duco beamed with delight from his piano stool. He cleared his throat and regained his composure, somewhat embarrassed by his outburst.

Sawwse repeated the tune, hoping to make her tutor laugh again. Instead, Con Duco looked at the gnome seriously and held up his palm. By now, she knew that this was a cue to stop singing.

'I won't lie, it is impressive that you are able to do this so quickly.'

Sawwse began to fist-pump the air exaggeratedly.

'However. This only means that we can advance slightly faster than planned. Each of us in this world has a kind of will or *fortitude* or inner spirit. This *fortitude* is usually only referenced when one is doing something courageous.'

Sawwse thought back to Vadania fighting the drake or Osrik holding his own against Alla'fyr. 'It helps you fight?'

'It can do. But most people forget that it sits within you at all times. The strength of your spirit becomes important when playing music at the highest level. Try your melody again.'

Sawwse did as she was asked but was met by a solemn face.

'I have solidified my *fortitude* and you will now struggle to sway me with your music, no matter how well *imbued* it is. This was going to be for our next session, but let's see how strong your will is.' Con Duco spun back around to the piano and began to bash the keys: left hand striking loud chords, the right interweaving melodies.

Waves of fear began to wash over Sawwse. The room seemed to shrink and grow, shadows took on shapes of strange monsters and unusually shaped vegetables.

'What's the matter?' Con Duco called out. 'Focus your mind, stop this from affecting you.'

Sawwse tried to close her mind to the fear, but she couldn't stop it from flowing over her. She began to sink into the floor, until she cowered with her hands on her head.

DUNNNNNNNNN.

'Concentrate. This is a battle. My *imbuement* versus your *fortitude*. Let's try again.'

This time, Con Duco played a much quieter, slower melody, satisfied that he had wiped the smugness from Sawwse's attitude. In turn, Sawwse closed her eyes and imagined Con Duco's notes as bubbles floating down into her pool of water. As they were absorbed by the water, she found that she couldn't help but snicker, and then giggle, and then laugh.[45]

'Perhaps you aren't as talented as I first thought,' said Con Duco, dismissively.

Sawwse's resolve hardened. She began to imagine the pool of water freezing over, until it was a gleaming mirror. The bubbles hit the mirror and bounced off. Sawwse stared at Con Duco triumphantly. She'd done it. But this only seemed to egg her tutor on.

'Try this.' The gentle melody picked up speed, chopped, changed and became a jazz movement. Sweat poured from Con Duco's brow as he made the challenge more difficult.

Sawwse scrunched her eyes closed, concentrating hard, but instead of the still black pool, she only saw the dancing particles that painted the black landscape of her mind. They moved and shifted until they began to group together to form a solid shape. Sawwse gasped and opened her eyes to find the white-horned mask and generally beetle-y vibe of Convener sat opposite her in the music room. 'What are you doing here?'

---

[45] "The metric of laugh varies from location to location, but the most common scale goes something like this: snicker > chuckle > giggle > laugh > belly laugh > crying laugh > can't breathe laugh > stroke." (Gnomeopedia, p. 157)

DUNNNNNNNNN.

Con Duco slammed his hands on the piano and spun around on the stool. 'Clearly this is more difficult for you than it first appeared.'

'Sorry! It's not that, it's… that.' Sawwse pointed to Convener but was met with an irritated and impatient glare from her tutor.

'Let's try again.' Con Duco began to play once more.

He cannot see me, said Convener, directly into Sawwse's mind.

Yep. Put that one together myself, said Sawwse.

'You must really concentrate on each note as I play them. Feel them taking shape.'

'Mmhm.' *Crimp, this is harder than it looks*, thought Sawwse. *How do telepaths do it?*

With great effort and patience, said Convener. *Apologies for intruding upon your mind like this, but it is an emergency. You are under threat. As is the guild. You must leave Rhyddinas immediately. It is not safe, and I cannot guarantee your protection if you stay here.*

Sawwse's eyes widened with panic.

Meet the others outside. Hurry. After this command, Convener's image dissolved into wisps of semi-transparent smoke stuff.

Sawwse stared at the space vacated by Convener as her mind spiralled. *Emergency? Under threat? What on Esh was happening?* It took Sawwse a moment to realise that Con Duco had stopped playing.

'What is it?' He could sense her fear.

'I… I have to go. I'm sorry.' Sawwse stood up to leave.

Disappointment radiated from the older man. 'Rhinoholms and adventuring guilds have no place in the life of a true student of music. There will come a point where you will have to make a choice about what you really want.'

'I'm sorry,' repeated Sawwse. Abashed, she grabbed her bag and ran down the stairs as fast as she could. Her mind raced with all the possible eventualities. It raced with all the impossible eventualities too.[46]

Outside, she saw her guild mates waiting for her inside a horse-drawn cart. She jumped in and found a space next to Ruby. Osrik tapped the driver on the back, and they shot out of the city.

Before Sawwse had a chance to ask, Vadania turned to her and confirmed her worst fears. 'It's Dorienne and Alla'fyr. They're coming for the map fragments and for Mirrah. Somehow, they know about her.' She gave Rangrim a dirty look.

'I'm loose lipped, but I'm not a spy!' shouted Rangrim.

'It might be prudent to keep our voices down,' said Corinne, gesturing toward the driver. 'We are trying to sneak away, after all.'

'The monk.' Osrik grumbled from the front. 'I should've recognised your description earlier. It was probably Francesco. He had a habit of–'

'Wearing a habit?' Sawwse winked at Osrik and nudged Ruby in the ribs. They stared at her blankly. 'I make jokes when I'm nervous, okay! Convener popped into my head and told me I was "under threat" or something.'

'And you are.' The voice came from the driver. He turned around to face the others. His expression was

---

[46] Rollerblading horsies, candy floss sharks, Alla'fyr is secretly nice etc. etc.

conflicted, like he was suffering from extreme cognitive dissonance. In his case, this was exactly what was happening. He was trying to hold onto his own thoughts while something else was jockeying for position inside his mind.

'Everything okay?' asked Osrik, wrapping his hand firmly around the axe at his side.

'Yes, I'm fineeaarrrgh!' A stark white light suddenly beamed from the driver's eyes and mouth.

'Ew!' Sawwse sprang back in her seat.

'Kill it!' shouted Ruby.

'What sorcery is this?' Osrik raised his axe.

But the white light seemed to stick in the air. It solidified. And then, like a Surrealist painting of Crocks, it melted. The guild mates sat in a stunned silence as the melting light reformed as a white-horned mask that floated about an inch in front of the driver's face.

Driver-Convener cleared his throat. 'As I was saying, you *are* under threat.'

'Er, no,' said Sawwse. 'We're going to need a little more time to process what on Esh just happened. You've just taken over the driver's body like some kind of possessive ghost.' She turned to the others. 'He'll probably suck all the energy from him until he's all withered and gross.'

The guild mates began shouting protests.

'I can assure you that is most certainly not what happens!' Driver-Convener shuffled in his seat, clearly uncomfortable in both having to raise his voice and defend himself. 'I treat my vassals with the utmost respect. There was just a temporary disagreement.' Driver-Convener stared down each of the guild mates in turn through the eyes of the white-horned mask. 'Now that that is resolved, let me explain the situation.'

Despite it not really being resolved in any way, the guild mates collectively decided under the circumstances that it was probably worth putting Convener's "vassalage" to one side, and to listen to what he had to say. During the explanation, there were raised eyebrows, some gasps, and some grumbling.

Sawwse summed up. 'Essentially, Alla'fyr and some Dorienne elite knights are coming to Rhyddinas to take the map fragment and Mirrah by force. We're relocating to a city called Spearca. Osrik wears a nightdress and has embarrassing tattoos. And you're leading Alla'fyr to Spearca to spring a trap on her. Does that cover everything?'

'I have a question, but I think I already know the answer.' Corinne pointed to a tarp in the back of the cart. 'Is everyone else aware that Mirrah is under there?'

The others recoiled once more.

'There's a bomb on the bus!' screeched Rangrim.

'You're purposely putting us in harm's way,' said Vadania.

Ruby curled up into a spiky hedgehog ball, while Sawwse whipped off the tarp to see Mirrah. She was still unconscious and looked no better than the previous day.

'As predicted, I have not been able to remove her curse,' said Driver-Convener. 'Unfortunately, due to Princess Eugenie's aggressive movements, I was also unable to remove the map fragment from her hand. Hence why she is travelling with you.' Before the guild mates had a chance to protest, Driver-Convener continued. 'Believe me, it is the only way. You are taking Mirrah to a safehouse in Spearca.'

'It won't be hard for Alla'fyr to trace Mirrah's magical signature,' said Corinne. 'You are hardly masking it.'

'No. That is where the trap comes into play.' Driver-Convener stared at Sawwse and pulled out a wanted poster. It was another one with Sawwse's face drawn on it in remarkable detail. This one read: "Stupid Gnome Wanted DEAD." 'It seems Princess Eugenie holds a grudge against you. She believes you murdered her father, King Poht.'

'But that's ridiculous!' protested Sawwse. 'I'm not stupid.'

'It works to our advantage.' Driver-Convener's white-horned mask smiled simply. 'I believe Alla'fyr won't be able to resist killing you and will do so before going after Mirrah.'

'You're using me as bait, aren't you?'

There was a short pause and then: 'Yes.'

'Unbelievable!'

'It is too risky,' said Osrik. 'Alla'fyr is too powerful. I won't let you put Sawwse in danger.'

'It has to be Sawwse,' said Driver-Convener. 'She is the one that both Alla'fyr and Eugenie hate. It's that hate, which will drive them to make mistakes. We will use their hatred for Sawwse to our advantage. Hate–'

'Alright! We get it.' Sawwse shook her head in disbelief. 'What's the plan then?'

Driver-Convener explained his plan. The guild mates took it in.

'Let the record show, I am *not* happy about this.' Sawwse crossed her arms in front of her chest.

'I'll add it to the minutes,' said Corinne.

'Crimping bait,' muttered Sawwse under her breath.

'Good luck.' Up front, Driver-Convener leant his head back. The white-horned mask burst into a million particles of light before sucking inside the driver's mouth. The driver began coughing. A lot. Osrik slapped his back and he recovered. 'Sorry 'bout that. Must've swallowed a fly or something.'

'Or a beetle,' muttered Osrik.

'What?'

But Osrik didn't elaborate. In fact, none of the guild mates spoke again. They continued their journey north toward Spearca in silence. Their minds stewed on the possibilities of the Ancient Device falling into the wrong hands. For all of them but Sawwse, the wrong hands meant anyone else's but their own. And as it occupied more and more of their waking thoughts, the Ancient Device licked its lips in anticipation. Well, it would've done if it had had lips. Instead, several pistons moved up and down gently, and an important-looking dial clicked into position. It wouldn't be long now.

Chapter 23:
A Warm Welcome

Spearca seemed near deserted when Alla'fyr flew into the city. She could've teleported, but she wanted to reserve some magic. It wasn't that she was worried, but if Mirrah woke up, she'd want some extra power at her disposal. She ported a whole city for goodness' sake. As for the guild, she'd systematically kill them one by one, and then have fun burning Sawwse Bohge alive.

'*So, what? Does that make me twisted?*' said Alla'fyr, accidentally out loud.

'Pardon?' It was a peasant woman walking with a cane.

'Vile woman! How dare you address me.'

'I'm sorry, miss. I thought you'd said something.'

Alla'fyr looked down her nose at the woman. "*Who does she think she is to talk to someone as powerful as me?*'

The woman looked up at Alla'fyr, saw the broken oath floating behind her, but couldn't quite resist. 'It really sounded very much like you said something that time.'

Alla'fyr shrugged and clicked her fingers, lighting a fire on the ground beneath the woman's feet. She chuckled as the woman hot-footed it away.

Spearca was normally so full of life, but there were no lights in the houses, and the only faces she saw were misanthropes, strays and the destitute. She felt no pity for the poor. As far as she was concerned, they could work their way out of poverty as she had done. '*I was dealt a poor hand, but that didn't stop me*,' she said. Alla'fyr knelt beside a man sleeping rough below a shop front.

'You. Where is everyone? Tell me what's going on in this place.' She grabbed the man's arm and shook him awake.

The man scrunched around in place and turned his back on her.

With her hand still clutching the man's arm, Alla'fyr began generating heat through her body and channelling it into her hand. It took the man a few moments to feel the pain, but when he did feel it, he tried desperately to shake free of her grasp. He shouted at her. 'What are you doing?'

Alla'fyr yanked the man to standing and then gripped his neck with her free hand. 'Where is everyone?'

'The fireworks,' he blurted out, desperately. 'They're at the fireworks.' He signalled toward the city centre.

Alla'fyr released his neck and smiled, sickly sweet in an instant. 'There. Nothing difficult about that, was there?'

The man tripped over himself to run away, clutching at the flesh of his seared arm. Alla'fyr watched him scamper off. The thing she knew about hard work was that it didn't matter after all. You could spend your life working as hard as you could, but you'd just be passed over in the end for someone less deserving. Alla'fyr screeched into the air, fire streaming from her feet. The buildings here were mostly one or two storeys tall, so she easily found her way around the city. She shot over alleyways, traders' yards, and markets, speeding along the roofs to the large church in the centre of Spearca. Here she settled at a distance and saw the firework display being set up. The city folk were laughing, readying themselves for a spectacle.

'*Simple pleasures for simple folk.*'

This externalised thought got a queer look from a nearby pigeon, who, a moment later, became a luxury roasted treat for a nearby cat.

Alla'fyr leapt from a roof down to street level, her thoughts whirring. It was the whole system that was wrong and that was why it needed to be burnt to the ground. She produced a blue flame in her right hand. '*Perhaps I should give them a real show,*' considered Alla'fyr. '*But no, I shouldn't get sidetracked. I can't afford to draw any undue attention to the Agents of Chaos.*'

Alla'fyr extinguished the fire in her palm and approached the crowd. Meandering through, she watched for any sign of the fool Osrik or his pathetic little gnome friend. She took out one of the wanted posters depicting Sawwse. It had galled her to see the gnome's naiveté elevated to notoriety in Dorienne, so she knew that she'd take particular pleasure in ending her life. Putting on her most demure voice, she sidled up to a local. 'Excuse me. Have you seen this gnome?'

'Lemme have a looksee,' said a goblin with an eyepatch. He snatched the poster from Alla'fyr and held it up to his uncovered eye. 'Yeah, I did see her. Where was it?'

'Weren't she hanging around that decrepit building?' said a nearby dwarf.

'That's right,' said the goblin. 'The abandoned lot. Wonder what she was doing sniffing around there?'

'And where is this abandoned lot?' asked Alla'fyr, all innocence.

'Two blocks west of here,' said the dwarf. He pointed. 'That way.'

'You have been most helpful,' said Alla'fyr with an attempt at a pleasant smile.

The goblin and dwarf watched her leave. They were standing stock still. A tiny image of a white-horned mask glinted in their eyes, and then vanished. They shook their heads.

'What were we just talking about?' asked the goblin.

'I think you'd just said something about your lawn being full of gremlins,' said the dwarf.

'Bleeding everywhere, these critters!'

As the city folk continued their conversations and prepared for their firework extravaganza, Alla'fyr walked to the abandoned lot. She was no longer conserving energy, she just thought it would look cooler.

A pleasant lute chord rang out around the lot, bouncing between the half-constructed pillars.

'Sawwse.' Alla'fyr spoke through gritted teeth. '*Playing music without a care in the world like some kind of… No. Three… two… one… and release the rageful feelings. I mustn't let her get a rise from me.*'

That would be tricky. The two brief encounters Alla'fyr had had with the gnome were enough to find her completely infuriating. Alla'fyr was suffering from 'I can't believe she said "hi" like that' syndrome, to the extent that a simple chord played on the lute was enough to set her eye twitching and teeth grinding.

Alla'fyr calmed herself down by imagining the surprise and horror on the gnome's face while she burned her alive. It didn't last long. Strung up in front of one of the large decrepit buildings was a white banner. It read:

WELCOME ALLA'FYR.

Before she could react, Sawwse appeared from behind an empty doorway and yelled, 'Surprise!' She wore her woodland party hat and played a jaunty tune on a harmonica. 'Wait. It's not your actual birthday, is it? That would be AMAZING.'

The tips of Alla'fyr's ears began to glow red hot. She chastised herself. '*Stop it. Don't give her the satisfaction. Do this on your terms.*'

'Er, right.' Sawwse gestured Alla'fyr to follow her into the building. She spoke as though she were an old friend. 'Come on, just through this way.'

'I'm walking this way because I want to walk this way. *Little does she know she's leading herself into a trap.*' Alla'fyr followed. She created a small flame inside each of her palms. 'Where are you keeping the wizard?'

Sawwse talked back over her shoulder while leading Alla'fyr further into the abandoned building. 'Corinne? Oh, she'll be busying about somewhere. Probably making health and safety overtures at the fireworks.'

'You're an imbecile. You know that's not the wizard I'm talking about.' Alla'fyr felt her throat burning. '*It's fine. She's doing it on purpose. Just relax.* Where is the map fragment?'

'It's the map that I need to talk to you about.'

'I'm not convinced there is anything to discuss,' said Alla'fyr. 'Unless of course, you have an offer for me?'

'That's-a bingo!' Sawwse winked at Alla'fyr.

'Oof. That's incredibly annoying.' Alla'fyr almost lost it, right there and then. But a little bit of deep breathing helped her keep her head.

Sawwse led her into an office at the back of the building. A small, square room, with a desk and two chairs on opposite sides. There were various box files stacked up in neat rows behind the desk.

Alla'fyr should have queried why there was an office in an abandoned building, but against her better judgement, she put out the fires in her hands and sat down opposite Sawwse. 'Go on then. What could you possibly offer to change my mind?'

'Thank you for coming today, Ms. Alla'fyr.' Sawwse spoke like an official, despite not fully grasping the concept of a job interview. 'What first attracted you to this position?'

Alla'fyr drew out a long sigh. *'Do not give her the satisfaction.'*

'Right. That was… enlightening.' Sawwse pretended to jot down notes. She raised her eyebrows. 'Perhaps you could tell us a little about your strengths and weaknesses?'

'Your Gnomish tricks may amuse others, but for a moment I thought you were prepared to be serious. This is all much bigger than you know. Feral times are approaching. There are actors more powerful than me operating across the world to bring about complete and total chaos. These world-defining shifts are bigger than all of us, but especially you. Let me make it perfectly clear that you are but a speck of dirt on the bottom of my shoe. Once I've taken the Ancient Device, we'll rewrite history and chaos will reign.'

Sawwse left a deliberately long pause. 'I'll put down "don't know."'

'Oof! Give me strength!' Alla'fyr closed her eyes. *'Three deep breaths and centre yourself. One… two… three… and release the negative energy. Which would be easier if I wasn't sat across from an unsufferable little – stop! Do not let her win. More deep breaths. Five. Let's do five deep breaths. One… two…'*

While Alla'fyr was busy externalising her anger management and relaxation techniques, inside Sawwse's mind was a cacophony of competing thoughts, most of which weren't her own. This was because Sawwse's mind was currently being used as a telepathic relay for the guild.

Stick to the plan, said Convener.

But what if I can change her mind, said Sawwse.

You can't, said Osrik. *Some people are evil through and through.*

She's already almost killed you once! said Ruby.

Yes, but that's before we properly knew each other, said Sawwse.

I told you she wouldn't go through with it, said Vadania.

I would go through with it if I could be sure that she was uncomplicatedly evil.

She is! A chorus of voices rang out in her head.

Please can we get back on track, said Convener. *You're doing really well with antagonising her.*

I wasn't even trying to antagonise her, complained Sawwse.

Keep it up and she'll lose her composure. Then she is ours.

'What are you doing?' Alla'fyr stared at Sawwse blankly.

'Er, what do you mean?'

'Your eyes keep twitching.'

'Oh. I'm just concentrating.'

'On what?'

Don't say telepathic conversations. Don't say telepathic conversations. Don't say telepathic conversations. 'Telepathic conversations. Crimp!'

Alla'fyr jumped up from her seat and spun around, searching for anyone else in the room. 'I should've assumed your guild would be around here somewhere. No matter.' Flames sprouted from Alla'fyr's palms. 'I had wanted to savour killing you, but I have wasted enough time here already.' She thrust out her arms and shot beams of hot fire directly toward Sawwse.

Sawwse did not react normally. She should have reeled backwards screaming in agony, cursing her gods, and wetting her kecks. That was what normally happened. Instead, she just looked a bit sad. 'I thought I could maybe change your mind about the whole 'killing people for a living' thing, but clearly not. Sorry about this next bit.'

'What is this? What are you? *It couldn't be true. She couldn't actually be a powerful wizard, could she*?'

Sawwse's face blurred and flickered in the heat, but then disappeared. It was Alla'fyr who reeled backwards in shock, cursed her gods, and wet her kecks (just a little). In Sawwse's place floated a white-horned mask. It grinned creepily before melting in the heat.

'You!' gasped Alla'fyr.

Suddenly, everything in the room disappeared: the desk, the chairs, the box files, and in the same moment, the actual contents of the room appeared: stacks and stacks of barrels, all marked in the same bold block lettering that read, 'GUNPOWDER.'

'Oh, for fu–'

The room exploded.

Chapter 24:
Alla'fyreworks

The last of the sky's ochre colour had dissolved, darkening the city. Night rushed in without a second thought for dusk, which was ideal on the imaginatively named 'Fireworks Night.' A curated selection of fireworks was held back to be lit when the church bell chimed. There were of course independent-minded city folk who fired theirs up to the heavens in small flurries ahead of schedule – it was important for them to keep all the dogs and sleeping babies in a constant state of peril. Speaking of peril…

Stupid, stupid, stupid plan, thought Sawwse as she ran through the streets of Spearca. *Absolutely crimping stupid plan!*

Boom! The first explosion startled Sawwse as the street briefly glowed bright red. She looked skyward and saw a second rocket shatter, splintering golden embers. Her surroundings faded, becoming gloomy once more.

Why had she agreed to be used as bait again? Okay, so she hadn't technically been in the room with Alla'fyr, and therefore hadn't been under much threat earlier. But that was all before. Before Alla'fyr had survived

Convener's trap. And before Convener's telepathic relay system had suddenly stopped working. Now Sawwse was running as if her life depended on it – and it did – with only a loose-knit plan of how to take Alla'fyr down.

Ba-koom-boom! Dazzling emerald fire reflected off the shards of metal in the blacksmith's yard, glimmering in Vadania's eyes. It was just like that fateful night all those years ago. Well, it wasn't. But the green fire in the sky was similar and that was enough to make Vadania snarl. Normally, this would be perfect. Keeping the rage simmering was what made her such a potent hunter, but recently it felt different. Sadness had sneaked into her memory along with the question: what if the dragon had never attacked in the first place? Vadania didn't know it, but the Ancient Device's claws were further wrapped around her throat.

Fffyeeew! Fffyeeew! Fffyeeew! Osrik could've sworn he'd seen someone turn down this alleyway. He clutched two hand axes, quicker to launch than his wizened battle-axe. Was it that he had spent so many long years fighting in skirmishes and wars overground, or was his eyesight finally fading? Dumpsters, rubbish bins and other detritus all glowed an incongruously pretty amber colour. Osrik breathed in. Osrik retched. The light did nothing to improve the smell of the alley. The scent was familiar. But he mustn't remember why. He clapped the side of his head to dispel the unwanted memory, and then he edged forward into the shadows.

Skriiii-skriiii-skriiii! Long tails of vermillion rushed through the sky. Fifty miles away a meteor trailed a dazzling likeness. Although she was terrified by the prospect of coming face to face with Alla'fyr, Ruby forced herself to concentrate. Too nervous and she could end up a moose with flamingo's legs, which is rarely a helpful combination.[47] The others had told her that it was very unlikely Alla'fyr would be on the rooftops. Ruby tried to keep that reassuring thought circling through her head, though she couldn't help thinking things would be easier if she were only more normal.

Pfffft-pop! Rangrim stood sentry by the main square, trying to ensure that the city folk weren't dragged too deeply into this potential disaster. This was an opportunity to prove himself if he could just stay focused. He had *Slaepan Gigas* strapped securely to his back. Vadania wasn't around to distract him with her luscious curls. It was perfect. He'd protect the city folk and be proclaimed a hero. They'd probably write songs about him: "The Hero of Spearca." Unless he couldn't do it? What if Thrimbald was right and he was never meant to pick up the sword in the first place? The Ancient Device whispered doubt into Rangrim's mind.

Fzzzz-snap! The sounds whizzed past Corinne as she paced across the rooftops. The darkness she was so used to became textured as the fireworks screamed into the air. Corinne calculated their trajectories and deduced that they were all just about within her regulations. She kept trying to make this new career as much like her previous one as possible, but there'd always be someone like Alla'fyr who broke the rules and someone like Larn who tested them to their limits. Perhaps there was no point. She chastised herself again for transmuting that loaf of bread all those years ago.

---

[47] The exception to this is the heavyweight ice-skating competitions on the frozen lakes of Svinhilla, where the moose are always scored low on grace and poise.

In its hidden chamber, the Ancient Device whirred and clanked. It knew that its evil magic was working. It was calling to them: the shifter, the administrator, the hunter, the hero, the scholar, but most of all, the ex-mercenary with a mountain of past sins, the bereaved princess who can't see the present, and the amnesiac wizard who forgets herself more with each passing moment. If the Ancient Device could have laughed, it would have given the world's preeminent pantomime villain a run for their money. But it couldn't laugh. Instead, its motor purred in anticipation. It was almost time.

But not quite. First, the guild had to deal with something less complex. Namely, the psychopathic wizard that wanted them dead…

There was a lull in the fireworks. Silence fell upon the city centre while the city folk waited for the huge firework display to commence. Sawwse stared down the street ahead of her. The buildings were drunk, leaning at crooked angles. Sawwse darted from one side of the street to the other, desperate to stay under cover.

In the alley, Osrik inched his way forward to a brick wall. A dead end. *When did it get this warm?* Beads of sweat began rolling from his forehead. He turned quickly on his heel, but Alla'fyr wasn't there. *Must be imagining it.*

Osrik ran his fingers across the coarse bricks, and for a moment he lost himself. No longer in a dark alley in the city of Spearca, he was transported back to his first home, The Ironforge. Running around the walled garden surrounding the mansion grounds, he trailed his fingers along the stonework and looked up at his smiling mother.

Had that really happened? Maybe. A long, long, long time ago. But why was that memory resurfacing now?

Osrik had no idea that this was the work of the Ancient Device. Of course, it didn't really matter why it was happening, just that it was happening long enough for Osrik to let his guard down. And as we know, terror seeks the infirm.

'Hells,' growled Osrik.

A great swirling column of fire suddenly rose above the buildings. Corinne heard the roar of the flames and began skimming and gliding over the rooftops towards it. The sky burned on the other side of the city from Ruby. She wanted to shift into cheetah-form and bolt over there, but in another, realer way, she wanted nothing more than to cower on the spot, which is what she did.

Sawwse turned a corner just in time to see Osrik engulfed within a wall of golden and crimson flames. 'Osrik!'

She froze. The heat from the fire shifted and distorted the alley, and she couldn't focus on what should happen next. Her eyes darted around looking for some kind of clue as to what she should do to help but came up with nothing. The buildings either side of Osrik caught fire.

'Play him a song, why don't you!' Alla'fyr stood between Sawwse and Osrik, controlling the flames swirling around the dwarf. 'See if that helps!'

Sawwse didn't move. She was stunned. Not just from the comment, which was clearly going to be circling her head at 3am while she was trying to sleep, but because she was watching one of her guild mates die.

It was unfortunate timing that one of the overeager city folks had consumed slightly too many dragonfire cannonballs. It was also unfortunate that this individual happened to be the one in charge of starting the firework display at the agreed signal: the bonfire. With his vision blurred, Simon Tattersdale saw Alla'fyr's column of fire rise into the sky over the tops of the nearby buildings and assumed it was the signal. Stumbling forward, he looked up at the church bell tower and could've sworn he saw the bell rocking back and forth. He didn't *hear* the bell, but that didn't mean crimp. His hearing was dodgy at the best of times after working at the Ministry of Unnecessarily Loud Noises for so many years.[48]

Taking out his matches, Simon Tattersdale bent down and swayed towards the waiting piles of fireworks. He struck his match along the ground and lit the fuses.

Back in front of the towering inferno, Alla'fyr laboured over her breath. She was badly injured from the gunpowder explosion and knew that she should regroup while she still had the chance, but she'd let the foolish gnome live once, and wouldn't make the same mistake again. It would only take a moment. She should have known that it only takes a moment of hubris to unmake a person.

Flames whipped this way and that, blurring and shifting as Alla'fyr walked slowly towards Sawwse. Deep within the fiery pillar, Osrik felt ashamed to have been caught off guard. He was blistered and burnt and felt like this must be the end, but he held onto life through sheer force of *fortitude*. Just long enough to do one last thing.

---

[48] "Sounds tested at the Ministry of Unnecessarily Loud Noises include, but are not limited to, alarms that go off before the sun is up, creaks in floorboards outside sleeping baby's rooms, dwarven snores, the laugh of a person you hate, and your neighbour's son practicing violin." (Gnomeopedia, p. 1292)

Alla'fyr approached Sawwse.

It's not right, thought Osrik. *She's innocent. Incredibly annoying, ill-suited to the adventuring life, and mentioned my nightdress too often. But innocent.* Summoning the very last of his energy, Osrik roared and launched one of his axes.

Turning suddenly at the scream, Alla'fyr dodged to her left. She avoided the full force of the axe but wasn't quick enough to escape completely. The blade of the axe, white with heat, caught her shoulder: seaming through her cloak and searing the flesh underneath as it cut.

The pillar of flames was dispelled and Osrik fell to the ground. But his peril wasn't over.

'You old fool,' hissed Alla'fyr. Her arm hung limply to one side. She took a step toward him. 'You think hanging around in a poxy little guild will absolve your sins?'

Osrik could barely even raise his head off the ground.

'You think anything could undo what you've done?'

'No, I–' Osrik coughed up blood.

'Pathetic. You can't even speak.' Alla'fyr stepped closer. 'I'll make this quick for you.'

Boom! The firework shook Sawwse out of her stupefied state. She needed to get Alla'fyr's attention and quick. She cupped her hands. 'Oi, skull 'ead!'

Alla'fyr continued walking. 'I'll deal with you in a moment.'

Sawwse thought for a second. 'But it's me! I'm *very* annoying… apparently. Wouldn't you rather kill me while you have the chance?'

Alla'fyr was not deterred. She produced a flaming ball in her hand and closed in on Osrik.

What was left? Sawwse needed something that would truly antagonise Alla'fyr, and she needed it now. '*Play him a song, why don't you!*' Alla'fyr's comment boomeranged back into Sawwse's head. '*See if that helps!*' Sawwse grinned.

'The moment you came to boiling point,' sang Sawwse. She made a loud trumpet noise with her mouth. 'I could see you were hell-bent on extinction. A first-rate offender.'

Alla'fyr's eye twitched.

'Skull lookin', so unkind.' Sawwse clicked her fingers and swung her hips to the tune. 'Say, wouldn't you like to come with me and see what you find?'

Alla'fyr's jaw was clenched as tightly as if it had been in a vice. '*One… two… three…*'

'Let me make a couple of points: I don't pop and lock for every skull I see.' Sawwse was now 'doing the Robot,' as annoyingly as she could manage. And then she belted out her pièce de résistance. 'You're a hellbender! Beeeeend a little time with me.'

This didn't really make any sense. But it didn't need to. Alla'fyr snapped. She whirled around and lanced a flame at Sawwse, who ducked out of the way and scampered out of the alleyway. Alla'fyr shot off the ground to follow.

Osrik smiled. He lay on his back and watched the flames overcome the buildings beside him. His *fortitude* had saved him from the worst of the blaze, so if he could just get back up, he'd be able to help Sawwse. But his body would not let him. He lay looking up at the stars. They began to explode and dance across the sky in every colour imaginable. These colourful patterns began to stick and merge in the skies, until the heavens looked like a paint-spattered canopy. *There are worse things to see before you die.*

Bolting out of the alley and onto the street, Sawwse knew that she would be outpaced by Alla'fyr in a matter of seconds. She didn't know what seconds were, but she knew they stood between her and becoming a charred piece of gnomeat.

The city stretched out in front of her, blooming in strange hues: magenta begat cyan begat jasmine begat other shades of less interesting colours. The fireworks popped and whizzed, and Sawwse began to pick out their rhythms. She joined in with their noises and raised her arms to the sky as if conducting. 'Ba-ba-ba frrrooom fzzz bap!' Sawwse concentrated on the sounds and *imbued* them with speed, willing herself to escape. Her legs moved faster and faster as she increased the distance between herself and Alla'fyr.

Fwoomph! A bolt of fire surged just inches from Sawwse's head, igniting a timber-framed building. *Fwa-fwumph!* Flames lanced past her setting the right arm of her tunic alight. Patting the fire out as she ran, Sawwse stole a glance behind her and saw a face full of hatred. Alla'fyr's hands burned with a red-hot force and her crimson robes billowed behind her: a fireball hurtling down the street.

Fzzz-boom! Ba-boom! The sky continued its thundering as Ruby did her best not to be startled. The more nervous she was, the less in control of her shifting, and the firework display was relentless. It was all she could do to keep running, crawling, scampering, slithering, swinging, rather than cowering, but if she stopped, she might turn into that *thing* again.

Ffyeew! Ffyeew-po-pop-pop-pop! Disoriented and frustrated, Corinne knelt atop a slanted tiled roof. She thought she'd have more time before the main fireworks display knocked her off balance. The unceasing explosions around her left imprints in the sky and in her mind. Where one faded, five more appeared. Corinne focused and slowly tilted her head this way and that. *What's that?* Away from the roofs, away from the sky, she could hear fire, working its way up a building: crackling and burning, but not yet roaring. *There.*

The fireworks melted away as Corinne focused her mind and flew from the roof, following the crackling fire's sonic trail of destruction.

Sawwse turned sharply into the blacksmith's yard. Her eyes darted around, desperately searching for Vadania or Corinne or, at a stretch, Rangrim, or at the farthest stretch, Ruby. 'No, no, no, they're supposed to be here!' She could feel the burning doom of Alla'fyr approaching but couldn't see any of her guild mates anywhere. Sawwse tucked herself behind a stone slab in the workshop facing the forge.

Alla'fyr flew into the yard and stopped. She held fire in each hand and her ears burned, both literally and metaphorically – a tiny enclave of goblin granite farmers she'd thoroughly terrorised in the past were cursing her name and spitting at an Alla'fyr-shaped effigy. But also, tiny flames sat atop her ears.

'The chase is at an end, Sawwse Bohge.' Alla'fyr stomped her foot and a small pillar of fire shot up from the ground, before melting back into the asphalt. Another stomp, another pillar. 'Which crevice did you crawl into?'

Sawwse's heart was racing. If the others weren't here, there was nothing to stop Alla'fyr from killing her. She tried to keep as still as possible. Long, slow breaths.

'You and your pathetic guild won't win, you know.' *Fwoomph. Fwa-fwumph.* Alla'fyr scattered her flames around her, as though she were planting seeds. Not even the best gardeners in the world could expect results as quick as this. The flaming roots took hold and fire sprouted from the ground all over the blacksmith's yard. 'You did well to trick me. I'll give you that. Had I known you were working with someone as devious as… Convener? Was that his name? It's hard to keep up with all his identities. Anyway, had I known, I would've been more prepared.'

Ba-koom-boom! Ba-boom-boom! The strobes of greens and blues from the sky above mixed violently with the crimson fire blazing in the yard's buildings, like the most sinister nightclub.[49] Sawwse's heart was beating faster and faster. Pinned in like this, she was like a mouse in some kind of contraption designed to catch mice. She was hidden for now, but it was only a matter of time before Alla'fyr found her. Where on Esh was Vadania?

Fwa-fwumph! Alla'fyr stomped her foot and another pillar of fire sprouted in the centre of the yard. Reaching into the flames, Alla'fyr began to shape the fire into an orb. She casually tossed the orb into the air where it slowly began to orbit, burning all the shadows in the blacksmith's yard to nothing.

Sawwse was small enough to stay hidden by the forge, if she could only keep her composure.

Alla'fyr changed tack. 'Perhaps when I return to Dorienne, I should tell Eugenie to set the Blue Forest ablaze.'

---

[49] "The most sinister nightclub in the world is Club Vampyre. The lights stay low throughout the night so that patrons can partake in 'necking' at their discretion. Yes, unfortunately that's exactly what it sounds like." (Gnomeopedia, p. 28)

Sawwse's throat tightened. Wasn't the Blue Forest hidden? How could she know about it? This was terrible. Yes, the Blue Forest was full of annoying crimplords who played pranks in almost all waking moments, but they were *her* annoying crimplords. And at least they weren't trying to roast her alive!

If only I knew magic, I wouldn't have to hide like a yellow-bellied coward. Sawwse closed her eyes and thought back to Con Duco's last lesson. If she could strengthen her *fortitude*, perhaps she could *imbue* a song and make Alla'fyr burst into tears or something. She pictured the familiar still black pool, but immediately knew something was wrong. Rather than rippling gently, the pool was bubbling and boiling over. Sawwse desperately tried to think of something to stop it, something that could overpower Alla'fyr. But she didn't stand a chance.

'Foolish gnome,' said Alla'fyr scathingly. 'You've given yourself away.'

Sawwse opened her eyes and watched as the forge hearth began to glow. Pale yellow at first, but soon it burned a familiar crimson.

'You lack the *fortitude* of an adventurer.'

Sweat rolled from Sawwse's forehead. The workshop shifted and swayed in the haze. It took everything she had to stay conscious.

Corinne followed the fiery trail, closing in on the furnace of the blacksmith's yard. Something was wrong. The fire was spreading too quickly, too violently. Not only was it a health and safety nightmare, but Sawwse was in serious danger. Piercing through the air, she closed in on the yard when- *Dunnn-dinnn-dunnn-dinnn!* The cathedral peal rang out throughout the city and shattered Corinne's orientation. Her mind shook-shimmered as she fell out of the sky.

The heat of the blacksmith's hearth had begun to burn Sawwse's skin, browning the bridge of her nose.

Alla'fyr walked slowly towards the forge. The orb of white fire fissured in the air behind her, haloing her like some kind of corrupt angel. The buildings about the yard were being consumed by raging flames, and once the orb cracked apart completely, the whole yard shifted with dancing red shadows.

'That old fool, Osrik died with honour.' Alla'fyr gestured behind her. She turned an invisible dial and the fire in the hearth slowly turned from crimson to violet to ferocious blue. 'But you'll die like a rat in a hole instead.'

Sawwse covered her face with her scarf. She tried to open her mouth to speak, but her lips had started to scab; she tried to hum, but her mind wouldn't fix on a tune; she tried to open her eyes, but didn't want to burn them; she tried to breathe, but the intense heat scolded her nostrils. Sawwse forced herself to count, to force her mind into some kind of focus. *One… two… three…*

A scream of anguish rent the air, cutting through the roar of the yard's fire. It was Vadania. Not the source of the scream. That was Alla'fyr. Vadania was the cause of the scream. More specifically, the twin short swords she'd just planted within Alla'fyr's shoulder blades. Vadania drew them down the fallen wizard's back.

The fire in the hearth disappeared and Sawwse gasped for air, somehow summoning strength to crawl away from the forge. Alla'fyr collapsed to her knees as Vadania withdrew her swords and quickly ran towards Sawwse.

'Are you okay, my friend?' Vadania looked on Sawwse with kindly eyes. It was rare that she looked upon anyone with a gaze that was nothing short of furious. She placed a water skin to Sawwse's lips.

'Thank you,' mouthed Sawwse. She drank the water. It was incredibly cold but invigorating too. 'Is this special Elven water?'

'What?' Vadania narrowed her eyes.

'I don't know. I just thought… Elves might have special water.'

'Why did you have to make it weird?'

'Okay, it sounds weird now, but the water is so cold! That's not normal!'

'I carry it in an ice pack.' Vadania frowned.

While Sawwse and Vadania continued to bicker, the blood streaming down Alla'fyr's back steamed and hissed and began to resemble a lava spill from a volcano. The molten blood hardened and crystallised, until it looked like a kind of shell.

'That does not look great,' said Sawwse.

Without another word, Vadania quick-stepped her way towards the fallen wizard. She'd hoped to kill her in one blow, but it seemed she'd have to finish the job.

There was a bright blue flash and Vadania went flying through the window of a burning building. Alla'fyr was not done yet. She rose to her feet slowly. She was now surrounded by a bright blue flame. As Alla'fyr walked towards Sawwse, the extra weight on her spine caused her to stoop. The calculating evil had gone from her eyes, leaving only brute magical power and desperation. She shot into the air: a firework stuck in perpetual explosion.

From Sawwse's perspective, there was a beauty to this. Her eyes still hurt, so the flickering cyan, sapphire, and ultramarine flames, came in and out of focus against a night sky of fuzzy, exploding colourful lights.

So, she was about to die. Again. Sawwse hadn't really thought joining an adventuring guild would involve this much peril. Yes, she'd been told adventurers risked life and limb, but she'd hoped there'd be more emphasis on the limb side of things, and preferably a non-important one at that. You know, like an extra toe or something. It didn't really matter now. Because there was Alla'fyr, screeching through the air towards her. Sawwse closed her eyes.

Bonk.

'I thought being burned alive would sound more fearsome than that,' said Sawwse. 'And be more painful.'

Bonk. Bonk. Bonk.

She opened her eyes. Alla'fyr was still there, but she was now behind a pane of glass. The wizard was bashing into the glass, but it deflected her each time. She looked more like a confused fly than a fallen wizard.

Bonkbonkbonkbonkbonk.

'There are about a dozen Level Four health and safety violations at work here.' Corinne placed a hand on Sawwse's shoulder. They were both encased within a thick glass sphere of Corinne's creation. 'I had to take emergency measures, I'm afraid.'

Sawwse grinned wide.

'She's wearing no protective gear of any sort, and between you and me, I'd be very surprised if she even had a permit for such extensive use of fire magic.'

Alla'fyr howled: half rage, half agony. Whatever magic was keeping her going was finally wearing thin. Rationality had returned to her eyes, and with it a double dose of dread: at failing in her mission, but also that she'd lost to Sawwse Bohge's guild. A deep knot in her throat forced out a gob full of tarry blood and black saliva.

'Absolutely disgusting,' said Sawwse.

Vadania emerged from the building and brushed herself down.

At the sight of the elf, Alla'fyr placed her feet on the ground before bursting to the other side of the yard. Panic bloomed in her eyes. 'I can survive this.'

The colours hitting the sky had begun to peter out, but there was still the occasional amber or lapis or emerald. Firing into the air, Alla'fyr flew to the roof above the yard. Her feet touched down on slate, and she saw the tiny frame of Ruby. Even amidst all her pain and humiliation, she found time for scorn. 'Let me pass, reject.'

Ruby stood ten feet from Alla'fyr, braced against the slanted roof. She desperately wanted to stand her ground. Ruby screwed up her face. 'No.'

Alla'fyr snorted. With one arm limp by her side, and the other clutching her shoulder, she walked past the tiny shapeshifter.

Ruby willed herself to change into something useful, something fearful, but her nerves played havoc with her system. She focused inward. She tried desperately to form her hand into a sharp claw, but only managed a miniature poodle's paw. Ruby tensed her jaw hoping to summon vicious fangs, but all her teeth fell out leaving her grimacing gummily. Finally, she tried to shape a stinger, but instead brought forth a stinker – the anal gland of a beaver. An unpleasant aroma filled the air between Ruby and Alla'fyr.

'Pathetic.' Alla'fyr laughed and spat blood onto the ground. Then, with a sharp shove, she pushed Ruby off the roof. 'Fly away, little bird.' With the last of her energy, she created a fiery portal to safety and threw herself through it. Alla'fyr had failed her mission and if she wanted to keep her life, she'd have to run far, far away. She could be a difficult taskmaster, but *her* boss was something else. And there were some things that were worse than death.

Sawwse and the others saw Ruby fall from the building. She shrank and shrank until they lost track of her. A moment later, there was a loud crash from a nearby wooden cart. Vadania rushed over to investigate.

Ruby sat in the cart holding her knees and trembling. 'I let her get away.'

'You survived,' said Vadania, offering her hand to Ruby. 'We survive so we can do more.'

Ruby took Vadania's hand and climbed out of the cart. They regrouped with Sawwse and Corinne when another figure entered the yard. Vadania drew her swords once more. 'What now?'

But it was Larn. He stood facing the others, burns across his face, cloak torn and singed, and a large claw mark across his chest. Around his neck hung a pendant, and trapped within the pendant was something that sparkled as bright as a star: another map fragment. 'Look what I can achieve… on my own.' Larn swayed this way and that, and then collapsed in a heap on the floor.

The others rolled their eyes.

Chapter 25:
My Own Hands

'What do you see?'

'It is… unclear.'

'Try again.'

'Of course.'

Cribbins took out a handkerchief and squeakily wiped the surface of a large turnip. He leant forward, bringing his face inches from the white and pink vegetable. He closed his eyes, mumbled something incoherent, and thanked his Aunt Julie for taking him to that naff séance so that he at least had something to base his impression on.

'Anything? Do you see anything?' asked Eugenie.

The Rhyddinian Council looked on in disbelief. One of them spoke up. 'Perhaps, it's better not to rely on… what was it you called it? Turnip scrying?'

'It's making me want to scry, I'll tell you that for nothing,' said another one.

'Shouldn't we wait a little longer for Alla'fyr to return,' said a third.

'It's been five days.' Princess Eugenie stalked around the table. 'If we wait any longer, then Sawwse Bohge and her evil minions will have the Ancient Device in their hands.' She placed a hand on Cribbins' shoulder. 'What of the turnips?'

Several beads of sweat rolled down Cribbins' forehead. He needed to hustle. And he needed to hustle hard. 'Mmmhhhmmm. Fire. Lots of fire. Mmmhhmm. Burning buildings. Running. Maps.'

'Maps! The maps to the Ancient Device? What about them?'

'HMmhhmmm. Three pieces to make a whole. MMMhhhmmm. Three pieces retrieved elsewhere. MHMmmm. Three pieces of turnip at a discount rate–'

'Retrieved elsewhere...' Eugenie looked stricken. 'So, it is already too late?'

'I wouldn't say that.' The Council turned as one to locate the voice. It was a proboscis monkey, sat with its legs dangling from a window ledge and its nose dangling from its face. The monkey tossed an apple in the air, caught it, and took a bite.

'Your turnip didn't say anything about this,' muttered one of the more jealous councillors.

'How did you even get in?' Another councillor addressed the intruder before thinking better of it. 'Guards! Arrest this louche monkey and get its disgusting nose out of here at once!'

'Wait.' Eugenie approached the monkey. 'You're the agent Alla'fyr sent to Zell. I sense her energy on you.'

'Francesco.' The monkey tipped an imaginary hat. 'A pleasure.'

'What of the five knights I sent to accompany you?'

'All perished at the hands of Sawwse Bohge.'

Eugenie didn't need Francesco's nose to grow – and gods forbid it did, it was disgusting enough as it was – to know that this was a lie.

'But I know how you can get your revenge.' Francesco took another bite of the apple. He tossed it in the air, slipped down from the window ledge and transformed into his human form before his feet touched the ground. It was all rather slick up until the point he held his hand out to catch the apple and missed. It landed on his foot instead. 'That's not important.'

There was a series of low grumbles, dark mutterings, and murmurs of, 'Rhubarb, rhubarb' from the less clued-up members of the Council.

'Where is Alla'fyr?' asked Eugenie.

'She's not around anymore.'

'She's dead?'

'Oh no.' A wicked smile spread across Francesco's face. 'Much worse than that.'

The Council didn't like the sound of that. One of them cleared her throat. 'Ahem. I think it's perhaps time we distanced ourselves from mercenaries. Especially monkeys disguised as humans!'

'No,' said Francesco. 'This is my true form.'

'Seconded. A blanket ban on all long-nosed monkeys!'

'The monkey was the disguise.'

'Thirded!'

Francesco grimaced.

'Fourthded!'

Eugenie ignored them. 'You implied it wasn't too late. Meaning?'

'Wouldn't you like to know–'

Before Francesco could finish curling his lip into a smirk, Eugenie was on him, a sword pressed against his throat. 'I'm tired of this. I let Alla'fyr plot and scheme–'

'Often loudly,' added a councillor, helpfully.

'–because it was useful to me. But I'm tired. I'm tired, and sad, and angry, and ready to tear the whole world apart if it means bringing back my dearest papa. So, you'll tell me what you meant, and then you'll do everything in your power to help me retrieve the Ancient Device, or else I'll ensure your end is sharp and unpleasant.'

'Said the actress to the bishop.' A tall councillor with grey hair stood up. 'I'll see myself out.'

Francesco gulped. He'd significantly misread the situation. He had assumed Alla'fyr had been exerting influence on a weakened princess and enfeebled council. She had not mentioned that Princess Eugenie was extremely capable, nor that her council were stark raving mad. One of them was wearing a turnip on his head, for goodness' sake! 'Fine. I'll help you. I'll lead your knights to her.'

'No.' Eugenie took the sword from Francesco's neck. 'I will do this with my own hands.'

This caused a furore amongst the Council, with shouts of protest and pleas to what remained of Eugenie's rational brain. But it was all for naught. She had that look in her eyes again.

'Assemble the army. We will depart post-haste.' Eugenie scrunched up her face and ran a finger along her blade. 'I will personally make sure Sawwse Bohge regrets murdering my papa.'

Chapter 26:
The Path Forward

In a safe house on the outskirts of Spearca – house being an extremely generous description of this abode what with its barely-there roof and its ready-to-fall-apart walls – several members of the Actum Tempus adventurer's guild were resting, recuperating, and really, really bored.

'What's the rhyme again?' Sawwse was lying on her back on the floor of the dirty shack. She was bouncing a small rubber ball off the wall. It made a dull *thud* each time. *Thud. Thud. Thud.* 'I'd like to know a bit more about the Dorienne kingdom before they seek me out and murder me. Know thy enemy and all that.'

'They're not going to murder you,' said Rangrim, from a perch on a hay bale.

'Oh, yes. Of course.' *Thud. Thud. Thud.* 'My sworn protector will stop me from being murdered. Just like with Alla'fyr.'

'I said I was sorry!'

'Remind me what was so important that you felt like it'd be fine if I burnt to death in the most gruesome way?' *Thud. Thud. Thud.*

'There were…' Rangrim flushed red. 'Free cocktails.'

Sawwse pretended to strain to hear him. 'Sorry, did you say, "three cockatrices?"'

'Come on, Sawwse.' Ruby tugged at Sawwse's sleeve. 'It's been five days. Hasn't he suffered enough?'

'I'll tell you who crimping suffered.'

'Actually, your injuries all turned out to be superficial in the end, and only needed various ointments and low-level cantrips to heal.' Corinne appeared at the doorway to the shack. 'It was Osrik that felt the worst of Alla'fyr's wrath. Even Larn needed a short spell in the ICU.'[50]

'I would have been fine.' Larn lurked in the corner of the room with his arms folded across his chest.

'Except that the poison flowing through your body would certainly have killed you had it not been for Ruby's potion.'

'It tasted like burnt socks.'

'How would you even know what burnt socks tasted like?' asked Sawwse. *Thud. Thud. Thud.* 'Can you not just say "thank you" like a normal person?'

'Actually, I think I *did* put burnt socks in that potion,' said Ruby.

While Larn coughed to cover up a dry heave, Rangrim sidled closer to Sawwse. 'I am really sorry, you know.'

'Ugh. It's fine, Rangrim.' Sawwse punched him on the arm playfully. 'It's exhausting staying mad at someone, anyway.'

Rangrim smiled bashfully. 'In that case, the one thing I know about Dorienne is that rhyme to remember the six husbands of Queen Harriet: "Divorced, hung drawn

---

[50] Intensive Corinne Unit.

and quartered, atomised; divorced, stake through the heart, shrunk to the size of a shrimp."'

'I don't think any of that rhymes,' said Corinne.

Sawwse sat up. 'Er, it also makes them sound absolutely terrifying!'

'I'm misremembering.' Rangrim scratched the back of his head. 'I think it's actually: "Divorced, head fell off naturally, died unsuspiciously; divorced, head fell off naturally, survived and definitely isn't being followed."'

'That's not a lot better!'

'When can we leave this godsforsaken shack?' growled Osrik from the shadows. He was lain down on a sheet across several hales of bay.

'Ah, the patient is awake again.' Corinne hummed happily as she made her way over to Osrik. She hovered her hands a few inches over his body and made several 'hmm' and 'ahh' sounds. 'Your vitals are almost fully stabilised. And–'

'Good enough for me.' Osrik pushed Corinne's hand away and made to stand up, but his knees buckled. He muttered under his breath. 'You should've let me die.'

Corinne ignored him. 'As for why we haven't left yet, it's because we're waiting for some kind of message from Convener. It's more than likely that his long-range telepathy took a lot out of him, and he'll be in touch again soon once his energy is restored.'

Larn scoffed. 'And in the meantime, we're left sitting here twiddling our thumbs while Princess Eugenie grabs the Ancient Device!'

'Except that we have all the map fragments,' said Sawwse.

'Sort of.' Ruby pointed to a corner of the room where Mirrah was lain down still unconscious. A shining piece of the map was still clutched within one of her hands.

'I don't understand why you continue to let her live.' Larn looked down his nose at the others. 'If it were up to me, I would've killed her as soon as I had the chance.'

'Everyone already suggested that.' Sawwse shook her head in frustration.

'And it was Convener who rejected the idea?'

'Convener and I rejected it, yes.'

An awful smile played on Larn's lips. It said that without Convener here to stop them, why not kill the wizard and take the map fragment for themselves? After all, if they didn't kill her now, it would only be a matter of time before she killed them, accidentally or otherwise. It also literally said: 'I'm going to kill her now.'

Osrik, Rangrim, Corinne, and Ruby looked conflicted, but offered no resistance as Larn slowly walked towards Mirrah. His metallic legs whirred and clanked as he strode past the others. It was only Sawwse that stood in his way.

'I'm not beyond forcing you out of the way,' said Larn.

'I don't doubt it.' Sawwse crossed her arms in front of her chest. 'And I'm not beyond kneeing you in the gonads.'

'Well, I don't think there's any need for that.' Mirrah opened her eyes. The others recoiled in shock as she got up slowly and casually brushed the straw from her clothes. She looked at Sawwse and grinned. 'Helbo.'

'Mirrah!' Sawwse's eyes lit up. 'Are you okay?'

'Strangely, I feel absolutely fine. Oh. One moment. *Hurrrggghhh.*' She vomited out a rainbow of strangely shaped coins, feathers, and tiny statuettes of hippopotamuses. 'Ah, that's better.' Mirrah suddenly became aware of the cautious stares of the others. 'Why are they looking at me like that?'

Osrik, Larn, and Rangrim were holding tight to their weapons, Ruby was cowering behind Corinne's cloak, and Corinne was bracing herself for something bad to happen.

'Sorry, where are my manners.' Sawwse grimaced as though she'd committed a faux pas. 'This is the Actum Tempus guild. Well, most of it. Vadania is out hunting. Again. Everyone, this is Mirrah.'

'Greetings.' Mirrah knelt on one knee and placed a hand flat on the ground. She looked up. 'They're still staring.'

'Guys, don't be rude.'

Corinne coughed. 'Apologies. We are slightly awestruck at meeting a member of The Twelve, slightly trepidatious about sharing the same roof with someone who accidentally – we hope – caused the city of Zell and all of its citizens to vanish, and slightly anxious about your designs on the map fragment that you are holding in your right hand.' She turned to the others. 'Does that cover it?'

There was a nervous murmur of assent.

Mirrah nodded patiently, scratched her cheek, and then counted out Corinne's points on her fingers. 'What's "The Twelve?" Where's "Zell?" And what do you mean by "map fragment?"'

'Your memory's maybe gotten a smidge worse,' said Sawwse.

'I haven't forgotten you, Sawwse Bohge.' Mirrah smiled and a galaxy somewhere far, far away exploded. Sawwse could've melted right there and then, but she forced herself to concentrate. She pointed to Mirrah's right hand. Mirrah saw the shining object clutched within her fist for the first time. 'Curious.'

'It's a map to something really important.' Sawwse walked to Corinne and held out her hand. Reluctantly, Corinne handed over a scroll of parchment. On it was Convener's imprint of the first map fragment. Sawwse approached Larn. She gave him a look. 'Do you want to find the Ancient Device or not?' Larn sneered. He took off his pendant containing his piece of the map and placed it gently in Sawwse's palm. Sawwse made her way back to Mirrah's side and showed her the sketch and the pendant. 'I think you know how to find the way.'

'But… I can't remember anything,' said Mirrah.

'You remember me.' Sawwse smiled and took hold of Mirrah's hand. She guided it to the parchment. 'I think it'll work.'

Mirrah held the map fragments together and concentrated. She didn't really know what she was supposed to be concentrating on, but she sensed a general focused vibe would be a good thing. If there was a sound to perfectly accompany a bright, glowing golden light, that would be the sound that now rang out about the shack.[51] When she opened her eyes, the map fragments were gone, and she held the parchment in both hands. Sketched on it in golden ink was a detailed map to the Ancient Device.

'You did it!' Sawwse gazed at Mirrah tenderly.

Mirrah looked back at Sawwse and smiled her world-spinning smile. But then… she sneezed. 'Achoo!' And with that sneeze, she vanished from the shack.

There was a brief pause while the guild mates checked that what they thought had happened, had happened.

---

[51] *Shhhweeeaaaaammmm*. Or something like that.

'So, granted that's not ideal–' began Sawwse, but she was interrupted by a cacophony of complaints and insults.

'You imbecile!' shouted Larn.

'For goodness' sake!' growled Osrik.

'Oh no,' squeaked Ruby.

Vadania stepped through the door of the shack holding three hares bound together by their ears. She looked at Rangrim. 'What has he done this time?'

'Come on.' Rangrim threw his arms up in exasperation. 'That's not entirely fair.'

Vadania glowered at him. It was her that'd found him in a drunken heap during the fireworks festival after all. Dragging him to a safe place had distracted her from her sentry. This did not please her.

Rangrim sulkily pointed at Sawwse.

'Okay, let's look at the facts,' said Sawwse. 'Mirrah woke up and *didn't* explode or cause the world to end. That's massive, that is.' She coughed and muttered the next bit very quickly. '*And then I gave her the map fragments and she disappeared.*'

'What was that?' Vadania's brow furrowed.

'Oh, I just said that I *gave Mirrah the map fragments and she disappeared.*'

'So, it is you who has caused the world to end.'

'That's a bit much.'

'We're doomed,' said Ruby.

'There are *less* gloomy ways to look at it,' said Sawwse.

'I needed that Device,' muttered Larn.

Sawwse looked at the others. It was clear that they were thinking along the same lines. There was hunger and doubt and regret in their eyes. Except Corinne, who was on her hands and knees crawling through the bed of straw.

'Aren't you going to take your turn berating me?' Sawwse pouted childishly. 'Corinne? What's wrong?'

'I thought something was strange when all the clamour started, because I didn't sense any kind of teleportation magic.'

'But we saw her disappear,' said Sawwse.

'Exactly. You saw her *disappear*, but you didn't see her *teleport*.' Corinne stood up suddenly holding a very thin thread of cotton between her forefinger and thumb. It clearly came from Mirrah's cloak. 'I believe Mirrah turned invisible and left the shack on foot.' She pulled at the cotton fibre causing it to glow bright pink. When she removed her fingers, the thread floated in the air and then, as in a cartoon, twisted into an arrow and pointed out of the shack. 'With a bit of luck, this should – literally – point us in the right direction.'

'Achoo!'

'Oh. She's right there.'

About fifty metres away from the shack, in the middle of a woodland path, stood an un-disappeared Mirrah. She was holding the map above her head and turning it this way and that to try and decipher it.

'Mirrah!' Sawwse waved her arms about wildly, before turning back to the others. 'Don't worry, this will all have been a misunderstanding. Mirrah's the best. Watch.'

Mirrah clocked Sawwse. She held up a hand in recognition and then turned on her heel and ran in the opposite direction.

'For the love of crimp,' sighed Sawwse. She met the unimpressed scowls of the others. 'Save it. Let's just get after her.'

The guild mates ran out of the shack, following the cotton thread which now zipped through the air after Mirrah, while Mirrah sprinted down a woodland path leading further away from Spearca and towards the large, looming presence of the Blue Mountains.

Mirrah was fast, but Vadania and Larn were faster. The others watched as they closed the gap and then caught up with Mirrah just as they reached a dense thicket of trees and brambles. There were the sounds of a kerfuffle: yelping, scrapping, twanging. A bright flash of purple light. And then nothing.

'What happened?' asked Osrik.

When the rest of the group reached the thicket, there was no sign of Mirrah, Vadania or Larn. Instead, there were two large, neatly wrapped presents.

'Ooh presents!' Sawwse was about to open one of them when a rapier poked through it and stopped just short of one of her eyes.

Larn and Vadania burst out of their cardboard boxes, looking around desperately for Mirrah. The thin cotton fibre pointed the way forward, so they raced ahead behind it. Corinne, Rangrim and Sawwse did their best to keep up, but Osrik wheezed and spluttered. It was all still too much, too soon.

'Should've just let me be,' he muttered.

But then he felt hot breath on his hand and a long, flat head nuzzling his side. It was a horse. What were the chances? Quite slim if you discount the fact that he was travelling with a shapeshifter.

'Come on,' said Ruby. 'I don't shift for just anyone. Hop on before I lose my nerve.'

A slow grin spread over Osrik's face. And then they were away, through twisted barks and brambles after the others.

Though they'd lost sight of Mirrah again, it was easy to track her. Even the least successful hunter in the world could find her. That was because she had left a trail of utter chaos in her wake: there were brambles that writhed around and moaned about getting old, little wind-up birds that fell out of trees and duplicated each time they tweeted, and snooty snakes that wore monocles and top hats and said things like, "Pip pip!" "Tally ho!" and "Be a good dear and eat this apple."

Corinne desperately tried to reverse the chaos while keeping up with the others, and the others did their best to avoid the nastier magical miscellany i.e. a hornet grown to the size of a bear demanding a pollen tribute, and a bear the size of pollen demanding to be put out of its misery.

'This is hopeless!' said Sawwse. 'We're never going to catch her.'

'As long as we follow all this weird magic, we'll be fine,' said Rangrim. 'We'd be as well taking a rest. What's the rush?'

'She's going to find the Ancient Device!'

'Oh yeah.'

'Follow me!' Vadania shouted back to the others. 'I know a shortcut.'

'A shortcut to where?' Sawwse pointed out the obvious. 'We don't even know where she's going!'

They emerged through the thicket to face a long, wide stone path that led in one direction: *Slaepan Wiga.* The mountain towered above them, dominating the scenery.

'Gods. It really does look like a sleeping knight.' Sawwse was staring up at the figure in the mountain. That rounded boulder was the helmet, a craggy outcrop made up hands resting against its chest, a huge shard of gneiss for a sword.

Vadania tilted Sawwse's head down back to the path. Though Mirrah was too far in the distance to see clearly, her magic was continuing to spill out. There were hundreds of small dots either side of the path.

'What are they?'

'I do not see them clearly, but they appear to be woodland animals,' said Vadania.

'It's faint, but I *think* I hear them singing,' added Corinne.

'You're telling me there's a thousand woodland creatures following Mirrah and singing at her?' Sawwse sounded sceptical. But then she thought that that was exactly the sort of thing that could happen to Mirrah. 'That. Sounds. Amazing!'

'What doesn't sound amazing is *Slaepan Wiga*,' said Ruby, trotting alongside Vadania. 'You're not really considering leading us up there at night, are you?'

The sun was teetering over the edge of the mountain like a perfectly round orange atop a table shaped like a mountain.

'What's the problem?' asked Sawwse.

Ruby stared at her with a long face. 'There's all manner of beasties that come out at night.'

'And savages,' grumbled Osrik. 'More savages than before. More *savage* than before.'

'Plus, conditions are almost always favourable during daylight hours,' added Corinne. 'Of course, I could generate a simple light spell to help us find our way, but that would certainly attract the aforementioned beasts and savages to us.'

Sawwse was beginning to understand. 'So, what you're saying is, it'd be a really bad idea to climb this mountain while it's dark?'

Vadania stopped walking and turned to face the others. 'Need I remind you all how much I… *we* need the Ancient Device?'

She needn't, thought Sawwse, looking round the group. The hunger in their eyes was still present, but there was a desperation there too now. It was her responsibility to stop them from using the Ancient Device. And Mirrah too. *If I can just be with her, I'm sure I can make things right.*

'This way.' Vadania led them away from the stone path into a pine forest further along the base of the mountain. They moved through the pines without stopping: the path was less clear than the other route, but well-trodden enough that there were no real obstructions.

After a while, the ground beneath their feet became softer and then the forest abruptly ended. A large lake opened out before them, ringed by a sandy beach. It was the first time Sawwse had come across anything like it. Sure, the Blue Forest was near to the coast, but because of the travel ban she'd sooner have seen pigs fly than visit a beach. She rushed onto the sand, kicking it, rolling in it, and letting it run through her fingers.

The others watched this display with bemusement. How was it that Sawwse was able to take joy in something at a time like this? Wasn't the regret gnawing at her too, like a constant drip drip drip of Ancient Device acid dissolving the foundations of her mind until nothing else mattered but finding it?

'This is SO fun!'

Clearly not.

'Keep your voice down!' hissed Larn. He pointed to a timber-framed hut that stood about thirty feet back from the water. It was modest in size, but clearly well looked after.

'I know who lives here,' said Vadania unsmilingly. 'An old friend.'

'Yes, you seem positively thrilled,' said Sawwse, as she was dragged away from the sand by Rangrim.

'It has been many years, and it is complicated.' Vadania signalled for them to walk past the hut, but they had already been spotted.

'Too complicated to say hello?' The voice came from a blindfolded elf sitting cross-legged on the roof of the hut. It was weird that none of them had seen her there. Something to do with the dimming light and the fact that the elf hadn't wanted to be seen.

'My apologies.' Vadania bowed quickly in an act of deference that shocked the others. 'Time is of the essence, and we didn't want to intrude–'

'If you are referring to the powerful wizard traipsing up *Slaepan Wiga* then you do not need to worry.' A faint smile played at the lips of the elf. She rose and then backflipped from the hut, landing in front of the others. 'I thought I taught you to listen more closely than that.'

'Of course.' Vadania shook her head. 'My mind is not focused.'

'Then your mission will fail.'

'Keep it light,' said Sawwse.

'What do you mean we need not worry?' asked Rangrim.

'Mirrah has stopped moving.' Vadania pointed beyond a sheer rock face. 'Somewhere over there.'

Sawwse scratched her cheek. 'So, either she's taking a break, or…'

'She's already found the Ancient Device,' muttered Osrik.

'You may rest here,' said the blindfolded elf. 'I will offer you protection for this night, and alert you if the wizard moves.'

'We do not need your protection,' said Larn, crossing his arms in front of his chest. 'I alone will sufficiently ward off any intruders.'

Sawwse laughed. 'No offence, Larn, but she seems like a badass and you… well, you're one of the least trustworthy people I've ever met.'

'It is a great honour to be worthy of Prysta's shelter.' Vadania bowed once again and then stared at the others until they did the same. Even Larn.

Sawwse began strolling towards the door of the hut. 'Dibs on the top bunk.'

Vadania grabbed the neck of Sawwse's tunic. 'We will treat your beach with respect.'

Prysta nodded her head and then walked inside the hut. After she was gone, Vadania directed the others to set up camp outside. She walked Sawwse to the last empty tent and offered it to the gnome.

'But where will you sleep?' asked Sawwse.

'I'll meditate tonight.'

Sawwse watched Vadania stalk away from the camp. Inside her tent, Sawwse got herself as cosy as she could – this was difficult, because she was camping[52] – and tried to drift off to sleep. It took a while, which is often the case when the crazy wizard you've possibly, maybe, developed romantic feelings for has run away from you,

---

[52] Camping: be at one with nature, bugs, Dutch ovens, and bad backs.

and is heading towards an incredibly powerful machine that might destroy history itself. But eventually, she drifted off, unaware that another threat was approaching and that this threat wanted nothing more than to see Sawwse Bohge dead.

Chapter 27:
Slaepan Wiga

Across the other side of the mountain from Sawwse Bohge and co, an army had amassed. An army attacking a mountain would have looked ridiculous were it not for the sheer scale of said army. From above, you could hardly see the terrain for the rows upon rows of soldiers. From below, you could only see the soles of their boots, which was less impressive. Regardless, if this army was going to wage war on the mountain, you wouldn't fancy the mountain's chances. It was good then that the army was being mobilised for something else entirely, something that the Dorienne Council found even more ridiculous: to find a dangerously powerful wizard called Sawwse Bohge and follow her to a mysterious Ancient Device in order to reverse time and bring back the former king of Dorienne. Unfortunately, the one person in the world that didn't find this ridiculous was the one leading said army.

Princess Eugenie stood at the head of the Dorienne infantry. Her plated metal had been polished so much that she'd had a wizard cast a protective barrier around it to stop pigeons smashing into her headfirst. The blood red cloak fastened to her armour fluttered in the wind, which had the dual function of looking incredibly cool and keeping the bull-men regiment at a useful level of rage. A look of fierce determination was set in Eugenie's eyes. There'd been enough delay, so she'd taken matters into her own hands. Those hands now held a leash. Eugenie tugged at it.

'Gargh!' The collar at the other end of the leash tightened, briefly choking Francesco who wore the collar around his neck. He was in his human form, which made the whole thing much more humiliating. A look of wild desperation was set in his eyes. What the hell had he gotten himself into? He had no idea where Sawwse Bohge was and nor did he care! He'd simply led Eugenie to the mountain out of instinct. It was worth a punt. And if Bohge wasn't here, surely there'd be an opportunity for him to escape amidst the beasts, the savages, and the blizzards. The leash tightened again. 'Gack!'

'Come on, doggy. Show me the way.'

That's if he didn't die of embarrassment first…

…Further up the mountain, Mirrah felt a rough tongue licking at her cheek. Her vision was bleary. 'Wha'stha'?'

It was a fox. And a squirrel. And a badger. And a cramble knadger. In fact, there were any number of woodland animals surrounding her in this… cave? Mirrah looked around. It wasn't a very large cave. More like a crevice. Was this a normal way to wake up? She couldn't remember. She assessed the animals who stared back at her with big eyes, and then, as one, began to sweetly serenade her.

Aaaaahhhhh aahhh laaaa baaaahhh aaahhh laaaa.

No. This was not normal.

'Okay, that's probably enough of that.' Mirrah held up a hand to quiet the animals. They did so. Even the otters, who clearly had the best singing voices. 'Can any of you tell me what I'm doing here?'

The animals stared back at her blankly.

'You can sing, but you don't know how we got here?'

'Exsqueeze me, ma'am.' A vole next to Mirrah tugged at her cloak. 'But would it be a possibwility to send us home now? I've dwedfully enjoyed all the singy-winging, but I need to get back to my cosy-wosy ickle nest.'

'Well, that's probably the most irritating thing I've ever heard. But yes. Of course I'll send you home. You'll just need to remind me where you live.' Mirrah waved her hand idly as she spoke. There was a loud pop and all the animals vanished from the crevice. Mirrah cocked her head. She was about to assess what exactly she'd just done but thought better of it. There were more important things to do. Namely, getting out of a crevice that was absolutely covered in animal droppings, dung, manure, scat, and poop. Mirrah gagged and ran outside.

The scene was worthy of a postcard. There was the Spearcian woodland park, over there was a beautiful stream leading to an idyllic lake surrounded by a forest of pines, and behind was the *Slaepan Wiga* mountain extending into the clouds.

Once Mirrah had taken in the scene, she looked down at her hands. She was holding a map drawn in golden ink. And then she remembered something. She'd run away from Sawwse Bohge. She felt awful. 'It's because I didn't want her to get involved in this. It's too dangerous.' *But what's too dangerous*? thought Mirrah. She traced her finger over the golden ink and felt an awful movement within her head, as if someone was playing tug of war with her cerebral cortex.

If the Ancient Device could have talked it would've said: 'Oi! You! Muppet! I'm up here! Bloody get on with it!' Instead, Mirrah heard the guttural churning of machinery and suddenly knew exactly where she must go…

…'She's on the move.' Prysta sat cross-legged atop her hut next to Vadania in the dawn light. They had spent the night meditating. Well, Prysta had spent the night meditating. Vadania had spent the night replaying that crucial event from her past over and over. This would usually fill her with rage. The rage she needed to continue her quest of vengeance. But this was different. She only felt regret, remorse, grief, and a compulsion to turn back time before her village was ever destroyed.

In fact, all the guild mates had slept poorly. The Ancient Device was much closer now, so its power was unbowed. It would take a tremendous amount of *fortitude* to escape its clutches at this range. Or, you had to be Sawwse Bohge, who didn't really regret anything. Her bad night was simply camping related.

'People actually choose to do this?' Sawwse stumbled out of her tent holding her lower back. 'I feel like I've aged about a century.'

'We need to go.' Vadania jumped from the roof of the hut and bowed deeply to Prysta. She turned back to the others. 'Now.'

The others gathered their things and followed Vadania away from the hut, nodding, bowing, and waving thanks to Prysta with varying degrees of enthusiasm as they went. They trailed around the circumference of the lake until they reached the mouth of a river.

'Mirrah is heading that way,' said Vadania. 'Following the river will be our quickest ascent. We can intercept her near the river's source.'

'Lead on,' grumbled Osrik.

The guild mates trekked through dense woodland to stay alongside the river, so Rangrim and Vadania took it in turns to cut a path for the others. The river swelled and narrowed, thickened and thinned, bulged and dwindled throughout their journey, until it maintained a relatively rapid flow, cutting through a rugged mountain path. The treeline was replaced by jagged rocks and low grass. Occasionally, the path fell away, so they gripped the sturdy mosses growing on the rocks and shimmied along at the water's edge.

After a couple of hours, the guild mates paused to catch their breath. The river was simply a shallow stream now. Sawwse sidled up to Vadania, who knew that nothing good usually came from sidling.

'No, we're not nearly there yet,' said Vadania.

'That wasn't what I was going to say, actually.' Sawwse quickly thought of something else to say. 'I was going to ask about Prysta.'

'Oh.'

'Well, go on then. Who is she?'

Rangrim looked on. He would've cringed at Sawwse's lack of tact, but he was interested in Vadania's answer. At least, in whether Prysta was a past flame or not.

Vadania sighed. 'Prysta takes people in when they are lost and gives them purpose. She is also one of the finest swordswomen across the Four Continents.'

'Then why haven't I heard of her?' scoffed Larn.

'The name is not familiar to me either,' muttered Osrik.

'Fame does not equate to skill.'

'That's true!' Rangrim agreed enthusiastically. 'How else do you explain Swordington Jones? Most famous swordsman in the world? Pah! Doesn't even do his own stunts!'

'I was lost too.' Ruby spoke quietly and sadly. She didn't add that she didn't really know what it felt like to be found.

One way or another, the others all knew what she meant. Osrik grumbled in agreement, Larn scowled, Corinne twiddled with her cloak, Rangrim scratched the back of his head, and Vadania tensed her jaw.

Crimp. Sawwse sensed the mood was about to plummet. If it was up to her to keep morale up, then it was time to sing. It was also time to cheat. Sawwse didn't know what the Ancient Device was doing to her guild mates' minds, and she couldn't hope to compete against ancient magic that powerful, but she needed to at least try. As she sang, Sawwse *imbued* her lyrics with warmth, with fondness, with love, and, most importantly, with laughter.

Oh, the grand old duke of Blork,
She had ten thousand hens;
She bukaaaaawed! them up to the top of the hill,
And she bukaaaawed! them down again.

Rangrim was the first to go. Ruby followed swiftly behind. And then Corinne's polite chuckle turned into a full-blown belly laugh. The other three were a tougher audience, but Sawwse's *imbued* song was already softening Osrik's grumbles, gently relaxing Vadania's tense jaw, and even weaving its way behind Larn's scowl.

When they were ducks, they were ducks,

And when they were clowns, they were clowns,
And when they were only halfway duck,
They were neither duck nor clown!

This finished them all off. Whether it was that their *fortitude* had been weakened by the Ancient Device, or whether it was just exactly what they needed, it didn't really matter. They fell about laughing. Even Larn, whose laugh was high-pitched and manic, and sounded a bit like someone attacking a violin with a cheese grater. 'Again!' he shouted. But then, after noticing the surprised looks of the others, he added, 'If you absolutely insist on singing that is.'

'Gladly!' Sawwse scrabbled up onto Rangrim's back and began her song all over again, this time with accompaniment from the others. It was a joyous scene and just what they needed to take their minds of the Ancient Device…

…Sat within its chamber deep within the mountain, the Ancient Device lay in wait. If it had been capable of growing a moustache, the ends of its moustache would've been relentlessly twiddled. If it had had hands, it would have used them to stroke a fluffy white cat in as menacing a way as possible. If it had been capable of rehearsing a speech, it would have rehearsed the living daylights out of its 'Master Plan' speech, complete with evil laugh. Instead, the Ancient Device lay in wait and plotted. As much as an insentient machine could plot.

Fortunately for the Ancient Device, there was no need to do much plotting. Its magic had already done its job. It had found people with enough regret in their lives that they would ruin the world if it meant changing something. And now that those people were on the mountain, it could draw them in with relative ease…

…Princess Eugenie felt the tug inside her mind. It was unlike anything she'd felt before. It was as if a tiny man inside her brain had yoinked her cerebellum and shouted: 'This way!' She could have laughed. All that time and effort searching for clues, and the answer just popped into her head. Eugenie turned to the nearest army official, General Fandango. 'You're dismissed.'

'But ma'am, I've served the Dorienne crown for many years–'

'No, I mean all of you.' Eugenie gestured to the masses of soldiers. 'Send them home.'

'They've come a long way for you. To not see battle at this point… For a soldier that's like a cat not seeing inside a toilet bowl before it craps.' General Fandango was notoriously bad at similes.

'They are too slow. I know where I must go, and I must get there before Sawwse Bohge.' Princess Eugenie signalled to the knights who made up her elite guard to follow her. 'Go home, general.'

'And what do I do about… this?' General Fandango held up the leash connected to Francesco. The shapeshifter was resting his head on his fist, tapping his foot, and sighing, signalling in about as performative a way as possible that he was bored.

Eugenie waved her hand dismissively and then without another word began scrambling up a rock wall to reach a higher path along the mountain. Her elite knights followed swiftly behind.

'Er, right.' General Fandango scratched his clean-shaven cheek. He was usually very good at decision making, even though it largely revolved around shouting 'Attack it!' at the top of his lungs. Being stumped was new. Strangely, the army didn't have a process in place for how to handle the 'strange man the Princess kidnapped and held hostage but then released into your custody'.

Francesco watched as the general weighed up his options. 'I'll make it easy,' said Francesco with a tut. He grew one of his nails into a tiger's claw and unlocked the collar around his neck. Francesco tossed it to one side and then stretched his neck one way, then the next.

'Right. Yes. You are free to go. I'll allow it.' Something dawned on the general. 'Could you not have done that at any time?'

'Hah!' Francesco pointed to Princess Eugenie who was already quite some distance away. 'With that monster around?'

'Er, yes. Right. Of course.'

There was an awkward pause while each man waited for the other to leave first. After as much as this as Francesco could take, he rolled his eyes, shook his limbs into wings and burst into the air as an eagle. He should have left, there and then, flown back to his undercover operation in Magnarra and be done with it. But something was stopping him, and it rhymed with brevenge. *What harm could come from a quick look round the mountain for that gnome? She's the reason I suffered that humiliation after all.* As Francesco sliced through the air on the hunt, he caught a scent on the wind…

…'Would a shower have killed you?' Sawwse held her nose as she walked alongside Osrik. The company continued their ascent up the mountain. The river was now long gone. It had branched off and fallen away below them. They trekked higher until they reached the mountain's plateau, a sparse landscape of heather and not much else. Various peaks rose up around them. 'I know we're busy trying to stop the end of the world and everything, but even then, there are limits to what is socially acceptable.'

Osrik grunted.

This was about as much as he'd said since the singalong, and Sawwse was getting worried. Her lively song had cheered her guild mates up, but it turned out it was quite difficult to sing and climb a mountain at the same time, so she couldn't keep it up. Without her *imbued* music, the others were falling prey to dark thoughts. She needed to change tack. Distract them.

'Ruby, you're into plants. Maybe you could tell us about all this heather?'

Ruby flushed bright red. 'Won't people find that boring?'

'Yes,' said Larn.

'*No.*' Sawwse shot Larn a sour look. 'It'll be fun. Something to cheer us up!'

'Well, er, okay. If you're sure.' Ruby scratched the back of her head and then after a couple of false starts began talking. 'Heather plants are usually much more vividly coloured than this. The particular purple or pink pigments can be extracted and used in potions to cure colour blindness. But this heather doesn't look right at all. It's dying.' She carefully picked a stem from one of the plants. It was a faded rusty colour and clearly in ill health. Ruby rubbed the leaves between her fingers. The heather turned to a fine powder and floated away in the wind. 'Something's been sapping energy from this entire plateau.'

'Such fun,' muttered Sawwse under her breath.

'Savages,' said Osrik.

'It's not savages.' Larn scoffed. 'There's nothing up here for savages.'

'Trust me. I don't know what they want, but they're here.' Osrik pointed to the ground. It'd clearly been well trodden.

'I see tracks from humans, goblins, and horses,' said Vadania. 'But there's something I don't recognise. There.'

The others had to squint to see it, but in the distance the heather had been crushed by something that had left huge, ridged tracks deep in the earth.

'A monster?' asked Sawwse. She hadn't seen mention of such a thing in the Gnomeopedia.

'Probably best if we keep moving, just to be on the safe side.' Corinne ushered them towards the floating thread of fabric, which was still forming an arrow and pointing, but was running out of seam, and so only performed its function in the most half-hearted of ways. Corinne knelt beside Ruby while the others walked on. 'I have a task for you. Would it be possible to scout around the area in the sky? It'd be prudent to know if something heads in our direction.'

Ruby nodded bashfully. She handed her rucksack to Corinne and then shook out her limbs. Once she was ready, Ruby crouched into a ball and wrapped her arms around herself. Long, downy white feathers protruded from her skin. Her head puffed up with fur and then moved jerkily this way and that. Owl-Ruby leant her body forward, almost horizontal, brought her wings above her head and flew up across the plateau.

Gliding over the plains of sad heather, Ruby was uncomplicatedly anxious. What the hells was she doing in an adventuring guild? Let alone scouting for savages that quite probably had specifically trained to hit Ruby-shaped owls out of the sky! This was madness.

Ruby's eyes swivelled as she flew along her guild mates' circumference high above them in the sky. There was nothing of note. She could see the path continuing north, but there were no savages as far as she could tell. Ruby took a wider arc. Yes, this was an act of madness. And yes, she was petrified. But her mind was set on finding the Ancient Device. If she could only use it before the others, she'd have a chance at feeling, you know, normal. Whatever that was.

Huh. What's that? There was a black speck in her peripheral vision. She swivelled her eyes round to focus. 'Oh no.' It was a huge eagle heading straight for her. Ruby arced through the sky. She'd gone too far from the others. She pivoted right and dove fast. Whipping her head back, Ruby instantly understood it was too late. The eagle's severe, cold eyes were upon her. It grabbed her wings with its talons and ripped through them. Ruby squealed in pain.

'I'm after yer friend,' said Francesco, clacking his sharp beak close to Ruby's ears.

Francesco was forcing Ruby down through the air at such speed that she could barely breathe. She spluttered out sounds, but no words. Ruby desperately tried to shift into something smaller, something able to escape his clutches, but she was in too much pain to concentrate.

'But it looks like something bad's coming this way, and I ain't got time to get mixed up in that.' Francesco released his talons. 'Tell that gnome it's not the last she'll see of me!'

Ruby careened towards the ground. She tried as hard as she could to catch a wind current but couldn't spread her wings fast enough. She was going to crash land. Ruby wrapped her wings around her body, tucked her claws inside her fur, and folded herself up as small as she would go.[53] She skidded along the ground through the heather, leaving a trail of dust behind her.

The madness wasn't over. A deep vibration shook the earth.

Ruby raised her head pitifully, scratched behind her ear with a spare talon, and then slowly shifted back to human. 'Afleghm!' She coughed out a handful of feathers and then assessed the damage to her arms. They were very sore. She couldn't move the right one very well at all.

And then the vibrations became more violent.

And then Ruby saw what was making them.

And then Ruby ran.

Slightly further up the mountain, Sawwse was continually checking a mime watch on her wrist. 'She said she'd be back by now.'

'I'm sure she's fine.' Corinne smiled reassuringly. 'It's been ten minutes at most.'

'Ten minutes! Oh no!'

'That's not a very long time.'

'I think we should check on her.'

Corinne stopped walking and paused beside the gnome. 'Not to state the obvious, but I think you are probably better equipped to do that than me. Just look up.'

'Yeah, right. And then you flick my chin or something. I wasn't born yesterday!'

'I don't see her in the sky,' said Vadania.

---

[53] Following the age-old advice: In the event of a crash, put your tray table up, put your head between your legs and kiss your arse goodbye.

'I saw her get taken out by some kind of eagle,' said Larn.

'Larn!' Sawwse gave him an exasperated look. 'Why didn't you say something?'

'I've got other things on my mind.'

'There, in the distance.' Vadania suddenly pointed at the western horizon. She drew her blades. 'Movement.'

The others squinted. A tiny smudge gradually emerged at the farthest edge of their vision. The smudge began to take shape. It looked like a gazelle. In fact, it was a gazelle. And it was running towards them rather quickly. And it was screaming.

'Is it shouting something?' asked Sawwse.

'Strangely, my PhD isn't in gazelle,' said Larn.

'Ha! In gazelle!' Rangrim laughed.

Sawwse crossed her arms in front of her chest. 'Since when are we rewarding Larn's bad manners?'

Rangrim scratched his beard. 'Sorry.'

'We need to go,' grumbled Osrik.

The gazelle was making ground quickly, despite a slight limp in its front right leg. It screamed again. 'Ruuuuuuun!'

'Oh, it's fine!' Sawwse clapped Osrik on the shoulder. 'It's saying "Fuuuuun!" I think it just wants to play with us.'

An awful tremor shook the ground around the plateau, and a not unrelated deep sense of dread and unease spread amongst the guild mates. Ruby's gazelle form was closer again and this time her voice was entirely intelligible. 'RUUUUUUN!'

'Or "Run,"' said Sawwse. 'It could've been "Run."'

Over the western horizon, giant vehicular machines roared towards them. Diseased rust covered their bodies, heavy duty tracks ran underneath them, and sharp, spider-like legs clawed along the ground. They looked almost shambolic, but less in a 'quaint seaside town' kind of way, and more in a 'diseased rusty truck about to run you down' kind of way. Outpacing the machines were smaller groups of savages on horseback. They were catching up with Ruby.

Vadania and Larn shot away along the path to the north. Osrik and Corinne followed swiftly behind. Rangrim grabbed Sawwse, flung her onto his back, and then also began running.

'We need to wait for Ruby!' shouted Sawwse.

Ruby wasn't far from them now, but Francesco's attack had left her too injured to run any faster. She couldn't close the distance between her and Rangrim, and the savages drew nearer with every breath.

Sawwse shouted to her. 'Turn into a goldcrest!'

'But I can't use my wings!'

'The momentum will fire you forward! I'll catch you!'

With tears streaming down her long gazelle nose, Ruby looked up at Sawwse's smiling face. Not for the first time, she decided to put her faith in her weird friend. Ruby pushed herself one last time, leaping as far forward as she could. She shrank from gazelle to goldcrest mid-leap and aimed towards Sawwse's hands.

Sawwse snatched Ruby's tiny goldcrest form from the air. 'I caught the snitch!'

'What?' asked Rangrim.

'Doesn't matter.' Sawwse clutched Ruby close to her chest and felt her little heart beat so fast. But she wasn't ashamed of running away.

It was necessary. The savages drew closer. The great towering machines were still some way off, but the horse-riding goblins and humans had closed the gap significantly.

'At this speed, they'll reach us in no time.' Vadania pointed to a craggy outcrop in the distance. 'Look. There's a cave up ahead.'

The savages fired arrows, which, in the law of all chase sequences, missed or glanced off the guild mates' armour. But they were also now close enough to see the glint of their gold teeth and tacky jewellery. The savages brought their horses alongside the group, encircling them, and then took it in turns to lean in close and swipe at them with their scimitars.

'Corinne, how far along are you in writing your 'no death on quests' policy?' asked Larn, between ducks and dodges.

'I am so proud of you for asking!' Corinne blushed. 'It'll take a few more revisions before I'm finished, but best practice dictates that we adhere to–'

'Good.' Larn jumped into the air and kicked out with both of his metallic legs, stunning the savage off of her horse into the ravine below. Then, he slashed his rapier to the now riderless-horse's legs, causing it to stumble and fall, crashing into three more of the savages who fell into the gorge as well.

'Not quite what I had intended.' Corinne caught the horses mid-fall in a magical bubble. 'Only to be expected from the rogue in our group, though in no way condoned. So long as the rest of us maintain restraint–' A spray of green goblin blood painted Corinne's robes as Vadania dispatched two more of the bandits with her twin blades.

The remaining bandits pulled back to the roaring machines, just as the guild mates reached the cave. Larn bolted inside, but Vadania faltered at the entrance. 'I don't know where this leads.'

‘It leads away from the savages.’ Osrik barrelled through the cave mouth.

‘It’ll be fine.’ Rangrim caught up. ‘I grew up on a mountain just like this. We’ll find a path one way or another.’

‘They’ve stopped.’ Corinne rested her hand on the hard rock that made up the cave entrance and felt the vibrations cease. She took out her spell book and rifled through the pages. ‘I’ll put a ward on the entrance.’

The others watched as the rusty, blood red bodies of the giant vehicles slowly opened. Inside each one, there were at least two hundred more bandits waiting. Loud trumpets sounded from the tops of each machine. With one huge roar, the savages inside charged towards the cave.

‘There’s no time.’ Vadania snapped Corinne’s book closed and shepherded the others into the cave.

They found Larn and Osrik up ahead, slowed by tight, winding, inclining passages. They squeezed through and continued along the rising paths, hampered by the low ceilings. Sawwse slunk down from Rangrim’s shoulders and finally found an advantage to being a “short arse” in this world of big people. She led the way further into the cave system, which continued to elevate.

Behind them, the sound of the savages grew louder. It was clear they’d entered the cave. Also, one of the savages shouted, ‘We’ve entered the cave!’ The savages slipped through unseen tunnels and crawled across the walls to catch up with the guild mates.

Sawwse screeched to a halt as a chasm appeared in front of her. A chunk of rock fell into the void below. She didn’t even hear it land. Not because the drop was so vast – although it was – but because Osrik pointed out a hastily constructed rope bridge, and her attention was immediately taken by the narrow, crumbling ledge that led to it. It wasn't ideal, but it was either that or the savages. She had to at least ask the question. 'What will the savages do if they catch us?'

'Flay you alive. Eat you alive. Burn you alive.' Osrik casually walked along the thin edge. 'Play with your body like you're some kind of meat puppet–'

'–Alive, is it?'

Osrik grunted.

'Thought so.' Sawwse shimmied towards the rope bridge.

'There must be another way.' Panic was clearly audible in Larn's voice. He turned away from the chasm back towards the passageway they'd just come out of. 'I'll fight my way through them.'

'There's too many of them.' Rangrim followed Vadania along the ledge towards the bridge. 'Are you scared of heights or something?'

'Of course not, you insolent fool!' Larn's voice was growing shrill.

Rangrim shrugged. He wasn't going to try too hard to persuade Larn.

'I believe I may have bought us some time.' Corinne was standing next to Larn. She was holding her flat palms out in front of her, but… nothing was happening. 'Hm. Curious.'

'What was that? What did you just do?' Larn was now at his shrillest. Sheer panic partied across his face as he patted his body all over. 'I will not be ballooned again!'

Corinne scratched her chin. 'Well, I had assumed a torrent of water would burst forth from my hands, flooding the savages in the tunnels before they could reach us. But that clearly hasn't happened. Unless I misplaced the morpheme relating to location while uttering the incantation, which would result in the water starting, not at my hands, but somewhere else entirely.'

Larn and Corinne stood together in silence for a few moments. The panicked shrieks of the savages echoed through the caves, before being completely subsumed into a noise so loud that it was impossible to make out anything else. It was the sound of gallons of water rushing towards them.

'BALLOON MEEEE!' shrieked Larn.

Corinne pushed him onto the narrow ledge and shimmied round herself, just as a biblical-level flood gushed out of the cave and flushed dozens of savages into the depths below.

But the threat was far from over.

As Corinne and Larn made it to the other side of the rickety bridge, dozens more savages crawled lizard-like along the cave walls, their cloven feet almost hewed to the rocks. If this wasn't disturbing enough, they took out short bows and fired arrows wrapped in razor wire across the chasm. And if *that* wasn't disturbing enough, some of them had mullets and nose studs.

Osrik held up his large oaken shield to give the others cover as they found a way forward: another escalating passage. As soon as they reached it, Vadania dragged Osrik through the entrance.

The slopes in the next cave were very steep, elevating up past jagged protrusions of rock. Sawwse and the others followed the tight passageways around until they came to a giant slab of gneiss. It completely blocked their path forward. The exact opposite of what they needed.

'This is the exact opposite of what we need!' shouted Sawwse.

Corinne put her hands to the gneiss for any sign that it might give way. 'Even with magic, this would prove very difficult to move.'

Down at the bottom of the slope, Vadania and Osrik were holding off the hordes of bloodthirsty and tasteless savages. But there were simply too many of them: they were on the walls, on the bridge, in the mouth of the cave.

Osrik smashed his battle-axe through three of the savages. 'Maybe I'll regain some of my honour if I die fighting.'

'And what? Lose your chance at using the Device.' Vadania spoke through gritted teeth while she slashed at the barbed-wire arrows.

It was the first time anyone in the guild had spoken with each other about using the Ancient Device, and it instantly created an uneasy feeling between the elf and the dwarf. If camaraderie was a physical thing, it would've plummeted into the gorge below.

Osrik grunted.

Vadania growled.

Back at the other end of the passage, Rangrim was whispering something to himself.

'Did you just fist pump?' asked Sawwse.

Rangrim beamed at the others. 'I think it's finally time.' He gave Sawwse a thumbs up, unsheathed the gigantic sword from his back and said, 'Get back,' in as deep and heroic a voice as possible. And then, with a huge roar Rangrim drew his sword in a large overhead arc and crashed it through the gneiss. The slab of rock immediately fissured, splitting down the middle. 'And that, my friends, is called being a hero.'

Sawwse shared a rare knowing look with Larn. As the gneiss cracked and widened, the cave floor started vibrating, and not in a relaxing foot massage kind of way. It was going to split open.

At the entrance to the cave, the savages stopped their assault. Even the savages, who were fuelled by rage, and seemed to have so little brain capacity that they found eating human skin a reasonable pastime, were aware of the gravity of the situation. They stared, horrified, as fractures appeared on the walls, ceilings, and floors all over the cave. The savages frantically clambered over each other to escape.

Vadania and Osrik caught up to the others.

Rangrim's cheeks glowed scarlet. 'Why's everyone looking at me like that? I split the gneiss, didn't I?'

The gneiss had indeed split, but so had the floor. And the gap in the floor was rapidly getting wider.

'Look!' Sawwse pointed ahead at a faint white light glowing in the distance.

Larn sprinted through the newly formed gap in the gneiss. The others swiftly followed, dodging sharp rocks that fell from the ceiling, and jumping from one side of the now gaping void in the floor to the other. The white light grew brighter and stronger until they burst out of the cave back onto the mountain proper.

Sawwse scurried and scampered away from the collapsing cave. Spinning around, she shouted, 'Look out below!' Her voice echoed into the distance, as the cave consumed itself and disappeared into an avalanche.

A thick blanket of snow covered the mountain's surface. The biting cold wind cut through the guild mates' clothes and armour. A thick mist engulfed their entire view. But views didn't matter to those that were no longer looking.

Osrik was the first. He crunched through the snow into the mist.

Vadania followed, striding alongside Osrik without acknowledgement.

'Er, guys?' said Sawwse. The mood felt very different from their singalong further down the mountain. 'Where are you going?'

Larn scowled and walked away.

'Weren't we supposed to follow Corinne's thread?'

Rangrim bowed his head and trudged into the mist.

'I'm sorry, Sawwse,' said Corinne. 'We no longer need to follow Mirrah, because the Ancient Device is now in here.' She tapped the side of her head. 'I tried to stop it, but it's no use. I imagine this might ruin the working relationships we've spent time building, but it feels unavoidable.' Corinne glided away through the snow.

With some effort, Ruby lifted her head out of Sawwse's pocket and then fell out, turning human the moment her feet touched the ground. She looked back at Sawwse sadly, and then hurriedly caught up with the others.

Sawwse watched in disbelief. The others were silently clawing, climbing, shuffling, slogging, tramping, and trekking through the snow. It was all she could do to keep up with them.

'Come back!' Sawwse ploughed on. She had no idea what to do. 'How about another song? We could sing one about not using an insanely dangerous machine to turn back time?'

Over a ridge and a short scramble up a rock face, she came to a long, flat pathway. Curiously, no snow lay at her feet. At the end of the path, Sawwse's guild mates stood in front of another cave mouth. It glowed invitingly.

'Right, let's come up with a plan of how to shut down this Device,' said Sawwse, catching up. 'Corinne, you love a plan. How about it?'

No one acknowledged her. Ruby stepped inside the cave. The others followed. Slowly at first, but then they grabbed and shoved at each other to get inside first. Sawwse had to run to keep up.

'Stop it! This isn't like you!' Sawwse paused. 'Except maybe Larn. But you should stop too!'

They ran further into the cave and emerged into a large chamber. And there it was. The Ancient Device. A gigantic metal machine built into the craggy walls of the cave. The large circular body of the machine was fitted with hundreds of instruments, gauges, and gizmos. Pistons protruding from its core. Rust had eaten large swathes of the Device, but its glowing heart shone a menacing red. Forgotten runes danced along the machine's surface. If it could have spoken, it would have said: 'Yet more have arrived for my pity party, how exquisite! Let me see which one of you will be of most use to me.' Instead, it emitted a metallic screech like a brass band thrown into a woodchipper. Its pistons roared into life. Thick mist hissed out from tiny holes all over the Device and surrounded the stupefied guild mates. As the mists swallowed them, the machine reached out its shadowy tendrils and clawed hold of their minds…

Chapter 28:

The Ancient Device

Pale moonlight filtered through a grove of ash trees, a gentle stream ran softly into a pool, and a weird bird made an irritating hooting noise. The scene was the same as Vadania always remembered it, except for the thin layer of milky white mist which now covered everything.

Vadania saw herself sitting by the water's edge. She remembered clearly every moment of that day: the white, loose-fitting robes, Soldi's symbol painted on her forehead, and the cooling refreshment of the soaked cloth on her face.

Gathering water for the temple had once been her favourite activity. Sitting alone by the pool had brought her great peace over the years. But knowing this moment as well as she did, Vadania also knew that that peace would be shattered very soon. She watched her younger self sighing contentedly, before picking up the bucket and walking back to the temple.

The shadow appeared sooner than she had realised. Vadania chastised herself for not sensing it. It lingered over the woods, blocking out the light. She looked up and for the first time, saw it clearly. It filled her body with dread. The massive scale of the dragon had been lost to memory's trickery, but here it was presented as clearly as on that fateful day. Its huge scales still glistened green and black under the moonlight, but Vadania now also took in the malevolent, malicious face. It spoke through a grin of endless daggers, and it said, '*No Hope.*'

It was true. It *was* hopeless. All that questing for vengeance now seemed ridiculous. The scale and power of the dragon was too much.

The scene skipped forward, and her temple was ablaze, her village crushed. The dragon reared its head back and screamed a merciless roar into the night sky. How could she possibly compete with such overwhelming power? Vadania slumped to her knees, broken.

That was when the Ancient Device posed the question. Well, it made a metallic gurgling sound by grinding its gears together, but somehow the screech of metal-on-metal resembled words, and somehow Vadania knew exactly what it asked.

'*WILL YOU RETURN?*'

The white mists flurried…

…When they cleared, Larn saw a ring of light encircling his younger self, kneeling on the floor. Forbidden books lay open, sprawled across the room. Watching this scene unfold from the perspective of a spectral essence, Larn understood immediately what was happening. He looked at the fourteen-pointed chalk circle, the occult books and all the ritual materials with scorn. Spectral-Larn spoke into the memory. 'Was I really this primitive?'

Reading from his notes, the younger Larn recited an exiled language. It was forbidden, almost forgotten, and sounded a bit like a frog playing a harmonica. Larn had pieced together fragments from various artefacts over the years, and now breathed fresh life into the language, the first to speak it since it had become extinct. The Larn of the present was still a little proud of that, at least.

A light breeze began to blow, turning the pages of the books. Something went quickly wrong. There was a loud sucking noise, like a drain capturing water or a troll eating spaghetti. The breeze turned into a sharp wind, which whipped at Larn's clothes and bit at his head, shoulders, knees and toes (knees and toes). Larn held onto his notes with one hand and steadied himself with the other. He couldn't catch his breath. Then, an ear-splitting pop and a horribly evil laugh.

'Pathetic.' Spectral-Larn looked on at his younger self. He laughed at the panic spreading over his face and through his body. 'Don't worry, it'll be over soon.'

Shelves snapped, candles melted, glass smashed under the incredible force. The memory of the demon's dark eyes and pale face was summoned up. It laughed as it arrived back in the world from which it had been banished.

Spectral Larn watched the rest of the scene play out: the contract was given (that he hadn't read), payment was taken (his legs and his soul), and his room was set ablaze by the callous monster.

A bright orange glow flickered in Larn's spectral eyes as he stared at his cowering younger self. Then, the image changed. The white mists swirled around him, resetting the scene. And then the deep, guttural machine language spoke: '*WILL YOU RETURN?*'

Larn smirked, looking around the room once more. 'I don't know, what do you think?'

A cold, menacing voice issued from deep within Larn's mind. *Interesting gambit, little human*, said the demon.

'Yes, I thought so too.'

This magic is ancient. It predates me.

Of course, Larn already knew all this. It was why he had been so desperate to reach the Ancient Device. There would be nothing the demon could do to stop his reversing of time, because the Device outpowered it. Obviously, it wouldn't have been ideal had the machine fallen into the wrong hands, but he was here for this moment. The moment when the sickening, self-satisfied grin was wiped off the demon's face.

Larn sneered. 'It's time to renegotiate the terms of our contract.'

Hssssssss. The demon hissed like a livid goose.

And then the mists swirled and spun…

…and danced and rocked around Ruby until she found herself watching her most hated memory.

Ruby watched as her younger self entered her parent's house. Her shoulders hunched and her arms tightened to her sides. Ruby felt the tension in unison. It came from a deeply depressing and dangerous place.

'Please, no. I don't want this,' pleaded Ruby to the Ancient Device, but it fell on no ears. Her voice was silenced. Also, the Ancient Device didn't have ears.

The memory played on.

'Where have you been?' Her father did not look up from his paper.

'I was in school,' said memory-Ruby. Not technically a lie.

Her father picked his bulbous nose and flicked a ball of snot at Ruby. 'I meant afterwards, dumb-oh.'

The younger Ruby stared into the soup in front of her and sighed.

'What's the matter? *Cat* got your tongue? Hah!' Ruby's father smacked his hand down hard on the table causing her to jump.

'No! Nononono! I won't watch this!' Ruby tried to shout, but no sound came out. She tried to shut her eyes, but without a corporeal form, there were no eyes to shut. Even trying to imagine hands with which to wave away this memory was futile. All it did was speed up the inevitable, reaching her least favourite part of the memory sooner. She watched helplessly.

Smack! Ruby's father rapped the cane across memory-Ruby's tentacle-hands. They turned human, but a howl of pain burst from Ruby's lips. Not the scream of a young child, but a cacophony of anguish. 'Silly *goose*, what did your mother just say. Be normal!' Her father raised the cane again and brought it down hard. *Smack*!

Ruby winced as her younger self released a growl-screech-yell-roar. She frantically repeated the same mantra as her younger self: *I am normal, I am normal, I am normal.*

Since she'd met Sawwse Bohge and the others, Ruby had begun to feel like she, well, not exactly *fit in*, but that she didn't *stick out* either. But the memory was undoing any scraps of confidence she felt.

Memory-Ruby sobbed and pleaded with her parents. 'I'm sorry, I'm sorry! Please don't do it again. I'm not sure I can control it–'

'Bad *doggy*.' Her father's rough calloused hands grabbed memory-Ruby's arms and Ruby felt herself losing control all over again. Her younger self shoved her parents out of the way, but it was too late. Memory-Ruby's body tripled in size. Striped, purple fur coated her body. Drool poured from the fangs hanging out of her mouth, and claws lengthened to the size of daggers. She screamed a scream that would haunt her parents for the rest of their lives, which happened to end approximately two seconds later.

Ruby's heart stung and her body sagged.

If the Ancient Device could talk, it would've said: 'This one's definitely a goer.' But it couldn't talk. Not really. Even so, its weird, twisted metal croak did manage to communicate something to Ruby. It posed her a question: '*WILL YOU RETURN?*'

The mists billowed around Ruby…

…and parted from Rangrim. His spectral presence now hovered over Hero's Point, the grassy mound that overlooked his mountain village. This memory was only a few years' old, so its wound was still fresh. Head in a fug, eyes bagged and crusty, Rangrim gradually became aware of a heavy shoe kicking his bum.

'Mhmph.' The younger Rangrim tried to speak, but his mouth felt glued together.

'Wake up, you lump.'

Rangrim cringed at himself. Memory-Rangrim looked disgustingly hungover, faltering as he tried to open his eyes against the too-bright sun. Rangrim surveyed the crowd of people that had come to watch this pathetic spectacle. They all looked so disappointed, and was that a surprise? They had every right to have expected more.

'What's going on?'

'Get up, you stupid oaf. Look at what you've done.' Thrimbald chastised the young dwarf.

Memory-Rangrim raised himself up with some effort, rocked unsteadily, and then stumbled back onto one knee. The world spun wildly around him. He raised a finger in the air, and, after a brief pause, vomited up all the previous night's ale onto Thrimbald's shoes.

'Oh, Rangrim.' Rangrim cringed at his mother's voice. It was her disappointment that made the whole memory so painful.

Memory-Rangrim was yanked to his feet by the surprisingly strong elder. 'Anything missing?' The elder shook him. 'Do. You. See. Anything. Missing?'

'The sword! It's been lifted.'

'Yes. Yes, it has, hasn't it.' Thrimbald thrust Rangrim forward and he fell to his knees once more. An extremely large sword lay flat on the ground in front of an ancient stone block. 'Rollo and Khanan's stores were both raided last night. Do you think that's a coincidence?'

'But… the legend?'

'I'd rather the sword lay dormant for twelve more centuries than for you to be the hero.'

Memory-Rangrim sunk his head in shame. He glanced up to look for his parents, but they had already begun to walk away, shaking their heads in disappointment.

Rangrim had had no idea what he was doing when he'd drunkenly raised the sword from its block the previous night. He was just trying to clear a space to rest his head and had pushed aside what he'd thought was a tree branch or an old shepherd's crook. *Slaepan Gigas* had somehow chosen him as its hero, and replaying this memory had reminded him of how little he was up to the job.

The memory unspooled, rewinding through the cringe, the shame, and the weird cucumber-headed village elder, until it reached the night before. Now, memory-Rangrim sat on Hero's Point alone, and *Slaepan Gigas* stood erect, back in its ancient, immovable stone block. The barrel of ale he had brought with him stood untapped.

A loud clunking, churning metal sound entered Rangrim's head and spoke to him in an ancient nonlanguage. It asked: '*WILL YOU RETURN?*'

Rangrim did not immediately say no…

…Corinne heard the mist whooshing past her, fizzing in her ears. Its touch felt cold on her upper lip.

'The Regularis Section VI District Court with Responsibility for Magical Misdemeanours, Unlicensed Transmogrification, and Unsanctioned Grape Eating finds the defendant guilty.'

How interesting, thought Corinne. *A simple conjuration? But no, it feels too real. I can feel the beige of the court room. How is this possible?*

As Corinne pondered this, memory-Corinne pondered her judgement. Wasn't it… wrong? 'Pardon?'

'We therefore decree that you are expelled from office permanently and with immediate effect.'

Corinne tuned back into the memory. Her job had been everything. She'd excelled at it. But her career had been cruelly snatched away from her.

'Surely there's been a mistake.'

'It was you who made a mistake, Ms Brightwood. It is our right to determine the correct punishment.'

'All I did was transmute a loaf of bread.'

'Unsanctioned use of magic carries heavy consequences, as you well know.'

'She was homeless. I took the ingredients from my own supply. I'm certain this should be counted as a misdemeanour. I have clerked on several cases whose outcomes have all been the same.'

'We have already heard your defence, Ms Brightwood. Verdict so ordered.' The judge banged his gavel in the least dynamic way possible. 'You can hand in your lanyard, clipboards, badge, and gun at the door. And by gun, I mean retractable pencil.'

Her whole collection of clipboards. Gone. Even the novelty one that played showtunes when you tapped it on its side.

And that was it. Corinne's lifelong career was over without fireworks, pomp, or ceremony, and with no special retirement pencil. It was a moment completely and utterly devoid of magic.

Would she have acted differently if she'd known how it would play out? She was about to find out.

The mists swished around her again, wiping the memory and returning Corinne to the previous week. She heard two voices. The first was meek and needy, it said: 'Please miss. Will you help me?' The second voice was whatever the opposite of meek and needy was and sounded like metal nails on a metal chalkboard. It said: '*WILL YOU RETURN?*'

Corinne sighed. The mists whirled around the chamber…

…Osrik knelt on the floor, head clutched in his hands. He had spent years shielding himself from his past and prided himself on his mental *fortitude.* It was why he'd survived as a mercenary for all these years. Back in Spearca, he'd dropped his guard and Alla'fyr had seized upon it. But this, what was happening to him now, was unlike anything he'd experienced before. The ancient magic running the device was more powerful than he could have imagined. It prised into his head and grasped hold of a life full of regrets.

The mists circled around the old dwarf. His eyes rolled into the back of his head as the mists rushed in. Suddenly, he saw himself as a young child. Heir to the Ironforge dynasty. Boy Osrik heard his parents shouting at one another yet again. He set aside his toys and ran past the walled gardens, disappearing into the vast acres of land on their estate. Boy Osrik returned as the sun began to dip, just in time to see his mother's carriage pull away from the manor. It was the last time he'd see her.

Osrik jerked his head. He tried to shout, but no words left his mouth.

A flurry of mist.

Osrik's father did not beat him, but nor did he show him any affection. Drabik Ironforge had spent the year since his wife's departure withdrawing into himself, drinking, and making promises he couldn't keep.

The mists blew in again, revealing faces and figures that Osrik had tried so hard to banish forever. Debtors seeking payment. They stood over Drabik as he signed a piece of parchment, and turned to look at the boy. There was now a deep sadness in Drabik's eyes. The debtors turned to face Boy Osrik, who stood there awkwardly.

Run, you fool. Run! thought Osrik, as he watched the men march his younger self out of the manor, debt settled.

Osrik focused his mental energy, trying to block the conjuration. He roared, swishing, and swaying his arms around him. A flash and he was in the Ancient Device's lair, but just as quickly his vision was once more obscured by the mists.

Another memory. This time it was Awkward Teenage Osrik being shoved into the back of a wagon. Slavers had brought him to one of the mines that used to belong to his father. They relished the irony as they set him to work.

Osrik tried to slap himself in the face, but his hand passed through his spectral form. He roared again but could do nothing against the ancient magic.

The Ancient Device clunked and whirred, and the mists thickened, swirling more furiously now about Osrik's head. They cleared and Osrik saw himself, a young adult now, cleaving rocks in a wide-open pit. There were many other slaves around him: hunger in their eyes, apathy in their spirits. The image changed again. Osrik was kept in a cage. The slavers cackled as they fed him scraps of barely edible jerky.

'Get out of my head!' screamed Osrik. He bashed the ground with his fists. The mists receded and he saw the cave once more. His breath quickened. The Ancient Device towered over him. Its single red eye glowed malevolently. Osrik raised his battle-axe ready to strike, but the Ancient Device had not finished its assault. It began to clunk and whir faster: pistons firing, cogs and wheels spinning, dials turning. Osrik didn't understand what was happening, but his fear was justified. The mists returned with renewed vigour. They span, swirled, swished all around Osrik. As he gasped, a torrent of mist forced itself inside his throat and he was lost to the visions again.

The dwarf was now much older. He was riding a horse alongside a man named Joseph. They stopped in the middle of a dirt path. The curtain covering the wagon blew in the wind and Osrik glanced inside. Groups of families clutching each other looked fearfully at the dwarf. His stomach turned. No one had told him. But did he do anything about it? No.

A man arrived. Money was exchanged. And then they left. Joseph slapped Osrik on the back, grinning. 'Another successful job.'

Back in the cave, Osrik's stomach jolted with guilt. He doubled over and threw up over the cave floor. The mists, momentarily flushed out, now rushed back inside the dwarf.

Osrik now saw a mirror image: a white-haired, haggard, old dwarf. He stood on top of a mound with the small mercenary outfit he had joined the previous year. They looked out over a burning field.

'I was very impressed with how you worked,' said Alla'fyr.

'You weren't too shabby.' Francesco smirked.

'We make a good team,' added Mauro.

Osrik grunted in acknowledgement.

'However,' Alla'fyr raised her finger, 'the job specifically stated we'd only get the money if there were no survivors. That was the deal.'

They looked to the group of orcs cowering beside them. It hadn't taken them long to surrender. Osrik supposed they may have even been coerced into fighting in the first place. What did it matter now? He sighed and raised his battle-axe.

Osrik threw up once more. The mists now span all about him, sending him flashing through his life of regrets, and the scraping metal sound spoke directly into Osrik's head.

'*WILL YOU RETURN?*'

His mother's face in the carriage.

'*WILL YOU RETURN?*'

The families holding each other in the wagon.

'*WILL YOU RETURN?*'

The scared, surrendering orcs.

Tears rolled down Osrik's cheeks. It was no use. He couldn't resist. His *fortitude* was gone. And he regretted everything. Every creaky old bone in his body knew the Ancient Device was evil, but this was his only opportunity to put things right. He had to.

'Stop!' Sawwse Bohge's voice echoed around the chamber…

…Back when the Ancient Device had begun its assault on her guild mates' memories, so too had the mists approached Sawwse, covering her vision in a blanket of white. But… they came up empty.

The mists furiously swam around her head, diving inside her mouth and ears. The Device's wispy tendrils tried to latch onto remorse and regret, but Sawwse had none. It rifled through her memories of being teased and pranked within the Blue Forest, but Sawwse believed this had made her stronger. It tried to remind Sawwse of when she fled her home, but she thought it was the best decision she'd ever made. It pushed her to imagine Marius finding the Gnomeopedia's nasty depiction of ogres, but Sawwse merely chuckled – there'd be another chance to explain the misunderstanding. True friends never lost sight of each other for long.

The Ancient Device posed Sawwse the question, but sounded much more uncertain than with the others: '*WILL YOU… RETURN?*'

'Return to what? Pimples and anxiety?'

'*ER, SURE?*' it rasped unconvincingly.

'Gods no! Crimp that. Life is for living.' The mists withdrew from Sawwse. 'Not that you'd know, being a machine and all that. No offence. Though I suppose you wouldn't be able to take offence being a… stop talking Sawwse.'

There was a shout from Osrik. Sawwse turned her attention away from the Device. It was then that she understood she was having a very different experience to the others. Her guild mates were stood stupefied, crying out, whimpering, and generally not in a good way. The ill-judged treehouse party at Findon Umlock's had left people in a similar state, except there it was only the fate of social worlds in the balance.

There was an awful, screeching sound.

Sawwse spun back around. The Ancient Device was shuddering with anger. Its pistons fired, its cogs whirred, and the runes covering its body glowed ominously. It seemed that, in fact, machines could take offence.

'I think there may have been a misunderstanding.' Sawwse scratched the back of her neck nervously, but then remembered why she was there. 'Oh! Please could you stop whatever it is you're doing to my friends and maybe turn yourself off forever. Er, please.'

There was a pause.

Then, a loud groaning creak from the Ancient Device, followed by a series of noisy thumps that sounded like a troll dancing on top of a typewriter. A small sheet of parchment spat out of a tiny slit on the machine and shot towards Sawwse.

She snatched it out of the air. There was some kind of script written on it. It was indecipherable at first, but then the runes on the sheet shifted and merged until it spelled a simple word, two-letters long:

NO.

'Right. Well, I'm probably still going to try to help my–' Sawwse made to move over to the others, but found her feet stuck in place. A patterned circle of light formed around her on the cave floor. It was some kind of complicated hex. She tried to move again but this time her foot sunk into the floor as though it were quicksand.

The machine stared at her from the wall. If it could've talked properly, it might've said something annoying like, 'How do you like dem apples?' Instead, it ground its gears together in a kind of harsh metallic laugh.

Sawwse panicked, but the more she moved the further she sank into the ground. It had swallowed her up to her waist. She looked at the others. They were more helpless than she'd ever seen them.

So, this was its plan, thought Sawwse. *Reduce them to their most vulnerable state and then offer them the chance to correct the past. But Convener tasked me with protecting them, so that's just what I'll do.*

'STOP!' Sawwse shouted at the top of her lungs. It wasn't the most graceful of plans, but she needed to get the attention of the others quickly. 'Ruby! Osrik! Corinne! Somebody, listen to my voice!'

None of the guild mates noticed. Their minds were elsewhere.

The ground was now at her chest.

The machine rasped its awful laugh again.

The ground was constricting her breath, but Sawwse breathed in as much as she could and then focused her mind.

'*WILL YOU RETURN?*' The Ancient Device posed the question to Vadania, to Rangrim.

Sawwse pictured the still black lake and then hummed, sending ripples along the water's surface.

'*WILL YOU RETURN?*' The Ancient Device spoke directly to Corinne, to Larn, to Ruby.

Sawwse felt the pain inside her guild mates' hearts. The Device had weakened their *fortitude* for her, so all she had to do was get through to them.

'*WILL YOU RETURN?*' The Ancient Device was inside Osrik's mind. He was crumbling. He would accept the offer.

The ground was up to her neck. Sawwse only had one chance. One word. One syllable. 'Stop!' She sung the word but hidden within her voice she wrapped a message of hope. A bubble of possibilities. A note to say that the future is what holds potential, not the past.

The word ricocheted around the cave. It zoomed through Vadania's devastated village. 'Stop!' Vadania heard it and snapped out of her self-pity, her sorrow, her paralysing sense of loss, and remembered that she'd promised to *never* stop until her vengeance had been satiated.

After Vadania, the word whistled past Ruby's ear, and shouted into her memory. Memory-Ruby pleaded with herself to stop shifting, but Sawwse's *imbued* command told her to stop denying her truth. Ruby suddenly found herself asking what was ever so wrong with shifting? And more to the point, where was the fun in being normal?

The word bounced off a wall and collided with Rangrim, piercing through the conjured representation of his memory, and altering it in the process into something… *more.* A prideful Rangrim, clutching the sword high above his head, fully deserving of the relic regardless of the manner in which he acquired it.

From Rangrim, the word flew toward Corinne. It crashed into the drab courtroom scene, added a dynamism that was sorely missing, and reshaped Corinne from a down-on-her-luck administrator to a strong, self-assured wizard whose role was integral to the guild.

'Stop!' The word echoed around the chamber, and this time it penetrated through the thick fog surrounding Osrik. The memories of his traumatic life resurfaced again: the awfulness of his abandonment and the horror of his subsequent actions. But the word shook up Osrik's sense of self, reshaping him from down and out, and revealing an opportunity, a second chance, so late in life, to make amends for all the wrongs he'd done.

And then the word passed by Larn. He barely heard it. He was too busy finalising the details of a contract with an interdimensional demon.

One by one the mists withdrew from the guild mates, and they could see clearly now that the Ancient Device wouldn't solve anything. It would take what they had and ruin the world. Without the mists, they could also *see clearly*. They were back in the cave, and Sawwse was… gone.

Vadania drew her twin blades and faced the huge machine. 'Where is she? What have you done with her.'

'There!' Ruby pointed to the circle of runes on the ground. She took Corinne's arm and guided her to it.

Corinne knelt on the ground and felt the runes. She sighed frustratedly. 'It's too complex. I can't unpick it.'

'Step aside, novice.' Larn snarled. There was something different about him. It was an aura. Not the usual aura of unpleasantness, but something else. Something more powerful. He placed his hand on the runes and incanted an ancient spell whispered to him by the demon inside his head.

The runes on the ground cracked, splintered, and shattered into a thousand glinting fragments of light. Sawwse was jettisoned from the ground like a dolphin jumping out of the ocean, albeit without the whistling and clicking sounds. Instead, she was emitting an excited humming sound while hugging one of Larn's legs. 'Thank you, thank you, thank you.'

Larn was aghast. 'It's fine.' He peeled Sawwse away from his leg.

There was an almighty metallic shriek behind them. The Ancient Device shuddered with rage, but then its machinery slowed, slowed, stopped, and the red light at its centre faded.

'So, did I do it then?' asked Sawwse. 'We… won?'

Osrik, Vadania, Larn, and Rangrim stood shoulder to shoulder facing the machine, weapons raised. They knew these things were rarely that simple.

'It's offered me something…' The voice came from behind the machine. Sawwse recognised it straight away. Mirrah! She slowly walked into view and placed a palm against the Ancient Device. Its red light began to glow once more. 'And I think I'm going to accept.'

Chapter 29:
Battle for Time

'I don't suppose it offered to stop?' Sawwse smiled awkwardly. 'You know, in a "you say potato, I say world-devouring time machine, let's call the whole thing off" kind of way.'

Mirrah chuckled. 'It did offer to stop. But it was more in a "use the Device to stop this awful erosion of my mind" kind of way.'

'Different.'

'We can't let you use it,' said Vadania.

'It's not as simple as it makes out,' growled Osrik.

'Once you use it, it won't stop until it has taken everything,' said Corinne. 'Time will be reversed to the very beginning.'

'To whichever space egg hatched the first galaxy.' Sawwse scratched her chin thoughtfully. 'Or space chicken. Whichever came first.'

'I… know all of that.' Mirrah pressed her palm harder against the Device. The red light at its centre began to glow a deeper red. The machinery whirred quietly. 'This is my only chance to put things right. Call me selfish, but if I don't do this, I'll lose myself completely. *Ego incognita.*'

'I thought that was a genital condition.'

'Sawwse!' scolded Corinne.

'I can't help it! I'm very nervous!'

Mirrah laughed. It was her full-bodied, tilt the head back, electrifying laugh, and it tugged at Sawwse's heart. They stared at one another with such intensity it was like the chamber faded away, and with it, all their worries.

It didn't last.

An arrow screeched through the air and pierced straight through Mirrah's hand. It struck the machine behind it with a sharp *ping*. Mirrah stared at the arrow for a moment, dumbfounded. 'Ouch.'

Sawwse and the others span around to find Princess Eugenie at the entrance to the lair, flanked by her elite knights. Eugenie narrowed her eyes. 'I don't know who you are, but the Device is mine to use.'

'Probably should've thought about that before you fastened her hand to it,' muttered Sawwse.

'You…' Eugenie faltered. There she was. The evil gnome, Sawwse Bohge. Her father's killer. She'd finally caught her. Eugenie knew that she was irrelevant in the grand scheme of things. Once she got her hands on the Device, she could go back in time and kill the gnome before she even got close to her father. It would be simple. But now that she was right here in front of her, surely it'd be disrespectful to her father's memory not to punish her. What harm could it do to kill her now *and* kill her again in the past? Eugenie notched another arrow to her bow. 'Anything to say for yourself before you die?'

'Yes! Why is everyone trying to kill me?'

'You turned my father into a frog and then murdered him.'

Sawwse cast her mind back. Wasn't there something back then? Back near the very start of her crazy adventure? Her eyes lit up in recognition. 'King Frog!' A beat. 'You don't look like a…' Vadania elbowed Sawwse hard in the ribs. Osrik shook his head vigorously. 'What? It's true! She doesn't look half frog, does she?'

Three things happened in an instant:

1. Eugenie loosed an arrow aimed at Sawwse's head with hawk-like accuracy.

2. Taking advantage of the distraction, Rangrim swung his gigantic sword in an overhead arc straight towards the Ancient Device.

3. Mirrah pulled the arrow out of her hand, and it turned into a flamingo.

In the next instant, Mirrah threw the flamingo through the air at such velocity that it burst into flames. It knocked the arrow aimed at Sawwse out of the way with its beak and then landed, screaming, in one of the Dorienne knight's arms, who also began screaming.

The instant after that, Mirrah held up a single finger and stopped Rangrim's blade just as it was about to strike the machine. She flicked it and the blade swung all the way backwards. It landed in the ground behind Rangrim and released a massive wave of energy that shook the whole chamber.

Mirrah turned her back on the room and placed both her palms against the Ancient Device. It roared into life, pistons firing wildly like a steam train whose driver is late for chippy dinner.

This time a volley of arrows rained down on Mirrah.

'Watch out!' shouted Sawwse.

'It is you who needs to watch out.' No one had noticed Eugenie approaching with graceful agility, but now she was upon Sawwse with her blade raised.

Mirrah didn't hear Sawwse's warning over the sound of the machine, screeching its metallic squall into the chamber, but it didn't matter. She batted away the arrows without looking up, and those bats fluttered around the chamber annoying everyone throughout the ensuing battle.

Vadania blocked Eugenie's attack on Sawwse but was dragged backwards by one her knights. Eugenie sliced through the air again but met Osrik's shield. She spun around with incredible speed and kicked Osrik to the ground.

Sawwse scampered away, but Eugenie was too quick. Sparks flashed from the floor of the cavern as Eugenie scraped her blade along it and chased after Sawwse.

Before Eugenie could raise her sword again, a powerful gust of wind blew her backwards. Her feet skidded along the ground as she fought to maintain her position.

'Nice one, Corinne!' Sawwse rolled out of the way of the spell.

Corinne channelled the spell with both her hands. Two Dorienne knights charged at her. She pivoted and brought her left hand to face the knights, keeping her right hand directed at Eugenie, but it wasn't enough.

As the wind weakened, Eugenie knew not to waste her opportunity. She took three great strides toward Sawwse and lunged forward with her silver sword.

Clang!

Rangrim met Eugenie's attack head on. He blocked once, twice, three times a dwarf, but Eugenie was too quick, and *Slaepan Gigas* too unwieldy. Rangrim couldn't launch an attack of his own and was being forced onto the back foot.

Sawwse looked around for the others. Vadania, Osrik, Corinne and Larn were all busy keeping the Dorienne knights at bay. She locked eyes with Ruby who was cowering within a crevice. Sawwse mouthed the word: 'Help.'

Ruby swallowed nervously. Rangrim wouldn't last much longer and then Sawwse would be unprotected, but what could she do? So long as she didn't turn into *that* it wouldn't be a problem, would it? And it'd be easy not to turn into *that*, wouldn't it? She'd just turn into a bear or something, and definitely under no circumstances turn into *that*.

A huge screech-yell-roar thundered around the cavern.

Ruby had turned into *that*.

Princess Eugenie turned on her heel, but too late. A huge purple, striped claw smacked into her chest plate and sent her flying across the chamber. Another swipe knocked Rangrim into the cave wall.

'Er, Rubes?' Sawwse faced Ruby's gigantic beastly form and slowly backed away. Beast-Ruby snarled at Sawwse, drool dripping from her jaws. 'You still in there?'

Beast-Ruby dived towards Sawwse. When she was mere millimetres away, Mirrah shot away from the Device and tapped Beast-Ruby on the shoulder. There was a tiny *pop* and Ruby had turned into a hamster, who instantly ran up Sawwse's tunic to her shoulder and licked her cheek apologetically. 'Sorry, sorry, sorry!'

'That's okay,' said Sawwse. 'Lucky Mirrah was there though. And it distracted her from the Ancient Device!'

Vadania disentangled herself from two comatose knights she'd just knocked out and watched Mirrah strolling back to the Device. She shouted to the others. 'Go after Sawwse!'

'Oh, I see.' Corinne casually walked past three ballooned knights that were slowly floating up to the ceiling. 'Mirrah cannot help but intervene.'

Sawwse looked at her in disbelief. 'Is bait literally all I'm good for?'

'Don't worry, we just need to be convincing enough to get Mirrah's attention.'

Larn booted one of the knights away from him and hacked at another with his rapier. Then, fixing his attention directly on Sawwse, he grinned wickedly. 'This should be cathartic.'

'Remember, don't pull your punches.' Osrik bashed his helmet against a knight and then brought his axe down hard against another knight's oaken shield.

'Do pull your punches!' shouted Sawwse, as Larn charged full tilt towards her. 'Please pull them!'

As Larn was about to strike, a hand grabbed his wrist. He pivoted to slash at Mirrah, but she was too quick, and strong! Larn buckled at the knees as a sharp pain shot through his arm. Mirrah flung him aside like a bag of nothing.

One after the other, and in between fighting the Dorienne knights, the guild mates took it in turns to attack Sawwse. They hurled daggers, cast spells, slashed, chopped, and swung at her, and each time, Mirrah left the Device in a flash to come to Sawwse's aid.

'Crimp,' whispered Sawwse. Was it just her imagination or was Mirrah getting more and more brutal each time she protected her? She looked between her guild mates, who were battered, beaten, pummelled, pounded, trashed, and thrashed, and whose strength was clearly waning; and Mirrah, who looked immovable, as though this was taking almost no effort out of her. But when had her eyes shifted from electric blue to storm cloud grey? And where was that chaotic warm energy she'd given off when they'd met? Sawwse tried to say something, but Mirrah wasn't listening.

Meanwhile, the Ancient Device's red eye glowed and its machinery rattled, but it would only fully power up if it had someone's full attention. The Device couldn't feel, but if it could, it would've felt a lot like Mirrah was leading it on, teasing it, baiting it, and other misogynist things like that. It was lucky then that someone else was prepared to step into Mirrah's vacuum.

Princess Eugenie slid over to the Ancient Device amid all the distractions and placed her palms against its side. Its power was unlike anything she had experienced before. A shock wave jolted Eugenie's body. It was all she could do to keep from passing out. But then, she got it. What was at first an indecipherable wall of sound became intelligible. As she parsed what the Device was telling her, she understood how to get what she wanted, and it would only take a few seconds.

But seconds were a luxury she didn't have.

Feeeeeeee-crack!

An enormous beam of rippling white energy sent Eugenie hurtling through the air. She smacked against the cavern wall. Her armour split.

Mirrah's hands smoked. Her brow was furrowed. She turned to the Dorienne knights. A silent spell later and two forks of lightning cracked from her palms and jolted round the knights' metal-plated armour, sending them spasming until they hit the floor.

Sawwse's eyes widened in horror.

Mirrah faced the guild mates. As she raised her hands, Sawwse shouted: 'Stop!'

Mirrah paused. A flicker of recognition flashed in her eyes like she'd suddenly remembered where she was. But instead of lowering her palms, she flicked her wrists, and the guild were instantly bound with glowing restraints. She smiled sadly at Sawwse.

It was no use. She felt more in control of her magic now than since the curse first struck. This wasn't unusual. Often when wizards are knocking on death's door, they exhibit a strange virtuosity, presumably born from a desire to get as far away from death's door as wizardly possible. Either way, Mirrah didn't know how long this control would last, so this was likely to be her final opportunity to put things right.

Mirrah stood in front of the Ancient Device once more.

It was now or never.

Now and *forever* if the Device got its way.

Mirrah stroked the machine's red eye. It hummed. She placed one hand and then the other onto the Device. The only thing Sawwse and the others could do was watch in fear as the Ancient Device whirred, clanked, and roared into furious motion. Its pistons fired so fast that they almost looked still.

The air around the Device shifted and blurred. It was like a mirage in a desert or like a machine capable of destroying the world has touched the fabric of reality and begun to peel away its temporal layers. The second one.

Sparks flew from the Ancient Device's machinery and little fragments of light flaked from its surface. Whatever Mirrah was doing was clearly having the desired effect. The Device purred with pleasure. This was what it wanted, in so much as an insentient machine could want for anything.

'I will not let you do this!' Princess Eugenie dropped from the ceiling. The sharp point of her silver blade aimed directly towards the top of Mirrah's head. But before she could even get close, Eugenie froze in mid-air.

Mirrah continued to control the Ancient Device with one of her hands, while the other was held open towards Eugenie. Without registering any emotion on her face, Mirrah bent her little finger.

Eugenie howled in pain as the metal armour encasing her left leg crushed around her thigh.

Mirrah bent her thumb.

A large dent appeared in Eugenie's other leg brace, as it compressed her right leg. She screamed again.

'Stop this, please!' Sawwse was horrified. This wasn't like Mirrah at all. This was cruel. Beyond cruel. Sadistic. If there was anything left of the Mirrah she knew, she had to try and get through to her. 'Please, Mirrah!'

But Mirrah wasn't listening. She bent her ring and index fingers, causing the plated metal around Eugenie's arms to crumple and crunch around them.

Another wail of agony rang out around the chamber.

Sawwse winced.

Meanwhile, the Ancient Device was generating so much energy, its machinery now glowed bright red. The chamber was charged with untamed magic: dust motes caught fire, crumbling rocks were zapped by stray bolts of lightning, everyone's socks suddenly felt damp and gross.

Not just that, but its properties as a time machine were becoming clearer. The area around the Device no longer resembled the cave. It was like looking into space.

There were stars and galaxies and fires burning far, far away.

The guild mates were stunned. They were viewing time. Deep time. It was hypnotisingly beautiful. They could do nothing but watch.

Except Sawwse. She'd never taken her eyes from Mirrah. Sawwse watched now as Mirrah began slowly bending her middle finger, squeezing Eugenie's chest plate around her body. She closed her eyes and thought back to when they had met, and then again in the tomb. *Hadn't Mirrah said she'd been thinking of my song before she teleported to the tomb? It's worth a shot. It's either that or watch someone get crushed to death and then watch the world end.*

Sawwse closed her eyes, took a deep breath in, and then began to sing.

They were Emmeline Flowerdew's lyrics, but as Sawwse sang them she thought of Mirrah, and of their brief but beautiful time together. She thought of their electrifying connection, unlike anything she'd felt with anyone else. And despite the peril and certain doom facing her, she smiled and opened her eyes.

Mirrah was staring at her. She was also smiling.

This time the chamber really did fade away. As did the Ancient Device, Princess Eugenie, and all the Dorienne knights. Even Osrik, Ruby, and the others were gone. The vines creeping over the walls of the cavern. The cavern walls themselves. The ground beneath their feet. Nothing remained. It was just Sawwse and Mirrah.

'Helbo,' said Sawwse.

'Bwilp,' said Mirrah.

They grinned at each other and stayed like this for several moments.

'I could stare at your eyes all day,' said Sawwse.

'I'd have liked that. If only we'd had the time.'

Just then, there was a flicker. It lasted for a split second, but in that moment Sawwse saw everything as it was. The Ancient Device ready to turn back time, Mirrah about to crush Eugenie, and the guild mates staring into a temporal abyss.

'This can't last, can it?' Sawwse's smile faded. Whatever this reprieve from the chaos of the chamber was, it was clearly temporary. 'You're still going to use the Ancient Device, aren't you?'

Mirrah nodded. She made to speak, stopped, tucked a strand of hair behind her ear, and then tried again. 'You know, that's not me using the machine, right?'

'You mean it's some kind of trickster shapeshifting demon?'

'Well, no. I mean, it is me. It's just not *me*.'

Sawwse scratched her head.

'I mean, I wouldn't normally act like that.'

'Are you blushing?' Sawwse's grin returned.

'I don't normally hold people up with bananas either.'

'More of a satsuma girl?'

Mirrah's smile returned too. 'Carrots, actually.'

Sawwse giggled. 'Is it wrong to be having such a lovely time when the world is about to end?'

'Oh. That whole thing.' Mirrah gestured broadly at the space where the Ancient Device was currently about to irrevocably change the world. She shrugged. 'I'm sure it's fine.'

They laughed at this, but then there was another break. A tear in whatever magic Mirrah was using to create this pocket of time and space for the two of them.

'What happens next?' asked Sawwse, a slight quaver in her voice.

'Hm. That depends on a few things.' Mirrah let out a sad sigh. 'Largely it depends on whether or not your song has attracted the attention of enough of my brain.'

'But you paused time for us, so… it worked?'

'I cannot pause time. This is merely a pocket universe.'

'Pocket universe, sure, sure, sure.'

'Time works differently here.' The scene flickered again, twice in quick succession. Mirrah frowned. 'Unfortunately, it's unstable. The curse has taken most of my mind. We'll simply have to hope that enough remains to stop things before it's too late, or that someone comes along and puts a stop to me.'

'That's cheery.'

Reality broke through the spell once more: the Ancient Device roaring, Princess Eugenie howling, the guild mates cowering. The flickers were getting more frequent. Mirrah's magic was faltering.

They stared at one another again.

'It's not enough,' said Sawwse.

'I know.'

'It's no way near enough.'

'But perhaps it would never have been enough.'

Sawwse smiled weakly. 'No. It'll never be enough.'

Mirrah walked to Sawwse then. With her thumb, she traced Sawwse's jawline, and then, cradling the back of her head with one hand, she kissed her. It was perfect: slow, smooth, firm, and a complete lack of teeth.

Sawwse's heart fizzed, but when she opened her eyes, it was over. Not just the kiss, but everything.

Chapter 30:
The Two

There was nothing but a bright, white light.

Well, I guess this is what dying feels like, thought Sawwse. *Less painful than Alla'fyr led me to believe. But I suppose she didn't reverse time to before I was born, or whatever the crimp just happened.* Sawwse sighed deeply. *That's odd. You can sigh when you're dead?* She'd never considered that dead people could sigh. But now that she thought about it, she presumed they probably had more to sigh about than the living. Sawwse also reflected that there was a heck of a lot more thinking that happened after you died. And it was also much, much louder than she'd assumed.

The noise was akin to that of a runaway train finally screeching to a halt when stopped by a spider-related superhero.

'Sawwse, are you okay?'

'Ruby? Are we sharing an afterlife?'

'We're not dead, you dolt.'

'Larn's here! How did *he* make the cut!?'

'We are not dead.'

'Oh. Vadania. That's a little more reassuring. Though, don't elves have a separate thing going on? Something something fancy boat?'

'Sawwse.' It was Osrik now. 'Open your eyes!'

She hadn't realised her eyes were closed. When she opened them, the light was so bright that it stung. Sawwse raised her hand to shield her eyes, and after she'd gotten used to the light, she realised it was coming from two huge shafts that beamed through a newly formed hole in the ceiling. A shadowy figure stood within each of the light beams. An aura of deep and steadfast power radiated out from both. The only thing that had ever come close to approaching this immense aura had been Mirrah.

'Mirrah,' gasped Sawwse, quickly turning to face her.

Mirrah was looking right at her, a slight smile at her lips. But any relief Sawwse felt was instantly washed away as she realised Mirrah was completely motionless. Strands of her golden hair were frozen like there'd been an accident in the hairspray factory. There was something else too. A sparkling, glinting sheen, like a thin film of magic had wrapped around her.

Beside Mirrah, Eugenie lay crumpled at her feet.

Ruby nudged Sawwse and drew her attention back to the shadowy figures now emerging from the light. One of the figures was large, substantially bigger than any of the adventurers, and the other was very small, similar in size to Sawwse in fact.

Vadania, Osrik, Rangrim, and Larn withdrew their weapons once again, unsure what new threat they faced, but the two figures didn't even seem to notice.

'Such a shame.' The smaller figure spoke in an irritatingly nasal tone, like a chirruping cricket was lodged up his nose. 'A truly great talent wasted on archaic nonsense.'

The larger figure grunted in acknowledgement.

'I do wonder whether there was more we could have done, intervened earlier, paid more attention to Mirrah's requests for help, discovered she'd been cursed etcetera, etcetera.' Rather than expanding on this point, the smaller figure just shrugged and said, 'Oh well!'

The figures stepped closer to Mirrah's immobile body. As they moved farther from the shafts of light, Sawwse was able to make them out more clearly. The smaller one was a gnome, just like her. His skin was the colour of jet, and his clothes were incredibly ostentatious: a highly decorative doublet, bright blue puffy trousers, topped off with a white ruff around his neck. By comparison, the larger figure wore a simple green travelling cloak, the hood of which covered their head.

The gnome placed a hand on Mirrah's back. Within seconds, Mirrah's body and clothes were crystallised, as though she'd been fossilised centuries ago. 'Right then, we should probably–Oh, I wouldn't stand too close to that.' He gestured apathetically to the Ancient Device without even looking at the guild mates. 'We've only temporarily shut down the machine, and we'll be sealing everything away shortly.'

Sawwse and the others shared blank looks with one another, shuffling on the spot awkwardly.

'Move it. Come on. Move, move, move.' The unpleasant gnome spun to face them and gesticulated wildly with his arms. The guild mates shuffled away from the Ancient Device and stared dumbfounded at the gnome, who sighed. 'This is so far beyond your woeful little adventuring troupe. What are you even doing here? That was a rhetorical question, please don't answer it.'

The larger figure began to chuckle, a deep laugh that vibrated the ground underneath their feet. He turned to face the guild mates and drew back his hood. Sawwse instantly recognised his big, toothy ogre grin.

'Marius!' Sawwse ran forwards and threw her arms around him. They held each other in a warm, comforting embrace, much to the astonishment of the others. Sawwse launched into an explanation, speaking a mile a minute. 'I'm so sorry for the ogre drawing it wasn't me, I borrowed the book and wrote in it of course but lots of it was already there and I don't know who wrote it, but they're obviously mean and wrong and smelly and poopy.'

Marius simply patted her on the head and grinned from ear to ear. He had absolutely no idea what she was on about.

There was a cough from the other gnome.

Sawwse spun around to face him. She placed her right arm at her breast and outstretched one leg below the other. 'My name is Sawwse Bohge, and it is so pleasurable to meet you.'

The other gnome frowned, wrinkling his nose and forehead. Sawwse realised that any hope of kinship was dashed when he spoke. 'It's the other arm. Unsurprising that they don't teach proper manners in whatever backwater village you're from.' He mimicked Sawwse's bow exaggeratedly, placing his left arm at his breast. 'I am Funndus Broxley. And it *is* your pleasure to meet me.'

'Well, he's hateful,' said Sawwse.

Marius looked apologetic, but Sawwse didn't seem too bothered by Funndus' discourtesy, excited as she was to have met her ogre friend again. She quickly turned to the others and set about introducing them to Marius, but before she could say "this is my friend Osrik, and he wears a funny nightdress," Funndus had interrupted her.

'No, no, no. Absolutely not. There's no time for this. Come on, Marius.'

'It's true.' Marius smiled sympathetically. 'We'll have plenty of time to catch up.'

'But what about Mirrah? What's happened to her?' asked Sawwse.

'We are Two of The Twelve,' said Funndus with genuine indignation. 'It is not for us to give you answers!'

Marius raised his big bushy eyebrows at Funndus.

Funndus rolled his eyes and sighed impatiently. 'Fine. I'm only going to explain this because I owe Marius one.' The pompous gnome cleared his throat. 'We presume Mirrah was attempting to use the Ancient Device to reverse time to a point before she went loopy, but that infernal machine wouldn't have stopped at that. It would've kept going until a point before *anything* ever existed, and then where would we be! No, no, no. It's silly magic and needs to be confined to the bin for eternity. So, it was important to… how to put this tactfully… make sure Mirrah was… dead. Otherwise, she'd have destroyed the world!' Funndus looked satisfied with himself. 'That should cover it. Come on, Marius, you grab her legs.'

'So, she's definitely gone then?' Sawwse's eyes filled with hot tears. Mirrah looked like some kind of crystalline sculpture, as though she'd never been real, like their connection had never happened. 'Surely, you can bring her back.'

'No,' said Funndus.

Marius shook his head sadly.

'Aren't The Twelve the most powerful wizards in the world?'

'We're not court magicians. We don't take requests.' Funndus spoke with a detached air of arrogance. 'And anyway, bring her back as what? A husk of her former self? No, that would be insulting to her memory.'

Sawwse scowled at Funndus.

'What's it to you, anyway?' Funndus flicked his finger and Mirrah's body began floating towards the shafts of light.

Sawwse stumbled over her words. 'I… well, we… there was something. We had something! I should at least be with her, wherever you're taking her.'

Funndus was about to respond when Marius put a large hand on his shoulder and signalled for him to return to the light. He mumbled as he walked away: 'This is why I don't get involved with the feeble people. Dreadfully moany the lot of them.'

Marius shuffled his feet uncomfortably while Funndus walked away. He crouched down next to Sawwse and met her pitiful look with his kind eyes. 'I'm sorry, little one. I too was very fond of Mirrah. She was my most trustworthy colleague.'

'Better than that pillock.' Sawwse stuck her tongue out at Funndus.

'Well…' Mirrah had contacted Marius back when she was first cursed. She'd stressed that there must be a saboteur within The Twelve. Someone who'd plotted her demise and laid a curse on the Ancient Device. This information troubled Marius greatly. It would be the first time that such a subversion had happened in the long history of The Twelve, but he trusted Mirrah completely.

She'd made him promise to investigate this conspiracy in secrecy. Now, he eyed his companion cautiously, but allowed no suspicion to show on his face. Funndus was examining his teeth in a small hand mirror. It was more likely that he was simply a pompous buffoon than a double agent. But this needed further consideration, and now was not the time.

Marius wanted to tell Sawwse that Mirrah had sworn him to stay away until she'd lost control. He'd desperately wanted to help, but if he'd gotten involved sooner, he might've aroused the suspicion of the rogue agent. Obviously, he couldn't tell Sawwse any of this. In fact, she was already far too involved in these dangerous matters than he'd ever hoped she would be. 'We're going to take Mirrah away now.'

Sawwse nodded sombrely. She cast her eyes down and saw the comatose body of Princess Eugenie, bent, and twisted out of shape. 'Can you heal her?'

Placing one of his large hands on Sawwse's back, Marius gently gestured to Eugenie's head. 'It will take more than magic to heal what is in here.'

'Sure, but you can do the gross legs and stuff?'

Marius chuckled. He hovered his raised palm over Eugenie's body and Sawwse watched in awe as the plated metal armour popped back out, like a used tin can uncrushing itself. The sweat from Eugenie's brow receded and her face flushed with colour once more.

'Tick-tock, Marius.' Funndus called from within the shaft of light.

Marius grunted in acknowledgement.

'How can we help?' asked Sawwse.

Marius grinned again and tousled Sawwse's hair. 'You have already done far more than you could imagine. But now, you need to leave. We need to seal the Device away and close this chamber forever.'

Vadania walked over to Eugenie. After studying her limp form for a moment, she picked up the princess and walked out of the chamber's entrance.

'Hooray. Finally. You've got the right idea.' Funndus made a shooing gesture with his hands. 'Go on, go.'

The others turned to follow Vadania out of the cave. All except Sawwse. She continued to stare back at Mirrah's frozen body. 'Well, this is properly goodbye then.' Suddenly, Sawwse ran to the shaft of light and threw her arms around Mirrah. Mirrah's body was so bitingly cold that it hurt to touch, but Sawwse continued to hold her face against it, ignoring the searing pain. After a few moments, she pulled her face away and whispered in Mirrah's ear, 'It will never be enough.'

Marius slowly walked over to Sawwse and wiped the tears from her face. He whispered something in her ear.

Sniffling, Sawwse managed a small smile. 'I'd like that.' She gave a final glance at Mirrah, before running to catch up with her guild mates.

After the guild mates had gone, Funndus chuckled to himself. 'I honestly don't know how you put up with the sentimental nonsense these mortals come out with.'

Marius rolled his eyes. 'We are not immortal.'

'As good as,' said Funndus, but then he caught Marius' glare. 'Oh. Mirrah. Perhaps a little tactless, but then she shouldn't have gone investigating such a relic in the first place. Speaking of which…'

Funndus thrust forward his hand toward the Ancient Device. The machine began to freeze and crystallise, just as Mirrah had done. Then, Marius bent down and placed his palm flat on the ground, summoning a thousand vines from cracks in the rock, which rushed to smother the Device.

Satisfied with their work, Funndus clicked his fingers and the cave rumbled, shook, and fell apart around them. Inside the shaft of light, Marius placed his arm around Mirrah, and then The Two disappeared.

Outside the chamber's entrance, Sawwse and the others waited and watched. A loud rumbling sound issued from within the cave, followed by a series of high-pitched chimes. The entrance slowly dissolved, leaving a snowy slope in its place. It looked natural, like it had always been thus, and like everything that had happened within had been but a dream or a distant memory.

But the entrance quickly reappeared, and twenty Dorienne knights that everyone had forgotten about were chucked out at great velocity, followed by a dozen or so unhappy bats.

Then, the entrance disappeared again. This time for good.

Corinne cleared her throat. 'I will save the full mission report for once we have returned to the guild headquarters, but it's perhaps worthwhile to acknowledge that our quest was completed successfully, albeit with some unexpected interventions.'

'*Deus ex* Marius, am I right?' Sawwse said this with little enthusiasm. She rubbed at her eyes and grumbled, 'Doesn't feel much like a victory to me, anyway.'

The guild mates looked at each other awkwardly.

'We're sorry, Sawwse.' Ruby sidled up next to her. 'We know she meant a lot to you.' Despite having just been in one of the most unbelievably scary moments of her life, Ruby was now feeling great, and it was all down to Sawwse. The heavy burden of her memory had been lifted and replaced by hope. Not even almost eating Sawwse by turning into *that* could bring her mood down. Slowly, Ruby began shifting her weight until her stomach expanded. She dropped to all fours and morphed her hands and feet into trotters. Pig-Ruby nudged Sawwse's leg. 'If it'll cheer you up, I'll give you a piggyback ride down the mountain?'

Sawwse tried her best not to smile, but she couldn't help it. 'That. Sounds. Amazing!' Sawwse jumped in the air and landed on Ruby's piggy back, who squealed and bolted haphazardly down the mountain.

'I want a go!' yelled Rangrim, chasing after them.

'Be careful!' growled Osrik, marching through the snow.

'Let them have their fun.' Corinne glided down a slope to keep up with Osrik and Rangrim. 'A little bit of merrymaking can be an important factor in building positive post-quest intraguild relationships.'

Vadania stayed back a moment. She still held Princess Eugenie in her arms, though her mind was currently occupied by the expression on Larn's face. He almost looked… happy. 'Enjoying the fun?'

Unsurprisingly, Larn wasn't thinking about Sawwse and Ruby. His thoughts were reeling from the immense power exhibited by Mirrah and The Two. But there was more. He was also thinking that such a concentration of power couldn't just disappear with Mirrah. It had to go somewhere else, to some*one* else. He grinned his special grin, which he reserved for moments where he was truly brilliant. 'Fun? Yes. Something like that.'

Vadania watched bemused as Larn trotted gleefully down the mountain after the others. In her arms, Eugenie stirred. Her eyelids fluttered open, but she couldn't quite summon the energy to talk. Vadania leaned close to her ear. 'You are broken. But I know someone who fixes people.'

'You can't mend people,' whimpered Princess Eugenie. But after some gentle shushing from Vadania, she closed her eyes again and drifted back off to sleep.

Without saying another word, Vadania set off after her guild mates and began the descent down *Slaepan Wiga*.

Chapter 31:
Sabbatical

The journey down was much less perilous than their ascent had been, but that was a low bar. There were no raids by savages, no murderous shapeshifting eagles, and no cave-ins. They descended through the snow, past the rocky outcrops and fields of heather, and down by the river that intertwined with the pine trees, with nothing but fatigue to bother them. Dawn broke as they walked, ran, and frolicked, so the mountain was painted first in the ambiguous blues of the half-light, then in the gloriously vibrant tones of an untroubled sun, and finally in that magical golden glow that precedes the night.

The beach outside Prysta's hut was a welcome sight.

Sawwse yelled at the top of her lungs. 'Honey, we're home!'

Osrik took off his bag and began erecting a tent. 'Don't get comfortable. We need to get back to the guild.'

'What's the rush?' Sawwse picked up one of the tentpoles and pretended she was throwing a javelin. 'We stopped the Ancient Device, didn't we? Surely, we deserve a rest!'

'Once again, you have decided to set up camp before asking permission.' Vadania glared at each of them in turn, before heading inside Prysta's hut.

'Unfortunately, we must return to Convener,' said Corinne after Vadania had gone. She gestured with her fingers and the tentpole left Sawwse's hands, hovering into place in the sand. 'We lost contact with him in Spearca, so we have a duty to check that he is okay.'

'I think you mean that *he* has a duty to check that we are paid what we are owed.' Larn busied himself with his own tent. It wasn't going very well. 'If Convener is dead, then I will take up my grievance with Grimiser.'

'Oh gods.' Sawwse dropped a ground sheet, which blew away in the breeze. 'You don't think he's dead, do you?'

Osrik grunted as he ran stumbling after the sheet. 'We shouldn't rule out the possibility.'

'I don't wish him dead,' began Ruby, who had already finished setting up her own tent, 'but there was something sinister about him. It might be for the best if someone else took charge.'

'I never pegged you for a usurper, Ruby!' Rangrim gave a hearty laugh, as he struggled underneath a large camping sheet.

Ruby flushed red and drew her hood over her head.

Inside Prysta's hut, Vadania stood facing her former master. Princess Eugenie rested unconscious on the floor. Prysta didn't say anything for a while. Instead, she opened a cabinet and took out a large glass bottle with a clear spirit inside. When Prysta took the stopper out, Vadania flinched at the smell. It was potent stuff. You could always tell when a spirit was going to be strong, because the label was handwritten and said: 'Wodka.' Prysta poured the liquid into two tumblers. 'A toast.'

'Hm.' Vadania stared into the glass. She wanted to say that she didn't feel like toasting while her personal quest remained uncompleted, and that she'd gotten involved in things she shouldn't have, which had only served to distract her from finding the dragon. But she didn't say any of this because judging by Prysta's face, she already knew. Vadania raised her glass, and then necked her measure in one go. She pointed to Eugenie. 'This one speaks of having no purpose.'

'My sword training days are far behind me.'

'Her skills with the sword are exceptional.' Vadania pointed to her chest. 'It is here that she needs help.'

'I guess I could help with a bench press programme.'

'No, that's not what I… her heart is broken.'

'I'm no surgeon. Perhaps a stent in her wrist?'

'I mean with grief!' Vadania cleared her throat, composed herself again. It'd been a long day. 'When you found me and my heart was full of grief and rage and torment, you fixed me. Eugenie needs your help.'

Prysta paused. 'I never could fix your rage.'

'Perhaps she will be different.'

The two Elven warriors smiled then and placed the palms of their hands together in a traditional farewell.

Vadania walked back outside with tired, heavy feet. She smiled as she took in the scene: the tents were unmade, and instead her guild mates were lying spreadeagled on the sand, sleeping comfortably in the warm air. Laying next to Rangrim in the sand, Vadania closed her eyes and instantly fell into a deep, untroubled sleep.

It took another whole day to get back to Rhyddinas, so it was evening by the time they arrived. The lantern lit streets reminded Sawwse of her first night in the city. It was strange to think that back then Convener had just been a strange beetle-y man who wanted people to join his guild. *And now he was, what?* thought Sawwse. *Dead? Unlikely. Ruby's right, of course. There is something sinister about him. But haven't we just saved the world, and wasn't it Convener who set us on that path?*

The guild mates mostly walked in silence back to the Happy Hearth, unsure what they'd find when they arrived. The quest had been so all consuming, and they'd learnt so much about themselves during it, that the Hearth felt like a memory, a place where some other adventurers met and went on missions.

Contrary to the mood of the adventurers, the Happy Hearth was full of laughter and life, with groups of cheerful punters stood around outside, tankards ready to drain. A new sign hung above the inn. It depicted a group of seven figures warming their hands by an open fire, sharing stories. There was even a small gnome playing a lute.

'My ears aren't that pointy,' muttered Sawwse.

There was also a large white banner of a golden hourglass set against a shield. The writing underneath said, 'Home of the Actum Tempus guild.'

The guild mates took a few moments to stare up at the banner in silence, before making their way inside. They had to squeeze through the heaving crowds to get to the bar.

'Well, I'll be dashed, darned, and doodled.' It was Grimiser. He looked ecstatic to see them, clearly no longer the miserable landlord they'd first encountered. Grimiser rushed over to them, clapped Rangrim on the shoulder, squeezed Corinne into a big hug, and tousled Sawwse and Ruby's hair. 'Convener will be so pleased you're back.'

'He's alive then?' asked Sawwse.

Grimiser chuckled. 'Yes, but he's *dying* to see you. Wheeey. Come on, this way.'

Sawwse exchanged wary glances with the others, before following Grimiser to the back of the pub, past the dingy storage room where they had first encountered one another, and to the door of the dining room.

Inside, they found a large, well-decorated room, with ornate candlesticks and fancy-looking paintings lining the walls. The huge oaken table that had been squashed into the storage room was here but looked completely appropriate in this space. The dining chairs were embellished with twisted wood.

Sawwse shook her head in disbelief. 'This was here the whole time?'

Grimiser held up his hands defensively.

'Welcome back.' Convener's voice came from the head of the table. He swivelled his chair round to face the guild mates. There was his big black glittery cloak, and his familiar, white-horned mask, which now contorted into a wide grin. 'The last few days have been quite restless for me. I was not sure whether you would succeed or whether I would wake to a world I no longer recognised. Or whether I would wake at all.'

The others stood stupefied, but then Sawwse said, 'Your chair rotates? That's so cool!'

'We lost contact with you after Alla'fyr's attack in Spearca.' Corinne whipped out a clipboard from within her cloak and began filing through it. 'I think I have the relevant form in here somewhere.'

'Never mind that.' Larn folded his arms across his chest. 'What about our reward?'

'I see the quest has not changed any of you too much.' Convener placed his fingertips together. 'It takes a tremendous amount of magical energy to communicate over great distances, and doing so leaves one's body vulnerable. It was a calculated risk not to get back in touch after Spearca.' He stood from his chair, which rolled backwards.

'So cool,' murmured Sawwse.

'As to the reward–'

Corinne cleared her throat. 'Would it not be best to first deliver my analytical report of the battle?'

There was a chorus of groans from the others.

Convener placed a large hand on Corinne's shoulder. 'There is much to discuss. You have all worked incredibly hard, and that hard work has strengthened the spirit of our humble guild. Many more challenges lie ahead. The Twelve are currently missing a representative, and that will have serious repercussions for the balance of the world.' He paused, seemingly lost in thought for a few moments. Then, he clapped his hands together. 'But that can wait until tomorrow. For now, you have all earned a rest. Grimiser will take you to your upgraded sleeping quarters.'

The guild mates filed out after Grimiser. Sawwse followed, but then changed her mind. There were too many questions she still had to ask Convener. Mostly about the revolving chair. However, when she turned back into the dining room, Convener had already disappeared. Sawwse shrugged and followed the others upstairs.

Once he was sure Sawwse had gone, Convener crept out from behind the door and returned to his seat at the table. He waved his hands and a large cheese and pickle sandwich appeared in front of him. 'Now, where were we?'

Back up the stairs, Grimiser gestured to a recently refurbished corridor. It couldn't have been described as luxurious because it was still The Happy Hearth after all, but it certainly had a cleanliness to it that had been missing before. Furthermore, instead of taking them to the shared dorm, Grimiser opened a series of doors to new, bespoke rooms.

'Our names are on them!' said Sawwse excitedly. 'Although, that is *not* how you spell Sawwse.'

Vadania, Rangrim, Osrik, and Larn each walked into their new lodgings. A loud yelp of joy followed Rangrim's entrance to his; a simple, 'this will do fine,' from Osrik; a sceptical hum sounded from Larn's room; and silence from Vadania.

Sawwse's room was next along the corridor. She raised her eyebrows to Ruby and squeezed Corinne on the arm. She stepped inside, and for once she was lost for words.

A huge, twisting tree trunk was suspended between floor and ceiling, books of all shapes and sizes lined three of the four walls, and then a whole host of musical instruments hung from the fourth. There was even both a space for her to practice *and* a nook built below the window where she could read to her heart's content. A package on her bed contained a sizeable amount of gold pieces.

Stunned, Sawwse backed out of her room. She wandered next door and into Ruby's, where the little shapeshifter stood with her hands clasped on her head. Her room was made up just like an apothecary: jars, beakers, and vials lined the walls and there was a full workspace complete with a hot plate and an enormous cauldron.

'Incredible,' murmured Ruby.

Back in her own room, Sawwse lay back on her cosy bed beside the tree. She thought about how Convener could create a room so perfect, and more importantly, for what purpose. *It feels like a lot of effort to go through when we might leave the guild*, thought Sawwse. But before she could question it anymore, or delve deeper into Convener's motives, she descended quickly into a deep sleep.

Early the next morning, Sawwse Bohge awoke. It had been one of those dreamless nights, comfortable and restorative, albeit short. It was still dark out, but she knew she'd slept as much as she could. She got out of bed, grabbed a book and a candle from the shelf, and headed downstairs.

As Sawwse reached the bottom of the stairs, she made her way to the hearth, stopping suddenly as she saw a figure in shadow by the front door. 'Who's there?'

'I had hoped to slip away unnoticed,' said Vadania.

Sawwse brought the candle closer to Vadania. She recognised the steely look in her eyes. 'You're leaving?'

'This was always meant to be a temporary stop.'

'But what about the guild?'

'It has been a distraction.'

'You call saving the world a distraction?'

'Yes.'

'But I thought the moral of the quest was to have no regrets or something.' Sawwse scratched her head. 'Let murderous dragons who destroy villages be bygones, and all that.'

'I wish you well, Sawwse.' Vadania smiled. 'May we meet again.'

'You know your name is embossed on that room upstairs, don't you?'

Vadania smiled again, and then left without another word.

Sawwse took up a place by the cold hearth. She wrapped herself in a blanket and read by candlelight.

It was hours later once the others finally woke up and gathered downstairs. Sawwse explained to them that Vadania had left. Most of the group were disappointed, and said as much, but it was Rangrim that looked most crestfallen. They ate breakfast and compared each other's rooms and plans for the days ahead. Suddenly, Sawwse sat upright in her chair and ran to the staircase. She sprinted upstairs to her room, and came back down with her large bag, full to the brim with books and instruments. Sawwse made her way back into the dining room and found Convener sitting, once again, at the top of the table. As usual, he seemed distant, as though his mind was elsewhere.

'Thanks for the room,' said Sawwse.

'You are most welcome,' answered Convener distractedly.

'And for the substantial sum of gold you awarded us.'

'Well deserved.'

'Anyway, I just wanted to come and let you know that I'm taking a short sabbatical.'

'Excuse me?' Convener's attention snapped back to the room.

'I'm taking a sabbatical. That's allowed, right? It should be. Let's say it is. I need to go see an ogre about a horse. And by horse, I mean stories of my lost love who was actually one of The Twelve and nearly destroyed the world.' Sawwse took in a deep breath and then bolted from the room. A second later, she popped her head back round the door for a second. 'Oh! And Ruby's coming with me. Okay, thank you again. Byeeeee.' She left again.

Convener's white-horned mask curled its mouth into a grin.

Back by the hearth, Sawwse burst into the room like a ball of energy. She grabbed Ruby's hand and pulled her towards the entrance. 'Goodbye everyone. We'll be back soon. Come on Ruby, hurry up!'

Osrik, Corinne, Rangrim, and Larn looked on with confused expressions, while Sawwse and Ruby ran outside holding hands. Sawwse whispered something in Ruby's ear causing her to break into a huge smile. Her mouth continued to extend and then her body elongated into a pony. Sawwse jumped on and Ruby galloped them all the way out of Rhyddinas.

It took the best part of the day, but finally they arrived at Marius' humble abode. The heavy stone door was ajar just like he said it would be. Inside, Sawwse guided Ruby through the circular hole in the stone and out into Garmish, Marius' beautiful garden. Marius spotted them immediately and walked over, flashing his toothy grin. 'Here already?'

'We can come back if it's not convenient,' said Sawwse.

'Maybe we could… rest for a… moment,' said Ruby, panting.

'You can stay as long as you like,' said Marius.

Ruby couldn't believe this place existed. It was like an encyclopaedia of flowers and herbs. The amiable ogre, who also just happened to be one of the most powerful wizards in existence, placed his hand on Ruby's back, and guided her around Garmish, pointing out anything that was particularly rare or interesting.

Meanwhile, Sawwse sat back in a low-slung chair. She emptied out the contents of her bulging bag. Twenty books fell out onto the ground, along with her flute, her lute, a tiny trumpet, and a brand-new hand drum. The gnome carefully picked up all the books and placed them into a pile.

That should keep me busy, she thought. 'But first...'

She retrieved the Gnomeopedia and thought of temples and tombs, sleeping knights and Ancient Devices, Rhyddinas, Spearca, and Zell. She thought of music and of magic, of friends and of enemies, of love and of evil. She thought of Mirrah.

'First, I have a lot to write.'

Epilogue

Far away from Rhyddinas, and moderately far from Garmish, the streets in Doriana were flooded with people. They had travelled from all across the Dorienne kingdom to raise banners, sound trumpets, let off fireworks, sing songs, and generally make merry in as many ways as possible. This was because there was a celebration taking place the likes of which the city hadn't seen for decades. And why not? After all, in a kingdom as safe as Dorienne, coronations don't come around very often. The Poht dynasty had been popular, but not in this way. The crowds were wild with an almost feverish support of the new king, perhaps because they were crying out for change, perhaps because he had risen from nothing to assume the throne, or perhaps simply because they too were fond of turnips.

The chant of the crowds reverberated through the streets, through the alleys, avenues, terraces, cul-de-sacs, boulevards, parades, out of windows, out of doorways, from rooftops, from trees, from bushes, and from everywhere it was possible to chant. And they chanted this: 'The King is dead, long live King Cribbins!'

THE END

Acknowledgements

My most heartfelt thanks go to all my family and friends, for their love, support, time, and attention. I'm particularly grateful to Dominic Burgess, Ellie Collins, Jim Grigg, and Katherine Graham, who gave lots of brilliant advice at various stages of writing the original version of this book. A notorious BIG thank you goes to Karen Quigley, who, as ever, was the perfect sounding board for all my ridiculous ideas; and to Iolo Roberts, who amplified all my ridiculous ideas and made them even more ridiculous. My parents and brother always deserve thanks for generally being brilliant and specifically for their everlasting encouragement.

Finally, the seeds of this story, and specifically the characters, originated from a game of Dungeons & Dragons, so I send special thanks to the original campaign group: Darius (Corinne), Mao (Larn), Jim (Osrik), Kev (Rangrim), Fraser (Ruby), Katherine (Vadania), and, of course, Karen (Sawwse), without whom this book simply wouldn't exist.

Readers' Club

What can you expect from the Actum Tempus Readers' Club? Well, probably not much. I have a normal office job *and* a toddler, so I am not time rich. However, when I'm not managing data, wrangling a three-year-old gnomeling, or writing silly jokes about spherical sheep and cubicle cows, I'm usually found discussing current affairs. And by current affairs, I mean such things as the recent spate of robberies by the sweet-toothed bandits on the Gateau Plateau, or the worrying murders at the troll factory.

Basically, I'll be talking rubbish.

If that's your bag, sign up to the readers' club via my website below. You'll get a free short story set prior to the Actum Tempus Saga. There's also a free bonus gift for you to claim. (Hint: it's another short story. I'm a writer, what did you expect? Sweets? No, that'd be creepy.)

If you join the club, you'll also be the first to know of any upcoming releases. Get ready for the Cribbins spinoff: *Tur-nip or Not Tur-nip*.

Join the club below!

Printed in Great Britain
by Amazon

61747965R00234